INTRODUCING

KATIE MAGUIRE

KATIE MAGUIRE was one of seven sisters born
to a police Inspector in Cork, but the only
sister who decided to follow her father
into An Garda Síochána.

With her bright green eyes and short red
hair, she looks like an Irish pixie, but she is
no soft touch. To the dismay of some of her
male subordinates, she rose quickly through
the ranks, gaining a reputation for catching
Cork's killers, often at great personal cost.

Katie spent seven years in a turbulent
marriage in which she bore, and lost, a son –
an event that continues to haunt her. Despite
facing turmoil at home and prejudice at
work she is one of the most fearless
detectives in Ireland.

Graham Masterton was a bestselling horror writer who has now turned his talent to crime writing. He lived in Cork for five years, an experience that inspired the Katie Maguire series. Visit katiemaguire.co.uk

ALSO BY GRAHAM MASTERTON

Ghost Virus

THE KATIE MAGUIRE SERIES

White Bones

Broken Angels

Red Light

Taken for Dead

Blood Sisters

Buried

Living Death

Dead Girls Dancing

Dead Men Whistling

Begging to Die

THE BEATRICE SCARLET SERIES

Scarlet Widow

The Coven

GRAHAM
MASTERTON

BEGGING
TO
DIE

Leabharlanna Poiblí Chathair Baile Átha Cliath

Dublin City Public Libraries

HEAD
ZEUS

First published in the UK in 2019 by Head of Zeus Ltd

9 7 5 3 1 2 4 6 8

A catalogue record for this book is available from
the British Library.

ISBN (HB): 9781784976477
ISBN (XTPB): 9781784976484
ISBN (E): 9781784976460

Typeset by Adrian McLaughlin

Printed and bound in Great Britain by
CPI Group (UK) Ltd, Croydon CR0 4YY

Head of Zeus Ltd
First Floor East
5–8 Hardwick Street
London EC1R 4RG

WWW.HEADOFZEUS.COM

BEGGING TO DIE

Author's note on Irish pronunciations

Caoilfhoinn = Key-lin
Caoimhe = Kee-va
Cathal = Ka-hal
Sadhbh = Sive (as in 'five')

Gaelic song '*Mo Ghille Mear*' from Katie's iPhone:
www.youtube.com/watch?v=c2q2pslNDCc

For Professor Sabina Brennan
of Trinity College Institute of Neuroscience, Dublin,
for her charm, her energy and her dedicated drive
against dementia

and for Caroline Delaney of the *Irish Examiner*
for her sweetness, her wit and for answering every
impossible question that I ask her.

One

Katie was walking past the iron gates of the Huguenot cemetery on Carey's Lane when she heard a child crying. She stopped and listened, because she recognized that this wasn't a cry of frustration, or hunger, or tiredness. This was a cry of loneliness, and desperation.

She pushed open the gates and stepped inside. The cemetery was small, surrounded by high walls all the way round, and meticulously tended. Most of the gravestones lay flat, with stone chippings filling in the ground between them, and wooden tubs with bay trees were arranged at intervals around the walls.

A tawny-haired girl was sitting on the edge of one of these tubs, sobbing. Katie guessed that she was about eight or nine years old. Her hair was braided in a single thick plait that hung over her left shoulder and she was wearing a grey plastic raincoat and yellow rushers. She was thin and pale and her face was dirty, so that her tears had left streaks down her cheeks, but she was pretty in an elfin way, with limpid brown eyes.

Katie approached her along the flagstone path. 'What's the story, sweetheart?' she asked, crouching down beside her. 'Are you all on your own?'

The girl's mouth turned down and she let out a heart-wrenching wail.

'*Unde e mumia mea? Nu-mi găsesc mumia!*'

'I'm sorry, I don't understand you,' said Katie. 'Do you know any English at all?'

'*Nu-mi găsesc mumia!*' the girl repeated, and more tears ran down her cheeks. Katie took her handkerchief out of her bag and gently dabbed them.

'Your mama, is that it? You've lost your mama?'

The girl nodded. '*Nu ştiu unde este! Sa dus în colţ şi a dispărut!*'

'She disappeared?'

The girl nodded again. Katie stood up straight and held out her hand.

'Come on, sweetheart, we'll find her for you. You don't have to worry. I'm police. Do you understand that?' She pointed to herself and said, 'Police?'

The girl stood up too, and quickly, and now she appeared to be panicking. She looked towards the cemetery gates as if she were thinking of running away. Katie snatched her left hand and held it tight and said, 'It's all right, sweetheart! You don't have to be frightened! I'll help you to find your mama, I promise you! You're not in any trouble.'

At the same time she thought, *Jesus and Mary, I wish I knew what language she was speaking. It's not zizzy enough for Polish and it doesn't sound like Russian. Maybe Bulgarian or Czech.*

'What's your name?' she asked her. Again she pointed to herself and said, 'I'm Kathleen. That's my name. Most people call me Katie.' Then she pointed to the girl and said, 'What about you?'

'Ana-Maria,' the girl told her. Katie wiped her eyes once more. She was almost tempted to spit on her handkerchief and clean the girl's dirty face, the way her mother used to do when she was little.

'Ana-Maria, that's a beautiful name. Well, I'll tell you what we're going to do, Ana-Maria. We're going to walk to the place where I work and we're going to find out what language you're speaking and where you come from. Then I'm going to put out a call for your mama and see if we can find her for you. And while we're waiting you can have a wash and a drink and something nice to eat. Okay?'

Ana-Maria may not have understood a word of what Katie was saying, but Katie smiled and nodded and tried to look encouraging, and she mimed washing her face and drinking and eating, and Ana-Maria seemed to grasp the gist of it. She held Katie's hand tighter, and the two of them left the cemetery and walked down Carey's Lane to St Patrick's Street.

It was Tuesday, mid-morning, and the pavements of St Patrick's Street were swarming with shoppers, as well as the usual buskers and living statues and chuggers, and the cars and buses were nose to tail. As they crossed over to Winthrop Street, Katie said, 'Look out for your mama, Ana-Maria. If you see her, call out to her, won't you?'

Winthrop Street was pedestrianized, so they could walk down the middle in between the shops. Katie swung Ana-Maria's hand a little and kept on turning her head to smile at her, trying to make her feel reassured.

'You like McDonald's?' she asked her. Ana-Maria nodded, and Katie thought, *At least there's one language that every child in the world understands.*

They had almost reached The Long Valley Bar when, about fifty metres up ahead of them, Katie saw a tall man with tangled grey hair and a grey leather jacket striding across the end of the street. His shoulders were hunched as if he were in a hurry, but he glanced towards them and when he caught sight of them he stopped as abruptly as if he had walked into an invisible lamp post.

As soon as Ana-Maria saw him, she let out a whimper and tugged hard at Katie's hand.

Katie said, 'What's the matter? Who is that?' but Ana-Maria only tugged harder.

The grey-jacketed man started to run towards them, with an extraordinary limping lope, and Katie immediately swung Ana-Maria behind her, to shield her. She raised her right hand ready to fend the man off, if she had to.

The man's face was grim, his eyes narrowed and his lips tightly puckered. He came galloping up to Katie without slowing down and even though she managed to strike his shoulder with a glancing karate chop, he was so big and so heavy and he had such momentum that she was sent sprawling on to her back on the pavement, hitting her head against one of the metal stools outside O'Flynn's sausage shop.

She lost her hold on Ana-Maria's hand as she fell, and Ana-Maria immediately started to run away, back towards St Patrick's Street, dodging in and out between the shoppers. The grey-jacketed man went loping after her, colliding with a young woman pushing a baby buggy, and forcefully shoving aside an elderly man who stopped to help her.

Katie scrambled to her feet and sprinted after him. She caught up with him outside the Hallmark stationery shop and jumped up behind him like a racehorse taking a fence to give him a running kick in the small of his back. He stumbled forward and collided with the postcard display stand outside the shop door, scattering postcards across the pavement. He managed to keep his feet, though, and he swung his fist at Katie, snorting through his nostrils.

Katie spun herself around and gave him the hardest round-house kick in the groin that she could manage. He shouted out, '*Dah! Futui!*' and doubled up, falling backwards into the shop doorway and shattering the glass door with a splintering crack.

'Stay down!' Katie shouted at him, as he tried to get up. 'I'm a garda officer! You're under arrest! I said *stay down*!'

'*Dute dracu, scorpie!*' the grey-jacketed man snarled back at her. He started to climb to his feet, and when Katie approached him to push him back down, he reached out and grasped a long triangular piece of glass from the broken door, pointing it at her like a dagger.

'You try to kick me again, bitch, I kill you to death,' he warned her, in a thick, phlegm-clogged accent. He stood up, jabbing the piece of glass towards her again and again, even though it had cut him and there was blood dripping from the heel of his hand.

Katie backed away, taking out her iPhone and prodding the

number for emergency backup. The grey-jacketed man started to limp off towards St Patrick's Street, waving the glass dagger from side to side to ward off anybody who might try to stop him. He backed his way into the side door of Brown Thomas, the department store, and then he was gone.

Katie hurried to St Patrick's Street, looking left and right to see if Ana-Maria was still in sight among the crowds. She jumped up and down, trying to see over the heads of the shoppers all around her, and she was still jumping when two gardaí in yellow high-viz jackets came running up to her, a man and a woman.

'There's some gurrier in a grey leather jacket tried to snatch this young girl,' she explained. 'He ducked into Brown Thomas and he might still be in there. He's violent, though, and he's carrying a piece of broken glass that he's using as a knife.'

At that moment, a squad car came around the corner from Merchants Quay with its blue light flashing.

'Go inside there and see if you can find him,' Katie told the two gardaí. 'I'll have these fellers watch the doors in case he tries to make a run for it.'

The squad car parked next to the statue of Father Mathew and two more gardaí climbed out. Even as they did so, another squad car arrived from the direction of Grand Parade.

Katie quickly briefed all the officers and then she called in to the station so that they could put out a citywide description of Ana-Maria. She had just finished doing that when Sergeant Nicholas Kearns turned up, along with two more gardaí. Sergeant Kearns had only recently been promoted but he had already proved himself to be level-headed in a crisis. He had a broad, sensible face with bushy blond eyebrows, and he walked with the confident gait of a man who spends an hour in the gym every morning.

'So who's this suspect we're looking for, ma'am?' he asked her.

'Eastern European, by the sound of him,' said Katie. 'And violent. And armed with a shard of glass that could almost cut your head off. So be doggy wide, I warn you.'

Katie left him in charge of searching for the grey-jacketed man while she herself went looking for Ana-Maria. She weaved her way through the crowds along St Patrick's Street, peering into every shop and every side turning, but Ana-Maria could be hiding in any one of a hundred doorways or could have run streets away by now. By the time she had reached Finn's Corner on Grand Parade, Katie had to admit to herself that Ana-Maria had disappeared, and that there was very little hope of finding her.

She walked back to Brown Thomas, breathing hard. The officers who had been looking for the grey-jacketed man were gathered on the pavement outside the front door.

'No luck?' she asked Sergeant Kearns.

He shook his head. 'Ere a sign. We even searched the ladies' jacks, but he could be anywhere at all, like, do you know what I mean? But I'll put the word out, specially among the immigrants, like. Somebody must know who he is, and where he hangs out.'

'It's the little girl I'm worried about,' said Katie. 'I have no idea why he was after her, or why he frightened her so much, but I'm praying that he doesn't find her before we do.'

Two

When she had heard Ana-Maria crying, Katie had been on her way to Cari's Closet to pick up an evening dress that was being altered for her. She wouldn't need it until next month so she decided to collect it tomorrow instead, and she asked Sergeant Kearns to drive her back to the station at Anglesea Street.

'It's some handling, like, keeping tabs on all these immigrants,' said Sergeant Kearns, as they drove along by the river. 'I know we're supposed to be politically correct, like, but it's growing worse. There's so many more of them flooding in and half of them illegals or asylum seekers – or making out that they're asylum seekers anyway.'

'I don't know what language that little girl was speaking,' said Katie. 'It sounded central European but who knows?'

'We hauled in a feller the other day and he could only understand Uzbek. Or claimed he could. It took us half the effing day before we could find an Uzbek interpreter, if you'll excuse my French. At least I know now what the Uzbek for "pickpocket" is. *O'g'ri.* That's something they don't teach you at Templemore.'

Before she went back up to her office, Katie called in to see Detective Inspector Fitzpatrick. He had been working lately on an operation to identify and keep immigrant suspects under surveillance. She found him sitting at his desk staring morosely at a long list of names on his laptop.

'How're you going on, Robert?' she asked him, pulling a chair around and sitting down beside him.

Detective Inspector Fitzpatrick shook his head. He was grey-haired even though he was only fifty-three, but built like a rugby forward, with a broken nose. He was unfailingly courteous to Katie, and respectful, but she was always disturbed by his cold, expressionless eyes. She found it impossible to tell what he was thinking, and sometimes when he appeared to be calm she was taken aback by the ferocity of what he came out with.

'It's like trying to find a needle in a halting site, tracking any one of these scummers,' he complained. 'There's so many of them coming in separate, like, making out that they're tourists, and then joining together and going on the rob for a week or so. But before we can pick them up on the CCTV or put a name to them, they're out the gap, back to whatever godforsaken countries they came from. They're highly organized, though, no question about it.'

'Well, we'll just have to make sure that we're even more organized than they are,' said Katie. 'But right now there's one of them I'm trying to locate in particular.'

She told Detective Inspector Fitzpatrick about finding Ana-Maria, and gave him a description of the grey-jacketed man. She even drew him a sketch, although she had never been very good at art. All the magic kingdoms that Katie had drawn when she was little had been populated by stick fairies and dragons that looked more like fire-breathing donkeys.

'I'll have Brogan go through all the CCTV mugshots we have on file and see if he can't pick him out,' said Detective Inspector Fitzpatrick. 'Don't you have any idea at all what language it was the little girl was speaking? That would be pure helpful in locating him, like. You know how all the different ethnic communities tend to stick together in locations that we know about. All the Somalis, for instance, down the lower end of Shandon Street and all the Romanians in Orchard Court in Blackpool and most of the Poles in their bedsits on the Lower Glanmire Road.'

'I'll try to remember some of the words she used,' said Katie. 'She definitely said "mammy" – although it sounded more like "*moo*-mia" – and I'm sure she also said "disappeared", which sounded like French. You know, "*disparu.*"'

'I wouldn't know. My French only stretches as far as "derby ears, seevo play".'

'Oh. You mean, *deux bières, s'il vous plait.*'

'That's what I said.'

Katie went up to her office. She had already eaten one half of the chicken sandwich that she had brought with her for lunch, and she opened her desk drawer and looked at the other half. Somehow, after rescuing Ana-Maria and then tussling with the grey-jacketed man, she had lost her appetite. She took out a pear, turned it this way and that, and then dropped it back in her lunchbox.

Her assistant, Moirin, came in, with her dyed-black hair tied back with a yellow band, so that she looked more like Disney's Snow White than ever, if Snow White had aged ten years and put on six kilos.

'Superintendent Pearse asked if you could drop in to see him as soon as you're back,' she said. 'He'll be in Chief Superintendent MacCostagáin's old office.'

'Thanks, Moirin. You couldn't be fetching me an espresso before I go to see him? I'm in dire need of caffeine.'

'I will of course. Oh – and there's something on your desk there, in that envelope. It was handed in as lost property but Sergeant O'Farrell thought you might want to take a sconce at it. He couldn't find it in the inventory but he thought it might be one of the rings that was robbed from the Public Museum last month. He said you'd never believe where it turned up.'

Katie picked up the clear plastic envelope that had been left beside her desk lamp with a slip of paper inside it stating GOLD RING and its PEMS reference number. She opened it and shook out a braided gold ring into the palm of her hand. Although it was quite heavy, it was quite small, so it was probably a woman's ring, or a ring that a man would wear on his little finger. It was embossed with a tiny face, which looked like a woman with her eyes closed. The ring was well-worn: it was finely scratched and there was a deep cleft in one side of the woman's forehead.

'It *is* unusual, isn't it?' said Katie, holding it up and examining it closely. 'I wouldn't say it's worth much, though. I doubt if it's real gold even. I'll have to ask Diana Breen to take a look at it. She knows her onions when it comes to antique jewellery, if you know what I mean.'

'It reminds me of a ring my grandma used to wear,' said Moirin. 'It had the face of Saint Samthann on it, and she used to kiss it regular.'

'Oh, yes? And who was Saint Samthann?'

'She was the abbess at Clonbroney. The story goes that when a monk waded across the river to have his way with one of the virgins in her abbey, a giant eel bit his nether parts and wrapped itself around his waist and wouldn't let go of him until he had presented himself to Saint Samthann and begged her forgiveness.

'My grandma told me that when she was younger some scummer tried to rape her but she prayed to Saint Samthann and next door's dog came bursting in and took a bite out of his backside. I don't know how true that was but it made for a good story.'

'Did Sergeant O'Farrell tell you where the ring was found?'

'No, but he said he'd talk to you later so.'

'Okay, thanks, Moirin,' said Katie, and put the ring down on her desk. Her iPhone pinged and she saw that she had a text from Conor, her husband-to-be. He was following up a tip-off about a stolen Weimaraner in Mallow and would be home late. Katie typed back: *No worries. I'm making fishcakes.* But then she wondered if she had bought enough breadcrumbs.

The nameplate had been removed from the door to Chief Superintendent MacCostagáin's office, leaving only four screw holes, and the door itself was half open. When Katie walked in she found Superintendent Pearse sitting on the edge of the desk with his arms folded. Another officer was standing in front of the window, with his back to her. He was wearing a pale blue shirt with the epaulettes of a chief superintendent – three red-and-gold pips over a red-and-gold bar.

He was tall, about the same height as Conor, with short black hair that was greying at the sides. He was saying something about recruitment, and how he wanted to see the number of sergeants up above forty again.

'And I don't only want to see our numbers improved, do you know? I want to see our public relations improved, too. It's no good at all closing our eyes and sticking our fingers in our ears. We've lost the respect of the man and the woman in the street and we're going to have to work hard to win it back.'

Katie stopped where she was. She was sure that she recognized his voice. Deep, with meaningful pauses, as if the pauses were just as important as the words, and with a slight but distinctive Sligo slur.

'Ah, Katie, how's it going on?' asked Superintendent Pearse, hopping off the desk. 'I gather you've been having some fun and games.'

'Nothing too serious,' Katie told him. 'Just some Eastern European feen cutting up rough.'

The officer facing the window turned around, and, yes, it was him, Brendan O'Kane. He was older, of course, than when she had known him at the Garda College at Templemore, but he still had that aquiline look about him – those sharp features and those mischievous eyes, as if he were always thinking what trouble he could stir up, if only for the hell of it.

He was rarely a troublemaker, though, except when he wanted to have his own way. He had been promoted more quickly than any of Katie's other contemporaries, and the last she had heard about him he had been the superintendent in charge of the Operational Support Unit, overlooking the Garda's helicopters, dog teams, boats and divers and mounted patrols.

For three-and-a-half months, during Katie's second summer at Templemore, she and Brendan had been lovers. She had been strongly attracted by his aura of risk and unreliability, but sure enough he had proved to be unreliable, and one afternoon she had come back early from her martial arts class to catch him in bed with her room-mate, Éama.

He came towards her now with one eyebrow slightly raised as if he were expecting her to make some vitriolic comment about what had happened between them all that time ago.

'DS Maguire,' he said, in that rich melted-chocolate voice. 'I've been hearing some remarkable reports about you.'

'I've not been idle, no, sir,' said Katie. 'Can I assume that you'll be taking over here in place of Denis MacCostagáin?'

'Poor Denis, yes. Well, *reckless* Denis, more like. I'm starting from today. This assignment came as much of a surprise to me as it obviously is to you. I'll miss the boats and the dogs and the helicopters. The helicopters most of all, because they could get me around so quick. But what you have here in Cork city is a challenge all right, and I must say that I'm looking forward to rolling up my sleeves and getting my hands dirty.'

'Oh, you'll do that for sure. But I think you can safely say that the force itself is pretty much spotless now. Given a little time, I think you'll be winning that respect from the public that you're after.'

'Well, all credit to yourself from what I hear,' said Brendan O'Kane. 'I was talking to one of the inspectors from the NBCI's anti-corruption unit only a couple of days ago about everything you'd done to clean things up in Cork. Arresting Denis Mac-Costagáin – that was the icing on the cake.'

He gave her a slanted smile, and added, 'He told me to watch my step around you, DS Maguire.'

Holy Mother of God, thought Katie. *He's giving me that exact same expression that he gave me when he looked over his shoulder and saw me standing in the bedroom doorway while he was naked as a goat on top of Éama. That expression that says – fair play, you've caught me misbehaving myself, but what are you going to do about it?*

'I'll be convening a general meeting early tomorrow morning so that I can introduce myself to everybody here at Anglesea Street,' Brendan O'Kane told her. 'Maybe you're free this evening, though, DS Maguire. We could discuss long-term strategy over dinner.'

'Not this evening, sir. Sorry. I have to go home and make fish-cakes for my fiancé.'

Brendan O'Kane gave her a resigned shrug. He knew exactly what he was telling him: that he would have to earn her trust all over again.

Superintendent Pearse caught the tension between them, but smacked his hands together and said, 'Fishcakes! It's donkey's since I've had fishcakes! You have my mouth watering now so you do! I'll have to have a word with herself so!'

Three

'Third fecking time this month,' said Darragh, as he weaved their ambulance through the traffic jam that had built up alongside the Blackpool shopping centre. 'I reckon there's a Satanic curse on this junction.'

'And always on a Tuesday,' Brianna remarked. 'My grandmother always said that Tuesdays were bad luck because Michael Collins was shot on a Tuesday.'

On the third day of January an elderly couple had been killed as they crossed over Commons Road, the main road north to Mallow, and only nine days ago a fourteen-year-old boy had been knocked off his bicycle and fractured his skull. This morning a yellow Ford Fiesta had come speeding out of Popham's Road through a red light and collided with an Expressway bus heading south.

The red-and-silver bus remained at an angle in the middle of the junction, its wing mirrors sticking out like the antennae of a giant wounded wasp. The Ford Fiesta had catapulted over the steel barrier on the corner of Commons Road and was now resting on its roof in the shopping centre car park. Darragh and Brianna had been told that the driver and his passenger were still trapped inside.

'Holy shite,' said Darragh, steering the ambulance through the crowd who were milling around in the road, an assortment of shoppers and Expressway passengers who were waiting for another bus to come and collect them. It looked as if the passengers would have a long wait because Commons Road was blocked for at least a kilometre in both directions.

'Watch out for that eejit with the head,' said Brianna. 'You don't want to be causing any more casualties than we have already.'

Two gardaí in high-viz jackets beckoned them towards the entrance to the car park. As they turned into it, they heard sirens and Brianna saw the flashing blue lights of two fire engines making their way down towards them from Ballyvolane. She felt a sense of relief, because there was nothing worse than having to tend to road accident victims who were so smashed into their vehicles that it was impossible to give them first aid.

They parked, and Brianna lifted up her resuscitation bag, climbed out, and crossed over to the wreck. The Fiesta's roof had been crushed so low that the driver and his passenger were not only hanging upside down from their seat belts but were hunched up, with their heads bent forward. Even though their airbags had inflated, Brianna suspected that they could both have sustained severe neck injuries.

Three more gardaí were gathered around the Fiesta. They had managed to wrench open the passenger door a few centimetres, although not far enough to lift out the young woman who was trapped inside. Her eyes were closed, and there was dark blood sliding out of the sides of her mouth. Brianna thought that she couldn't have been more than seventeen years old. Her short hair was dyed shocking pink and she was wearing a denim mini-skirt and a denim jacket.

Brianna knelt down beside the car, rolled up her sleeve and managed to squeeze her right arm through the gap in the door to feel the young woman's pulse. It was twenty-eight beats per minute, which was dangerously slow, and indicated that she could have suffered internal injuries and be in cardiogenic shock. Her eyelids fluttered and she bubbled blood between her lips and whispered something, but then she closed her eyes again and her pulse rate dropped even further.

Darragh, meanwhile, was crouching down on the opposite side

of the car. The driver's door was wedged tight but a garda had smashed the window with his baton and Darragh was checking the driver's heart rate and trying to assess what injuries he might have suffered. The steering wheel had been rammed into his chest and he was letting out little mouse-like squeaks when he breathed.

Brianna guessed that he was only three or four years older than the girl in the passenger seat. His hair was shaved up at the sides and a snake was tattooed around his neck. His left arm must have been torn in half by the impact of the crash, because the two long bones from his forearm had burst through the elbow of his green JD Sports tracksuit and were protruding from it.

The two fire engines drew up alongside the ambulance with their lights flashing. Six firefighters jumped out and hurried over to the crushed Fiesta. A few seconds later a red Ford Ranger Rapid Response Vehicle pulled up behind them and out climbed Assistant Chief Fire Officer Stephen O'Grady. He was Cork Fire Brigade's specialist in major disasters – big-bellied, jowly, with fiery red cheeks and a bristly little moustache.

The leading firefighter leaned over to assess the state of the wreck, and how they might extricate the driver and his passenger who were tangled up inside it. He was very tall, and black-haired, and doleful-looking, and Brianna could almost picture him carrying a scythe in one hand and an hourglass in the other.

'We'll be needing the spreaders, Michael!' he called out. 'And the cutters – and two rams!'

'Are these two the only casualties?' asked Assistant Chief Fire Officer O'Grady, as he joined them. 'How about the bus passengers?'

'The bus driver's a bit shocked, like,' said one of the gardaí. 'His passengers all had a fair jolt, too, but there's nothing worse than a couple of bruised knees, and a lump on the head. Most of them are pure vexed because they're late for wherever they're supposed to be heading to. There's Christian sympathy for you.'

'Well, it's a blessing I suppose, that nobody else has been

injured,' said Assistant Chief Fire Officer O'Grady, although Brianna thought that he sounded slightly disappointed.

'It's critical we extricate both of these two as quick as we can,' said Darragh, brusquely. 'Even if their vertebrae aren't fractured, they'll be suffering from acute compression of the neck and that could lead to permanent cord lesion.'

'The rear oyster is going to be the best way,' said the leading firefighter. 'We'll take the doors off first. Then we'll cut through the back and lift up the floor with a couple of rams.'

The firefighters brought over two Holmatro spreaders. With chugging hydraulic pumps and loud creaking noises that set Brianna's teeth on edge, they forced off both the Fiesta's doors. Then they passed a canvas strap from one side of the car to the other, underneath the patients' thighs, tightening it up with a ratchet so that their weight would be taken off their necks.

Brianna was watching them, biting her thumbnail. They were both unconscious, and blood was still dripping from the girl's lips.

'Come on,' she said. 'You have to get a groove on. This is the golden twenty minutes.'

The firefighters cracked out the Fiesta's rear window, and then used cutters like huge black lobster claws to crunch through its two roof pillars. After that they set up two hydraulic rams inside it, just in front of the back seats. They started up the pump and with an agonized metallic groaning, the rams gradually lifted up the floor, so that the back of the car opened like an oyster shell. As soon as it was gaping wide, the firefighters slid two long boards along the roof, one under the driver and one under the girl. Then they reclined both front seats as far as they would go, unfastened the ratchet strap, and sliced through the seat belts.

As gently as they could, Darragh and Brianna and two of the firefighters lowered the driver and the girl so that they were lying face down on the long boards. Now they could slide them out of the car and carry them across to the ambulance.

Inside the ambulance, Brianna fitted a Kendrick Extrication

Device on to the girl, fastening the straps around her torso and waist and behind her head. This was a kind of jacket to keep her anatomically immobile and lessen the chance of any further injury. At the same time, Darragh strapped another KED on to the young man. Once they had done that, they gently rolled both patients off the long boards and on to their backs on the ambulance's trolleys.

'Right,' said Darragh, making his way forward to the driver's seat. 'Let's hit the bricks.'

With their blue lights flashing and their siren whooping, they sped out of the car park, turning sharp left at the junction and heading back towards the city.

Bracing herself against the swaying of the ambulance, Brianna fitted oxygen masks and pulse oximeters on to both the girl and the young man. There was a time when she would have put them on an intravenous atropine drip before they set off, but the current thinking was that more victims were saved by getting them to hospital as fast as possible and not wasting time by treating them at the scene of the accident.

She checked the girl's pulse again. It was slightly stronger now, up to forty-eight, and blood was no longer running from the sides of her mouth. Depending on the compression damage to her neck, and whatever internal injuries she may have suffered, there was a reasonable chance that she would survive.

She had to hold on tight to the side of the trolley as Darragh crossed over the Christy Ring Bridge and took a sharp right along Lavitt's Quay, beside the river. Once she had steadied herself, she went across to the young driver. Underneath the oxygen mask his face was the colour of congealing porridge and his breath was coming in tiny snatched gasps. She laid her hand flat on his chest and she could feel the distinctive scrunching of a crushed ribcage.

She staggered slightly as Darragh swerved around some parked cars, and then she checked the young man's pulse. It was thirty-two, and irregular. The oxygen was helping to keep his heart going, but because of his chest injuries she couldn't give him manual CPR, and she wasn't sure if a pacemaker would only make his injuries worse. In her experience, it was ten to one that he wasn't going to make it.

'How are they doing?' Darragh shouted, over the blaring of the siren.

'The girl's not so bad, but it looks like the feller's touch and go.'

'Sure listen, only five more minutes and we'll be there,' Darragh told her. 'Tell him to hold on, will you? We've the worst survival record out of the whole fecking stack.'

'The state he's in, like, I don't think he'll pay me any mind,' Brianna shouted back. At the same time, quite calmly and deliberately, she reached over and turned off the young man's oxygen supply.

'Will you move out the fecking way, you gowl!' Darragh screamed at a rental-van driver who had decided to stop and reverse right in front of them. 'Holy Jesus, they must be deaf and blind and half a bubble off true, some of these eejits!'

Brianna took no notice. She was watching the young man dispassionately as his gasps became fewer, and weaker, and when the ambulance started moving again she ducked her head down now and again so that she could look out of the window and see how close they were to arriving at Cork University Hospital.

The young man stopped gasping just before they turned into the hospital entrance. Brianna checked his pulse again and his heart had stopped beating.

'Thank you, Jesus,' she whispered. 'Perfect timing, as usual.'

She waited until Darragh had backed the ambulance up to the entrance to the emergency department and hurried around to open up the rear door. Then, just as calmly as before, she turned the young man's oxygen supply back on again.

'What's the story?' asked Darragh, as he climbed up the steps.

'He's gone,' she said, lifting up both of her hands as if to say, *I did everything I could, but—*

'Oh well,' said Darragh, looking down at the young man's body. 'Another one bites the dust. That'll learn him that your red light means stop.'

Four

Conor was already at home by the time Katie turned in to the gateway of her bungalow on Carrig View, twenty kilometres to the east of Cork city and overlooking the estuary of the River Lee. He must have heard her pulling up outside, because he opened the front door with Barney, her red setter, and Foltchain, her red-and-white setter, both of them excitedly flapping their tails. As she climbed the steps up to the porch, though, she saw that he was also cradling a small black-faced pug dog in his arms.

'I thought you were going to be late,' she said, as she tugged affectionately at Barney and Foltchain's ears.

'I know. But the Weimaraner turned out to be a red herring, if you know what I mean. I was given a tip-off about this little feen instead.'

'Mother of God, Con. Are we after setting up a home for rescue dogs? Where did he come from?'

'Ballincollig,' said Conor. 'The woman who had him helps out in the kitchen in The Darby Arms. Walter, his name is. She told me that some fellow came into the pub about two weeks ago looking to sell him, because he was off to start a new job in England.'

'A likely story,' said Katie, hanging up her pointy-hooded raincoat. 'How much was this fellow asking for him?'

'Only a hundred and fifty euros. That's less than a quarter of what you'd normally expect to pay for a pug puppy. If they're show quality, they're over a thousand. But because Walter was so cheap, your woman didn't ask for any paperwork, or if he'd been wormed or inoculated, or if he'd been chipped.'

'But he turned out to be one of the dogs you've been looking for?'

'That's right,' said Conor. He followed Katie into the living room, where a fresh log fire was snapping and crackling. She sat down on the couch to ease off her ankle boots and both Barney and Foltchain came nuzzling up to her, one on each side, eager to have their ears stroked.

'Will you two please stall the ball for a second to take my boots off!' she protested, and both dogs cocked their heads to one side as if to say, oh, come on, who's more important, your boots or us?

'Where's Walter's owner?' asked Katie. 'Aren't you going to take him home?'

'His owner's a young woman who works for the county council's library service, Caoimhe O'Neill. She still lives with her parents in Douglas.'

'So, what, hasn't she paid you?'

'Not yet, but I'm not going to ask her to. It's Walter's condition that worries me. She says she bought him from the Foggy Fields puppy farm up at Ballynahina, and they assured her that he was one hundred per cent healthy, but you only have to look at him to see that he's in fierce poor shape, the same as a lot of brachycephalic dogs like him.'

Katie looked up at the pug puppy in Conor's arms. He was silver-grey with a black mask, and from the way he was staring back down at her she thought he was adorable.

'He's a darling,' she said, blowing him two or three kisses. 'What's wrong with him?'

'You name it. Everybody thinks pugs look so cute with their squashed-up faces, but if they've not been carefully bred and well taken care of, they can suffer a whole rake of problems. Walter has trouble breathing, because his nostrils are so narrow, and upper airway issues, and he has bulging pockets of tissue in the back of the throat that could choke him.'

'Now you come to mention it, his eyes look pure bulgy, too,' said Katie, peering at Walter more closely.

'That's right. They're so protuberant that his eyelids don't quite cover his lids, and that's why he has all that discharge. He could even be prone to proptosis.'

'If I knew what that was, I'd probably feel even more sorry for him than I do already.'

'Well, you would, because it means that his eyes are liable to pop right out of his head, even when he's just playing or rolling around. I've seen it happen a few times. You can push them back in again, but as he grows older he'll almost certainly end up blind.'

'So that's why you haven't returned him to his mistress.'

'I'll take him down first to Domnall O'Sullivan at the Gilabbey Veterinary Hospital – you know, the same fellow who took care of Barney. He needs a thorough check-up and he'll maybe need surgery to help his breathing and get rid of those everted laryngeal saccules. That's if Caoimhe's prepared to pay for it.

'I really want to find out a whole lot more about this Foggy Fields, though. There's far too many of these illegal breeders these days, and the puppies they're churning out are almost always sick and miserable and over half of them die after only a few weeks. Do you know how many puppies this country produced last year?'

'No, but I'm sure you're going to tell me.'

'Nearly a hundred thousand! That's how many! Even though we have only seventy-eight registered breeders! In England they have nearly nine hundred registered breeders, and do you know how many puppies they produced?'

'Go on.'

'Seventy thousand, that's all. That means our breeders are turning out sixteen times as many. It's a scandal.'

Katie tugged on her fluffy pink slippers and went through to the kitchen. Conor and Barney and Foltchain all followed her.

'Con,' she said, as she took out the cod and the smoked

haddock that she'd put in the fridge that morning to defrost. 'I know how dedicated you are to protecting animals, but don't you think you're doing enough to help them as a pet detective?'

'Katie – just listen to this little fellow! He's struggling with every single breath! If he was a human, we'd be rushing him off to the emergency room!'

'We would, yes, but you're taking him to see Domnall to-morrow, aren't you? And if you start going after those illegal dog-breeders you could find yourself in desperate trouble. You're already on a suspended sentence for setting fire to Guzz Eye McManus's mobile home. You'd only have to get yourself involved in one more incident like that and you could find your-self banged up in Rathmore Road, sharing a cell with a bunch of druggies.'

'McManus was a sadistic monster. When you think of all the dogs that got torn to pieces in his dog fights.'

'That was still no justification for you burning down his home. And it was only because the judge was such a dog lover that you got let off so light. The puppy-breeders are something else, though. We tried to prosecute one only last summer. He had thirty-one breeding bitches but he said that he was mad about dogs and he hadn't realized that he wasn't allowed more than six. He pleaded to apply for a licence and they gave him one.'

'They didn't fine him?'

'No, Con. There's no will to,' Katie told him. 'Dog wardens can give you a spot fine of a hundred and fifty euros if you don't pick up your dog mess, can't they, but the courts won't penalize you for breeding seven hundred illegal puppies and selling them off when they're only two weeks old. You saw what happened when Pat Murphy tried to raise the question about puppy-breeding in the Dáil. Nobody showed up, except for the minister. Nobody.'

Conor watched her in silence as she peeled potatoes and put them on to boil, and then mashed up the fish.

'I know you're fuming,' she said. 'When you find out more about Foggy Fields I can talk to the ISPCA for you and see if it needs to be investigated. But please, I'm begging you, Con, stay out of it yourself. I don't want us to have to postpone our wedding because you're locked up in jail. And I don't want you getting on the wrong side of the puppy-breeders. They're a hard lot, I can tell you. But then you know that already.'

'They don't scare me, Katie. What they're doing is wrong and incredibly cruel. And it doesn't do our country's reputation much good, either. Irish-bred puppies are notorious in America for being sickly and difficult to train.'

Katie put down her fork and went over to him and touched his beard. Walter looked up at her and she could hear the laboured whining in his stenotic nostrils.

'Con, sweetheart, I know you want to save every dog in the world. Saint Conor of the Canines. I love dogs as much as you do, but I don't want you to risk your freedom or your life.'

They sat down at the kitchen table to eat their fishcakes while the dogs wandered off to lie down by the fire. Barney and Foltchain seemed to accept Walter as if he were a visiting cousin, and let him lie between them.

Katie told Conor how she had found Ana-Maria in the Huguenot cemetery, and how she had been attacked and Ana-Maria had run away. 'The Lord only knows where she is now. I just pray that she has some shelter because it's lashing out there tonight, and something to eat.'

'The whole world's going to hell in a sulky,' said Conor. 'A kennel-owner friend of mine texted me from Sligo this morning and said that his farm had been ransacked. There's gangs coming down from Dublin into the countryside and robbing every house they come to. Where are the guards these days, that's what he asked me.'

Katie ground black pepper over her fishcake and shook her head. 'I know we're letting people down. We've suffered so many budget cuts in the past few years, though, and we simply don't have the manpower any more. Oh – I shouldn't be saying "man-power" these days, should I? Let's say we're seriously under effective staffing levels.'

When they had finished eating, they went into the living room and sprawled on the couch together. *First Dates Ireland* was showing on the TV but they had turned the sound off.

'Your beard needs a trim,' said Katie, tugging at it. 'You're starting to look like one of them what's-their-names. One of them fellers from ZZ Top.'

'I'll go up to Crew Cuts tomorrow, I promise you, as soon as I come back from the vet's.'

'I think I love you, straggly or not.'

'You only think?'

'I love you but you scare me. I don't think you realize how dangerous they are, some of the scumbags you keep challenging. I don't want you ending up in the river. Not for all the sickly puppies in Ireland.'

Conor kissed her, and then kissed her again. 'I swear to God that I'll watch my back, Katie.'

She was about to warn him about one illegal dog-breeder in particular, up in Labbacally, who she knew to have five hundred bitches on his farm, when her iPhone played the chorus from 'Mo Ghille Mear' – *My Gallant Hero*. She had chosen that ringtone especially for Conor.

'Ma'am? Sorry to disturb you so late.' It was Detective Sergeant Ni Nuallán.

'Not a worry, Kyna. What's the story?'

'That little girl you found today. She's turned up.'

'Ana-Maria? That's a pure relief. Where was she?'

'She walked into Burger King on Pana about an hour ago and asked for a burger. "Burger" was about the only English word she knew. She had only thirty cents on her, and of course she was unaccompanied, but the manager used his brains and let her have the burger and a milkshake, and while she was eating it he gave us a ring.'

'Thank goodness there are some people with decency in this world. Where is she now?'

'She's right here, in the station, fast asleep in bed. I've rung Margaret O'Reilly at Tusla and she'll be coming over first thing. She'll fetch one of the social workers who specializes in separated foreign children. Meanwhile, Garda McGuinness is going to be keeping an eye on her during the night, in case she wakes up distressed.'

'How is she?'

'Beat out, I'd say. But she wolfed her burger, apparently, and drank all her milkshake, and she'll be given a good breakfast tomorrow.'

'We still don't know what nationality she is?'

'She hasn't said a word since we brought her here. But the social worker will know.'

'Thanks, Kyna. That's taken a load off my mind. I'll come in early tomorrow to see her.'

She put down the phone. 'That was Kyna,' she told Conor. 'Ana-Maria has turned up.'

'I gathered that. Good news.'

Unexpectedly, Katie's eyes filled with tears. Conor reached out for her but she flapped her hand and said, 'I'm all right, Con. I'm grand. I think I'm feeling a bit like a little girl lost myself, since my da passed away. I'll be all right.'

Conor said nothing but put his arms around her and held her close. After a while she sniffed, and then she laughed.

'What's so funny?' he asked her.

'Your beard. It tickles.'

Five

As they drove slowly past the entrance to the Savoy Centre on St Patrick's Street, Garda Megan Cavey said, 'Gearoid's not up yet. What's the time? Looks like he's having himself a lie-in, the lazy fellow.'

Garda Jimmy Brogan drew the squad car into the kerb, beside the bus stop. The beggar they knew only as Gearoid was lying in the doorway of the empty shop underneath O'Brien's Photographers, covered from head to foot in a thick blue blanket. It was eight oh-five and by now he had usually peeled off his blanket and gone to the toilets in Dunnes Stores and bought himself a cup of coffee and a cheese roll. He should be sitting up in his khaki anorak with his cardboard sign saying, *Homeless But Not By Choice Please Help.*

Garda Cavey climbed out of the squad car and crossed the pavement to the shop doorway. She was a sturdy girl with a big bottom, thick ankles and short gingery hair and so many freckles that her face looked as if it had been liberally sprinkled with paprika. She crouched down beside Gearoid's blanket and said, 'Gearoid? You're not still dreaming are you there, Gearoid? Time to wake up and start shaking your paper cup, sham!'

There was no response. Gearoid's head was completely covered but his feet were sticking out from the end of the blanket in their worn brown boots with thick grey socks. Garda Cavey was inclined at first to let him sleep on, but then she noticed a dented green tin of Peterson's Irish Oak tobacco beside the wall. This was the tin in which he kept the cigarette ends that he salvaged from the gutter, and she couldn't imagine that he would leave it out in full view while he was asleep, in case some other beggar hobbled it, or it was picked up by a council street cleaner.

She pulled her black latex gloves out of her jacket pocket and snapped them on. Then she reached out and shook Gearoid's shoulder.

'Gearoid? Come on, Gearoid, it's morning! How about stirring yourself?'

There was still no response, so she grasped the top of his filthy blanket and tugged it down. He would normally sleep with the hood of his anorak raised, especially on such a cold January night, but this morning his hood was folded back, exposing his thick tangled mess of auburn curls, mingled with grey.

She shook him again, harder this time, but all he did was jiggle lifelessly and she realized that he was either drunk or drugged or more likely dead.

She turned around and called out, 'Jim! Jimmy! We're after needing a white van here, boy! And the technical experts! I think Gearoid's left us!'

While Garda Brogan called for an ambulance and the Technical Bureau, Garda Cavey dragged the blanket completely off Gearoid and heaved him over on to his back. When she did that, an empty vodka bottle rolled away across the pavement. There was no question now that he was dead. His eyes were wide open but they had already turned dark and flat. His dry, cracked lips were parted, and the tip of his yellow-furred tongue was sticking out as if he were showing the world for the very last time that he didn't care what it did to him. He stank of faeces so his bowels had obviously opened when he died.

Although he was so filthy, Garda Cavey pressed her fingers underneath his scraggly beard to check if there was any sign of a pulse. She had once believed that a middle-aged woman who had collapsed in Paul Street Tesco was dead, but on the way to hospital the woman had suddenly sat up and asked where in the name of Jesus she was being taken to.

Garda Brogan came over and looked down at Gearoid. He was in his late thirties, Garda Brogan, with a sooty six o'clock shadow and black eyebrows that met in the middle.

'Been dead for at least three hours, I'd say. Probably more. Oh, well, poor Gearoid. He always said that he'd be happier in Heaven. Used to be a folk singer, that's what he told me. Even made a record. He's probably crooning away with the choir invisible already.'

'I can't see any obvious signs of trauma,' said Garda Cavey. 'No blood on his clothes. No bruises.'

Garda Brogan nodded towards the empty vodka bottle. 'Alcoholic poisoning, plus hypothermia, I'll lay money on it.'

Garda Cavey stood up. 'What a way to end your life, do you know what I mean, like? Dead in a doorway.'

'Could have been worse, I suppose,' said Garda Brogan. 'He reckoned that this is one of the most profitable doorways in Cork, when it comes to begging. What – you're right next to the Savoy Centre, and slap-bang opposite Debenhams and Brown Thomas. Even on a bad week he told me he could clear seven or eight hundred euros, easy, and he'd make a heap more than that during the Patrick's Day Parade or the LGBT Pride Parade, or Easter or Christmas. This doorway, it's like a fecking franchise.'

'He was still on his own, Jimmy, with no roof over his head and no bed to sleep in.'

'True, but you can't judge other people's happiness by your own, like, can you? Some fellows are happy being priests, or monks, but you wouldn't catch me being celibate. I wouldn't give up women even if they offered to make me the Pope.'

'That's about as likely as me being asked to be Mother Superior.'

Five or six people standing at the bus stop were now staring at them and at Gearoid's body, and several shoppers had stopped to see what was happening. Garda Brogan said, 'Right. I'll cordon this area off if you take a few pictures. Then we can cover your man up until the white van gets here.'

He ushered all the bus passengers away from the bus stop with his arms spread wide as if he were herding sheep, and told the shoppers to toddle along and go about their messages. Reluctantly they shuffled off, although a small crowd of curious onlookers had already gathered on the opposite side of the street.

'Nothing to see here!' Garda Brogan called out, but they didn't move away.

He went back to the squad car and took out a roll of crime tape and a digital camera. While he tied tape around the bus-stop railings, Garda Cavey was taking a series of photographs of Gearoid from all angles. The forensic technicians would do the same, but this was part of the new first-response kit that was gradually being issued to gardaí all over the country. It was especially helpful in cases of domestic abuse or accidental death, or the homeless found dead in doorways.

Ten minutes later an ambulance arrived, followed shortly after by a van from the Technical Bureau, two more squad cars, and an unmarked car bringing Detective Sergeant Sean Begley and Detective Garda Bedelia Murrish.

'So what do we have here?' asked Detective Sergeant Begley, turning up his coat collar and sniffing loudly.

'Homeless fellow, name of Gearoid,' said Garda Brogan. 'Looks like he died sometime late last night or early this morning.'

'Poor beggar,' said Detective Sergeant Begley. 'Didn't even get the last rites.'

Six

Katie had eased herself out of bed at six a.m., while it was still dark. She showered and dressed as quietly as she could, because Conor was still asleep. Before she left, though, she brought him a mug of tea, switching on the bedside lamp and kissing him on the forehead to wake him.

'Jesus, what time is it?' he blinked.

'Too early for chasing lost dogs. You don't have to get up yet.'

'Oh. That's a relief,' he said, sitting up. 'I'll ring you later so, after I've taken Walter in to Gilabbey. Maybe you'll have time for a bite of lunch with me, even if we only go across the road to The Market.'

'Let's play it by ear. It depends what heinous crimes the good people of Cork have decided to commit during the night. Brendan O'Kane's holding a meeting this morning to introduce himself but I doubt if that will take too long. He's not a man of many words.'

'You knew him from Garda College, didn't you say? Do you think you and he are going to get along okay?'

'You know me, Con. I'm the Angel of Resilience.'

'If "Resilience" was a brand of concrete, I'd agree with you.'

Katie kissed him again, on the lips. She had told Conor that she had trained with Brendan O'Kane at Templemore, but she hadn't told him about their affair, or how it had ended. She didn't believe in causing pain or jealousy when it wasn't necessary.

She arrived at Anglesea Street just after seven twenty. It had rained during the night but the clouds had cleared away now and the pavements were shining. Ana-Maria was still at the station, and Katie found her in the canteen, swinging her legs as she was eating a breakfast of Flahavan's porridge and toast, with a young female garda, Maebh Cassady, looking after her.

Ana-Maria dropped her spoon when she saw Katie walk into the canteen, jumped down from her chair and ran over to hug her. She looked up at her and said, '*Mătuşa... îmi pare rău că am fugit!*'

Katie smiled and gave her an affectionate squeeze. 'Whatever it is you're saying, sweetheart, I'm happy to see you safe. And I love your dress!'

Ana-Maria's hair had been washed and braided into two separate plaits, and she was wearing a bottle-green corduroy dress with a cream lace collar, which Katie guessed had been found in the station's lost property room, because it was two sizes too big for her.

'Here, go back and finish your breakfast,' she said. 'I'll have a coffee myself to keep you company. Maebh, thanks for taking care of her. Do you know what time Margaret O'Reilly's coming over?'

'About eight, she told me,' said Maebh. 'She's fetching an interpreter, too. No, you're grand – it's been a pleasure to look after her. She's a darling. I only wish I could understand a word of what she's saying. We've been playing noughts and crosses, though, and that's kept us laughing.'

Ana-Maria had just finished her toast when Margaret O'Reilly appeared, accompanied by a young balding man in rimless spectacles and a black Puffa jacket. Margaret O'Reilly worked for Tusla, the department of child protection, and her particular concern was lost or abandoned foreign children. She was a tall woman, with wispy grey hair, and a voice that grew louder and then faded away from time to time as if she were standing on top of Knockboy mountain in a fitful breeze.

'So this is Ana-Maria,' said Margaret, pulling out a chair and sitting down next to her. 'How're you going on, Ana-Maria? Have you enjoyed your porridge?'

Ana-Maria looked across at Katie with a worried frown, as if she were asking who this woman was, and what she wanted. Katie gave her a reassuring smile and said, 'Don't you fret, sweetheart. This is Margaret and she's a lovely woman and she's going to take good care of you.'

'*Vreau să rămân cu tine, mătuşă,*' said Ana-Maria, holding out her hand across the table.

'Romanian,' declared the balding young man with satisfaction. He turned to Katie and said, 'She just called you auntie – *mătuşă* – and says she wants to stay with you.'

'She's going to break my heart, this little one,' said Katie. She smiled again at Ana-Maria but she almost felt that by smiling at her she was betraying her, because there was no possible way that she could adopt her. 'Let's go upstairs to my office and we can ask her a few questions about her background and why she was wandering around by herself.'

The balding young man crouched down beside Ana-Maria so that he was on the same level as her. '*Salut, Ana-Maria! Numele meu este Murtagh şi o să vă spun ce vă spun aceste doamne.*'

To Katie, he said, 'I've just told her that my name's Murtagh and that I'll be able to translate whatever she says, so that you'll understand her.'

They all went upstairs to Katie's office and sat on the beige leather couches beside the window, although Ana-Maria almost immediately stood up again so that she could look out at the passing traffic and the hooded crows that were perched on the roof of the building opposite.

'*Mierle!*' she said, pointing.

'*Nu, ciorile cu capişon,*' Murtagh told her. Then, to Katie, 'She said they were blackbirds.'

'Ask her where her father and mother are,' said Katie.

Ana-Maria was silent for a few moments after Murtagh had asked her that, twiddling with one of her plaits. Eventually, she said, 'Daddy's still at home.'

'Okay. But where's your ma?'

'I went around the corner and then she wasn't there. I went back and called her but I couldn't see her anywhere. I didn't know what to do. I asked a lady if she had seen my ma but the lady didn't know what I was saying.'

'When did you come to Ireland?'

'I don't understand.'

'This country is called Ireland. Did you know that?'

'No. Ma said that we were going away for three weeks but she didn't say where.'

'Did she say why you were going away?'

'I don't understand.'

'Did she say what you were going to be doing when you got here? Did she say it was like a holiday, or did she say that you were going to be working, or what?'

'She said we had to ask people in the street for money.'

Katie said, 'Ask her how many people came from Romania along with her and her ma.'

Ana-Maria counted on her fingers, whispering names. '*Caturix... Bogdi... Minodora...*' At last she said, 'Twenty-one, I think.'

'And you were all going to ask people in the street for money?'

'Yes.'

'That man in the grey jacket who you ran away from – did he come with you from Romania?'

'Yes. He brought us here. My ma hated him. She said he was a *lupul*. That's what she always called him, Lupul. But not when he could hear her.'

Murtagh said, 'Lupul. That means wolf.'

'If she hated this Lupul so much, why did she come to Ireland with him?' asked Katie.

'I'm not sure. I think it was something to do with my daddy. I think Daddy owed Lupul some money.'

'Do you know what Lupul's real name is?'

'I think Dragos.'

'But you don't know his second name?'

Ana-Maria shook her head.

Murtagh turned to Katie again and said, 'Dragos is short for Dragomir.'

'Ask her when they arrived here in Ireland, and if they came by air or by ferry. If Dragomir's the name on his passport, the immigration service should have a record of his full name and what kind of a visa he was travelling on, C or a D.'

'We came on a plane and then we came on a ship,' said Ana-Maria. 'We've been here... four days and four nights.'

'Where have you been staying? Do you think you could show us where it is?'

'It's a big house up on a hill,' said Ana-Maria, angling her hand to indicate that the hill was very steep. 'It's cold and damp and it smells like *varză*.'

'Cabbage,' said Murtagh.

'How long have you been there?'

'Three days and two nights. Yesterday was the day we were supposed to go out into the streets and start asking people for money.'

'So you went out with your ma to ask people for money... but she disappeared?'

'Yes.'

'You don't know why she might have disappeared? Did she have an argument with Lupul?'

'I don't know. She and Lupul were always shouting at each other.'

'Ask her if she knows what town Lupul comes from,' said Katie.

Ana-Maria shook her head again.

'What town do *you* come from?'

'Târgovişte.'

Murtagh said, 'Târgovişte... I've been there. It's about eighty kilometres north-east of Bucharest. It has its cathedral and its historical bits but a lot of it's fierce run-down. All those Communist-era blocks, do you know what I mean? It's where they executed the Ceaușescus, out of interest. Out of the court-room, up against the wall, and bang, all in five minutes flat.'

'What's your ma's name?'

'Doamnă Bălescu.'

'And her first name?'

'Sorina.'

'What does she look like? What colour is her hair?'

'The same colour as mine. She's pretty. With brown eyes and red lips. But a little brown spot just there, on her cheek.'

'She means a mole,' said Murtagh.

'And what was she wearing when she disappeared?' asked Katie.

'A red coat. And a brown woolly hat. And brown boots. And she was carrying a big knitted bag.'

'All right, Ana-Maria,' said Katie. 'I'm going to tell all the police officers in the city to start looking for your ma. If she's still here in Cork, I promise you that we'll find her for you.'

Ana-Maria nodded, and whispered, *'Mulțumesc,'* although Katie could see that she was very close to crying.

'Come on, sweetheart,' Katie told her, taking hold of her hand. 'I have to talk to Margaret here for a few minutes. How would you like to do some drawing? Moirin… could you fetch in some paper and some of those coloured pencils, please?'

Moirin came in with a legal pad and a mug filled with assorted crayons. She took Ana-Maria over to Katie's desk and sat her down and said, 'There, pet. Why don't you draw me a pussycat?'

'Doamnă întreabă dacă ai desena pisoi pentru ea,' Murtagh translated.

Ana-Maria nodded again, and said, *'Da.'*

She folded back the first page of the legal pad. As she did so, she caught sight of the braided gold ring that Katie had left lying on her desk. She let out a funny little squeal, clapped her hands and picked it up.

'What's wrong, sweetheart?' Katie asked her.

Ana-Maria slid off the chair and came back to her, holding the ring up high. Now the tears were streaming down her cheeks, and her mouth was turned down in anguish.

'*Acest inel... acesta este inelul mamei mele. Ea nu-l scoate niciodată.*'

'What's she saying?' Katie asked Murtagh. 'Something about her mother. Is it her mother's ring?'

'Yes,' said Murtagh. 'She says it's her mother's ring but her mother never took it off.'

Katie held out her arms and held Ana-Maria close. Ana-Maria was trembling and sobbing and squeezing the ring tightly between her finger and thumb as if somehow that could magically make her mother reappear.

'This ring was handed in as lost property,' said Katie. 'Maebh... can you go down to the front desk and see if they have a record of who handed this in, and when, and if they told the duty officer where they found it. Apparently Sergeant O'Farrell said there was some kind of a story behind it, but I haven't yet found out what.'

She said to Ana-Maria, 'May we borrow this for just a few minutes?' but Ana-Maria shook her head, clutching the ring tight in the palm of her hand and holding it close to her chest.

'Okay, not a problem,' said Katie. She took out her iPhone and said, 'At least let me take a picture of it.'

Ana-Maria reluctantly held it up while Katie took three or four quick photos. While she was doing that, Murtagh leaned over and peered at the ring over the top of his spectacles.

'Since she's Romanian, I'm pretty sure I know whose face that is,' he told Katie, as Maebh left the office. 'You see this cut in her forehead... that's not damage to the ring. If this is who I think it is, it's part of the story.'

'So who do you think it is?' asked Katie, stroking Ana-Maria's plaits to calm her down.

'Saint Philothea of Argeș.'

'That's a mouthful.'

'She's the most famous saint in Romania. In fact, they call her the Protectress of Romania, although she was born in Bulgaria. She was only a young girl when she died. It was her job to fetch her father his food when he worked in the fields. Every day, though, she used to give some of his food to poor children that she met on the way. When her father found out what she'd been doing, he was so thick about it that he hit her in the head with an axe. Hence this cut.'

'Mother of God, what a monster,' said Katie, although Murtagh had reminded her uncomfortably of what her own father had done.

'The story goes that her father couldn't move her body,' Murtagh went on. 'He couldn't shift it for love nor money and nor neither could nobody else. So he called for some priests and they read out a long list of possible places to bury her, and when they came to the monastery of Curtea de Argeş in Romania, her body suddenly became light and they could pick her up. Her remains are still there today, in Curtea de Argeş. It's a fantastic building all right, massive.'

'I'm sure it is,' said Katie. 'But what we need to know is who took this ring off Ana-Maria's ma, if she never took it off herself, and where she is now. Tell Ana-Maria she can keep the ring, would you, but she'll have to give me a few minutes to talk to Margaret. We need to find somebody to take care of her, but it must be somewhere safe. For some reason this Lupul wants to lay his hands on her.'

Maebh said, 'Maybe he's after her because she knows something incriminating about him, like, do you know what I mean, even though she doesn't know herself that she knows it. Do you remember that little Tommy Kelly last year? Only four years old, poor innocent little fellow, and he told me where all of his uncle's guns were buried. His uncle was only after trying to run him over with his tractor.'

Margaret leaned forward. 'There's a couple in Glanmire who could take her in – Michael and Sadhbh Flynn. They're youngish, in their early forties, and they've taken in emergency cases for us before. The husband's an IT specialist and works from home now, so he's always around, but he's ex-Navy so he's no stranger to security.'

'They sound perfect,' said Katie. 'I'll make sure that the Glanmire gardaí know that she's there, though – at least until I know more about this Lupul and why he tried to grab her. Meanwhile, I'll see if we can't contact her father in Romania. We can start by contacting the Romanian embassy in Dublin. Murtagh – you could help us with that.'

'I will of course.'

'Right – if you could tell Ana-Maria that Margaret is going to take her to meet some really friendly people who are going to look after her. We'll have to find her a coat, too, otherwise she'll be foundered outside.'

Murtagh quietly told Ana-Maria what was going to happen, and Ana-Maria nodded, although she never took her eyes off Katie, as if she were expecting Katie to interrupt and say, *No, forget that, you'll be coming to stay with me.*

'There'll be a rake of paperwork,' said Margaret. 'But I'll sort everything out with the immigration. INIS have always been pure understanding when it comes to stray children.'

Maebh returned a few minutes later, accompanied by Sergeant O'Farrell, who was holding the lost property logbook under his arm.

Sergeant O'Farrell came over to Katie and opened the book, but before he showed her what was written in it he nodded towards Ana-Maria and said, 'Cassady told me she doesn't understand English. Is that right?'

'That's right. She speaks only Romanian.'

'Well, then, here's the entry for that gold ring. It was fetched in at seven forty-nine yesterday evening by Patrick Devlin of St Anne's Terrace. He said his ma was making meatballs in the afternoon for her family's supper and she found the ring in the mince.'

'In the *mince*? Serious? Where did she buy it from, this mince?'

'Buckley's on Shandon Street. She always buys her meat there, so he said. She thought that one of the butcher's assistants might have dropped it into the mincer accidental-like. She couldn't take it back to the shop to complain because they would have been closed by then, and apparently they're closed all day Wednesday. He was coming into town clubbing anyway so she told him to fetch the ring in here. She's fierce superstitious and she thought it was bad luck or something with that creepy face on it and she didn't want to have it in the house.'

Sergeant O'Farrell thought for a moment, and then he shrugged. 'Maybe she hoped that if the ring was handed in to us, we'd be giving the butcher down the banks when he came to claim it. You know, for contaminating his meat, like.'

'But now we know that the ring *didn't* belong to one of the butchers,' said Katie. 'So how did it get mixed up in the mince? I hope to God you're not thinking what I'm thinking.'

Sergeant O'Farrell glanced across at Ana-Maria again. 'You're sure she doesn't understand us?'

'We need to test that mince,' said Katie. 'I'll send Markey and Scanlan up to St Anne's Terrace to see if they can get a sample, even if Mrs Devlin's already binned it. I'm presuming that she didn't make meatballs out of it.'

'No, she didn't. But her son said she flushed it all down the toilet.'

'Oh, perfect. In that case, they can find out where this Buckley lives and have him open his shop up for us. Bill Phinner can send a couple of technical experts up there to take traces from their mincer, and see what he might have stored in their fridge, heaven forbid.'

Sergeant O'Farrell said, 'You don't really believe – well, you don't really think—'

'Let's see what the test results tell us. But do you know something, Ryan – I have a fierce uneasy feeling about this. You know what it's like when the sky turns a funny colour and you feel that a storm's brewing up? That kind of a feeling.'

Seven

'Here he is, the poor little cub,' said Conor.

He lifted the grey plastic dog-carrier crate on to the table in Dr O'Sullivan's treatment room and opened it up. Dr O'Sullivan reached inside and lifted Walter out, holding him up as if he were a newborn baby and staring intently into his squashed black face.

'Well, I can tell you for starters, Con, he's having desperate trouble with his respiration. And you're right about his eyes. Classic example of proptosis. I hate to say it, but this unfortunate pup should never have been born at all.'

'If you could give him a thorough once-over for me, Domnall, and let me know how much you'd be charging to set him to rights. Or as near to rights as you can manage. Then at least his owner will have a choice. She can leave him to suffer, or fix him – whatever that's going to cost – or she can have you put him to sleep.'

'I'll do what I can so. Leave him with me.'

'I'll come back in a couple of hours if that's okay. I'm going up to Ballynahina to see his breeders.'

'Not the dreaded McQuaide sisters?'

'The very ones.'

'Well, watch yourself with Blánaid. She's the pretty one but she's sharp all right. You'd think she'd been sleeping in the kitchen drawer with all the knives. Caoilfhoinn's not so bad but a bit on the slow side and she does whatever her sister tells her.'

'Anything else I should know about them?'

'They put up a pure respectable front but I have it on good authority that they're churning out illegal puppies by the hundreds. Oh – and be wide when it comes to their so-called trainer. I don't know what his name is but he's a second cousin to the O'Flynns. Bit of a hard chaw.'

'Okay. Thanks for the heads-up. I'll see you later.'

Walter turned his head around and looked at Conor as he walked away. In his seven years as a pet detective, Conor had handled scores of mistreated and miserable dogs, but there was something in the sad, hopeless way that Walter looked at him that touched him. Perhaps it was what Domnall had said about him, that he should never have been born at all.

Conor drove north from the city through the village of Dublin Hill and up the long straight ribbon of a country road that was Glenville Street. The morning was almost bright enough for sunglasses. He heard on his car radio that a rough sleeper had been discovered dead in a doorway on St Patrick's Street. He also heard that a young woman's body had been recovered from the River Lee, a suspected victim of the 'Lee Pusher', who was supposed to be haunting the river at night, pushing drunk or unsuspecting victims into the water.

He saw a sign at the roadside with the name Foggy Fields on it, so he turned off and drove down a narrow boreen with nothing on either side but low hedges and fields that were speckled with distant cows. After driving two kilometres he came to a metal gateway, with a larger sign for Foggy Fields, and a painting of a shaggy labradoodle puppy with a pink ribbon tied round one of its ears. A steep asphalt forecourt led up to a large stone farmhouse with a slate roof, and behind the farmhouse Conor could see a row of five yellow-painted sheds.

As he climbed out of his car, a woman appeared around the side of the farmhouse carrying a plastic bucket in one hand and a broom in the other. She was short and plump, with a round face under a purple headscarf, and she was wearing a shiny pink padded jacket that made her look even plumper.

'How're you going on there?' she called out. 'Is there something I can help you with?'

'I hope so,' said Conor. 'I'm looking for a puppy for my daughter as a birthday present, and I've heard good things about Foggy Fields.'

'Is it any special breed you're after?'

'She has her heart set on a pug.'

'I'm sure we can help you there. Let me just put away this bucket and brush, and you can come inside and see what we have on offer.'

She disappeared for a few moments around the other side of the farmhouse, and he heard a loud clattering. When she came back, she led him in through the front porch and into an office, where another woman was sitting on the edge of a cluttered desk, talking on the phone. This woman was no taller, but she was slim, with wavy blonde hair and a tip-tilted nose and bow-shaped scarlet lips. She was dressed in a loose cream boat neck sweater and tight black leather trousers, with high-heeled ankle boots. She smelled strongly of Estée Lauder Modern Muse.

'It depends how many you're after,' she was saying. 'We can send you fifteen at least in the next two weeks but you'll have to wait till the end of the month if you want more than that. Sure I'd buy more bitches if you paid me more, Stevie, but you can't have it both ways, like, do you know what I mean? You go up to three hundred for the cockapoos and then we can start to talk serious numbers. I don't care what Sammy says. Tell Sammy that if he wants them any cheaper he'll have to come up here and start siring them himself.'

She put down the phone and turned to Conor with a smile. Her front teeth were smudged with lipstick.

'This gentleman's come looking for a pug pup,' the plump woman told her.

'Now!' said the blonde. 'If it's a healthy happy puppy you're

43

looking for, you've come to the right place, I can assure you of that. I'm Blánaid McQuaide and this is my sister, Caoilfhoinn, if she hasn't already introduced herself, which I doubt if she has.'

'Conor MacSuibhne,' said Conor. 'A pal of mine has one of your pugs and spoke very highly of you. My daughter fell in love with the little fellow when she saw it and she's eleven years old next week so I thought I'd come up here and see if I can buy one for her, like.'

'You're in luck, then,' said Blánaid. 'We had a new litter of pugs just three weeks ago, and they're all such darlings you'll find it almost impossible to choose which one you want. Two of them have been snapped up already but there's still four left.'

'They're only three weeks old?' asked Conor. 'Isn't that too young to be taking them away from their mother?'

'Oh, they soon adapt,' said Blánaid. 'I'm sure your daughter will be giving her puppy more love and attention than its mother could ever have given it.'

'Fair play. You're the expert. How much are you asking?'

'For a pug, six hundred and fifty.'

'Phew. I never realized. I thought maybe a couple of hundred.'

'Six hundred and fifty – that's at least a hundred euros less than any other breeder will be asking from you. Why don't you take a look at them? Just imagine your daughter's face when she wakes up in the morning on her birthday and there's a dear little pug sitting on the end of her bed.'

'I don't know, like, at that price.'

'Look, I'll go down to five-seventy-five, but I can't afford to go lower. It's a fierce expensive business, breeding high-quality puppies and giving them the first-class care that we give them here at Foggy Fields. We make scarcely any profit at all and too often we make a loss. We only do it for the love of it, don't we, Caoilfhoinn?'

Caoilfhoinn had been biting her lip and staring out of the window. 'What?' she said. Then, 'Oh, yes. Totally for the love of it, like.'

'Fetch that new pug litter for us and bring them into the parlour, would you?' Blánaid told her.

She slipped off the edge of the desk and while Caoilfhoinn went to find the litter, she led Conor into a large room on the opposite side of the corridor. It was furnished with a reproduction antique sofa and two matching armchairs, and a peat fire was sullenly smouldering in the grate. The lime green walls were hung with paintings of Labradors and boxers and red setters, and with framed certificates from various Irish dog shows. In one corner stood an oak desk with a china statuette of a rough collie like Lassie and, next to it, a credit card terminal.

'It's insane how competitive it is these days, puppy-breeding,' said Blánaid. 'You may have seen some nasty comments about Foggy Fields on Facebook, but they're all posted by rival breeders, do you know? We always take the best care of our breeding bitches... I mean, it would be madness not to, wouldn't it? And we treat all of our puppies like the precious darlings they are.'

'That's reassuring,' said Conor. 'How many breeding bitches do you have here?'

'Oh, a whole variety. You name them. Pugs, labradoodles, cockapoos, Lhasa apsos... all the most popular breeds. There's bigger puppy farms in Cavan, I'll admit that, but we're easily the leading breeders in Cork.'

Conor nodded. Blánaid hadn't really answered his question, but he was posing as a simple, indulgent father who knew nothing at all about dogs. He didn't want her to start suspecting that he was trying to find out what shortcuts she was taking to save money. She had already admitted that she had no compunction about taking a puppy that was only three weeks old away from its mother. To separate them before they were at least six weeks old was not only cruel but bad practice. Any younger and the puppy could suffer severe health and behavioural problems, because it had not yet been taught by its mother how to socialize and how to take care of itself.

As Domnall had once said to him, 'A three-year-old child can walk and talk and feed itself and go to the toilet, but it hasn't yet learned what's right and what's wrong and how to live with other people. You wouldn't dream of taking a three-year-old child away from its mother, so why would you do it to a three-week-old pup?'

Conor went over to the fireplace and held out his hands over the peat. 'It's been desperate cold this month, hasn't it? I can't remember a January as bitter as this.'

'Thank God my partner and me are going to the Maldives the week after next,' said Bláinaid. 'We'll be needing umbrellas only to keep off the sun. Three weeks we're going for. It'll be divine.'

Caoilfhoinn came in, lugging a big soft padded bag. She set it down on the sofa and opened it wide so that Conor could see the four pug puppies sniffing and wriggling inside it.

'They're pure gorgeous, aren't they?' said Bláinaid, reaching into the bag and lifting one of them out. 'This one's the feistiest. He'll give your wee girl hours of fun, I can promise you. Here – hold him if you want to. Say "Hello there, sham – how would you like to come and live with me and my daughter?"'

Conor took the little pug awkwardly, as if he had never held a puppy in his life. He stared into its glassy, bulbous eyes, and the pug stared back at him. He could see and hear at once that it was having trouble breathing. It had undersized nostrils, so that it was breathing through its mouth rather than its nose, which made it drool. It sounded, too, as if it had an elongated palate, which would restrict its airway.

Even though it was so young, it already had crusts around its eyes, because it was suffering from the same problem as Walter, proptosis. It would only have to get involved in a rough-and-tumble with Conor's imaginary daughter and its eyes would be in danger of popping right out of their sockets.

'Well, he's a cute enough little fellow, isn't he?' said Conor. 'I'm sure Aoife will love him.'

'Do you want to take him now?' asked Bláinaid. 'We can also provide you with a pet carrier, a luxury dog bed, and a month's supply of Red Mills puppy food, all at bargain prices.'

'Well, you've won me over,' said Conor, handing the puppy back to her. 'But five-seventy-five... I'll have to make a transfer from my savings account. I could do that tomorrow morning, though, no problem at all, and come back and collect him. And, yes, I'll be needing a bed, won't I, and some food, I hadn't thought about that. Maybe I can take a picture so that Aoife can see what this little fellow looks like.'

'Of course,' said Blánaid, and set the puppy down on the sofa. Conor noticed that it was shivering. This could indicate that it was cold, or anxious, or that it was suffering from respiratory distress or canine distemper or some other neonatal illness. It let out a little squeak which Conor knew to be 'seagulling', and which was a sign of fading puppy syndrome. Whatever was wrong with it, it would probably die within a week or two.

He used his iPhone to take a series of photographs from several different angles, and also a video so that Domnall would be able to see how badly the puppy was quaking.

'Aoife's going to be over the moon when she sees these,' he told Blánaid. 'I'll be back with you in the morning as soon as my money's cleared.'

'We'll be looking forward to seeing you so. We'll have everything ready, especially this little dote.'

Conor drove out through the gate and headed off along the boreen. As soon as he was out of sight of the Foggy Fields farmhouse, however, he pulled his Audi into the side of the road, with two wheels tilted up on the lumpy grass verge, and climbed out. There was a soft breeze blowing, almost like somebody breathing on his face, but the silence out here was overwhelming.

He walked back as far as the high guelder rose hedge that surrounded the puppy farm. He jumped over the ditch at the side of the boreen and climbed up the tussocky hill beyond it, keeping his head down behind the hedge in case one of the McQuaide sisters happened to be looking his way.

He reached the back of the farm, where the five yellow sheds stood. He peered over the hedge and listened, but he couldn't see either Blánaid or Caoilfhoinn, and so he forced his way through a narrow gap in the hedge beside a fence post. He scratched the back of his hand and pressed it against his lips to suck away the blood.

As he was crossing towards the nearest shed, his iPhone warbled. It was Katie, wondering if he was still meeting her for lunch. *Holy Saint Peter,* he thought, *if she knew where I am and what I'm doing here, she'd go wild.*

Before he texted her back, he climbed up the grit-coated steps to the shed door and opened it. As soon as he stepped inside, he was met by an extraordinary noise. This wasn't the cacophony of yipping and yapping that he would have expected from newborn puppies. This was a high-pitched shrieking, more like a crowd of terrified children than dogs, and it was accompanied by the ringing of tiny claws against metallic mesh.

It was gloomy inside the shed, because the skylights in the roof had been painted over with yellow paint, and the air was almost unbreathable. It was suffocatingly warm and it stank of urine and faeces.

Conor saw that the left side of the shed was stacked with wire cages, three deep, and that each cage was crammed with puppies of different breeds – pugs and cockapoos and labradoodles and chihuahuas. They were all in turmoil as Conor walked along the length of the shed, jumping up and screaming and throwing themselves against the sides of their cages. The floors of each cage were covered with nothing more than a thick layer of ripped-up newspapers, soaked in urine, and even though each cage had a plastic water bowl, Conor could see that some of them had been tipped over and many were either empty or filled with urine.

On the right-hand side of the shed there was a row of plywood crates, with lids placed loosely on top. He heard scratching and whining from inside the crates, so he lifted one of the lids and used his iPhone to light up its interior. Lying on a bed of shredded paper was a brown-and-white pointer bitch, staring up at him with mournful eyes, like a tragic Madonna in a medieval painting, except that her eyes were so crusted with yellow gunge that she could barely see. Four newborn puppies were suckling at her, while a fifth was lying in a corner of the crate, half-covered with torn-up paper, its eyes open but clearly weak and sick.

The bitch appeared to be well-fed, but her coat was matted and filthy and she looked exhausted and miserable. Conor guessed that she had given birth to many more litters than was good for her. Seven litters in a bitch's lifetime was more than enough.

He took three or four photographs and a few seconds of video. The bitch looked up at him appealingly, but all he could do was carefully replace the lid on top of the crate and shut her up in darkness again, along with her suckling puppies.

He was about to lift the lid on the next crate when the shed door opened. Immediately the puppies started screaming and jumping and scrambling up against their wire-mesh cages. Conor looked quickly around, but there was nowhere that he could hide himself. All he could do was drop his iPhone back into his coat pocket and stand up straight.

A tall, bulky, broad-shouldered man stepped into the shed. Although he was silhouetted against the daylight from the open door, Conor could see that his head was shiny and shaven, but he had a drooping moustache and a beard. He was wearing a khaki parka with a fur-trimmed hood, and he was carrying a large cardboard box.

As soon as he saw Conor, he said, 'Hey! You! What in the name of feck are you doing in here, hoop?'

Conor raised both hands. 'Just being nosy. I was out for a hod, like, and when I was walking past here I heard dogs barking. I thought they sounded a bit distressed so I came in to see if they were okay. That's all.'

The man dropped the cardboard box on to the floor with a bang that made Conor jump. 'What the feck do you mean you was walking past? Nobody fecking walks past here. Never. This is all private land. Not even the fecking farmer walks past here.'

'Sure look, everything seems to be grand altogether. The dogs I mean. So I'll just be out the gap, shall I?'

Conor approached the man and tried to sidestep past him, but the man sidestepped too, and blocked his way to the door. The man smelled strongly of stale alcohol and body odour. Conor looked up at him and saw that he had a livid Y-shaped scar on the right side of his forehead, above his eye.

'Before you go, hoop, why don't you tell me what you was *really* doing in here? You're not one of them snooping inspectors, are you?'

'Ah, come on, do I look like it? Besides, they always wear the official jackets, don't they, the inspectors, and have badges?'

'Maybe you're one of them newspaper reporters, then. We've had enough fecking trouble from them, I can tell you.'

'I told you. I was walking past and I heard all these dogs barking hysterical-like, and I thought there might be something wrong. I mean, listen to them now, for the love of God. Why do you think we're having to shout to make ourselves heard?'

The man looked down at Conor with one eye half-closed. 'Let's you and me go to see the owners, like. Happen they'll want to call the guards and have you done for trespass. Maybe you was planning on hobbling one or two of our breeding bitches – is that it?'

Conor shook his head. 'Listen, I'm not the ISPCA inspector and I'm not a newspaper reporter and I'm not a dog-napper, either. I've stolen nothing and I've done no damage, so if you'll kindly step out of my path and let me get out of here—'

'I don't fecking believe you,' said the man. 'Come on, let's you and me go to see the McQuaides. They'll know what to do with you. If I let you go, hoop, and it turns out there's a fecking great piece in the *Echo* about Foggy Fields tomorrow, saying it's a shitehole or whatever, what kind of a hard time do you think they'll be after giving me?'

Conor hesitated for a few seconds. If he allowed this man to take him back to Blánaid and Caoilfhoinn, his whole investigation would collapse. They wouldn't sell him their little pug for sure, although he needed it as living proof that they were breeding puppies with total disregard for their happiness and, more importantly, their health. On top of that, he still lacked evidence that the McQuaide sisters owned far more breeding bitches than the law allowed, and that they were exploiting those bitches with unforgivable heartlessness.

'No, forget it,' he said, and tried to push the man out of his way.

The man immediately pushed him back, so hard that he lost his balance and slammed up against the wire-mesh cages right behind him. The little cockapoo puppies inside the cages shrieked and tumbled over each other. Conor grasped the mesh to pull himself upright, but then the man took two steps forward and hit him on the cheek with a left-handed punch. Conor's head was jerked sideways so violently that he felt the sinews in his neck crunch.

Stunned, he dropped on to one knee, shaking his head to clear it, and then trying to stand up again. He was fit, and he had taken judo lessons, but this man was far heavier, and far stronger, and far more violent. As Conor stood up, he punched him in the face, and Conor felt his nasal bone snap. Then he punched him on the right side of his forehead, so that he fell to the left, and as he fell he punched him on the jaw. Conor ended up lying on his back on the filthy wooden floor, and he spat two bloody teeth out of the side of his mouth. Although he was half-concussed, he still tried to lift himself up again, but the man kicked him hard between the legs, not just once but three times, until he doubled up in unspeakable agony and lay on his side, both hands cupping his genitals.

The man stood over him, rubbing his knuckles. 'Fancy another kick, hoop? Or have you had enough? I got plenty more if you want them, free of charge.'

Conor could faintly hear him over the shrieking of the puppies, but he couldn't speak. He was in so much pain that he could barely think. As he lay there on the planks he heard his iPhone warble, and he was vaguely aware that the man bent over him and took it out of his coat pocket, but his testicles hurt so much that he was unable to move. He heard the shed door open and close, but after that everything went dark and silent and he was sure that he was going to die.

Eight

Katie was worried now. She had texted Conor to tell him that she couldn't meet him for lunch because a homeless man had been found dead this morning in a doorway on Pana. She was waiting to be briefed about it, so that she could hold an impromptu media conference at two o'clock.

It was twenty-five minutes since she had texted and Conor had yet to come back to her. He must have heard his phone warble, and even if he had been driving he would have answered her by now. She texted him again. *Where RU? I cant meet 4 lunch.*

She waited, but there was still no reply, so she set her phone down and went back to the assessment that she was writing about last year's crime figures in Cork. There had been a disturbing increase in the number of knife attacks, as well as attacks with corrosive liquids, like drain cleaner and sulphuric acid.

Some of the acid attacks had taken place among the Asian community. At least three girls had been disfigured for refusing to marry the man of their parents' choice. But even more assaults had been committed by young thieves on mopeds, spraying acid into the faces of pedestrians and snatching their mobile phones.

Detective Sergeant Begley knocked at her open door and came in, followed by Detective Bedelia Murrish. Detective Sergeant Begley was looking as buttoned-up as ever, while Detective Murrish was as skinny as a catwalk model, and even walked like one, with an elegant lope.

Even though she hadn't heard it ping, Katie glanced at her iPhone to see if Conor had replied, but the screen remained blank. She pushed back her chair, stood up and said, 'Come on in, Sean – Bedelia. What's the story with this homeless fellow?'

Detective Sergeant Begley took out his notebook and held it at arm's length to focus on it. 'The deceased has been identified as one Gearoid Ó Beargha. Garda Brogan knew him well and said he'd been sleeping in that doorway next to the Savoy Centre for the past two-and-a-half years. He'd been offered at least temporary accommodation by the council and by the Simons, too, but he'd always turned it down.

'Garda Brogan said he came from Clon, originally. He was a folk singer with a band called the Shoot-On-Sights. He used to go drinking with Noel Redding from the Jimi Hendrix Experience, so Brogan said, because of course Redding lived in Clon in his later years, before the cirrhosis took him. The Shoot-On-Sights broke up because Ó Beargha was always langered and once he fell off the stage. He started a solo career, but he usually turned up wrecked for his appearances and so nobody would book him any more.

'His body's been taken to CUH for post mortem, but I'd say it was the drink that did for him, that and the cold. Vodka and hypothermia, that's a desperate combination.'

'There were no outward signs of injury?' Katie asked him.

'None that we could see. No bloodstains on his clothing or anything like that, like. We gave him a quick frisk once they'd put him in the ambulance. He still had money on him, about thirty-five euros in his pocket and ninety more rolled up in one of his socks. If anybody topped him, they didn't do it for the grade. Mind you, the bang of benjy off of his socks, Jesus. If it hadn't been my job I would never have taken his socks off, even if he'd had the winning lotto ticket stuffed inside them.'

'Here, ma'am,' said Detective Murrish, and handed Katie a clear plastic evidence bag. Inside it was a small dog-eared notebook with a green mock-crocodile cover.

'I've had a flick through it already, like, and he's written himself one or two reminders, like his daughter's birthday and his PPS number, but mostly it's full of songs that he's composed. "The Day I Sleep Forever", one of them's called, which is kind of sad.'

Katie gave her a wry smile. She had grown to like Detective Murrish. With her messy straw-blonde hair and her hooded blue eyes, she always looked sleepy and dim, but she had an acute, analytical mind, combined with a sensitivity to other people's emotions that would have done credit to a fortune-teller. This gave her an edge over some of her male colleagues, who were clever at deducing how and when and who, but often failed to give much thought to the deeper reasons why.

'I'm holding a media conference at two,' said Katie. 'I won't be saying too much except that I'll be appealing for any relations or friends of the deceased to come forward so that we can build up a fuller picture of his life and what may have led to his death. But I'm going to make sure that our foot patrols keep a constant watch on the doorway where he used to beg. If it gets taken over by another beggar, they should try and find out who they are – he or she – and what nationality they are. If they're foreign, they need to ask them where they came from and how long they expect to be staying here.

'They should check their ID, but even if they don't have any, they should just leave them be. I don't want them to think that we might be on to them.'

'Where are you going with this?' asked Detective Sergeant Begley. 'Are you thinking this Gearoid might have been offed by this Romanian feen – this Loophole, or whatever his name is?'

'Lupul, yes. I mean, think about it, Sean. Little Ana-Maria told us that he's fetched over twenty people from Romania to beg in the streets. Now if I'd gone to all the trouble and expense of doing that myself, I'd be making sure that I monopolized all the most lucrative begging spots in the city, wouldn't I?'

'I can't argue with that, ma'am. But if he *did* off your man, I'd be interested to know how. Like I say, there was no obvious sign that he'd been shot or stabbed or beaten. Let's just pray it wasn't the nerve agent, you know, like the Novichok, or else we'll be having to put half the city centre in quarantine. Anyway, the lads upstairs are already going through all of the CCTV footage. There's a camera only a few metres away outside of Eason's, and it's pointing towards the Savoy Centre. Nobody could have gone near Gearoid during the night without being recorded.'

'Thanks, Sean, that's grand,' said Katie. She handed the evidence bag back to Detective Murrish. 'Maybe it's worth taking a second look through this book, Bedelia, just to see if there's any indication that he might have been ill, or if there was somebody in his life who wished him harm. Maybe there's a clue in one of his songs. Singers do that sometimes, don't they – write about their troubles in their songs.'

'There's a line in that "The Day I Sleep Forever",' said Detective Murrish. 'It goes something like, "Everybody thinks you love me, just because we share a bed… But I know you'll only be happy when you see me lying stiff and dead." Something like that, anyway.'

'There you are. Maybe it was nothing more than a song he made up, but maybe he was writing about some ex-lover of his. There might be some clue in the notebook as to who it was. It's worth checking.'

'We'll shoot on over to Pana to check that doorway,' said Detective Sergeant Begley. 'If there's nobody there, maybe I'll take it over myself. The moth's nagging to go to Lanzarote for her holliers this year instead of Banna Beach and I could do with the extra grade.'

With only twenty minutes to go before the media conference, Katie had still received no reply from Conor, even though she had repeatedly rung him and texted him and emailed him. This wasn't like him at all. Usually he answered her immediately, and he would often text her during the day with jokes and comments about the news and just to tell her how much he loved her and couldn't wait for her to become Detective Superintendent Ó Máille.

She was thinking of going upstairs to the communications room and asking them if they could track his phone for her when Chief Superintendent O'Kane appeared in the doorway.

'DS Maguire,' he smiled.

Katie was standing by the window with her iPhone in her hand, trying yet again to get an answer from Conor. Brendan came over and stood close beside her, closer than he would have done if they had been only work colleagues.

'Help you with anything, sir?' she asked him.

'Sure like, this homeless fellow that's been found dead. How are you thinking of presenting this?'

Katie looked up at him. She could still see the mischief in his eyes, and God, he was still handsome in that sharp hollow-cheeked way that had made her feel like mothering him and surrendering to him, both at once, all those years ago.

'I'm saying nothing special. Just the facts.'

'Don't you think this would be an opportunity to express our concern about the number of people sleeping rough in Cork every night? Maybe we could say that we're setting up a night patrol to make sure that they're as safe and well as possible, and to try to persuade them to try their luck at a hostel.'

'It's our job to protect them, sir, but I don't think their welfare comes under our remit. You can ask Superintendent Pearse, but I seriously doubt if he has the officers available for a night patrol, let alone the budget.'

'I just want us to come across as being more humane, Katie. Or is it against protocol to call you Katie?'

Katie said nothing, but looked at her iPhone again, and then dropped it into her jacket pocket.

'What happened between us at Templemore, Katie, I'm hoping that's all water under the bridge. You've done brilliantly well for yourself, and I respect you for that, and I'd like us to work as close together as we possibly can. We really have our work cut out, winning back the public's trust.'

'The best way we can do that is for us to be consistently truthful,' said Katie. 'In fact, it's the only way. No more fiddling the breath-test figures or wiping the points off celebrities' driving licences or taking backhanders to let offenders go free. We don't need PR stunts like a night patrol for rough sleepers.'

'Fair play, maybe you're right. But I'd appreciate any other ideas you might have for enhancing our public image. I want you to think that you can come to me at any time and talk over strategy.'

'Thank you, sir. Now I'd better be getting downstairs for the media conference. Will you be attending it yourself?'

'Katie – there's no need for you to be so official. You don't have to call me "sir". At least, not when we're alone together.'

Katie looked up at him again, but again she said nothing. She couldn't stop thinking about Conor, and where he was, and why he wasn't answering her texts.

'I won't beat about the bush,' said Brendan. 'The minute you walked into Michael Pearse's office I mentally kicked myself for having cheated on you all those years ago. You're even more attractive now than you were then, Katie, I don't mind telling you.'

He paused, as if he were waiting for her to thank him, but instead she went over to her desk and picked up the notes she had written for the media conference.

'I'm not suggesting for a moment that we pick up where we left off,' Brendan persisted. 'I'd like to believe, though, that we can be friends again – very close friends – as well as fellow police officers. That's all I wanted to say.'

'I'm engaged to be married, sir,' said Katie, tilting up her chin to challenge him.

'Yes. Michael told me. Lucky fellow.'

Katie buttoned up her jacket and left her office, with Brendan following close behind her. *Too* close behind her – as close as a husband or a lover might follow – but she didn't want to walk faster to increase the distance between them because that would turn this awkward moment into a comedy. Besides, why should she?

They went down in the lift together. Neither of them spoke, but Brendan didn't take his eyes off her once. Katie glanced from side to side, but she couldn't stop herself from looking back at him. What a bastard he was. Why did he have to be so handsome, and so charismatic? She could almost smell the pheromones that he exuded. She fixed her gaze on the orange pips on his epaulettes, but they, too, were a symbol of his power.

There were only a few reporters in the conference room when she walked in – Dan Keane from the *Examiner*, Douglas Kelly from the *Times* and Fionnuala Sweeney from the *Six One News*, as well as two freelancers. Brendan came in behind her, but not so close now. When she sat down, though, he sat beside her, and laid his hand flat on the desk, almost as if he expected her to lay her hand on top of his. Katie could see that the red tally light on the RTÉ video camera was switched on, and so she made sure she didn't look down at his hand and that her face showed no reaction at all.

'Sadly—' she began, 'sadly, a homeless individual by the name of Gearoid Ó Beargha was found deceased in a doorway on St Patrick's Street early this morning. He was forty-six years old, and previously from Clonakilty. The cause of his death was not immediately apparent, but his remains have been taken to Cork University Hospital for a post mortem by the deputy state pathologist.'

She gave the reporters the details of Gearoid's background as a musician, and asked for anybody who had any information about his health or his personal circumstances to contact her at Anglesea Street.

When she had finished, Brendan raised one hand for attention.

'I would like to add one thing more, one personal comment. Now that I've been appointed chief superintendent here in Cork city, I'm intending to work closely with the council, the social services and the relevant charities to address the increasing problem of rough sleepers. We don't want to lose any more Gearoid Ó Bearghas. Not one.

'No matter how destitute they are, no matter how disturbed or addicted or down on their luck, all of the men and women sleeping outdoors on these freezing cold nights are our brothers and sisters, and we owe it to them to protect them.

'Detective Superintendent Maguire has agreed to help me in this mission. She is an officer of exceptional ability and drive, not to mention charisma. I know that between us we can soon make a considerable difference to the streets of Cork – giving shelter to the homeless, sustenance to the hungry, and hope to the hopeless.'

He turned to look at Katie, and Katie was sure that the cameras captured the provocative expression on his face. She saw Dan Keane raise an eyebrow, and Dan Keane never missed a trick. She gave a quick, humourless smile, shuffled her notes and stood up.

Mother of divine Jesus, this man is after fetching me a heap of trouble on top of the heap of trouble I already have.

Nine

Brianna had only just poured out two cups of tea for herself and Darragh when the call came for them to attend an accident in Wellington Road, on the northside of the city.

'I think they do this deliberate-like,' she told Darragh, lifting her high-viz jacket off the back of the chair and shrugging it on. 'They have a sixth sense, so the second I have a cup of the scaldy in my hand, they go and crash their cars or set fire to themselves or fall down a well.'

'You're nearly right,' said Darragh, as they bustled out of the door. 'A young woman's fallen downstairs. She's pregnant so they're worried about the baby too.'

They climbed into their ambulance and drove out past Smyths Toys and headed for the city. Traffic was sparse this afternoon so Darragh didn't have to switch on the siren until they reached Merchants Quay and crossed the river by St Patrick's Bridge.

'I meant to tell you I saw that boyfriend of yours in town yesterday evening,' said Darragh, as he turned up MacCurtain Street.

'Braden? Oh, yeah? He didn't mention it.'

'We had only a brief natter, like. But he was saying that you two were buying yourselves a new car. One of them BMW X3s. Jesus, I wish. I'm still rattling around in that old Toyota.'

'Oh, you shouldn't believe everything that Braden tells you. He's had his eye on one of them ever since one of his pals from the football club showed up in one. He's been out of work since St Stephen's Day and can you see me affording one on my wage?'

They drove up York Hill and then turned right into Wellington Road, which led up to St Luke's Cross. Halfway up the road they saw an elderly man standing on the pavement outside a maroon-painted house, waving at them. Darragh pulled into the kerb and he and Brianna climbed out of the ambulance.

'She's inside,' the man gabbled. 'I'm their neighbour, from down below them anyway. I heard this bumping, like, and she's only fallen all the way down the stairs from the top to the bottom and she's lying there now because we didn't like to move her, do you know what I mean, in case we caused her more injury. The thing of it is, she's expecting, and her husband's terrified that she could lose it.'

The front door was open, and so Brianna and Darragh went straight into the hallway. It was dark in there, and smelled of damp, and the wallpaper was peeling off. Directly in front of them was a precipitous staircase, carpeted with sisal, and at the bottom of the staircase, lying on her back with her arms outstretched and her legs wide apart, was a dark-haired young woman. She had obviously been on her way out when she had fallen because she was wearing a brown overcoat and Ugg boots, although one of her boots had fallen off. The sisal carpeting was slippery, even though it was rough, and the treads of the stairs were very narrow, so it wasn't surprising that she had lost her footing.

Kneeling on the floor beside her was a pale, curly headed man of about thirty years old, wearing a mustard-coloured sweater and grey tracksuit bottoms. He was gently stroking her forehead and calling her name, 'Ailbe – Ailbe – Ailbe – can you hear me, Ailbe? *Ailbe!*'

When he saw Brianna and Darragh enter the hallway, he stood up and held out his arms like a religious supplicant.

'Thank God you're here. She fell all the way down from the landing and she's seven months' pregnant. She's breathing all right but she hasn't opened her eyes and she hasn't said a word.'

'And her name's Ailbe, yes? And yours is?'

'Peter.'

'Okay, Peter. If you can stand back now so that I can examine Ailbe and see what we can do for her. Darragh – we're going to be needing a neck collar here.'

Ailbe's face was so white that she could have been a marble angel in some cemetery. She was breathing, although her breaths were quick and irregular, little sips of air, as if the angel were trying hard to conceal the fact that she wasn't really marble, but alive. Brianna opened her resuscitation bag and took out her flashlight, and then she gently peeled back Ailbe's right eyelid and shone the light into her pupil. The pupil was dilated and it didn't constrict in response to the light, which was one indication that Ailbe was concussed. Brianna peeled back the left eyelid, and saw that the pupil was smaller, another symptom of concussion.

'Is she going to be all right?' asked Peter from the doorway, his hands clutched together.

Brianna was taking Ailbe's pulse, which was rapid but weak. 'She's knocked herself out, Peter, and they'll have to do a CT scan when she gets to the hospital to make sure that she hasn't bruised her brain. I haven't yet given her a once-over to see if she's broken any bones.'

'And the baby? What about the wain? He's a little boy.'

Once Brianna had taken her pulse and her blood pressure, she unbuttoned Ailbe's coat and then her thick pink home-knitted cardigan. Underneath her cardigan, Ailbe was wearing a dark brown corduroy maternity dress, and Brianna lifted up the hem and tugged down her tights so that she could check her white knickers. There was no trace of blood or fluid so it looked as if her amniotic sac hadn't been ruptured.

She laid her hand on Ailbe's distended stomach and she could feel the baby stirring inside her. Once they had carried Ailbe into the ambulance, she could use a Doppler stethoscope to measure the baby's heartbeat.

'You're all right,' she told Peter. 'I don't believe the baby's come to any harm.'

'Oh Jesus Christ in Heaven, I hope not.'

Quickly and carefully, Brianna felt Ailbe's arms and legs and pelvis. She seemed to have no bones broken, but her neck was at an awkward angle. As she tumbled down the stairs she must have twisted around trying to save herself and the back of her head had hit the hallway floor so hard that her chin was now pressed against her chest. It was possible that she had sustained a similar kind of lesion as the boy and the girl in the overturned Fiesta, or even dislocated her vertebrae.

Darragh appeared in the doorway with the trolley from the ambulance, with a cervical collar on top of it, which looked like the lower half of a knight's helmet made of hard white plastic. He knelt down on the other side of the hallway and gently raised Ailbe's shoulders so that Brianna could fit the collar around her neck and fasten its Velcro straps.

'She's going to be all right, isn't she?' asked Peter. 'She hasn't broken her neck, has she? Nothing like that?'

'Like I say, they'll be giving her a scan when we get to the hospital,' said Brianna. 'She's stable for the moment but I'll be keeping an eye on her vital signs until we get there. The baby's too.'

'Should I come in the ambulance with her?'

'Best not to. Health and safety and all that, like. You have a car, though, do you? You can follow us to Wilton but if we have to go through a red light you won't be able to go through it after us, I'm afraid. We don't want two casualties in one day.'

Brianna and Darragh lifted Ailbe on to the trolley and wheeled her out to the ambulance. Peter ran up the road to where he had parked his battered blue Kia.

Before he climbed into the driver's seat, Darragh nodded towards Ailbe. 'What's the form?' he asked Brianna. What he meant was, no matter what you told Peter, how seriously hurt is she really?

'Touch and go, I'd say,' said Brianna, as she unhooked the oxygen mask and fitted it over Ailbe's nose and mouth. 'I felt a soft lump on the back of her neck when I was fitting the collar and I'd guess she has a serious compression fracture. She could easy have damaged her spinal cord, and then who knows? She'll be lucky to end up a quadriplegic.'

Darragh looked down at Ailbe sadly and said, 'Jesus, you wouldn't wish that on anybody, would you? Poor girl. She's the bulb off my cousin Sinead.'

'Come on, Darragh, let's get going. Every second counts.'

Darragh started up the ambulance and they drove up to St Luke's Cross with the siren whooping and scribbling, and then turned south down Summerhill. Through the tinted rear windows, Brianna could see Peter following close behind them.

She took Ailbe's pulse and blood pressure again. Although she was still unconscious, her pulse was much stronger and more regular, and her blood pressure had risen. Her eyelids fluttered and her lips moved as if she were trying to say something. Maybe she was calling for Peter to help her. Maybe she was simply asking 'Where am I?', like most concussion patients when they eventually opened their eyes.

'Should have watched your step, shouldn't you, girl, being pregnant and all?' Brianna said, under her breath.

'How's it going back there?' Darragh called out.

'She's stable. I'm just going to check the baby's heartbeat.'

They crossed over the Brian Boru Bridge, heading for the South Ring Road, the fastest route to the hospital. Depending on the traffic, Brianna reckoned that she had less than ten minutes before they reached the emergency room. She lifted up Ailbe's dress to bare her stomach, and then she unzipped the case containing the Doppler stethoscope. It had a headset, like a normal stethoscope, but a hand-held battery-operated wand, which was pressed against the patient's skin to detect a foetal heartbeat. Brianna smeared Ailbe's stomach with gel, but she didn't put on the headset. She laid the stethoscope to one side so that it would look as if she had been using it.

Ailbe's lips had started moving again, and her left eye was half open. The last thing that Brianna wanted was for Ailbe to regain consciousness and see her, or to start speaking out loud. That would make it too much like murder, rather than euthanasia, which is how she preferred to think of it. When she lay in bed at night, wide awake while Braden snored beside her, she liked to consider that what she had done during the day were Christian acts of mercy. Her patients had very little hope of recovery, and even if they did recover, most of them would be physically maimed or brain-damaged and their lives would be almost intolerable. How would Ailbe bring up her baby, if she were paralysed from the neck down? She wouldn't even be able to hold it to her breast, to feed him.

Once Ailbe was brain-dead, her baby might survive if the doctors could keep her heart beating artificially, but they would have to start doing this the moment after she died. There would be only one outcome of what Brianna was intending to do, and that was two funerals.

They had reached the South Ring now, and Brianna had to hold on to the nearest grab handle to keep her balance while they tilted their way around the Magic Roundabout. As soon as the ambulance was steady, though, she ripped open the Velcro fasteners on the sides of Ailbe's cervical collar, lifted her head and took the collar apart.

Ailbe let out a high-pitched whistle through her nose, and then the faintest of moans, as if she were having a bad dream. Brianna held her head tightly in both hands, her fingers buried deep in her thick dark-brown hair, and wrenched it upwards, until she heard a crackling sound in her neck. Next she pushed Ailbe's head to the left, as hard as she could, and then to the right. Finally, she twisted it around in each direction, as far as it would go, like Regan's in *The Exorcist*, until she heard that same crackle from her fractured vertebrae.

Brianna bent over Ailbe, and listened. She was no longer breathing, but Brianna checked her pulse again, just to make sure. No pulse at all. Her heart had stopped. Her stomach bulged and rippled, but that was her baby kicking, and if he was no longer receiving oxygenated blood, he too would die, within only a few minutes.

They had nearly reached the hospital. Brianna fitted the cervical collar back on to Ailbe's neck and tidied her hair. She checked her pulse one more time to make absolutely certain that she was dead. Her baby was still kicking, although his kicks were feebler, and less frequent, and by the time they turned into the hospital entrance and backed up to the emergency entrance, he seemed to have stopped kicking altogether.

Darragh opened the back doors of the ambulance and said, 'How is she?'

Brianna burst into tears. 'Oh God, Darragh. She's gone. I did everything I could but she went out like a light. Let's get her inside quick. Maybe we can save her baby but I doubt there's much hope.'

Two hospital orderlies came out and helped them to lift Ailbe out of the ambulance and wheel her inside. Brianna stood on the ambulance steps with her hand pressed over her mouth and her eyes blurry with tears. She felt genuinely sad for what she had done, but what would Ailbe's life have been like if she hadn't finished it for her? And her baby would never know how his life might have turned out, because he would never see daylight. At least they would both be remembered with inscriptions on a gravestone, and that was more than was granted to most of the people who died in this world, whose names and lives were forgotten for ever.

Peter's blue Kia drew up next to the ambulance with a slither of tyres and Peter scrambled out, leaving the driver's door wide open. He ran over and said, 'She's okay, isn't she? She hasn't lost the baby or anything?'

Darragh laid a hand on his shoulder and said, 'Come inside, boy. They'll be giving her a full examination, the doctors, and they can tell you a whole lot more than we can.'

Peter turned around and saw Brianna wiping the tears from

her eyes with a crumpled tissue. He turned back to Darragh and said, 'Why is she crying? What's happened?'

'Come on inside,' said Darragh.

'Why is she crying? Tell me! Why is she crying?'

Ten

They had found an address for Eamon Buckley the butcher on the PULSE computer, but when they knocked at the door on Mount Agnes Road they were told by a plump young woman jiggling a fat baby in her arms that he didn't live there any longer and she had no idea at all where he had moved to.

They went to his shop at the top end of Shandon Street and although it was closed and the blinds were drawn down over the windows, the Pakistani newsagent next door knew where he was living now. They didn't tell him that they were detectives but he must have guessed because he called out, 'What's he done now?'

Detectives Scanlan and Markey had already seen Eamon Buckley's criminal record. He had been convicted and fined three times in the past five years for assault, and once for threatening to cause serious harm. That was when he had chased a customer halfway down Shandon Street brandishing a meat cleaver, although he hadn't managed to catch him.

His house was a large detached property on the corner of Farranferris Avenue and Kilnap Place, freshly painted a pale mushroom colour, with a white pillared porch added to the front to make it look even grander than its semi-detached neighbours. It was high up on the northside of the city in Farranree, with a distant view of the green hills to the south. A new red Mondeo was parked at an angle in the driveway.

'Why am I nervous about this?' asked Detective Scanlan, as she opened the wrought-iron front gate.

'Oh come on, Padragain. He's only a butcher with a record of violence and we're only going to be asking him how some woman's ring got mixed up in his mince.'

'Nothing to worry about at all, then? Even when we ask him to open up his shop so that we can look for evidence that he's been butchering human beings?'

'You have it. I'll bet you he's as docile as your auntie's pet poodle.'

'My auntie doesn't have a pet poodle. She has a marmalade cat that will scratch your eyes out as soon as look at you.'

Detective Markey climbed the front steps and rang the doorbell. Inside the house they could hear chimes playing 'My Wild Irish Rose'. At first there was no response, but then they heard a man's voice shouting, 'There's somebody at the door, for feck's sake! Is nobody going to see who it is?'

A woman's voice screamed something unintelligible in reply, and then there was the sound of somebody clumping angrily downstairs. Still the door didn't open, and Detective Scanlan said, 'Try ringing again.'

'I don't think I need to,' said Detective Markey. 'I think he knows that we're out here, like. Maybe he's just zipping his pants up.'

They waited almost a minute, but the door remained closed, and eventually Detective Markey pressed the bell button a second time. While the chimes were still playing, the door was flung open and Eamon Buckley was standing there, bald but unshaven, dressed in a sleeveless vest and a baggy pair of green corduroy trousers.

He was huge. He filled up almost the entire doorway. He had an overhanging forehead with deep-set eyes buried underneath it and a jutting jaw like an Easter Island monument. His shoulders and upper arms were writhing with tattoos, mostly dragons and snakes, but a GAA badge, too.

'If you're after selling something, I don't want it,' he said in a thick, raspy voice. 'And if you're debt collectors come about the car you can go and feck yourselves, the pair of you.'

Both detectives took out their ID cards. 'Detective Markey and Detective Scanlan, from Anglesea Street Garda Station,' said Detective Markey.

'Oh yeah? Well, if some skanger's told you that I give them a dawk, I never.'

'Nobody's complained about you assaulting them, Mr Buckley. But one of your customers found a gold ring in a portion of beef mince that you sold her, and we're interested to know how it might have found its way there.'

'What? What's their name, this customer?'

'We're not at liberty to tell you, sir. All we need to know is where the ring might have come from. For instance, could one of your assistants have dropped it in the mince by accident?'

'I have only the one assistant and he don't wear rings. And I don't wear rings neither. This is shite, this is. This is some gouger trying to get compo, that's what this is. I've had it before. They say they've found a dead wazzer in their tripe or a mouse's tail in their drisheen. Mind you, they've only fecking eaten it all before they discovered that there was anything wrong with it, so there's never any fecking evidence, like.'

'That's as may be,' said Detective Scanlan. 'But we'd appreciate it if you'd come down to Shandon Street and open up the shop for us, so that our technical experts can carry out a few tests.'

Eamon Buckley stared at Detective Scanlan with his beady near-together eyes as if she had suggested that he should drop his trousers, come out into his front garden and dance the High-Cauled Cap for them.

'Open up the shop? I will in my fecking gonkapouch, girl. The shop's closed Wednesdays. Now you can feck off and leave me in peace. I don't know nothing about no ring and to tell you the truth I don't give a shite.'

With that, he slammed the door shut, leaving Detective Markey and Detective Scanlan staring at each other, half in surprise and half in amusement.

Detective Markey pressed the doorbell again. There was no

response, so he pressed it again, and again. After the third chiming of 'My Wild Irish Rose', though, Eamon Buckley shouted out, 'Feck off before I have you for harassment!'

Detective Scanlan stepped right up to the front door and called out, 'Mr Buckley! It's no use at all your refusing to co-operate! We have a District Court warrant to search your shop, can you hear me? If you don't open it up for us, we'll have to open it by force and any damage that's done you'll have to pay for yourself!'

There was a lengthy silence. After a while, the front door opened again and Eamon Buckley stood there, glowering at them.

Detective Scanlan stepped back, but then she reached into her jacket, took out the warrant, and held it up in front of him. 'This is it, Mr Buckley. You can read it for yourself if you want to. Signed by Judge Gráinne Devins in person.'

'Okay, girl, whatever,' Eamon Buckley growled at her. 'Stall it there for a couple of minutes while I put on my coat and my boots. This is a fecking liberty, this is. I don't know nothing about no fecking ring. It's a scam, that's what it is. I'm being persamacuted.'

While Eamon Buckley went inside to finish dressing, Detective Markey rang the Technical Bureau and told them to meet him and Detective Scanlan outside the butcher's shop. After nearly ten minutes, Eamon Buckley came out wearing a tight-fitting Crombie overcoat with a moth-eaten velvet collar and a dark brown knitted hat like a tea cosy.

'I fecking warn you,' he said, as he followed them down the garden path, 'I'll be after complaining to Mick Nugent about this.' Mick Nugent was the Sinn Féin councillor for Cork City North West. Detective Markey said nothing, but opened the back door of their Vectra for him and stood patiently waiting while he squeezed himself in.

They drove down to Shandon Street by way of Redemption Road. Eamon Buckley reeked of stale cigarettes and every now and then he snorted with a catarrhal thump. None of them spoke. Detective Scanlan didn't even want to breathe the same air as him, let alone talk.

They parked outside his shop and once he had heaved himself out of the car Eamon Buckley took out a jangling bunch of keys that would have done justice to a jailer. He opened up the door and led the two detectives inside. The shop was chilly and dark and smelled of stale blood and bleach. Eamon Buckley let up the blinds and then stood in front of the empty glass display counter with his arms folded.

'Well, go on, then,' he said. 'Search all you like, but I can tell you for nothing that whatever you're looking for you won't find it.'

'I think we'll be the judges of that, sir,' said Detective Scanlan.

They waited uncomfortably for a few more minutes and then a Technical Bureau van drew up outside. Three technicians climbed out, two men and a woman, and one of the men gave them a cheery salute through the window. Once the technicians had pulled on their white Tyvek suits, they came rustling into the shop like three noisy ghosts, lugging their shiny aluminium cases of forensic equipment and a Lumatec ultraviolet lamp.

'How're you going on?' the woman technician asked the two detectives. Then she turned to Eamon Buckley and said, 'Are you the owner of this shop, sir?'

'What of it?' he retorted.

'Well – we'll be here for several hours yet,' she told him, look-ing around. 'There's no need for you to stay. In fact, we'd prefer it if you left us to crack on without you being here. We can lock up for you when we've finished, if you can give us the key.'

'If I leave you here by yourselves, how can I be sure that you won't be planting some evidence?' Eamon Buckley demanded. 'Like maybe some blood you've brought with you, or somebody's chopped-off fingers, so that you can leave prints all over the shop.'

'Jesus, I should have thought of that, shouldn't I?' said the woman technician. 'Serious, though, sir, we have a rake of genu-ine evidence from other investigations to be dealing with. We're up the walls with it. We don't need to be inventing any.'

She pointed to the cold-room door at the rear of the shop.

'I'm assuming you have a fair amount of meat stored in the back there?'

'What the feck do you think I have in there? Christmas trees? I'm a fecking butcher, aren't I? Of course there's fecking meat in there.'

'Sure, like. It's just that I have to advise you that we may be taking samples of meat away with us so that we can carry out more extensive tests in our laboratory. We'll provide you with a full list of what we've removed.'

'And you'll be paying me for it, won't you? Because I won't be able to sell it once you've been messing around with it. The eye of the round, that's fifteen euros the kilo, and fillet steak, the piece, that's thirty-eight euros. And I only take cash.'

Detective Markey said, 'How about giving us the key, Mr Buckley, and then we can drive you back home.'

Eamon Buckley hesitated for a moment, but then he took out his massive bunch of keys and used his thumbnail to prise the shop key off its ring. Once he had grudgingly handed it over to the woman technician, Detective Scanlan said, 'Let's be out the gap, shall we, Mr Buckley, and let these good people get on.' She ushered him out through the door, while Detective Markey stayed behind to have a brief conversation with the three technicians.

Outside on the pavement, Eamon Buckley snorted again, and coughed, and spat, and then he beckoned to Detective Scanlan and said, 'C'mere till I tell you something.'

Detective Scanlan was looking at her iPhone to see if she had been sent any new texts.

'What's on your mind?' she asked him.

He leaned close to her, and spoke in a harsh, soft voice, glancing over her shoulder from time to time as if he were making sure that nobody else could hear him.

'I'll tell you what's on my mind. I don't know what the feck you think you're looking for, but there's nothing for you to find, like I told you, and if you *do* find something, whatever it is, then it's a fecking fit-up. So what I'm telling you is, if you *do* find something, you'll need to be doggy wide, girl, twenty-four/seven. I'm one of the best butchers in Cork, do you know what I mean, and there's nothing I don't know about cutting up pigs and sheep and cows, and a woman detective wouldn't be too much different. Except for the fun bags, maybe.'

Detective Scanlan stared at him for a few seconds, her heart beating fast. When she answered him, her throat had tightened up, but she did everything she could to sound professional and unimpressed.

'Let me tell *you* something, Mr Buckley. Making a threat to kill or cause serious harm to a garda is a criminal offence. I could arrest you for what you've just said, and you could be sent to prison for a maximum of ten years, or have to pay a fine of fifteen hundred euros. But then you know that perfectly well already, don't you?'

Eamon Buckley raised both of his huge hands. 'What the feck are you on about, girl? I never said a word. Not a single fecking word. Prove that I did, go on! Arrest me if you want to, and take me to court, and I'll tell the judge that you're lying through your teeth and I never said nothing.'

He leaned close to her again. He gave her a grin that bared his snaggled, tobacco-stained teeth, and then he lasciviously licked his lips. 'Some cuts are juicier than others, did you know that? Rump, or flange.'

Detective Markey came out of the shop. 'Ready to go?' he said. Then, seeing Detective Scanlan's expression, 'What's the form, Pad? What's going on here?'

'Nothing at all,' said Eamon Buckley. 'We was just discussing the desperate high price of bodice, wasn't we, girl?'

Detective Scanlan opened the Vectra's rear door and said, 'Get in.'

Eamon Buckley climbed in, still grinning at her, and Detective Scanlan slammed the door.

'What's the story?' Detective Markey asked her.

'It's nothing. He threatened me, that's all.'

'The gobshite. We could haul him in for that.'

'Forget it, Nick. He doesn't scare me. What's he going to do, strangle me with a string of sausages?'

Detective Markey looked at Eamon Buckley sitting in the back seat and Eamon Buckley winked at him and gave him a thumb's up, as if to say, *I know what she's telling you, and believe me I mean it.*

'I don't know,' said Detective Markey. 'It kind of depends how that ring ended up in that mince, wouldn't you think?'

Eleven

It was nearly four o'clock before Conor rang her.

'Katie?' he said. He sounded stuffed-up, as if his nose were blocked. 'You're not in a meeting or anything, are you?'

'Jesus, Con, where have you been? I've been trying to get in touch with you for hours. I was beginning to think you'd had an accident.'

'I have in a way. I'm in the emergency room at CUH. I can't speak now because they're just about to take me through for an X-ray.'

He paused, and Katie heard him grunt in pain. Then he said, 'I was given a bit of a beating up at Foggy Fields. I'll tell you about it later.'

'What? No, you won't. I'll come over there right now.'

'Listen, you don't have to. It's not life-threatening. I can still drive, so I'll see you this evening when you get home.'

'Don't argue, Con. I'm coming over. I'll see you in fifteen minutes, if not sooner.'

Katie told Moirin that she was going to CUH, then she buttoned up her dark green hooded coat and hurried downstairs. As she was crossing the reception area she met Detective Sergeant Begley, who was carrying a plastic bag that smelled strongly of Chinese takeaway.

'Late lunch, Sean?' she asked him, taking out her car keys.

'I was coming up to see you once I'd had a bite to eat,' he told her. 'Garda Brogan rang me.'

'Brogan? He was one of the officers who found that homeless fellow dead outside the Savoy Centre this morning, wasn't he?'

'That's right. I'd asked him to call me if any other beggar had taken his place. And sure enough, they had already. Talk about jumping into a dead man's shoes.'

He set his bag down carefully on the floor, took out his iPhone and flicked it until he found what he was looking for. 'There,' he said, passing it over to Katie. 'That's your man.'

Garda Brogan had sent him a photograph of the beggar who was now sitting in the doorway where Gearoid Ó Beargha had died. He was a scrawny young man with a prominent nose and blond hair tied in a man-bun on top of his head. He was wearing a dirty bronze quilted anorak and a sad-looking grey mongrel was lying on his blanket next to him. Propped up next to him was a cardboard sign saying, *No Work Please Generos.*

'Brogan spoke to him. He said he was a coffin-maker and that he had come from Romania looking for work, but he hadn't yet been able to find anybody who would employ him.'

'A coffin-maker? That's fierce appropriate. But don't tell me there aren't enough people dying in Romania to keep him in business back home. They have a measles epidemic there, don't they?'

'Who knows? Maybe the Romanian undertakers don't pay as well as ours do, over here. Brogan said he spoke reasonable English and when he asked him for his papers, he showed him his Romanian ID card, and that was all in order.'

'So what did he do then?'

'Nothing. Let him be, like you told us. I'd briefed Brogan that if he found anybody he wasn't to move them on, and not to give them any cause to think that we might be checking up on them, like, to see if they were part of some organized begging ring.'

'Good work,' said Katie. 'But make sure we keep him under constant observation from the CCTV. If anybody comes up to talk to him like they know him, get in touch with me at once. I want to see what they look like. By the way – what about the footage of our deceased fellow, what's his name, Gearoid? Any results from that yet?'

'The lads upstairs are still scanning through that now, ma'am. Your man settled himself down to sleep real early yesterday evening, about half-past eight, so it could take them three or four hours before they find anything, even if they speed it up. Are you away out now?'

'I'm off to the Wilton Hilton. I'm not sure how long I'm going to be.'

'Okay, but I'll text you if anything interesting comes up.'

'Thanks. Now away with you and have your lunch. You don't want your chow mein going cold.'

She arrived at the emergency room just as Conor was being wheeled in from the X-ray department. She was shocked by how badly he had been beaten up, and if it hadn't been for his chestnut beard she hardly would have recognized him. His face was monstrously bruised, black and red and swollen, and a large white dressing was stuck across his nose with adhesive plasters. His left eye was almost closed, like an overripe aubergine, and his lips on the left side of his mouth were puffed up and split and crusted with scabs.

The porter pushed his trolley into one of the cubicles and tugged the blue curtain across to give them some privacy.

'Holy Mother of God, Con,' said Katie, taking hold of Conor's hand. 'Who did this to you?'

'It was my own fault, Katie,' he told her, in that stuffed-up voice. 'I was being too nosy, as usual.'

'Con, look at the *state* of you. What on earth happened?'

'I went up to Foggy Fields puppy farm. I told the McQuaide sisters that I wanted to buy a pug puppy for my daughter.'

'What? What daughter? You never told me you had a daughter.'

'I don't of course. I wanted them to incriminate themselves out of their own mouths, that's all, and they did. They offered to sell me a pug that was only three weeks old – far too young to be taken away from its mother. It looked pure sick, too.'

He stopped suddenly, clamped his hand over his mouth, hesitated, and then retched.

'What's the matter?' Katie asked him. 'Do you want me to call for a nurse?'

Conor took a deep breath and then he shook his head. 'No, you're all right. I've been gawking so much I don't have any gawk left in me. Give me a moment.'

'You have to tell me who did this to you, darling. I'll have them hauled in and charged with assault. They'll get time for doing this.'

'You can't. It was my own fault, like I told you. I went around the back of the farm to take a sneaky look inside one of their puppy-breeding sheds.'

'You went inside one of the McQuaide sisters' sheds without asking their permission?'

Conor nodded. 'I was about to take some pictures when this sham-feen the size of Tyson Fury came busting in and caught me at it. I can take care of myself, usually, but I didn't stand a chance against this fellow. He slapped me and kicked me all over the shop.'

He paused and swallowed, and then he said, 'You should have seen it in that shed, Katie. It's like hell on earth for those poor breeding bitches, and their puppies, too. Hell on earth.'

'I'm sure that it is, Con, and I know how desperate you are to stop this puppy farming, but you were *trespassing*, for the love of God.'

'I know. But how else was I going to get evidence against them? They wouldn't have let me take a look voluntarily, like, would they?'

Katie dragged over a plastic chair and sat down. She felt both sympathetic and exasperated. She didn't want to make Conor feel any worse, because it was obvious that he was in pain, but he had risked his freedom for the sake of those puppies.

'You know very well the conditions of your sentence being suspended,' she told him. 'What did the judge say? You're not to involve yourself in any more illegal activity against people you suspect to be mistreating dogs – no matter how justified you believe yourself to be. Leave it to the ISPCA, that's what he told you.'

'Well, I know, but—'

'Con – think about it. This fellow who beat you up could well go to prison, but you know what he's going to say in his defence. He found you trespassing on private property, and he'll probably say that you were causing damage, or that he thought you were after stealing some of the dogs. That means that *you'll* go to prison, too, no question about it, for violating the rules of your probation.'

She squeezed his hand tight. She was very close to tears. 'If you get yourself locked up, Con, how are we going to get married in the summer? I'm a Garda superintendent. I can't have a wedding ceremony in the prison chapel up at Rathmore Road.'

'Then for Christ's sake *don't* arrest him,' said Conor. 'I've admitted that it was my own stupid fault.'

'But look what he's done to you. When I first saw you just now, I hardly knew who you were.'

At that moment Katie heard the curtain being drawn back, and a polite cough. She turned around to see a consultant coming in, sympathetically smiling. He was dark-skinned, neatly bearded, with rimless spectacles. He was carrying a folder with several X-ray photographs in it.

'Bhavik Sandhu,' he announced. 'I am a consultant in urology. I will be taking care of Conor this afternoon.'

'Detective Superintendent Kathleen Maguire,' said Katie. The consultant's eyebrows lifted and he gave her a quick, evasive smile, as if he didn't quite know how to react to that.

'I see. Are you investigating how Conor came to be so badly injured?'

'Yes and no. He's my fiancé, as it happens.'

'I see. Your fiancé? Well, I'm sorry to have to tell you this, but your fiancé is going to require urgent surgery.'

He turned to Conor and said, 'The triage nurse tells me that you were kicked between the legs, Conor, is that correct?'

'That's right. Three times at least, so far as I remember. I mean, Jesus. I didn't know pain like that even existed. It went right off the register.'

'It is hardly surprising that it hurt so much. Your X-ray has shown that your testicles are badly bruised and that you're suffering from testicular torsion. Your spermatic cords have been twisted and this means that the blood supply to both of your testicles has been cut off.'

'I know what it means, doctor,' Conor told him. 'How serious is it?'

'Well, not to beat around the bushes, extremely serious, which is why we will have to take you into theatre straight away. Because of the length of time that has elapsed since you were injured, your testicles have already started to atrophy, and without a blood supply for so many hours there is a high risk that they could infarct. This means that they could die.'

'I know what that means too, doctor. In that case, the sooner you operate, the better, don't you think?'

'I will have you prepped for surgery within the next few minutes, Conor. Once we have sorted out your testicles, one of our maxillofacial surgeons can address your other injuries. You have a fracture of your zygoma, your cheekbone, and also a multiple fracture of the floor of your orbit, your eye socket. It's possible that we may need to insert a graft to rebuild your orbit – titanium, perhaps, or dissolvable plastic.'

'What about my nose? I can feel it crunching inside and I can hardly breathe.'

'We'll have to wait for the swelling to go down first. Then you'll need rhinoplasty to straighten it.'

'Oh, Con,' said Katie, and took hold of his hand again.

'Serves me right, doesn't it, charging around like Brian Boru?

I should have remembered that Brian Boru got pure creamed out of it, the same as me.'

They were still talking when a porter and two nurses appeared, one almost anorexically thin and the other chubby.

'Conor Ó Máille?' said the chubby nurse, cheerfully. 'We're ready to take you off to the theatre now, Conor.'

Conor looked up at Katie. 'I'm sorry, darling. For you, more than myself. I've made a right hames of everything, haven't I?'

'Oh, for God's sake, don't fret yourself about it,' said Katie, taking a tissue out of her coat pocket to wipe her eyes. 'You were haunted not to be killed. I'll be saying a prayer for you, Con, and I'll be back later when you're out of surgery.'

Conor caught the sleeve of her coat. 'Listen, just one more thing. Walter. I left him with Domnall at the Gilabbey. He's going to need picking up and looking after.'

'Okay, Con. No problem. I'll take care of him.'

She watched him being wheeled away. She felt as if the metaphorical storm that she had predicted had suddenly rolled in, and that the sky had blackened overhead.

She was sitting in the relatives' waiting room half an hour later when her iPhone played 'Mo Ghille Mear'. When she took it out, she saw that she had been sent a text by the deputy state pathologist, Dr Mary Kelley.

Gearoid Ó Beargha did NOT die of natural causes. I'll email you full post-mortem report shortly + photos CGI scans.

Katie immediately stood up and left the waiting room and walked quickly to the hospital mortuary. When she pushed open the doors and went inside, she found Dr Kelley standing in front of her computer, busily typing with two fingers. Katie thought she had lost some weight since she had last seen her, and she looked less like a Russian matryoshka doll than she had before, although she still had a double chin.

Along the left-hand wall of the mortuary, four trolleys were lined up. All of them clearly had cadavers on them but they were discreetly covered in green surgical sheets. In the centre of the room, Gearoid was lying naked on a stainless-steel autopsy table, face down. His skin was as white as candle wax, although he had two wings of dense dark hair across his shoulders. His arms and legs were hairy, too, and his buttocks were blotched by a mass of blue and yellow bruises. The downdraught ventilation system around the autopsy table was switched on, to minimize odours and to protect the pathologist from breathing in pathogens while she was working on him, but Katie could still detect the distinctive rotten-chicken smell of death.

'Kathleen! That was amazingly fast,' said Dr Kelley. She switched her computer to sleep and came over to Katie, holding out a green surgical mask.

'I was here in the hospital already, as it happens,' said Katie. 'A friend of mine has had a bit of an accident.'

'Not too drastic, I hope?'

'They're operating on him now. He should be fine by the time they've finished with him, God willing.'

'I'll tell you, Kathleen, if I didn't work here, you wouldn't get me near a hospital for love nor money. I wish I'd taken my old dad's advice and trained to be a chemist. And my ma – she thought I ought to be a teacher in high babies. She said I had the sympathy for it. But, oh no. I was determined to cut people up, more fool me.'

Katie tied on her mask and tugged it up over her nose, and then she crossed over to join Dr Kelley beside Gearoid's naked body.

'He has all the usual symptoms that you'd expect from a street sleeper,' said Dr Kelley. 'He has liver cirrhosis, hepatitis B, eczema and psoriasis. He also has skin infestations including scabies, foot trauma and dental caries, and a chronic lung infection. In any event I wouldn't have given him a life expectancy of more than three or four years, the condition he's in.'

'But he didn't die of natural causes?'

The tangled curls on the back of Gearoid's head had already been parted, but Dr Kelley leaned over and brushed a few stray hairs out of the way, so that Katie could clearly see a small red hole in his skull.

She peered at it closely. 'That's not a bullet wound,' she said. 'It doesn't look like a stab wound, either.'

'You're right, it's not. It's a drill hole. He's been *drilled* to death, with what I would guess is an ordinary cordless drill. You know – the sort you can buy in Hickeys or Clark's or any do-it-yourself shop.'

'Serious? You mean like one of those Black and Deckers?' Katie lifted her hand up as if she were holding one.

'Spot on. And whoever killed him, they knew exactly what they were doing, because there are no hesitation marks. I would guess that they felt for his occipital protuberance – you see this bump here at the back of his skull. Then they located the soft spot underneath it and drilled at an angle upwards, into his brainstem. I could tell from the CGI scan that they must have swished the drill around a bit just to make sure. His medulla oblongata has been drilled into mush, and that would have killed him instantly. Stopped his heart, stopped his breathing, stopped all sensory communication between his brain and his body.'

Katie was silent for a moment. 'What about forensic evidence?'

'If you look here, you can see these two wide bruises on his back and this was probably where his assailant knelt on him while he was drilling into his head. There's some bruising on his left wrist, too, although that might not be related. Bill Phinner has all his clothes and his shoes, of course, and the poor fellow's few possessions. There was a little bundle of love letters from some woman called Ailbe.'

'Has anybody from the Technical Bureau examined his body yet?'

'One of Bill's technicians is coming across here later to take some more pictures and some hair and skin samples, but to be honest with you I can't see how they're going to help us. You'd need to find the drill bit and see if it had any remnants of his brainstem on it. Of course, whoever killed him would only have to put the drill bit in a dishwasher and that would be that. There's nothing like a Finish Powerball for getting rid of evidence. They ought to say that in their ads.'

'All right, Mary,' said Katie. 'Thanks a million for that. I'd best be getting back to the waiting room. I don't know how long my friend's operation is going to take.'

'I'll be emailing the post mortem to the station for you in about twenty minutes, and I'll send you a hard copy too. I hope your friend makes a full recovery, anyway.'

'Thanks. Me too.'

As she walked back along the hospital corridor, Katie thought – *what if Conor doesn't* make a full recovery? *What if the surgeons can't save his testicles, and he turns out to be sterile?* She admitted to herself then that ever since she had accepted his proposal of marriage, she had been turning over and over in the back of her mind the possibility of having a baby with Conor, although she hadn't allowed herself to shape the thought into words.

Any child she had with Conor could never replace her little Seamus, and she wouldn't want that, anyway. But after she had come into his nursery that morning and found Seamus dead in his cot, she had always felt incomplete somehow because she had no children. Five out of her six sisters had families, and after all she was still young enough to be a mother. Hadn't that Gwen Stefani become pregnant with her youngest child at the age of forty-three and Janet Jackson had been fifty when she had given birth. So why shouldn't she? An Garda Síochána granted maternity leave, after all.

She went outside the front entrance of the hospital and phoned Detective Inspector Mulliken. It was dark now, and it was starting to rain, so she stayed close to the wall under the shelter of the portico. When Detective Inspector Mulliken answered, she gave him all the details of Gearoid Ó Beargha's post mortem.

'Oh, that's grand, that is,' he said, with a sigh. 'Now we'll be having to stop and search suspects for cordless drills as well as firearms. What's it going to be next? Food mixers?'

'Wait, there's more,' she said, and she told him about the young Romanian coffin-maker who had taken over Gearoid's begging site outside the Savoy Centre.

'You think he might have had something to do with this Gearoid being murdered?'

'We have no way of knowing, Tony, not yet – although yes, it's a fair possibility. But listen, I want us to check the passports or the ID cards of every Romanian national we find on the streets. We'll need to do it fierce discreet-like. Let's check on all the other rough sleepers as well, so it doesn't look like we're picking on Romanians in particular. I'm convinced there's an organized begging ring in the city at the moment, and I don't want them to get wide and melt away before we can haul them all in.'

'Okay, ma'am, I have you,' said Detective Inspector Mulliken. 'I'll go down right now and talk to Superintendent Pearse. I'll ask him if his foot patrols can make a start this evening. They could check up on a few of the homeless tonight, do you know, and then a few more tomorrow. That way, it'll seem like it's random.'

'Maybe they can arrange for a member of the Simon Community to go around them – or somebody from the city council's homeless emergency service. If they do that, it'll look much more like they're simply concerned about the rough sleepers' welfare. It should help to identify any professional beggars, too. If they're professional beggars they won't want to move and risk losing their site, even if it means they get a bowl of soup and a warm bed for the night.'

'That's good thinking, ma'am. I'll make sure it's done.'

Katie went back into the hospital and sat down in the waiting room. On the table lay a copy of an old *VIP* magazine with a picture of the Instagram star Tara O'Farrell on the cover, showing off her seven-month baby bump. *Oh thank you, Lord*, she thought. *Why don't you rub it in?*

An elderly woman on the opposite side of the waiting room gave her a smile, and said, 'All right?' But the reality was that Katie felt as if her mooring rope had come loose, and she was adrift.

Twelve

'Oh Jesus, Matty, I'm dying,' whispered Máire, huddling up closer to him. 'I can't feel my feet any more.'

Matty lifted his head so that he could peer down to the bottom of their sleeping bag. 'It's that fecking bin liner, that's what it is. It's only gone and blown away, like. No wonder your feet are so cold.'

The two of them were bundled up in the doorway of an empty shop on Cook Street, opposite the Vanilla Café. The temperature had dropped below freezing now, and the rain was dredging along the pavement like a funeral procession seen through a fog.

They were both in their middle thirties, although Matty was prematurely drawn and grey, and Máire's face was yellowish and bloated from cirrhosis. What now seemed like years and years ago, Máire had been a promising young dress designer and Matty had been studying at the School of Law at Cork University. They had bumped into each other at Gorby's nightclub one Freakscene Wednesday, and they had been attracted to each other almost at once. After the nightclub had closed, some old school friends of Matty's had invited them round to their flat in Togher for drinks, and in the early hours of that morning they had both first tried crack cocaine.

Their sleeping bag was ripped at the bottom, which was why Matty had covered it with a black bin liner. Now the bin liner had been whipped away by the wind, and the sleeping bag was drenched, and so were the three pairs of thick woolly socks that Máire was wearing.

She snuggled in closer. 'I can't feel my feet but the rest of me's aching something terrible,' she said, and then she started to cough. She coughed and coughed, bringing up sticky lumps of phlegm.

At last she stopped coughing and wiped her mouth three or four times with her tartan scarf.

'Do you think Scully's still around?' she asked Matty.

'Even if he is, he won't give us any. We've missed two tick Fridays and we'd have to settle up first.'

'What about Bimbo?'

'Not a hope in hell. He's most likely in bed by now with that molly pal of his.'

'How much grade do we have left?'

'Thirty-six euros and eleven cents.'

'Is that all? We shouldn't have bought those fish and chips. I'm probably going to puke mine up anyway. But that's enough for a screed of coke, isn't it? There must be somebody who'll sell us some. What about Billy Murphy?'

'Billy Murphy? His stuff's seventy per cent cattle wormer.'

'I know. But it's still thirty per cent pure.'

Matty shivered. He felt drained and exhausted, as if the endless rain had diluted his blood and turned it to pale pink water. He had a nagging ache in his lower back and underneath his maroon woollen hood his scalp itched so much that he could have scratched it until it bled. He didn't know if he could summon up the strength to go trudging around the deserted streets of Cork at this time of night, looking for somebody to sell him a rock of crack cocaine for €36.11. Even if he could find a dealer, a rock half the size of a thumbnail usually cost €50 or more.

There was a West African nicknamed Zoomer who hung around the entrances to the Voodoo Rooms and Chambers, the gay club on Washington Street, but both of those would be closed by now, and in any case he hadn't seen Zoomer in weeks. Maybe he had gone back to Nigeria or been lifted by an undercover drug officer or been stabbed by a rival dealer.

Although Matty was so tired and so reluctant to struggle out of their sleeping bag, Máire had triggered the need in him and he knew he wouldn't be able to settle down again until he had managed to find something to smoke or snort. In the crumpled plastic Dunnes' bag in which they kept most of their belongings there was a crack pipe, which he had made out of a Tanora bottle topped with tinfoil and duct tape. He could already imagine himself sucking on it and feeling the high.

Maybe The Hangout on Princes Street was still open, and maybe Billy Murphy was still there. Máire was right. Even if he only had snow, what did it matter if it was seventy per cent cattle wormer? As long as it wasn't seventy per cent baby laxative, which had made Matty fill his trousers almost as soon as he had snorted it.

'Okay, then, I'll see what I can find,' he said, and started to struggle with the zip fastener on the side of the sleeping bag, which was always awkward because several teeth were missing.

He managed to jerk the zip halfway down and crawl out of the sleeping bag on to the cold, wet pavement. He was still on his hands and knees when three men appeared out of the rain and walked up to him.

'You're going somewhere, my friend?' one of the men asked him, in a strangely musical foreign accent, almost as if he were singing it.

Matty reached out and gripped the sill on the side of the shop doorway to help himself on to his feet. As he did so, the men stepped closer, hemming him in. One of the men was tall while the other two were shorter, although all of them were heavily built. The tall man wore a grey leather jacket, while the others were dressed in black anoraks and jeans.

'What are you after?' said Máire, in a reedy voice. 'We've no grade if that's what you're after, and we've no gravel either.'

'We don't want no money, nor drug,' the tall man told her. 'All we want is you move.'

'What do you mean, move?' Matty demanded. 'It's the middle of the fecking night, for Christ's sake.'

'What does that matter?' the tall man asked him. 'You move, that's all.'

'You're not cops, are you?'

'Do we look like cops?'

'Well, if you're not cops you can go and jump in the river. We're not going anywhere. This is our pitch.'

The tall man turned to look at his two companions for a moment, as if he wanted their reassurance that he was being reasonable.

'What difference one doorway or some other doorway? Go find yourself and this *curvă* some other doorway.'

Matty was shaking now, and his knees were so weak that he had to lean against the shop window again. He didn't feel like arguing. He didn't feel like anything except creeping back into the sleeping bag and bundling himself up and going back to sleep. Why didn't these men just go away and leave him and Máire alone? He was too tired and disorientated to think about moving, and apart from that, this doorway was more than just a shelter from the rain. They had settled into it six weeks ago when the previous occupant had disappeared, and they had found it to be the most profitable spot for begging that they had ever known. Before this they had squatted in the entrance of an empty estate agent's office on South Mall, and they hadn't collected half the money that they were making every day here on Cook Street.

'Go,' the tall man repeated. 'Pick up all this crap rubbish of yours and sling hook.'

'Get stuffed,' said Matty. 'We're going nowhere.'

The tall man cupped one hand to his ear and leaned forward as if he hadn't heard. 'What did you say, my friend?'

'I said, get stuffed. Go on, up the yard with you. We're staying right here and there's no way you can budge us.'

'Marku,' said the tall man, quietly, taking a step backwards.

One of the shorter men slung a khaki canvas bag off his shoulder, unbuckled it, and lifted out a black cordless drill. Before Matty had a chance to say anything, or to react, the tall man took another step back and said, 'Danut!' in that sing-song way, like 'Dah-*nooot!*'

The other man stepped into the shop doorway, seized Matty's shoulders and twisted him around so that he lost his balance and staggered down on to one knee. He almost fell on top of Máire, and Máire tilted herself away and screamed out, '*What are you doing, you skanger? Leave him alone! Get off him!*'

The tall man ignored her and said nothing, watching dispassionately as Danut forced Matty face down on to the pavement and knelt on his back.

'*Get off him! Leave him alone!*' Máire kept on screaming, wrestling her arms out of the sleeping bag and taking hold of Danut's sleeve, trying to pull him off. Marku handed the cordless drill to Danut and then he slapped Máire hard around the side of her head – first with his right hand and then with his left.

'*Linişte!*' he snapped. 'You shut up your mouth!'

'You *bastard*!' she screeched at him.

'*Taci!*' he retorted, and slapped her again, so hard that she pitched backwards and hit her head with a loud *klokk!* against the shop door. She fell sideways, stunned, making a thin mewling sound.

Danut had tugged down Matty's hood and with his left hand he was feeling the back of his skull through his prickly grey hair. Once he had found the lump that he was looking for, he held his thumb against it as a marker while he pressed Matty's nose hard against the pavement. Matty was too weak to struggle. Like everything else in his life these days, he just lay there and accepted whatever was going to happen to him. He didn't even pray.

Danut looked up at the tall man and said, 'Okay? *Nimeni nu vine?*'

The tall man glanced up and down the pedestrian precinct and then nodded, and said, 'Okay.' Danut positioned the tip of

the drill bit up against Matty's neck, about a centimetre underneath his thumb. Then – with a sharp whine – he drilled into his
skin. Matty jumped as if he had been electrocuted, and let out a
strangely childish cry, more like a small boy who has lost something dear to him than a grown-up man in agony.

Danut waggled the drill up and down and from side to side,
and then carefully drew it out. Underneath him, Matty was lying
completely lifeless. Danut handed the drill back to Marku and
pulled Matty's hood up.

Máire was sitting up now, blinking in pain, with one hand
holding the side of her head. 'Matty!' she said, huskily. '*Matty?*'

'He said he would not go, but *see!* now he is gone,' said the tall
man. 'That is what you get when stupid.'

'Matty! Oh Jesus, Matty! What have they done to you? *Matty!*'

Máire kicked her legs out of the sleeping bag and climbed over
to Matty's body. She knelt beside him and shook his shoulder, but
when he didn't respond she tried to turn him over on to his back.

'Matty!' she wept, miserably. 'Don't leave me, Matty! You can't
leave me alone, Matty! I won't be able to live without you! Where
will I go? What will I do? I'm going to die without you, Matty!
Matty, wake up! Matty!'

'He won't wake up, *curvă,* not never,' said the tall man. 'So
time for you to go also, and to forget you saw us.'

Máire stood up, swaying as if she were drunk in her sagging
knee-length orange cardigan. '*Forget* you? How am I ever going
to forget you? You killed my Matty! I saw you! How am I ever
going to forget that? You scumbags!'

She lurched towards him, both hands lifted like claws. She had
taken only two stumbling steps, though, before Danut stepped
across and seized both of her wrists, forcing her back into the
shop doorway and up against the door.

'Get your filthy disgusting hands off me, you dirtball!' she spat
at him, and a long string of saliva and phlegm dangled from her
lower lip. 'You'll be locked up for what you've done to my Matty,
don't think that you won't!'

'Marku,' said Danut, tersely. '*Dă-mi burghiul electric. Apoi, vino aici și ține mâinile acestei femei.*'

Marku passed him the drill and then took over holding Máire's wrists. Máire twisted and thrashed and then tried to drop herself down to the ground, but Marku kept her pinned up against the door.

'*Întoarceți femeia în jur!*' Danut told him, and Marku tried again and again to turn Máire around so that she had her back to him, but again and again she twisted around to face him, spitting and gasping and swearing. He was strong but she was hysterical, bursting with fear and hatred and adrenaline.

With his left hand Danut grabbed Máire by the throat, forcing her head back. She spluttered and choked, her eyes bulging, but she still managed to spit at him. He lifted the drill and pointed it at the centre of her forehead, and when she spat at him again he drilled straight into her skull. The drill bit snagged for a second against her bone and made a high squeaking noise, and the drill stalled; but Danut jiggled it and pressed the trigger again and managed to pull it out.

'*Aaaahhhhh!*' Máire screamed at him. '*You murderer! You shitehawk! You bastard!*'

Danut said nothing, but moved the drill three centimetres to the right and drilled into her forehead again. She kept on screaming for a few seconds but then suddenly she stopped. Danut took the drill out, moved it up a further three centimetres and drilled a third hole. He drilled another and another and another, until Máire's forehead was riddled with them. Her eyes were still open but now they were glassy and focused on nothing.

Danut took his hand away from her throat and her head dropped forward. He lifted the drill as if he was going to bore more holes in the top of her skull, but the tall man laid his hand on his shoulder and said, '*Ajunge.* No more. She is dead now.'

Danut and Marku let Máire slide down to the pavement. The three men then stood over the bodies, discussing quickly and quietly what they were going to do with them. The tall man decided that they would leave Matty where he was, because he looked as if he had died from natural causes, but that they would have to carry Máire away with them.

They rolled her back into her sleeping bag, pulled up the zip as far as they could, and then Danut hoisted her over his shoulder, like a butcher carrying a side of beef. The three of them made their way along Cook Street to Oliver Plunkett Street, where their green Hyundai was parked in the loading bay outside Soundstore. Again the tall man looked quickly up and down the street to make sure that there was nobody in sight, and then they opened up the boot of the car and dropped Máire's body inside, so that it thumped on top of some plastic shopping bags.

Without a word, they all climbed into the Hyundai, with Marku behind the wheel, and drove away.

Back along Cook Street, a dishevelled stray cat came padding up to Matty's body and sniffed at it. Matty lay there with his cheek against the pavement, his eyes closed, not even dreaming of the life he should have had as a lawyer, smart and prosperous, with a house overlooking the River Lee and a family that would never be.

Thirteen

It was ten past one in the morning before Mr Sandhu came into the waiting room. Katie was sitting with her eyes closed and an open copy of *Stellar* about to tip off her lap. Mr Sandhu reached out and touched her gently on the shoulder.

'Are you sleeping?' he asked her.

Katie instantly opened her eyes and sat up straight, and the magazine dropped on to the floor.

'What?' she said. 'No... just resting, that's all. What time is it?'

'It has gone one o'clock. Your fiancé's operation took longer than I expected, but it is all over now, and he has been taken upstairs to a private room to recover. He is not awake yet, but you will be able to go up and see him if you like.'

'How did it go?'

Mr Sandhu sat down beside her. 'I wanted to talk to you about this before you saw him. As I explained before, he was suffering from torsion of his testes. If he had been able to reach the emergency room within an hour or two, it was likely that we could have untwisted his spermatic cords and we might have been able to save at least one testicle.'

'But what are you trying to tell me? That he left it too late?'

'Well, I'm afraid so. Not only had the blood supply to his testicles been cut off for more than five hours, but his left testicle was ruptured. This is quite a rare injury, but it can happen when the testicle receives a very hard direct blow.'

'Go on,' said Katie. She was beginning to feel that she was still asleep, and that she was dreaming this. She was the only person left in the waiting room, and outside the hospital was eerily quiet, except for the distant sound of trolley wheels squeaking and a phone endlessly ringing, unanswered.

'We did what we could, but I have to tell you that it was necessary to remove both testicles.'

'Mother of God. Poor Conor.'

Mr Sandhu could only sit with his hands together, blinking at her sympathetically. 'I have no idea what your future plans were – for your marriage, and perhaps the possibility of having children. But I regret that your fiancé is now unable to become a father.'

He paused, clearly uncertain about saying any more. But then he gave a brittle little cough, and added, 'For some time, too, he might also have difficulty in having conjugal relations.'

Katie hadn't even been thinking about that. She had only been thinking about Conor and how devastated he would feel when he found out that he was no longer fertile. Unlike her, perhaps he hadn't been considering that they could have a child together, and perhaps it was selfish of her to feel distressed that it was no longer going to be possible. Perhaps it was even more selfish of her to worry that he might no longer be able to make love to her. But what kind of a marriage would it be if they couldn't have sex?

'I'm sorry,' said Mr Sandhu. 'As I told you, we did everything we could, but it was hopeless.'

Katie nodded. 'I'd like to see him now, if I can.'

'Of course. It may be three or four hours before he regains consciousness, but if you would prefer to explain his condition to him yourself, before I talk to him—'

'Yes. But I think I'll need you there. It's not going to be easy.'

Mr Sandhu stood up. 'Whichever gods we believe in, it is sometimes difficult to understand why they punish us in the way that they do.'

Katie picked the copy of *Stellar* up off the floor. 'At this particular moment, doctor, I'm seriously thinking of becoming an atheist.'

She sat beside his bed in his dimly lit room, watching him steadily breathing. He was never as peaceful as this when they slept together. He was continually jolting and murmuring, as if he were dreaming that he was having an argument or chasing some dognapper headlong down a windy hill in Kerry.

She felt so sad for him that she couldn't even give her sadness a shape. He was so virile-looking: tall and fit, with his muscular gym-honed stomach and his dark chestnut beard. He could have been one of the Vikings who landed in Cork more than a thousand years ago. He was so original in his thinking and so passionate, too. She had thought that he was attractive the very first moment she had seen him walking into the station, but the more she had grown to know him, the more she had felt that he was the right husband for her. He cared for her, but he respected her independence, and he understood her devotion to duty, even when it made life difficult for both of them.

He also understood completely the grief she felt for her late father, because his own father had taken his life when Conor was only fifteen. Katie's father had committed suicide after he had shot the man who had defrauded him and scores of other elderly people out of tens of thousands of euros. Conor's father had embezzled money from his own life insurance business. But no matter what crimes they had committed, that didn't make it any easier to lose them before their time.

A nurse came in at two thirty-five to check on Conor's vital signs. Katie decided to leave him then and drive home. She was exhausted and, apart from sleep, she needed a shower and a change of clothes, and she wanted to make sure that her next-door neighbour, Jenny Tierney, had fed Barney and Foltchain, and taken them out for their evening walk.

'I'll see you in the morning, darling,' she said, and kissed Conor's swollen, purple-bruised cheek. Conor didn't stir.

She was awakened a few minutes after seven by her bedside phone ringing. She reached across for it, and at the same time switched on the lamp. Behind the curtains, she could hear rain pattering against the window.

It was Detective Sergeant Begley. 'Hope I didn't disturb you, ma'am,' he told her, and then he sneezed.

'Bless you,' she said.

'Sorry – I'm allergic to early mornings, like.'

'Well, you're not the only one. What's the story, Sean?'

'About half an hour ago another homeless fellow was found deceased in a doorway on Cook Street, between Pana and Oliver Plunkett Street.'

'Oh, Jesus.'

'We've cordoned that section of the street off both ends and Bill Phinner's sending a technical team out there shortly. I'll be heading out there myself in a minute with Bedelia.'

'Any obvious cause of death?'

'The fellow's body hasn't been touched yet, but Sergeant O'Farrell says he couldn't see any visible trauma and nothing at all in the way of blood, although it's been lashing all night to be fair. But it was the same with that Gearoid, wasn't it?'

'True.'

'There's one thing more, though. One of O'Farrell's officers knew the fellow well enough to chat to, although he never found out his name. He said that there was always a woman with him. There's women's clothing and other female bits and bobs in the doorway, along with the deceased fellow's things, but there's no sign at all of her.'

'Have you spoken to DI Mulliken yet?'

'I have, yes. It was him who said that I should ring you.'

'All right. I'm glad you did. For starters, we need to find this missing woman, don't we, if only to confirm that she wasn't on the scene when your man passed away. That officer who knew her – make sure he gets down to the lab asap and starts preparing an EvoFIT. And let's see if we can find anybody else who might be able to give us a description. Shopkeepers and café staff on Cook Street. Traffic wardens. Street sweepers.'

Katie pushed back the fat pink duvet and swung her legs out of bed. 'I have to go to CUH first, Sean, but I'll be into the station as soon as I can. There's CCTV covering Cook Street, isn't there?'

'Not that pedestrian stretch of it, although there's cameras on Pana and Oliver Plunkett Street, so they will have picked up anybody who went in or out of it.'

'Okay, if you can get the lads upstairs to start looking through all that footage. Have any of the media been in contact yet?'

'Not so far as I know. Mathew McElvey's not in to the press office yet, although they might have rung him on his moby.'

'If Mathew gets in to the station before I do, tell him that he can confirm to the media that an unidentified male has been found deceased on Cook Street. He can of course say that we're investigating, and that we'd appreciate hearing from anybody who might have witnessed anything unusual around that area last night. But that's all. He mustn't say that your man was homeless, or sleeping rough, do you know what I mean? If they ask him if there might be any connection between his death and Gearoid's, he should simply tell them that it's far too early to be speculating.'

'All right, ma'am. I have you. I'll see you later so. Nothing serious at the hospital is it, if you don't mind my asking?'

'What? No – I hope not, Sean. I sincerely hope not.'

Conor was sitting up in bed when she came into his room, attached to an intravenous drip. On the tray in front of him there was a plate of toast and raspberry jam and a cup of tea, and he was watching *Ireland AM*. His left eye was completely closed now and he still had a large plaster across his nose, but at least he was more recognizable than yesterday.

'Katie!' he said, picking up the TV remote and switching it off. 'Now here's a sight for sore eyes!'

Katie came up to his bedside and kissed him. 'I brought you these. I think under the circumstances you're allowed to break your diet.'

She handed him a cellophane packet of Wilde's chocolate fudge slices, as well as a folded copy of this morning's *Examiner*. Then she took off her bobbly dark green overcoat and hung it over the back of the chair, sitting down close to him.

'My God, Katie,' he said, holding up the packet of fudge. 'You know my deepest darkest weaknesses already, and we haven't even exchanged rings yet.'

'So how are you feeling?' she asked him. She was trying to smile and sound bright, but her throat felt tight and she was finding it more difficult than she had expected. 'Has the consultant been in to see you?'

'Not yet. I've had all my vital signs taken, and apparently I'm still alive. But I don't know for sure if they've been able to repair all of the damage. I'm not too worried. One ball can do the work of two. You can walk with only one leg, can't you, and you can still drive even if you have only the one eye.'

'Do you have any pain?'

'Kind of a dull throbbing ache down there, but they've got me on the oxycodone, so it's tolerable. I can tell you, though, I won't be riding a bicycle for a while. Not over cobbles, anyway.'

'Oh, Con.'

'You'll not be taking out a summons against the fellow who did it, will you? I'd say I've been given punishment enough for being a reckless obsessive eejit without being locked up in jail for eighteen months.'

Katie shrugged, and tried to smile, but said nothing. Because Conor had broken the conditions of his bail by trespassing on the McQuaides' property, she hadn't yet made up her mind if she should charge their minder for beating him up so badly.

Conor paused, and sipped his tea, and then he said, 'To tell you the truth, I've had the McQuaide sisters on my mind ever since I woke up this morning – how we can close them down.'

'Oh, yes?'

'I reckon we'll have to do an Al Capone on them… you know, get them for tax evasion or fraud or some other offence apart from puppy farming. Only two or three TDs have any serious interest in putting a stop to illegal dog-breeding. That's because there's scarce any public support for it and, more to the point, there's no votes in it, either. Apart from that, the ISPCA don't have enough funding to prosecute the McQuaides privately.'

'Con – you need to forget about the McQuaide sisters for a while. Concentrate on getting yourself better. When you're fully fit, we can talk about this some more.'

'That's all very well, sweetheart. But every minute that goes by, all over the country, hundreds of breeding bitches are suffering, all shut up in boxes without even seeing the daylight, and thousands of puppies are weak and sick and deformed and pining for their mothers, just so that monsters like the McQuaide sisters can have their fancy houses and their Mercedes and their holidays in the Maldives.'

'Con—' Katie began, but at that moment there was a tap at the door and Mr Sandhu appeared. He was accompanied by a nervous-looking junior doctor with fiery red hair and glasses, who looked the spit of Ed Sheeran.

'Good morning, Detective Superintendent,' smiled Mr Sandhu. 'The nurse told me that you had arrived. I hope you managed to get some rest overnight. Good morning, Conor. How are you feeling this morning?'

'Sore, and still battered about, but better, thank you.'

'We have sorted you out down below, although it will take a little while before the sutures can be removed and the swelling will subside. Next, of course, we need to address your nose and your cheekbone and your eye socket, and I am hoping that we will be able to do that tomorrow or the day after at the latest. Mr O'Connell will be dealing with that surgery, and he will be coming to see you later today. He is our leading maxillofacial consultant.'

'Well, I can't wait to have my face fixed. I've been eating my breakfast here and I don't know what's been crunching louder, the toast or these smashed-up bones in my nose.'

'I am sure Mr O'Connell will fix you up perfectly,' Mr Sandhu reassured him. But then he looked across at Katie and said, 'However, I think it is necessary now to make you aware of the full extent of the surgery that *I* have performed on you, and what its consequences might be.'

'"Consequences"?' said Conor, and he looked at Katie, too. 'That sounds like what the judge said to me when he was passing sentence for burning down Guzz Eye's mobile home.'

'I will explain what it was necessary for me to do in surgical terms, because of the seriousness of your injuries,' said Mr Sandhu. 'Then I will let your good lady explain to you what the long-term effects will be, and leave you to discuss between yourselves how you are going to manage them.'

'I'm not sure I like the sound of this,' said Conor. He had been about to take another sip of tea, but now he carefully placed his cup back on its saucer.

'The blood supply to both of your testes had been cut off for so long that they had suffered infarction, or necrosis. Tissue death, to put it simply.'

'Both of them?'

'I'm afraid so. Added to which the left testicle was severely ruptured, beyond any meaningful repair. I had no alternative but to carry out a radical inguinal orchiectomy.'

'You had to remove both of my testicles?'

'Yes, in essence.'

'So I'm a eunuch?'

'That is not a word we use in urological practice, Conor.'

'It doesn't matter what word you use, doctor. It's still what I am. A eunuch. A *castrato*. The next thing I know they'll be asking me to sing soprano in St Francis church choir.'

Mr Sandhu shook his head. 'No, no, no. Contrary to popular myth, a fully grown man who loses his testes does not start speaking in a high voice. This happens only when a boy is castrated before puberty, before his vocal folds have lengthened and thickened and his voice has broken.'

Although he was listening to Mr Sandhu, Conor kept his eyes fixed on Katie. He looked so devastated that she could have burst into tears, but she didn't want to distress him any more than he was distressed already, and she didn't want to make him feel that they had no hope of an intimate relationship together. He wouldn't be able to give her a child, but maybe he would still be able to make love to her.

'What about – you know – what about virility?' he asked.

'It's early days yet, Conor, and I am sure you understand that the effect of your surgery could be psychological as well as physical. But I know you have a supportive and understanding partner in Detective Superintendent Maguire, and there is plenty of help available to you, both in terms of counselling and also medication.'

'Like, Viagra?'

'That is one treatment, yes. There is also Cialis and Levitra, and they are doing experiments with stem-cell injections, too. But hopefully these will not prove to be necessary.'

There was a long silence in the room. Eventually, Mr Sandhu said, 'Do you have any other questions at this time? Perhaps I should leave you two together to discuss your next steps.'

Conor said, 'Yes. Thank you.'

Mr Sandhu hesitated for a few seconds, nodded to Katie, and then he and the junior doctor left the room, closing the door behind them.

Katie reached out and held Conor's hand, and squeezed it. 'You'll get through this, Con, with God's help.'

'I'll get through it, darling, with or without the Lord Almighty. But how about us?'

'I'm not going to abandon you. I love you.'

'You loved me as I was before I was a eunuch. But what about now?'

'Don't use that word. This has all been such a fierce shock. You have to give yourself time to recover. Mentally, like Mr Sandhu said, as well as physically.'

Conor tried to pull his hand away, but Katie held on to it tightly, and wouldn't let him.

'What do they say about men who don't behave like men?' said Conor. 'You know, cowards and wimps and suchlike? "You don't have the balls, boy", that's what they say. And now that's me.'

'Con—'

'You're the strongest, most passionate woman I've ever come across, ever. I knew I could never match you for determination, or confidence, or bravery. No – let me finish. I could never be your equal in those ways, ever. But I thought that I could make you feel loved, and looked after, and satisfied. I thought that I could give you a glow.'

He tried again to tug his hand away, but again Katie clung on to him, even though tears were streaming down her face, and she felt as if she had been punched so hard that she was breathless.

'I can't do that for you any more, Katie. I can't give you anything that a man should be able to give you. The glow's gone out for ever.'

Fourteen

When Brianna walked in, she found Niall Dabney bent forward at his desk, half-hidden behind a huge spray of plastic orchids, hounding down a sausage-and-egg McMuffin.

'Mmmph,' he said, with his mouth full. 'Bit of a late breakfast.'

Brianna said nothing, but crossed over to his desk and sat down in one of the two worn-out purple-upholstered armchairs facing him. Niall took one more bite and then pushed the paper-wrapped McMuffin to one side. The whole reception room smelled of sausage and damp and dust.

'Result,' he said, smacking his hands together. 'With your upside-down car fellow, anyway. It turns out that he was his parents' bar of gold, and they want to give him a grand send-off, with the horse-drawn hearse and all the trimmings. Seven-and-a-half thousand, plus VAT.'

'What about that Looney girl?'

'Oh, that one who died of an overdose? Her father rang me, like, and asked me if I could organize a funeral in Skibbereen, where most of her family are from, but he couldn't afford more than four and I couldn't have done it for the money, do you know? Not a hope.'

'Well, that's a disappointment.'

'Don't be too disappointed, Bree. The upside-down car fellow's parents have paid in full in advance and I have your cut for you.'

Niall leaned sideways and opened his bottom desk drawer.

He produced a manila envelope and passed it over. Brianna opened it, licked her thumb, and counted out the notes inside.

'This is only five hundred.'

'I have my overheads, Bree. I can only give you ten per cent of the net, like.'

'That's not what we agreed.'

'That's all I can afford, for the love of God. Look at the state of this place, do you know? It hasn't been redecorated since the millennium.'

Brianna didn't have to look around the reception room to know how tatty it had become. Even though Dabney's Funeral Home was only a small premises on Marlboro Street sandwiched in between Flynn's Donuts and Bootz Shoe Shop, it had once been quietly opulent inside, with purple velvet curtains and a thick-pile purple carpet. Now, though, the curtains were faded and the carpet was moth-eaten. The marble memorial plaques in the window display were laced with cobwebs and the gilt lettering on the glass had peeled so that it read, *abney's Fun ral Hom* .

Niall Dabney himself had been equally worn down by time and shortage of money. He was a short man, with a large head, but in early middle age he had been reasonably handsome, always immaculately dressed in black, with bouffant grey hair and a rich, solicitous voice. Niall Dabney's had been the place to go if you wanted to give your loved one an unusual and distinctive funeral, with a choir maybe, or a guard of honour, or girls in long white dresses showering the casket with white rose petals as it was carried out of the church.

But then Niall's wife, Aileen, had died of breast cancer, only forty-three years old. Although Niall was so experienced in dealing with the grief of others, he had found himself unable to cope with his own grief, except by drinking. A lavish funeral that he had arranged for the former TD for Cork South-East had turned into a shambles. The hearse had broken down on the Magic Roundabout so that it had to be towed into St Finbarr's chapel by John O'Leary's recovery truck, following which the coffin had been dropped halfway up the aisle and Niall had ended up screaming in a drunken rage at the priest and the TD's widow.

From then on, Niall could only attract enough business to stay solvent by offering cut-rate funerals to Cork's less affluent families. Years of alcohol and anxiety had taken their toll on him, and he looked ten years older than he really was, with thinning hair and a stained grey suit and hands that trembled uncontrollably. Even the areca palm in the corner of his reception room was shrivelled and brown, and had long ago lost its ability to purify the air.

'I could have another for you,' said Brianna. 'A young woman seven months' pregnant and the baby, too, which is kind of a bonus. The husband's not wealthy, but the young woman's parents live in Douglas and they're comfortably off, I'd say. I've been around to see them to offer condolences, as usual, and of course I recommended you for the funeral arrangements.'

'Good girl. Grand. A mother and baby funeral? I charged ten thousand for the last one of those I arranged, and that was ten years ago – at *least* ten years ago. I organized it so that we had three baby lambs around the grave when the little one was buried. There wasn't a dry eye in the cemetery.'

Brianna said, 'You can have baby alligators around the grave if you want to, Niall. This time I want my full ten per cent and no messing.'

Niall didn't answer but picked up his McMuffin and then put it down again.

'Do you know what I hate about this world?' he said.

'Let me guess. The commercial rates you have to pay on this dump of a funeral home. No? The price of Jameson's whiskey. No? Not that either?'

'No, Bree. What I hate about this world is that there are so many dead people in it. I hate death. I detest it. And yet every single one of us has to face it in the end.'

'I can't imagine why you hate it so much, Niall. You make your living out of it, after all.'

*

At the same time that Brianna was talking to Niall, Ailbe and her baby were being wheeled into the mortuary at CUH. The porter was accompanied by Mr Stephen O'Malley, the consultant obstetrician.

'How's it going, Mary?' he asked. He was tall and stooped and bespectacled, with bushy eyebrows, and a permanent frown on his face as if he were always trying to remember something important, but never could.

Usually, when she was carrying out a post mortem, Dr Kelley liked to listen to classical music, but this morning the mortuary was silent except for the sprinkling of rain against the clerestory windows and the fitful buzzing of a fluorescent light that was nearing the end of its life.

'Overworked, as usual,' she said, putting down her pen. 'They will insist on having fatal accidents, these Corkonians. You could almost believe they do it on purpose.'

She had just finished her examination of an eighty-three-year-old cyclist who had wavered into the path of a petrol tanker as he was leaving The Three Horseshoes pub on the Old Youghal Road. She had found that his blood alcohol level was 102 mg per 100 ml, over twice the legal limit for drivers. His skull had been completely crushed under the lorry's nearside front wheel so that his face was as flat as a pie dish, with his ears sticking out for handles.

Mr O'Malley took off his glasses, breathed on them, and polished them on his tie.

'As you'll see for yourself, Mary, I carried out a c-section. There was no detectable foetal pulse so I was fairly sure that we were going to be too late, and sadly we were, but it was worth a shot. The mother fell downstairs, apparently, and broke her neck.'

Dr Kelley lifted the sheet that was covering Ailbe and looked down at her for a long time. Her baby was lying on his side next to her, mother and baby boy who would never know each other.

'Good-looking young woman,' Dr Kelley said at last. 'She wouldn't have guessed for a moment when she woke up yesterday morning that she and her wain were going to end up here.'

Mr O'Malley nodded, abstractedly. 'What did somebody once say? "The world in its violence and its serenity will roll on through the endless indifference of space, and it will take only one hundred of its circuits around the Sun to turn us, who loved each other, into dust."'

'Well, thank you for that, Stephen. I've just carried out a post mortem on an auld fellow with a squashed head, and I was sorely in need of cheering up.'

'Oh, you're welcome.'

Mr O'Malley waited for a while, as if he had something more to say, but then he simply cleared his throat, turned around and walked off. Once the door had swung shut behind him, Dr Kelley called for Denis, her anatomical pathology technician. Denis came out from the back room where he had been writing up the notes for the elderly cyclist. He was a serious young man, Denis, whippet-thin, so that his lab coat always seemed to be on the point of slipping off his shoulders. He had a pointed nose and a prominent Adam's apple and hair that was brushed up vertically so that it looked as if he had stuck his fingers into an electric socket.

'We have a mother and a baby here,' said Dr Kelley. 'If you can store the baby away in the chiller for the moment, we should have enough time this afternoon to examine the mother.'

Denis raised the sheet and looked underneath it, but said nothing. He snapped on a pair of latex gloves and then lifted up the baby boy as carefully as if he were still alive. He carried him over to the cold storage units at the far end of the mortuary, slid out a stainless-steel drawer, and laid him inside.

When he came back, Dr Kelley was bending sideways, peering closely at the purple blotches around Ailbe's neck.

'Mr O'Malley said she broke her neck falling downstairs, but this bruising is highly unusual for an injury like that. I could almost believe that she was throttled.'

'Maybe she *was* throttled,' said Denis, gravely. 'Maybe she was throttled and then she was pushed downstairs afterwards to make it look like an accident.'

'Oh stop,' said Dr Kelley. But then she palpated Ailbe's neck with her fingertips, and turned her head from side to side.

'Her cervical vertebrae are dislocated all right, and I can feel a fracture, too. We'll have to do a CT scan to tell exactly how extensive the damage is. But it does seem excessive for a straight-forward fall downstairs. I'd say she's suffered an abrupt rotation of the head. Look at the way it flops over. This is what you'd expect from a fellow having his neck screwed around in a rugby scrum, or the victim of a T-bone car crash. Not a young woman tumbling down a flight of stairs.'

'So what's the plan?' asked Denis.

'Let's scan her neck first, before we make our abdominal inci-sion. I want to be satisfied that this *was* an accident, and that she wasn't throttled and thrown downstairs afterwards, like you said.'

'I'll bet you a hundred yoyos she was.'

'Denis – this is a mortuary, not a branch of Paddy Power. Have some respect.'

'Sorry,' said Denis, and genuinely looked it.

Fifteen

On her way back to Anglesea Street Katie had to pass Gilabbey Veterinary Hospital, so she stopped off to collect Walter.

She caught Dr O'Sullivan just as he was shrugging on his overcoat to leave. He went back to fetch Walter in his plastic dog carrier crate and set him down on the table in reception.

'It's a sin, and there's no other word for it,' he said. 'I've seen far too many brachycephalic puppies in this condition. Whoever bred him, they should be waterboarded. Then they'll know what it feels like to be gasping for breath.'

Katie could hear Walter wheezing inside his crate and leaned over to give him a little wave and blow him two kisses. Then she turned back to Dr O'Sullivan and said, 'You know as well as I do, Domnall, you'd only be fined for mistreating a dog, but if you did the same to a human you'd get six months in jail. Did you see that fellow who killed his dog in the Peace Park by stepping on its head – and what did the judge give him? Two hundred hours of community service, that's all.'

'Sure, but it's so wrong. Aren't dogs God's creatures too? Even this unfortunate little pug.'

'Well, thanks for taking a look at him,' said Katie. 'What do we owe you?'

'My usual fee is seventy euros for an examination, but let's call it fifty, plus twenty for the overnight stay. But don't bother yourself with it now. My secretary will send you the bill.'

'Is it possible to set him right?'

'It depends what you mean by setting him right.'

'Well, could you sort out his breathing, and take the swellings out of his throat, and make sure that his eyes don't pop out? And whatever else he needs, do you know, like vaccination and worming and chipping.'

'I could, yes. But it wouldn't be cheap. I'm not saying you couldn't find a vet in Cork less expensive than me, but these wouldn't be simple operations and I'm not blowing my own trumpet when I say that I'm one of the best. If not *the* best.'

'So how much are you talking about?'

'I've known Conor for years, so of course I'd give you a discount. Off the top of my head, I'd say three thousand. It could work out a doonchie bit more if there's complications. But three thousand should cover it.'

'As much as that?' said Katie.

'I'm afraid so.'

'Conor will have to have a word with Walter's owner, of course. She's only a library assistant, so I don't know if she'll be able to stretch to that. Maybe she has pet insurance. I simply don't know.'

Dr O'Sullivan gave her a rueful smile. 'I wish I could say that I could charge you less, but veterinary surgery can cost as much as human surgery, sometimes more so.'

He hesitated, still smiling in the same regretful way. 'I hope I'm not sounding morbid if I say that you could have him put to sleep for a hundred and twenty.'

As if he had heard what Dr O'Sullivan had said, Walter let out a thin, hopeless whine.

Katie looked in through the holes in his crate and said, 'It's all right, Walter. I'll take you home this evening and you can have some of those training treats and sit by the fire with Barney and Foltchain again.' Then she turned to Dr O'Sullivan. 'I hope to God that he didn't understand what you said then. I think he's suffered enough, if only by being born.'

★

Back in her office, Katie had only just set down the dog crate under the window and hung up her coat when there was a knock at her open door and Detective Sergeant Begley and Detective Bedelia Murrish came in.

'How's the form, ma'am?' asked Detective Sergeant Begley. 'And how's your Conor doing today?'

'He's on the mend, thanks, Sean.' Katie had told her fellow officers that Conor had been taken into hospital but she had given them no more details than that. She hadn't wanted to tell them that he had been beaten up, and how badly, or why, because then they would have been curious to know why she hadn't yet taken any steps to identify and arrest his assailant. She had thought about inventing some story about him falling off a ladder while he was clearing the gutters around her house, but she had never been able to tell even the whitest of white lies. As her father used to say, 'Telling a lie – that's like setting a rat loose. It'll always come back to bite you.'

She sat down at her desk. As usual, there was a stack of messages and files on her blotter. 'So – what's the story with our deceased rough sleeper?' she asked, quickly leafing through them to see if there was anything urgent.

Detective Sergeant Begley came around her desk and laid down his tablet in front of her. On the screen there was a photograph of Matty lying face down on the pavement, staring at nothing.

'I gave him a quick once-over, and would you believe it, he has a hole in the back of his head, in exactly the same place where our late friend Gearoid had a hole.'

He swiped to the next photograph, a close-up of the back of Matty's head. His scraggly hair had been parted so that Katie could just make out a small dark knobble of dried blood. 'There, can you see it? I couldn't tell for sure if it was done by a drill bit, but it would be one hell of a coincidence if it wasn't, wouldn't you think?'

'Mother of God,' said Katie. 'Did your man have any other injuries?'

'Minor bruising and scratches and contusions – only what you'd expect from somebody sleeping out on the street. His body's on the way to CUH now for an autopsy but I have plenty of pictures for you. There's something more, though. The technicians found bloodstains in the doorway that didn't seem to correspond at all with the position that your man was found lying in, or the hole in the back of his head. As you can see, the hole has scarcely bled at all.'

'So the bloodstains could have come from somebody else?'

'That's what it looks like.'

'And there's still no trace of this woman who was always with him?'

'Nothing so far. We haven't been able to find any witnesses, but we're checking through the CCTV footage and we should have the EvoFIT soon, if it isn't ready now.'

'Have we put a name to him yet?'

'We found this in his jacket pocket,' said Detective Murrish, and handed Katie a clear plastic evidence bag. Inside was a pale green Personal Public Service card, with a black-and-white photograph of an unshaven young man on it, with a strangely haunted look in his eyes. The name beside the photograph was Matthew Donoghue.

'We checked with the Intreo Centre on Hanover Quay. When he first applied for his PPS number he gave his parents' address on Military Hill, so we went up to see them.'

'They were in bits, of course,' put in Detective Sergeant Begley. 'Upset, but not totally surprised. Your man was studying to be a solicitor but he was only halfway through law school before he got himself hooked on crack and fentanyl and who knows what else. He kept fleecing money from his parents to pay for his drugs and in the end they kicked him out. They told us that everybody knew him as Matty.'

'But they didn't know who his woman friend was?'

'No. They hadn't seen Matty since the last St Patrick's Day parade, in the street. It was only by chance, and not to speak to, and so far as they could make out he was alone. But we'll be taking the woman's EvoFIT round to all the clubs this evening and showing it to some of the dealers. It's a hundred to one that she's a druggie too, so maybe some of them will reck her.'

Katie sat silent for a while. Then she said, 'That must be a pure profitable pitch for a beggar, that doorway. Plenty of footfall – plenty of shops and cafés and pubs all around.'

'I know what you're saying, ma'am,' said Detective Sergeant Begley. 'We'll be keeping our eyes peeled for whoever takes it over, once the technicians have gone, believe me, and I won't be altogether gobsmacked if it's a Romanian.'

'No, me neither. I have such a strong feeling it's this Lupul character behind this. Haven't we made any progress in finding out where he's based? Little Ana-Maria said it was a big house on a steep hill, didn't she? A big house that smelled of cabbage.'

'You're talking about half the old houses on the northside, ma'am.'

Katie pressed her fingertips against her forehead. She could feel the beginnings of a headache coming on.

Detective Sergeant Begley said, 'We thought of driving little Ana-Maria around to see if she could pick out the house for us, and Kyna asked Margaret O'Reilly at Tusla if we could do that.'

'What did she say?'

'Absolutely not. The poor little girl's still far too upset about losing her mother. The couple who took her in said she was screaming half the night with nightmares, that's what Margaret told us. She's worried that she'd only have to see the house and it could traumatize her even more.'

'What about estate agents? Doesn't anybody have a record of renting out a house to somebody Romanian? You wouldn't easy forget a fellow who looks like this Lupul, would you, and talks with such a thick accent?'

'We've checked with all the main ones, ma'am – Lisney and Savills and Charles McCarthy – and most of the smaller ones, too. Nothing so far. Of course, it could have been a private letting, like, or maybe it's just a friend's house.'

'And how about that Romanian coffin-maker who's taken over that spot beside the Savoy Centre? Have we seen anybody making contact with him? Giving him food or drink or collecting money from him? They could be tailed.'

'Not so far, ma'am. The only people we've seen talking to him at any length was one of the Simons and some fellow who came out of The Long Valley, so wrecked he could hardly stand up.'

'All right, keep trying,' said Katie. 'If it *is* Lupul, he's doing this so brazenly that we're bound to catch him one way or another.'

'That's what surprises me, do you know what I mean? It looks likely this Matty was killed the same way as Gearoid, and you couldn't make it more obvious, could you, that they'd both been murdered – and both been murdered by the same offender. He could have used a little imagination, don't you think, the murderer? I don't know – maybe given one of them an overdose and pushed the other one under a bus.'

'You'd make a first-class serial killer, Sean, no mistake about that.'

'Now, myself – if *I* wanted to get rid of a rough sleeper without anybody finding out that it was me – I'd knock him out first with a length of scaffolding, so that it would look like he'd tripped over and hit his head on a street sign. He might be drugged up or langered already, in which case I wouldn't have to. After that I'd simply sling him into the river. Nobody would be able to tell for sure if he was murdered, like, or if he'd fallen in by accident, or if he'd committed suicide. I mean, suicide's the favourite. How many people did the riverdance in the Lee last year alone? Fourteen, wasn't it?'

'Sure like, but maybe it's *not* so surprising,' said Katie. 'What's the usual procedure in Romania, when the police find vagrants deceased on the streets? It could be that they don't always give them such a thorough autopsy as we do. Without an autopsy we could easily have concluded that our two rough sleepers died of natural causes – hypothermia or liver failure or some such – and that the scabs on the back of their head were only that – just scabs. After all, they're covered in them. Needle tracks, psoriasis, scabies, rat bites, you name it.'

'So you think that our killers may have used a drill because they thought we'd never catch on how these fellers died?'

'It's a possibility, isn't it? And that makes me think they might have done it before, either in their home country or here. Listen, I've a friend in the international fraud unit at Harcourt Street – DI Jimmy Joyce. He has regular contact with the police force in Romania, as well as Bulgaria and the Czech Republic and all the other Eastern European countries. I'll ask him to check on their procedures, and whether they have any records of murders being committed with a similar MO.

'I'll also be asking DI Fitzpatrick to start nosing a bit more intensively around our immigrant communities here in Cork – especially Orchard Court. Maybe I'm wrong, and this Lupul is nothing more than a small-time gouger, but you have to ask yourself, don't you, who else could it be?'

'There's that fat fellow.'

'Oh… you mean that Ştefan Făt-Frumor. He's a piece of work all right, but he's been keeping a low profile lately, hasn't he? I don't know if he's still in business even – here in Cork, anyway. Patrick O'Donovan heard some rumours that he'd moved most of his drug-running up to Dublin. So many of the Kinahans and the Hutches have either been shot or banged up that he saw there was a gap in the market.'

'Lupul does seem to be our prime suspect, doesn't he? Most of the Romanians I've come across are perfectly law-abiding. About the most criminal thing they ever get up to is pocketing the tips they collect from the car wash and not declaring them to the Revenue.'

There was another knock at her door, and Chief Superintendent Brendan O'Kane came in. Katie could see that his hair was freshly cut, and there was a strange sly smile on his face, as if he had come to ask for a favour.

'Kathleen... I heard you were back. How's your – fiancé?'

'He's bearing up, thank you, sir. He might have to stay in hospital for three or four more days, but that's only so that they can keep him under observation.'

'You did tell me why they've taken him in, didn't you? Perhaps I wasn't listening.'

'No, sir, I did not,' said Katie. She paused for a moment to make it clear to him that she wasn't going to tell him now, either. Then she said, 'DS Begley and Detective Murrish have been briefing me about the homeless fellow who was found dead on Cook Street this morning.'

'Well, that's really what I came to talk to you about. That's the second rough sleeper who's died this week. I was wondering if there was any connection.'

'It looks likely, sir, although we'll have to wait for the autopsy. Gearoid Ó Beargha was killed with a drill bit into his brainstem, as you know, and this fellow Matty Donoghue has a similar wound on the back of his head.'

'The media have been pestering Mathew McElvey down in the press office, that's the thing, and he wants to know if we can release any details yet. And so do I. This is doing our image no good at all. The public don't like to see the homeless sleeping on our streets, but on the whole they feel sorry for them, or else they wouldn't give them so much money. And until they can find accommodation or shelter of some kind, we're supposed to be protecting them. I made that pledge at that media conference, didn't I? "No more Gearoid Ó Bearghas!", that's what I promised. What does this make me look like?'

'Superintendent Pearse has extra patrols out at night, sir. But like all of us, he has only a limited budget and his officers can't be everywhere at once. The ideal answer would be to clear all the rough sleepers off the streets, but where would they go? Apart from that, a fair number of them wouldn't even want to go into shelters.'

'So what do you intend to say to the media about this latest fatality?'

'I'm not going to announce that Gearoid was murdered, not yet anyway. Even if it turns out that this Matty was murdered, too, and in the same way, all I'm going to say is that in both cases we're still trying to ascertain the cause of death. For the time being I want our perpetrator to stay under the impression that he or she has got away with it, undetected. Of course there's no way of telling for sure if that's what they believe, but it's a possibility.'

'It's the use of a drill, see,' put in Detective Sergeant Begley. 'Why use a drill when you could just stab them or shoot them or bash them over the head with a shovel? The drill holes, they're well hidden in the victim's hair, and what with all the other lesions on their scalps, it's easy to overlook them, do you know what I mean?'

Brendan was about to say something else when Walter let out a plaintive yap, and then gave a miniature sneeze.

'Oh, you poor little dote, I nearly forgot you, didn't I?' said Katie. She got up from her desk, went over to the window and lifted him out of his dog crate. 'I expect you're hungry and thirsty, aren't you, and you could do with a tissue. Just look at you, snotty boy!'

'And who's this?' asked Brendan. 'Don't tell me you've added a sniffer dog to your team.'

'This is Walter, sir. He's a pug and sad to say he can't breathe well enough to be a sniffer dog. He was stolen from a young woman who works for the council and my Conor tracked him down to a pub in Ballincollig. His problem is that he's been over-bred to have this cute squashed-looking face but his airways are far too narrow and his eyes are in danger of popping out. He needs several operations, apart from vaccination and worming, and that's going to cost a small fortune.'

Brendan came up and stroked Walter's head. Walter snuffled at him and licked his lips and sneezed again. 'And what if he doesn't have the operations?'

'He'll have to be put to sleep. He's suffering now but his

suffering will only get worse as he grows older – that's if he survives for more than a few months. He was bred illegally, sir, and he should never have been born at all.'

'Well, that's a heartbreaking story and no mistake. His owner – can she afford all this treatment?'

'I don't know. I'll be taking Walter back to her tomorrow and I'll ask. If she can't – well, this is the last time you'll see him.'

Katie gave Walter a reassuring little jiggle in her arms.

'Moirin!' she called out. 'Could you fetch me in a bowl of water for our boy here?'

As she turned back, she saw that Brendan wasn't looking at Walter, but at her, and it was that thoughtful, concentrated look that she had seen in men's eyes before. That look that said: *What can I do to make her want me?*

Sixteen

Late in the afternoon, when it was dark outside, and sparkling raindrops were clinging to her windows, Bill Phinner came up to see her, accompanied by Detectives Markey and Scanlan.

Moirin had gone out earlier and bought a packet of Barking Heads puppy food so that she could feed Walter, and now he was asleep on one of the sofas, snoring like a two-tone whistle.

'What's this, ma'am?' asked Bill Phinner. 'Got yourself a guard dog?'

'That's right,' Katie told him. 'His name's Walter. One bold word out of you and he'll bite your leg off.'

'Oh, he's so *cute*,' said Detective Scanlan, kneeling down on the floor beside him and stroking him.

'He's cute, but he's not too well. I'm hoping that we don't have to have him put down.'

'You can't! That would be tragic!'

Katie shrugged. 'It depends if his owner can afford to have him operated on. But I agree with you, yes, it would be tragic.'

Bill Phinner said, 'I was going to text you but I was up here anyway. We've had all but one of the results from Buckley's the butchers.'

'And? Have you found out where that ring came from?'

'No, ma'am. The samples of mince we took from Eamon Buckley's fridge were all pork or beef, a bit on the fatty side but nothing else. A couple of cuts of meat looked suspicious, but they turned out to be goat. There's a crowd of Somalis living down the lower end of Shandon Street and it turns out they love their goat.'

'No other traces?'

'Blood spatters everywhere, like you'd expect in a butcher's. They'd been wiped off with disinfectant but it didn't look as if there'd been any deliberate attempt to eradicate them completely, not like painting over them or anything, and of course they all showed up with the luminol. And all of them were pig or cow or chicken blood. No human blood at all.'

'So the shop was clean and there was nothing to indicate that poor Ana-Maria's mother might have been disposed of there?'

'No, ma'am. We even took the mincer apart to see if there were any scratches on the cutters that might match up with that ring. The mincer was fairly new, too, so the blades were hardly marked at all.'

Katie frowned. 'When you think about it, though – even if the ring *was* dropped into the mincer, surely it couldn't have gone through all those little holes at the end?'

'That's called a mesh plate, ma'am. The holes are usually only six millimetres in diameter, so you're right, it wouldn't have gone through. When they'd finished mincing, though, they would have unscrewed the mesh plate to clean it, and maybe it dropped out then, mixed up with any minced-up meat that was still left inside. We don't have any way of knowing.'

'Ah well,' said Katie. 'It's a fierce pity that woman flushed the mince she'd bought down the toilet. If you'd been able to analyse *that*, maybe you could have proved it conclusively, one way or another.'

'I'd love to prove that Eamon Buckley was guilty of something – *anything*!' Detective Scanlan put in. 'The disgusting threats he made to me, I tell you! The biggest pig in Eamon Buckley's shop is Eamon Buckley himself!'

'I'm afraid we can't haul him in just for being gross,' said Katie. 'If being gross was an arrestable offence, we'd have half the men in Cork downstairs in the cells.'

Detective Markey was looking thoughtful. 'I was struck by one thing,' he said. 'Maybe it means nothing at all, like, but that's only a small butcher's, Buckley's, and he can't be making too much of a profit these days. After all, he's having to compete with Tesco's and Dunnes and all them butchers in the English Market, too – you know, like Bresnan's and O'Mahony's – and even they say that life isn't easy these days.'

'What are you getting at, Nicholas?'

'He has a brand-new Mondeo parked outside his house, and the house itself is fresh-painted and the double-glazed windows look like they was only recently put in. I'd say that the fridge in his shop is new, too, and he has a shiny glass counter that looks as if it was fitted not long ago, because you can still see the marks where the old one was. And like you say, Bill, that mincer was new – or almost new.'

'Maybe he's doing a roaring trade in goats,' said Bill Phinner.

'He could have got the grade from anywhere, couldn't he?' said Katie. 'Maybe one of his relatives passed away and left him an inheritance. Or maybe he won the lotto.'

'Sure like,' Detective Markey agreed. 'But if a fellow's well minted and has nothing to hide, why should he act so aggressive? That's what struck me. You don't often get that level of hostility, not from somebody who knows they've done nothing wrong. They might get narky and give out a bit, but they don't start saying that they'll hunt you down and cut you up into pieces, like Eamon Buckley did with Padragain here.'

'I know what you're saying, but unfortunately that doesn't prove anything. Maybe he's just a hard chaw, and he behaves like that all the time.'

'I did a background check on him,' said Detective Scanlan. 'He's been cautioned three times for domestic abuse in the past two years, but each time his wife wasn't prepared to press charges.'

'Well, even if he is a natural bully, I'm still not going to let this drop,' Katie told her. 'Ana-Maria's mother disappeared and she still hasn't been found and her ring turned up in mince bought from Buckley's shop. Even if Eamon Buckley had nothing to do with it, I still want to know how it got there. I believe in a lot of things – God, and the afterlife – but I don't believe in magic.'

'So what's the next step?' asked Detective Markey. 'Maybe we should stake out his shop for a day or two, and see who comes and goes.'

'What about that sexual assault case you're working on? The one at Flynn's Hotel? How's that progressing?'

'We're still waiting for one of the principal witnesses to come back from Gran Canaria. We have some video evidence but nothing that you'd call conclusive. A lot of shouting and hollering and blurry images that might be the accused but then again might not. The phone got dropped on the floor at the crucial moment, so we have five minutes of footage of the victim's left tackie and some grunting noises but that's about it.'

'All right,' said Katie. 'Let me think about a stake-out. This whole Romanian thing is breaking my melt, I can tell you. If the autopsy proves that Matty Donoghue was killed by the same drill as Gearoid Ó Beargha, I may have to pull our coffin-maker in for questioning, but I'm fierce anxious not to alert this Lupul and his gang or whoever's responsible. If they think we're on to them, they could vanish, just like that, *poof!* and then we'd never have a hope on God's earth of catching them.'

Before she went home, Katie rang Conor. He sounded slurred and drugged-up, but he assured her that he was feeling no pain.

'We have to talk some more, though, sweetheart,' he told her.

'Let's wait until you're out of hospital. I can arrange to take some time off and we could go down to Parknasilla maybe. A couple of quiet days by the sea would take the stress off both of us.'

'Oh... I meant to tell you this afternoon... I drove myself to the hospital, so my Audi's still here in the car park.'

'That's all right, Con. I'll send somebody over tomorrow morning to pick it up and take it down to Cobh.'

'Katie…'

'What is it, darling? Stop fretting for the moment and concentrate on getting yourself well. That's all that matters.'

'But I'll never get well, will I? All the doctors in the world can't give me back what I've lost. I'd have been better off having my legs cut off. Jesus – I'd have been better off having my *head* cut off. At least that would have put an end to me, and I wouldn't have to suffer for the rest of my life.'

'Con, shush. I stopped off at the vet's and picked up Walter. He's here with me now and I'll be taking him home tonight. If you can give me his owner's address I'll take him round there tomorrow.'

'What did Domnall have to say?'

'The poor little dote needs several operations, mostly to help him breathe more easily. But it's going to cost three thousand euros at least. Otherwise the kindest thing is to have him put to sleep.'

'Three thousand? Yes – that doesn't surprise me, although I can't see his owner affording that much. Maybe the kindest thing would be for Walter and me to be put to sleep together.'

'Con, for the love of God, don't talk like that. There's all kinds of amazing surgery they can do these days. Look at that fellow who had a whole new face put on him.'

'Don't think I didn't ask Mr Sandhu about that. He said it might be possible technically, do you know what I mean, but they can't do it ethically. If you fell pregnant, it would mean that I'd given you some other man's child.'

Katie was silent for a few seconds. Perhaps he too had been thinking about them having a baby, although he had never suggested it to her. The tragedy of his injuries seemed to become more unbearable every time she spoke to him.

'You sound beat out,' she said. 'Try and get yourself a good night's sleep.'

'I'll do my best,' he told her. 'But even if I sleep as long as Rip Van Winkle, it won't make any difference, will it? When I wake up I'll still be a eunuch.'

'Don't let me hear you use that word again, Con. Not ever.'

'All right. Gelding.'

'Goodnight, Con. I'll see you tomorrow.'

She left a note for Moirin that she might be late in tomorrow morning, and then she carried Walter in his dog crate down to the car park. It had stopped raining but the temperature had dropped and she could see her own breath. The city was unusually quiet, except for the sizzle of tyres on wet tarmac and the occasional distant parp of a car horn.

As she steered her Focus out of the Garda station car park, her attention was caught by a car behind her switching on its headlights and pulling away from the kerb. She had to stop at the traffic lights at the end of Old Station Road, and she frowned at this car in her rear-view mirror. There were double yellow lines on Old Station Road, which meant no stopping at any time, but it had been parked with its nearside wheels up on the pavement, so that it hadn't caused too much of an obstruction. But who would risk parking on double yellow lines right outside Cork's main Garda station, and who would suddenly switch on their lights and come nudging up behind her as she started to drive home?

She kept glancing at the car in her mirror as she drove up Albert Street and crossed over the south channel of the Lee on the Éamon De Valera Bridge. It stayed close behind her as she passed over Custom House Quay and then crossed the Michael Collins Bridge. It was still less than a car-length on her tail as she turned eastwards on the Lower Glanmire Road, the main route that would take her back to Cobh.

She tried to make out what model of car it was. She was fairly sure it was a Toyota SUV but it had dazzling halogen headlights and it was too close and too bright for her to be able to see it clearly. It was also too close for her to be able to see its number plate.

Driving along beside the River Lee, which was black and glittering in the darkness, she deliberately slowed down, until she was going no faster than 28 kph. The Toyota continued to follow her, but slowed down even more, widening the gap between them until she could see only its headlights. She carried on crawling until she reached the Dunkettle Roundabout, where the Lower Glanmire Road connected with the main N8. As she steered around the roundabout she saw in her mirror that the Toyota was having to give way to a cement lorry turning north. She jammed her foot down on the accelerator, speeding over the Dunkettle Bridge and undertaking three other cars as she slewed around the N8 roundabout to join the N25, which would take her due east, to Cobh Cross. She ignored an angry barrage of horn-blowing and kept on going with her foot pressed down hard on the pedal, weaving out into the outside lane and overtaking a bus and an Amber petrol tanker.

By the time she reached Harper's Island she was driving at over 150 kph. She kept glancing in her mirrors in case the Toyota driver had seen where she was going and was coming after her, but no headlights appeared to be gaining on her, or even keeping up. She slowed down only when she reached Cobh Cross and turned down towards Fota Island, and even then she was going fast enough to make her tyres scream out like a chorus of panicking schoolchildren.

Seventeen

Before she turned into her own driveway at Carrig View, she drove half a kilometre further down the road and turned into the narrow entrance to Dock Cottages, a terrace of flat-fronted houses that led down to the river. She turned her Focus around at the end of the terrace and sat waiting to see if she was followed. An oil-tanker blared out a low, mournful hoot as it passed behind her, which almost put her heart crossways, but after nearly five minutes she guessed that she had successfully given the Toyota the slip.

As she drove back to her house, though, her mind was whirring. Had that Toyota really been tailing her? Maybe it had simply been driving in the same direction, at least as far as the Dunkettle Roundabout. Yet if it *hadn't* been tailing her, why would it have been waiting outside the station, illegally parked, and why had it only started moving off when she came out of the car park? She was almost sure it had been tailing her, from the way it was being driven. But who had been trying to follow her, and why?

She was always alert to the fact that there were plenty of criminals in Cork who bitterly resented her for having arrested them, or who were anxious to prevent her from investigating the rackets they were running. Because of that she always looked under her car in the morning before she climbed into it, and she kept her eyes open for anybody who might be following her or watching her. When she was on duty she was always armed, too, with her Smith & Wesson Airweight revolver.

Despite the ever-present threat to her life, though, she always tried to live a normal or even a mundane existence, if only for the sake of her own sanity. She went out to pubs and restaurants with Conor and she took Barney and Foltchain for walks along the seashore, and she tried not to think that there might be a bomb planted under her chair in The Roundy or that she might be walking unknowingly into the crosshairs of a high-powered rifle.

She parked outside her house and lugged Walter's dog crate inside. Barney and Foltchain greeted her with their usual overexcitement, their tails whacking against the radiator in the hallway. Before she took off her coat she let Walter out of his crate, and they snuffled around him as fussily as if they were asking him, *Walter! It's you again! You're back! Where in the world have you been, boy?*

'Right, dog people,' she said. 'The number one priority is for me to light the fire. Once I've done that, I'll feed you.'

Katie had already laid the fire early this morning with crumpled newspapers and kindling, so all she had to do was put a match to the firelighters. Once they were flaring up, she switched on the television, although she turned it to mute, and then she went over to the window.

She had almost closed the curtains when she saw a white SUV glide past her driveway and come to a stop behind the dry brown beech hedge at the front of her house. She waited, and watched, and after a few moments she saw its lights switched off.

She couldn't have been sure, because the streetlights all along the Lower Glanmire Road were sodium, but the Toyota that had been following her out of the city had also appeared to be white.

'Wait here, you three,' she said to the dogs, but they started to follow her out of the living room and into the hallway and she had to snap, 'Stay! *Ná bogadh!*'

Before she opened the front door, she turned off the hallway light and the outside light, too, so that when she stepped out on to the porch she wouldn't be silhouetted, or lit up, and present herself as an easy target. She walked up to her driveway gate and cautiously looked around the hedge. The SUV was still there, with its engine running. Its interior was in darkness, but she thought she could see two men inside it, and the glow of a cigarette. Its nearside window must have been open, because after a few moments smoke billowed out of it, and was snatched by the chilly breeze, and blew away.

Katie wasn't quite sure what she should do next. These two men could be perfectly innocent, and had simply stopped for a break, or maybe they were lost and had stopped to get their bearings. But she couldn't see a satnav screen, or the light from a mobile phone, and if they were consulting a printed map, surely they would have had the interior light switched on.

She took her own phone out of her coat pocket and quickly prodded in the number from the SUV's index marks. Almost instantly, the response came back from the National Vehicle and Driver File. The SUV was a Toyota RAV4, first registered in October 2016 to William John Sweeney of Áit Síochánta Farm in Ballyshoneen Cross, County Cork.

She checked with the PULSE computer, but there was no record of this vehicle having been stolen. Yet what would a farmer from Ballyshoneen Cross be doing here in Cobh, outside her house, at this time of night?

Her answer came almost at once. The Toyota's engine was switched off, and the cigarette was flicked out of its window in a shower of sparks. Both its driver and its passenger doors were flung open and the two men swung themselves out. It was too dark for Katie to be able to make out what they looked like, even though there was a streetlight fifty metres further down the road. She could only see that they were both wearing shiny black Puffa jackets and both had shiny shaved heads.

The two men came striding in her direction, but they couldn't have been aware that she had been watching them from her driveway gate, because as soon as they caught sight of her they came to a shuffling stop, and almost collided with each other, like two comedians.

'Detective Magga-wire?' said one of them, in a harsh Eastern European accent.

'Who are you?' Katie demanded. 'Have you been following me here?'

'You are Detective Magga-wire?'

'Who wants to know?'

The men came closer. One of them was much taller than the other, but they both looked hard, with broad shoulders and faces as rough as concrete, and the shorter man's head kept twitching to the left, as if he were about to have a fit at any moment and start hitting out.

'We have come for girl,' said the taller one. He sounded as if he were reciting something that he had been taught to say by somebody else. 'You bring us out girl, okay?'

'What girl? I don't know what you're talking about.'

'You know what girl. Don't give us trouble.'

'Or *what*?' Katie demanded. 'Come here, you two – if you're not out the gap before I count to three I'll be calling for backup and having you hauled in for threatening behaviour.'

'No, we don't go. We have come for girl.'

'You listen to me, sham. I have no idea what you're talking about and if you don't leave *now* – like, *immediately* – I'll also have you arrested for failing to comply with a direction from a member of An Garda Síochána. In case you don't know, that's a Class D fine of a thousand euros or six months in prison.'

'*You* listen, *vacă*, we don't go without girl,' said the shorter man, in a thick phlegm-clogged voice. He took a step towards her, his left hand raised to grab her arm, but Katie took two quick steps backwards, her heels crunching on the shingle driveway. She thrust her hand into her open coat and tugged out her revolver, pointing it directly at the shorter man's head.

'Down on the ground, the both of you!' she barked at them.

The two men stared at her in shock, and then at each other. The shorter one tentatively raised both hands, but both of them remained standing.

'I said, down on the ground!' Katie repeated. 'Don't you eejits understand English? Face down, *flat*, and stay there until my backup gets here!'

There was a long, tense pause. Katie pointed her revolver at the taller man and then back towards the shorter man. The breeze had risen, and the dry beech hedge was furiously rattling, like some kind of mystical warning. The taller man was staring at Katie with deep hostility but then he glanced behind him, as if he were measuring up the distance between him and the SUV. He hesitated for a few seconds, and then he snatched at the sleeve of the shorter man's jacket and said, '*Alerga! Nu ne va împuşca! Alerga!*'

They both turned around and ran back towards the Toyota. They yanked open the doors and scrambled into their seats, and the taller man started up the engine. With a loud slithering of tyres they swerved away from the kerb and sped off down Carrig View, with the passenger door still flapping open.

Jamming her revolver back into its holster, Katie ran back to the porch and slammed the front door so that the dogs couldn't get out. Then she climbed into her car and reversed out of her driveway and on to the road. She pressed her foot down hard on the accelerator pedal and went speeding off after the Toyota. The two men had a start on her, but she knew all the roads in Cobh, every twist and turn and unexpected obstruction. She had also been trained up to CBD2 in high-speed driving when she was at the Garda College at Templemore.

Carrig View became the High Road that led straight into the centre of Cobh, and as she passed the Great Gas petrol station, Katie caught sight of the Toyota's red rear lights up ahead of her. It was travelling fast, but not as fast as her. She took several deep breaths to steady herself, and whispered, '*Do scíth a ligean,*' which her grandmother always used to say to her grandfather when he was overexcited or threw a rabie – *relax*. Her heart was thumping but she was confident that she had this situation under control. She could have fired at the two men as they ran away, but if she had wounded them or killed them the subsequent Garda inquest would have been a nightmare. *You shot two unarmed men in the back, Detective Superintendent Maguire?*

She supposed she could have shot at their tyres, but she knew that most tyres these days were either run-flat or self-sealing and so that probably would have been pointless.

As she passed Heidi's café, where she occasionally went for breakfast, Katie was only about a hundred and fifty metres behind the Toyota. She had no way of telling if the two men realized that she was chasing after them, but when they reached the junction with Whitepoint Drive they took a sudden right-hand turn. She could only guess that they were trying to be evasive, in case she had sent out a call to the local Garda station to look out for them, and given a description of their Toyota. But she doubted that they would have turned down that way if they knew that Whitepoint Drive led only to the Lower Road, which turned sharply east to run parallel to the High Road, and eventually met up with it again at the Cobh Heritage Centre.

She also doubted that they knew that Cobh Garda Station was sited halfway along the Lower Road, and that Cobh Garda Station was open twenty-four hours.

Katie didn't turn down Whitepoint Drive after them, but kept on speeding along the High Road. She switched on her r/t and had herself patched through to the communications room at Cobh.

'DS Maguire, from Anglesea Street. Come here to me, this is urgent.'

'What's the story, ma'am?'

'There's a white Toyota RAV4 heading east on the Lower Road. It'll be passing right by you in only a couple of minutes. I'm heading into town myself on the High Road and I'm hoping to cut it off at Westbourne Place. If you can send a car behind it, we'll have it boxed in.'

'We have a couple of cars parked right outside on the road, ma'am. Don't you worry – we'll be after it pronto.'

'Listen – there's two occupants in the Toyota, and they're both Eastern European fellows. I don't believe they're armed but tell

your officers to be dog wide anyway. They're wanted for threatening behaviour, and maybe other offences, too.'

'I have you, ma'am. Roger and out.'

Katie had to slow down for a moment before she could pass
an elderly couple in a mustard-coloured Volvo estate. They were
driving at such a crawl that she was tempted to blast her horn at
them, but then again she calmed herself down by saying, '*Do scíth
a ligean.*' As soon as she was able to overtake them, she pressed
her foot down again and it took her less than two minutes then
to reach the junction with Westbourne Place.

She did a sharp U-turn, which led to an approaching driver
flashing his lights and giving her the finger, which she ignored,
and then she sped down the slope towards the car park in front of
the Cobh Heritage Centre and Deepwater Quay beside it. It was
here that the *Titanic* had docked, and over the pointed rooftops
of the red-brick museum she could see that a huge white cruise
liner was tied up here this evening, festooned with lights.

As she neared the car park, she recognized the Toyota's halogen headlights approaching from the direction of the Lower
Road. It was travelling much more slowly than it had before, but
a Garda squad car was only about a hundred metres behind it,
and because of that the taller man was obviously taking care to
keep to the speed limit. She could see that a second squad car was
following, about three hundred metres further back.

Katie slewed her Focus sideways, stopped, reversed a little, and
then applied her handbrake, so that she was completely obstructing the narrow road that led up towards the town centre. The
Toyota slowed down even more when it reached the car park, and
then it, too, came to a halt. Katie could imagine what the two
men were saying to each other, as it must be dawning on them
that they had two Garda squad cars close behind them and that
their only escape route was blocked off.

She could also imagine what they were saying to each other
as she left her car and began to walk towards them, and what
they were saying probably included a stream of swear words in

whatever language they spoke. Since they had been demanding 'the girl', it was more than likely that they were Romanian. Meanwhile, the first squad car had stopped so close behind them that it was almost touching their rear bumper, while the other squad car drew up alongside. The squad cars' doors were thrown open and five uniformed gardaí climbed out.

'*DS Maguire!*' Katie shouted out to the gardaí, holding up her ID card in her left hand. '*I'm armed!*'

None of the officers had time to respond, though, because the Toyota's engine suddenly revved. It shot forward, hitting the side of a Volkswagen saloon and denting its door. It then careened around the car park, colliding with three or four more cars before it screeched around the side of the heritage centre and headed towards the quay.

Katie started to run around the corner after it, and three of the gardaí joined her, including a sergeant, while the other two climbed back into their squad car.

'They won't get away!' the sergeant panted. 'Dermot and Michael, they'll go back and cut them off at Whitepoint Drive!'

Although it was late and the temperature was almost down to zero, the quay was brightly lit and crowded. A row of five tour coaches had just returned from Cork city and they were parked up nose to tail beside the museum wall. Dozens of passengers were stepping down from them and filing across the quay. A square blue pontoon was tied up between the ship and the shore so that they could board the liner through a large door in its starboard side.

The Toyota headed straight towards the lines of passengers without slowing down, and Katie heard screams and deep soft thumps as at least four or five of them were knocked over.

'*For the love of God, look out!*' she cried, although she was breathless and she doubted that anybody could hear her over all the background noise. Because it was so cold, the coaches' engines had been left running and the cruise liner's generators were droning and the passengers were shouting in panic.

A dock worker ran forward in his high-viz jacket and threw

a traffic cone at the Toyota, which bounced off its windscreen. The Toyota slewed to the right and hit the front of the first tour coach. The impact sent it spinning around in a circle and it skidded over to the edge of the quay, rocking on two wheels for one queasy second before it toppled off and landed on its side on top of the pontoon. The bang was deafening, followed by a loud slap of seawater. Almost instantly, its petrol tank exploded and it was engulfed in flames.

Two dock workers and a crewman from the liner attempted to approach it, but the flames were already too fierce and the heat was too intense for them to get close. Katie could even feel it from where she was standing on the quayside, and she raised her hand to shield her face.

'We need ambulances – *now!* – and the fire service!' she called out to the sergeant, although when she turned round she could see that he was already talking on his r/t. When she turned back, she saw that three crew members had appeared in the liner's open doorway with fire extinguishers.

The crewmen started spraying the Toyota with thick white foam, although the flames seemed to swallow it up and leap even higher. After less than a minute, to her horror, Katie saw that the driver's door was gradually starting to lift up, like a trapdoor from hell. Even more flames poured out of the SUV's interior, and wrapped in these flames appeared the taller of the two men. His entire head was on fire, and the sleeves of his Puffa jacket were blazing, so that it looked as if he were wearing fiery epaulettes. The crewmen aimed criss-cross jets of foam at him, and he managed to push up the door a little higher. He reached out and gripped the rear door handle, trying to pull himself out, but then another billow of flames engulfed him. He dropped back inside the Toyota and the door slammed shut on top of him.

In the distance Katie could hear ambulance and fire engine sirens, so she left the quay and ran across the car park to move her car. She reversed it into the last remaining parking space, opposite the statue of Annie Moore, just as a fire engine with its blue lights flashing came down the slope. When she had done that, gasping for breath, she came back to see how many of the liner's passengers had been injured, and if she could help.

As far as she could make out, only one passenger was clearly dead, a black man with grizzled grey hair in a camel-hair coat. His glasses were lying on the concrete in a widening stain of blood, their lenses cracked, and an elderly woman was kneeling beside him, sobbing. A young Chinese woman had been badly hurt, and one of the ship's doctors was giving her a painkilling injection. Another white-haired woman looked as if she had been slapped across one side of her face with a bright red paintbrush, and she kept dabbing at her cheek in disbelief, while a big-bellied middle-aged man was lying on his back on the ground, rolling from side to side and groaning like a dying bull.

After the fire engine, three ambulances arrived, only seconds apart, and six paramedics came hurrying out of them, four men and two women, carrying their resuscitation bags. Katie could only stand back and watch, pushing her hands deep into her coat pockets because the wind that was blowing from the harbour was so bitter. The wind was pungent with smoke, too, and she hoped she couldn't smell charred human flesh.

She crossed herself as the paramedics got to work and whispered a prayer to Saint Raphael, the patron saint of healing. There was no other way she could help. She didn't want to ask herself if she had done the right thing by pursuing those two men. There was no question, though, that if she hadn't pursued them they would still be alive, and none of these innocent passengers would have been killed or hurt.

Inside her mind, she couldn't help hearing what her former Chief Superintendent, Denis MacCostagáin, used to say whenever any of his officers were accused of negligence or lack of foresight. 'If only time went backwards instead of forwards. We'd never make any fatal mistakes, would we, because we'd be wide to what was coming. But without fatal mistakes our lives would be dreary as all hell, wouldn't they?'

Eighteen

It was four thirty a.m. before Katie returned home, and she was exhausted and shaking with cold. She had stayed on the quay until the last of the injured passengers had been taken away for treatment, and a three-man technical team had turned up in their white Tyvek suits, yawning, to take pictures.

The firefighters had doused the last flames that flickered from the Toyota's tyres, and about an hour later a bright orange mobile crane had arrived on the quay to lift its burned-out shell off the pontoon and load it on to the back of a flatbed truck. The bodies of the two men were still inside it, but removing them without further damage was going to take the skill of a specialist pathologist, and that would be done at the Technical Bureau's workshop where vehicles were taken after serious accidents.

She hung up her coat and went into the living room. The fire that she had lit hours ago had burned down to ashes and so she turned on the central heating. Barney and Foltchain opened their eyes and Barney stood up and shook himself to greet her, but Walter stayed fast asleep on the couch. He had left a small curly turd on the tiles in front of the fire and he had scratched at the hearthrug in his attempt to bury it.

'It's all right, dog people, you can stay in here for the rest of the night,' she told them. 'Don't think you're sleeping in here tomorrow, though. Tomorrow, it's back to the kitchen.'

She undressed and showered to warm herself up and to wash away the smell of smoke. When she had pulled on her long brushed-cotton nightdress, she went to the washbasin to brush her teeth. She stared at herself in the mirror. Green eyes, Titian red hair, skin as pale as ivory. Her late lover, John, had teased her that she was like a selkie, one of the seal-women who lived under the sea but could shed their skins and come ashore to take on a beautiful human form and find a human husband. They made wonderful wives, but they were always secretly yearning to return to the sea.

John used to say that it wasn't the sea that Katie couldn't give up, but her life in the Garda. She couldn't hear a news report about an armed robbery or a civil disturbance or a missing person without having to drop whatever she was doing and drive immediately back to Anglesea Street to take charge. She couldn't even see a squad car speeding past with its blue light flashing without calling in to the station to find out where it was heading, and why.

She knew that, indirectly, her devotion to duty had led to John's death, and as she looked at herself in the mirror now, she could see that she was still asking herself if her commitment to her job was continuing to cost people their lives. That black man, lying on the quay with his broken glasses beside him – he was somebody's husband, somebody's father, somebody's grandfather. If she hadn't pursued those two Eastern European men, he would have enjoyed a good dinner on board the cruise liner yesterday evening and now be sleeping soundly in his cabin. Instead, he was lying in a refrigerated compartment in the ship's mortuary, waiting to be taken back to whichever country he had come from, for his funeral.

She went to bed and switched off the light and tried to sleep, but instead she lay in the darkness with her eyes open. As well as the chaos at Deepwater Quay tonight, she couldn't stop thinking about Conor. She adored everything about him, even his rashness. Perhaps his rashness more than anything. But what if he was never able to make love to her again? It was no good her pretending to herself that she could live without sex. Her sex drive was integral to what she was. It gave her determination, and the strength to stand up to those misogynistic officers who tried to belittle her. It gave her power, and courage. She would never have chased after those two men tonight if she hadn't been confident that she could face up to them once she had caught them.

Lying there, her thinking was distorted by tiredness and delayed shock, and she could almost believe that her sexuality brought nothing to those around her but disaster. If she was any creature from mythology, she was more like the Dullahan, the harbinger of death, than a selkie.

She made up her mind about one thing, though. She wasn't going to let Conor's beating go unpunished. He may have broken the conditions of his bail, but she doubted that any judge would insist that he had to go to jail and serve out the rest of his suspended sentence, not now that his injuries had proved to be so life-changing. Surely losing his manhood was punishment enough.

As her mind churned over, one thought kept surfacing again and again. Why had those two men demanded that she hand over 'the girl'? She had to assume they meant Ana-Maria, and presumably they hadn't realized that Tusla had taken her into temporary care, and thought that Katie was still looking after her. Lupul had risked arrest for assault in his attempt to get his hands on her, and these two had followed Katie all the way from Anglesea Street and threatened her. Why did they want this little girl so desperately?

Katie slept for about an hour, but in the middle of a strange dream in which she was floating about ten centimetres off the floor and somebody was laughing at her, her phone warbled. It was Detective Sergeant Begley.

'Sorry to ring you so early, ma'am. Patrick O'Donovan has just been giving me the latest about what's been happening down at Cobh. Three dead, that's what he heard. Are you okay yourself?'

'I'm grand altogether, thanks, Sean. I'll be giving you all a full briefing about it later this morning, as soon as I get in.'

'So long as you're not hurt or nothing. From what Patrick

was saying, it sounded like a fecking war zone. But – listen – the main reason I'm ringing you is about that dead fellow from Cook Street, that Matty Donoghue. We've identified his woman friend. We found a notebook among their possessions and it had a few phone numbers in it, as well as about a million sketches of dresses and jackets and hats and stuff. One of the numbers turned out to be her sister.'

'Stall it for a moment, Sean,' said Katie. 'I just need to switch on the light and blink myself awake.'

'Oh, sorry. Should I ring you later?'

'No, no. I'm conscious now. Go on.'

'The woman's name is Máire O'Connor. She's thirty-four years old, homeless now but used to live with her parents on Deanrock Avenue, by Clashduv Park. She was a fashion student at Mallow and showing a whole lot of promise. That's what her sister said anyway. But then she got herself mixed up with this Matty Donoghue and drugs and it was downhill all the way after that.'

'Any response to the EvoFIT?'

'One of the bouncers at the Sparkle Club recognized her and knew her by name. He said that she was always hanging around waiting for the dealers, and giving out to them because of what they were charging for crack.'

'But nobody's seen her since last night?'

'No. And judging by what she's left behind, I'd say that she didn't leave Cook Street voluntarily. Not just her notebook, but a couple of spare sweaters and underwear and soap and a tooth-brush and tampons even.'

'Oh, Jesus.'

'I've sent the EvoFIT down to Inspector O'Rourke so that he can hand it out to his beat patrols, and I'll be contacting the Missing Persons Bureau so that they can post it on their website. I expect you'll be wanting to have it shown on the TV news, and all the social media, too. I'll be having a word with Mathew McElvey as soon as he shows up.'

'Good man yourself, Sean. Give me an hour or so and I'll be in.

I have one small errand to run first and besides that I want to give this whole investigation some serious thought. What happened last night could have been connected to this Lupul character, too. I was confronted by those two fellows in the Toyota who died, and they sounded like they could have been Romanians. But it was all a total disaster, and I don't want to go rushing in blind and risk anything like that happening again.'

She went to hang up the phone but dropped it on the floor, so she had to get out of bed to pick it up. She was still tired but it was seven twenty-one now and she knew she would never be able to get back to sleep. She shuffled into the kitchen, filled the kettle and stood staring out at her garden. It was still dark outside and it was still raining. She couldn't remember when it had last been a pet day. In fact, she could hardly remember when it hadn't been winter.

The grey detached houses on Lime Trees Road were all identical, so Katie had to drive slowly along it peering at the numbers on the front doors. Eventually she reached Caoimhe O'Neill's house and parked outside. She carried Walter's dog crate up to the front door, rang the doorbell and waited. Walter let out one of his miniature sneezes and she bent over and said, 'You're grand, boy, don't worry. You'll be back with your missus in a minute.'

Caoimhe answered the door herself, a big, dark-haired young woman in a white blouse and a grey skirt, clearly dressed for her work at City Hall. Katie had already texted her to say that she was bringing Walter back to her, and she was flushed with excitement and almost in tears.

'This is so, *so* kind of you!' she said. 'Come on in... come through to the kitchen. Here, let me take the box for you.'

She led Katie through to the kitchen, where her father was sitting at the table with a mug of tea and her mother was standing at the sink, drying dishes.

'Pa, Ma, this is Superintendent Maguire.'

Caoimhe's father stood up and gave Katie an appreciative nod of his head. 'Caoimhe told us that you'd be fetching Walter over yourself because Conor wasn't too well. Nothing too desperate, I hope?'

'Well, he's recovering. But he wanted me to have a word with you about Walter. You know that he took him to the vet, for a check-up? I'm afraid it's not very good news.'

Caoimhe lifted Walter out of the dog crate and held him in her arms. Walter sniffed and wheezed and sneezed but he was plainly overjoyed to be home.

As gently as she could, Katie told the O'Neills what was wrong with him, and why he needed radical treatment if he was going to survive. Then she told them how much Domnall would charge for surgery.

Caoimhe's father slowly sat down again. 'Holy Saint Joseph. Three thousand euros? There's no way in the world we could manage that. I suppose we could try that what-do-ye-call-it. That crowd-funding. A cousin of ours had the prostrate cancer and he raised enough to be treated.'

Caoimhe clutched Walter tight, with tears rolling down her cheeks.

'I know it's a desperate expense but maybe you can find a way,' said Katie. 'All I can say is that Conor has agreed to waive his fee for finding Walter. He's totally passionate about illegal puppy farming and how people like Caoimhe are being conned into buying puppies that should never have been bred at all.'

She paused, and then she said, 'Have a think about what you want to do. When you've decided, give me a call at Anglesea Street. Look, here's my card.'

She left the family standing at their front door, miserable and numb, and walked back to her car in the rain.

Even before she had hung up her coat or switched on her PC or prised the lid off her cappuccino, Katie called down for Kyna.

Kyna appeared looking pale and tired. Her blonde hair was tangled and she was wearing no eye make-up. Katie didn't ask her what she had been doing last night, or where she had been, and who with. She didn't want to know, and in any case she had something more critical on her mind. As she was driving in to the station, she had decided that she was going to start taking positive and immediate action in all of the investigations that she had been considering up until now. No more caution, after last night's carnage, and to hell with the risks.

'Whatever Cairbre's working on, Kyna, can you tell him to drop it and go across to the District Court? I want a search warrant for the Foggy Fields puppy farm. Specifically, we're looking for forensic evidence of an assault causing serious harm.'

'You've decided to follow it up then?'

'I have, yes. Conor's injuries... well, let's just say that they're a fierce sight worse than the doctors first thought. I mean, it's possible that a judge might insist that he goes to jail for breaking the conditions of his bail, but I don't think any judge would be that hard-hearted.'

'Like, how bad is he really?'

'Let's just say that it's going to take him a long time to get over what's been done to him, and maybe he never will.'

'Oh, Katie. I'm so sorry. Give him my best wishes, won't you?'

'I will of course. And for his sake, I also want to see if I can prove that the McQuaide sisters ordered him to be beaten, or at least turned a blind eye to it. If I can do that, I may be able to close down their puppy farm. I know it's not going to be easy. There's no political interest at all in stamping out illegal puppy-breeding. But I can try my damnedest.'

'Okay. I'll go back down now and have Cairbre run over to Washington Street.'

Katie sat down at her desk and while she quickly shuffled through the memos and files that Moirin had left for her, she called for Detective Inspector Mulliken, Detective Markey and Detective Scanlan.

Detectives Markey and Scanlan arrived first, and a few minutes later Detective Inspector Mulliken walked in, carrying a cardboard cup of coffee.

'Change of plan,' she told them, standing up and ushering them over to sit on the couches by the window. 'After what happened at Deepwater Quay last night, I've decided to forget about the softly-softly approach. Bill Phinner tells me that we haven't yet been able to identify the two fellows I was chasing after because they were as good as cremated. But they both had Eastern European accents and I believe they followed me home because they thought I was still taking care of that little Romanian girl.

'I may be wrong, but I'd say that it's a bent cent to a euro that they were connected to this Lupul fellow, and I want to track him down now and haul him in before anybody else winds up getting themselves killed. We need to bring in that coffin-maker who's dossing down outside the Savoy Centre and question him about Lupul's possible whereabouts.'

'But Lupul's going to find out that we've lifted your man, isn't he?' asked Detective Inspector Mulliken. 'And if he's guilty, he's likely to pull a disappearing act, like you said he might.'

'Yes, he might. But if he does, we'll alert the immigration to keep their eyes peeled for him and notify the airlines and Stena Line ferries. I admit that he could still manage to slip out of the country and spirit himself back to Romania. If he does – well, we may be able to have him extradited back here, maybe not. At the very least, he'll no longer be a threat to Cork's rough sleepers.'

'I'm sorry, ma'am, but all of this is still pure hypothetical,' said Detective Inspector Mulliken. 'Like, we have no evidence at all that Lupul is responsible for killing Gearoid Ó Beargha and Matty Donoghue, do we? And even if those two fellows who ended up dead at Deepwater Quay *sounded* to you like they were Eastern European, we can't be sure that they were associated with Lupul, or even that they were Romanian. One Eastern European sounds very much like another – to me, anyway. I can't tell my Poles from my Czechs from my Bulgarians.'

'Fair play to you, Tony,' said Katie. 'But now the body count's doubled and as far as I'm concerned that changes everything. This investigation is going absolutely nowhere and I would rather find out that I'm wrong than find out nothing at all. Maybe Lupul isn't our killer driller, but there's a fair chance that he might be. We're never going to know for sure unless we find him and haul him in.'

'Sure like, but would a few extra days really make a difference? Can't we wait until Bill Phinner's put names to those two dead fellows – or their nationalities, at the very least?'

'I'd agree with you if Matty Donoghue's girlfriend wasn't missing. Hopefully, she's still alive, even if that blood in the doorway on Cook Street turns out to be hers. And if she *is* still alive, where is she? We need to find her, alive or dead, and urgent-like. I'm sorry, Tony. You may think it's rash to pick up our coffin-maker. *I* think it's rash. But after last night I don't see that we have much choice. I don't want to see any more innocent lives being lost.'

'Well... you're the boss,' said Detective Inspector Mulliken. He turned away to look out of the window as if he had only been half-listening to what she was saying, and had his mind on something else altogether.

Katie turned to Detectives Markey and Scanlan. 'Sean – Padragain – I've decided that we should keep a tail on Eamon Buckley for at least three or four more days. I'm with you, Sean, about Buckley's financial circumstances. There's definitely something that doesn't add up there, although it may turn out to be nothing at all. It's that ring that's still begging the question, do you know what I mean? How did it find its way into Mrs Devlin's mince? There could be some totally innocent explanation, like maybe a magpie dropped it out of its beak as it was flying over Mrs Devlin's kitchen and it dropped down the chimney and bounced into her mixing bowl.'

'I'll bet a month's pay *that* didn't happen,' said Detective Markey.

'Well, of course it didn't. And even if it did, how did the magpie get the ring off Ana-Maria's mother's finger?'

'I'm trying my best not to be prejudiced, but I'm one hundred per cent *convinced* it was that gobshite Buckley,' said Detective Scanlan. 'I'm sure it was him and when I can prove it, it'll make my day to see him in court. In fact, it'll make my year.'

'All right, then,' said Katie. 'Keep Buckley under surveillance until the end of your shift. I'll arrange with Superintendent Pearse to have a couple of uniforms watch him tomorrow morning until you come back on.'

When Detectives Markey and Scanlan had left, Katie tried ringing Conor. His nurse answered his phone and told her that he was downstairs having a CGI scan. Mr O'Connell, the maxillofacial consultant, was assessing how much reconstruction work would be needed on his cheekbone and his palate, and how his nose could be straightened.

'How is he in himself?' asked Katie. 'He was very down last night.'

'Well...'

'Please, tell me the truth. You know that we're going to be married.'

'I changed his dressings this morning and he's healing well.'

'But?'

'Don't tell him I told you this, but he's sad. I've been in nursing for eleven years and I swear I never saw a man as sad as him. I saw that statue of Jesus at Knock weeping real tears, but I swear that the Lord Jesus was the soul of cheerfulness compared to your Conor.'

Katie didn't know how to respond to that, so all she said was, 'Thank you, nurse. Thank you for being so honest,' and then she hung up. Afterwards she sat at her desk for a long time staring at the framed photograph of Conor and herself, a selfie they had taken in the grounds of Blarney Castle, one windy afternoon in October, with the dry leaves blowing in the air all around them like brown moths.

Kyna came back into her office. When she saw Katie sitting there, she walked around her desk, stood behind her, gently laid her hands on her shoulders and kissed the top of her head.

Katie reached up and took hold of one of Kyna's hands and squeezed it. 'Why does life do this to us, Kyna? Tell me that.'

'If I knew that, Katie, I'd be a billionaire, like, no question at all. I'd be on a beach in the Bahamas, and you'd be lying next to me. But I don't know, and so I'm not.'

Nineteen

'Bran!' shouted Saoirse. 'Bran, would you come back here, you stupid eejit!'

Her Wheaten terrier took no notice, but carried on scampering along the grass verge beside the river, chasing after three ducks that alternately waddled and flapped their wings to get away from him, letting out an occasional irritated quack. They seemed to regard him as more of a nuisance than a threat.

'For the love of *God*, Bran, would you do as you're told and come back here, otherwise it's no kelties!'

Saoirse started to jog after him. She was nineteen, with a plump, doll-like face and braided brown hair. She was studying beauty therapy at Cork College of Commerce, but she had taken the past three days off because of a rotten cold. This was the first time she had been outside since Monday, and she had wrapped herself up warmly in her thick red duffel coat and her knitted yellow scarf. She was small, only five feet one tall, and in her pink rushers she looked almost like a young child.

The three ducks eventually grew tired of being harassed, and they flopped one after another into the river and swam away. Bran reached the water's edge, but stayed on the grass, stock-still, watching them. He had been named after one of the two brave hunting dogs of the mythological Irish hero Fionn mac Cumhaill, but he lacked the nerve to jump into the chilly grey water of the Lee to go after them.

'You are the thickest dog ever,' said Saoirse, bending over to clip his lead back on to his collar. 'What do you think you were going to do with those ducks, even if you caught them?'

She was concentrating so much on fastening his lead that she wasn't aware of the tall, thin man in the loose grey tracksuit who was jogging in her direction. He crossed over the road on to the grass and as he did so he started to run faster, until he was almost sprinting. She looked up just as he collided with her, knocking her off balance and into the river. She was still holding Bran's lead, and when she rolled over in the water, splashing and gasping, she yanked Bran into the water, too. Bran yelped and went under, but almost immediately came up again, paddling furiously to keep himself afloat.

Saoirse tried to shout out for help, but when she opened her mouth she swallowed filthy cold water, and all she could do was splutter. She had never learned to swim, and even though she was thrashing her arms and legs wildly, she went under again.

She kicked and struggled, and managed to break the surface, desperately gasping for air. She tried to reach the concrete bank, which was less than two metres away, but her duffel coat was sodden now, and weighing her down, and even though she tried to make swimming motions with her arms, she made no progress at all, and went under for a third time.

The tall, thin man in the grey tracksuit had run off by now, turning the corner into the narrow entrance to Church Avenue, and disappearing.

Brianna had just tugged open the packet of cheese-and-onion Taytos that she had packed in her lunchbox when the call came that a woman had been pulled out of the river at Blackrock.

'I think the Lord's telling me to go on a diet,' she said to Darragh, as she climbed into the ambulance next to him.

'I think the Lord's telling me to move to a city where there isn't a river,' said Darragh. 'This is the fifth floater since St Stephen's Day and it isn't even February yet.'

They sped around the Magic Roundabout and headed north on the South Link Road, with their blue lights flashing. Traffic was mercifully light, and they reached The Marina in less than ten minutes. There was a small crowd of five or six people gathered beside the river, and as Brianna climbed down from the ambulance she could see a young woman in a red duffel coat lying on her back on the grass, and a middle-aged man kneeling beside her.

'Thank God,' the man said, as Brianna knelt down beside him. 'I've been giving her the kiss of life, like, and she's coughed up about three pints of water. She's breathing but she hasn't opened her eyes yet.'

'What happened?' asked Darragh. 'Does anybody here know who she is?'

'I've seen her before, walking her dog along here,' said a woman. She was holding Bran in her arms, wrapped up in a tartan car blanket. 'I think she lives in the village, right opposite The Leaping Salmon.'

'My neighbour Michael was putting out the rubbish and he saw her waving,' put in another woman. 'He ran straight over and jumped in and pulled her out. He's back inside now, getting himself dry. That's the third time he's gone in now to rescue somebody out of the river. They should give him a medal for it, do you know?'

Saoirse's lips were pale turquoise and her cheeks were reddened from the cold but she was still breathing. Brianna checked her pulse and then she and Darragh lifted her on to a stretcher and carried her into the ambulance. Once inside, they raised her up into a sitting position to drag off her soaking-wet duffel coat and her green Aran sweater, and Brianna wrapped a crackly foil survival blanket around her.

Darragh folded up the steps and closed the doors. As he was walking around to the front of the ambulance, a Garda squad car came around the corner, followed closely by another. One of the gardaí came over to him, a big beefy fellow, hitching up his belt.

'How is he?' he asked.

'He's a she, and with a modicum of luck and God's eternal mercy she'll survive,' said Darragh.

'Trying to drown herself, was she?'

'I have no idea. The dog was in the water, too, so maybe she went in after it. It's unbelievable, the number of people who jump into the river to save their pets. The pets usually manage to get out by themselves while their owners go under.'

'You're not joking. Christmas Day we had some auld wan who went into the water by the Shaky Bridge, trying to rescue his sheltie bitch when it went for a swim. He went straight down to the bottom while the sheltie paddled over to the other side. It could swim better than Michelle Smith, that bitch, I'm telling you.'

Darragh climbed up behind the wheel of the ambulance and started to drive off to the University Hospital. In the back, Brianna had fitted an oxygen mask over Saoirse's nose and mouth and was keeping a watchful eye on her pulse. Her heart rate was fast and erratic and Brianna thought it was quite possible that after her immersion in the freezing cold river she might easily be at risk of a cardiac arrest. That was what it would look like, anyway, if her heart were suddenly to stop beating.

Brianna thought for a moment, biting her lip. They had reached Victoria Road already so she knew she had only six or seven minutes at the most. But as they turned on to the South Link, she made up her mind. The girl lived in Blackrock, so it was likely that her parents would be reasonably well off, and could pay for a decent funeral.

'How's she coming along?' Darragh shouted.

'Not too good,' Brianna called back. 'Her pulse is ectopic and her temperature's down to twenty-eight point three.'

Quickly, she lifted off Saoirse's oxygen mask. Then she picked up a folded white towel from the shelf beside her, folding it once more to make it thicker. She pressed it over Saoirse's face and held it there, all the time watching the oximeter attached to Saoirse's finger to check her pulse and her oxygen levels.

Darragh was speeding along at almost 120, with the siren

blaring. Usually they were held up by the traffic at the Magic Roundabout, but today the road was completely clear.

'Come on,' Brianna whispered to Saoirse, keeping the towel pressed down hard. 'The Good Lord Jesus is expecting you, girl. Don't keep him waiting.'

Suddenly, however, Saoirse kicked her legs underneath the shiny foil blanket, and jerked her head violently left and right. She reached up with both hands and tore the towel away from her face, and when Brianna tried to press it down again, she seized her wrists and stared up at her, her eyes bulging and bloodshot, whining for breath.

'What are you *doing*?' she said, in a thin, piercing scream, almost like a whistle.

Brianna said, 'Drying your face, girl. You've just been fished out of the river, like, don't you know that? You're all soaking wet.'

She tried to press the towel down once more, but Saoirse forced her wrists upwards. 'Stop it! I can't breathe when you do that! Stop it!'

'Don't talk such nonsense, girl. I'm a paramedic. I've only saved your life, like. Now let me dry you.'

Brianna tried again to cover Saoirse's face with the towel. She pressed down as hard as she could, but Saoirse kept her grip on her wrists and strained against her, gasping with effort. There was a moment when the two of them were deadlocked, Brianna look-ing down at Saoirse with grim determination, and Saoirse looking up at Brianna in bewilderment and fear. Their breathing sounded like two lovers, close to a mutual climax.

They had reached the Sarsfield Roundabout now, and the hospital was only two or three minutes away. Brianna was begin-ning to panic now, and she grunted and leaned forward with all of her weight, no longer making any pretence that she was doing anything to Saoirse but trying to suffocate her.

Saoirse made one last desperate attempt to push her away, but she was still in shock and the effort was too much for her. She let out a strangely wistful '*ohhh*', and passed out. Her head fell back and her eyelids flickered and her hands dropped on to the blanket, and as the ambulance swerved around the roundabout, her body was jostled limply from side to side.

Brianna folded up the towel again and kept it pressed down hard over Saoirse's face. She held it there right up until the last few seconds when Darragh was backing them up to the hospital's emergency entrance. The oximeter had dropped off Saoirse's finger on to the floor while she and Brianna were struggling together, so Brianna couldn't tell from that if her heart had stopped beating. As Darragh was opening up the doors, however, she felt Saoirse's carotid artery with her fingertips and she detected no pulse.

Thank you, Saint Agatha. The patron saint of nurses has blessed me once again. And this girl is blessed, too. In return for helping me to find prosperity here on Earth, she'll surely find peace and joy and eternal happiness in Heaven.

Two porters lifted the trolley out of the back of the ambulance and wheeled it in through the hospital doors. Brianna and Darragh followed them, until they met the duty doctor coming towards them, Dr Ryan O'Keefe, prodding at his mobile phone. He was a big, ebullient man, more like a rugby forward than a doctor, with curly blond hair and reddened cheeks, and a way of stamping along when he walked so that his white coat flapped.

'One for the mortuary, I'm afraid, doctor,' said Brianna.

'Third fatality today,' said Dr O'Keefe, still prodding at his phone. 'We had two little kids run over by a bus on the Lower Glanmire Road, on their way to school. Only five and six years old. What's the story with this one?'

'She was pulled out of the river by Marina Park. She'd inhaled a fair amount of water, like, and she was hypothermic, but I'm not so sure if you can put her death down to drowning. I took her pulse and I reckon she could have experienced an autonomic conflict when she first fell in, do you know? Anyway, she suffered a fatal cardiac arrest on the way here from Blackrock.'

Dr O'Keefe dropped his phone back in his overall pocket and watched Saoirse's trolley being pushed away along the corridor.

'Okay, I'll take a look at her and pronounce life extinct. You could be right, though. More people die of heart seizures when they fall into the river than they do of actual drowning – especially now in the winter, when the water's so cold. But of course there's no way of telling post mortem.'

Darragh looked at his watch. 'We've time for a cup of tea, I'd say. I'm as dry as Gandhi's flip-flop. Do you want to go up to the Coffee, doc?'

'I'll catch you later so,' said Dr O'Keefe, and went stamping off along the corridor with an occasional skip, as if he were trying to catch up with some invisible friend who was walking faster than him.

'I'm thinking of going to Las Vegas for my holliers,' said Darragh, as they sat in the hospital café.

'Serious?' Brianna didn't look up. She was tapping away at her mobile phone, sending a text to Niall Dabney.

'Yeah, serious. Somewhere hot, and dry and deserty, anyway, where people don't keep on fecking drowning.'

'Darragh,' she said, 'I think you're forgetting that they have swimming pools in Las Vegas – hundreds of them. I'll bet you that even more people drown there than they do here in Cork. Too many margaritas, and then a midnight skinny-dip, and glug. The only difference is that the water's warm, so that when they find you floating around in the deep end in the morning, you're already half-poached.'

'You've a sick mind, you have, Brianna.'

'I'm a realist, that's all. There's a headstone waiting for all of us. It doesn't really make much difference how and when we go.'

She sipped her tea and waited for Niall to text her back. Once the dead girl had been identified, she would call round at her parents' house to offer her condolences and describe her last moments, which relatives always wanted to hear if they hadn't been present when their loved ones passed away. Sometimes she would invent last words that they had spoken, such as 'Tell my mother I love her' or 'I'm coming, Saint Peter! I'm coming!' Then she would leave one of Niall's cards and recommend him for his 'sensitive, respectful, personal services... not like one of those big undertakers who churn out their funerals like the black pudding factory down at Clon'.

Darragh finished his third shortcake finger and smacked his hands together. 'Right...' he said, with his mouth full. 'We'd better make tracks.'

They were buttoning up their jackets when Dr O'Keefe came in to the café.

'I'm glad I caught up with you,' he told them. 'This'll brighten up your day. That girl you fetched in – she's going to recover.'

Brianna stared at him. 'What do you mean, she's going to recover? She stopped breathing, and she had no pulse.'

'Her pulse was weak all right, and her breathing was so shallow that it was almost undetectable. Almost like hypopnoea. But once we put her on oxygen and she began to warm up, her pulse rate improved and she started to breathe normally.'

'Well, that *is* good news,' said Darragh. 'Lately I've been feeling that I've been driving a fecking hearse, like, more than an ambulance.'

'Is she conscious?' asked Brianna. Her iPhone pinged and she guessed that it was Niall, but she didn't take it out of her pocket and look at it.

'No, no, she's not conscious yet,' said Dr O'Keefe. 'She might have suffered some brain impairment if she was under the water for any length of time, but until she recovers consciousness it's too early to say for sure. As soon as I'm happy with her vital signs, I'll be sending her across for an MRI.'

'You truly think that she's going to survive?'

'Like I say, she could have sustained some brain damage because of oxygen deprivation. But I'm confident that physically she's going to pull through all right.'

Brianna suddenly felt as if she were going to faint. She saw tiny white sparks floating in front of her eyes and she had to pull out her chair again and sit down.

'Are you all right there, girl?' Darragh asked her, laying his hand on her shoulder.

'I'm grand, thanks. It's just – well, it's come as a fierce shock, like, finding out that she hasn't passed away. I was so sure that I'd lost her.'

'Not at all, Brianna,' smiled Dr O'Keefe. 'It seems like you saved her life. I'm sure that when she's recovered enough, Brianna, she'll be wanting to thank you.'

Brianna nodded, but said nothing. Her heart was beating hard and she was finding it difficult to breathe, almost as if she, too, had a folded towel pressed against her face.

Twenty

Katie was finishing off her report on Deepwater Quay when Detective Inspector Jimmy Joyce rang her from Dublin.

'How are you going on there, Kathleen? Listen – I've managed to have a word with my old friend Alexandru Salavastru. He's the Comisar-şef of the general directorate for criminal investigation in Bucharest.'

'Does he know this Lupul fellow?'

'Oh, yes. His name is actually Dragomir Iliescu. It seems like he's a long history of convictions, going way back to when he was a teenager... most of them for begging with menaces. He tried to set up a begging ring in Bucharest but he got chased out by a fellow called Bruce Lee.'

'Bruce Lee? Serious?'

'That's right. He's the king of the beggars in the capital there and that's his nickname. That's why Lupul upped sticks and went to Târgovişte. Alexandru wasn't aware that he was here in Ireland, but he said that it didn't totally surprise him. Things were getting a bit too hot for him in Romania, both from the cops and from rival gangs, too.'

'Did you tell your friend he's a possible murder suspect?'

'I did of course. And he said *that* didn't surprise him, either. The gang wars among the homeless are a serious problem in Romania. As you know, there's hundreds of them living in tunnels underground in Bucharest, and I mean like *hundreds* of them.'

'And what do the police do when they find one of them dead?'

'Unless there's obvious signs of serious assault, they don't bother to carry out a post mortem. Most of the homeless can't be identified or traced so they simply send them off for burial as quickly as they can. As you can imagine, their mortality rate is shocking. Every single one of those homeless men and women under the streets is suffering from HIV, and most of them have TB, too. Ninety-nine per cent of them are drug addicts of one kind or another. The ones who can't afford heroin or crack are addicted to Aurolac, which is a metal-based paint. They empty it into black plastic bags and sniff.'

'So if somebody had drilled into their brainstem with a cordless drill, it's unlikely that the police would notice?'

'Alexandru had to admit that they probably wouldn't. He's not saying that the Poliția Română are anything but scrupulous, but the sheer scale of the homeless problem in Romania makes ours seem like nothing at all by comparison. If you had to be lifting ten or twenty dead bodies every day out of the sewers in Cork, I don't suppose you'd be checking for doonchie little drill holes in the backs of their heads, either.'

'Thanks a million, Jimmy,' said Katie. 'You've been pure helpful. I needed to know if this Lupul believed that he could get away with killing rough sleepers without us realizing what their cause of death was. If it *is* him that's been doing it, like – but now I'm almost a hundred per cent sure that it is.'

'Are you any closer to finding your man?'

'Not yet. But I have a whole team out looking for him. We'll get him in the end.'

'Well, good luck with that, Katie. And if you do haul him in, you can come up to Dublin and buy me a drink or two at The Brazen Head, to show your appreciation.'

'You can hold me to that, Jimmy. I promise you.'

As Detective Inspector Fitzpatrick and Detective O'Donovan turned into Orchard Court, a small boy in a mustard-coloured sweater came running out into the road right in front of them, chasing his football, and they almost knocked him over. Detective O'Donovan blipped his horn and shook his head, but all the boy did was pick up his ball, give him the finger and shout out something unintelligible but probably obscene.

'Pure class, these Romanians,' said Detective Inspector Fitzpatrick.

'Oh, I don't know,' said Detective O'Donovan. 'I blew my horn at some fellow who stepped out in front of me in Fair Hill the other day, and do you know what? He was only after slinging a lump of dog shit after me.'

'Well, I suppose it depends on the area. They wouldn't be doing that to you in Montenotte now, would they? Or if they did, they'd at least wrap it up neatly in leftover Christmas paper.'

Detective O'Donovan parked and the two of them climbed out. Orchard Court was a small, dull estate in Blackpool, on the west side of the N20, and the noise of passing traffic was constant. Most of the houses were terraced or semi-detached, with a few odd ones built to three storeys high, and they were all painted a washed-out yellow and white. It was a freezing cold afternoon, with low grey cloud. Apart from the boys kicking a ball around, the streets were deserted.

The house they wanted was right at the end of the cul-de-sac. If a red Lexus IS hadn't been parked outside, Detective Inspector Fitzpatrick would have thought that its residents were out, because the curtains upstairs were all drawn and the windows downstairs were all in darkness. Detective O'Donovan went up to the blue-painted front door and rang the bell.

'What's the Romanian for "any china white, boy?",' he asked, chafing his hands together.

'There's no point in trying to make out that you're an addict,' said Detective Inspector Fitzpatrick. 'You're too fecking healthy-looking by half.'

'Okay, I'll forget it, then. But thanks for the compliment.'

'Besides that, Făt-Frumor knows me by sight. Only a couple of years ago I lifted him for stealing drugs from the Mercy Hospital pharmacy. If he hadn't had that crafty hoor Bernard Fágán representing him, I reckon he would have got at least three years.

'"My client was suffering from agonizing back pain", that's what Fágán told the judge. "His doctor refused to believe him so he was forced to self-prescribe." Self-prescribe my arse. Only to the tune of fifty-three bottles of oxycodone, which he conveniently forgot to pay for. I reckon I'll go to the offie after this and self-prescribe myself half a dozen bottles of Jameson's – see if I can't get away with them without settling up.'

Nobody had answered, so Detective O'Donovan lifted the flap of the letter box and leaned forward to peer inside. As soon as he did, the front door suddenly opened and Ştefan Făt-Frumor was standing there, with a cigarette in his mouth, holding a newspaper.

He was a short, big-bellied man in his mid-fifties, with prickly white hair and cheeks that were creased like a partially deflated beach ball. His left eye was milky white and blind, and there was a small hook-shaped scar underneath it. His right eye was chestnut, with amber flecks in it. He was wearing a baggy maroon tracksuit with stains on the pants and his feet were bare, with lumpy toes.

'So?' he demanded, without taking his cigarette out of his mouth. 'What are you two pigs after?' He spoke in a high, harsh northside accent, and if the two detectives hadn't known that he was Romanian, they would have guessed that he had been born and brought up in Croppy Boy or Farranree.

'We're trying to find one of your fellow Romanians,' said Detective Inspector Fitzpatrick. 'He's known as Lupul, although we understand that his given name is Dragos or Dragomir. We believe he may be trying to set up a bit of business here in Cork, and we need to ask him a few questions about it.'

Ştefan Făt-Frumor took his cigarette out of his mouth and spat sideways on to the front path. 'You think I'd sneak on him, even if I knew?'

'We're not asking you to sneak on him, Ştefan. All we're asking

is, do you know him, and if you do, do you know where he usually hangs out?'

'I know him, yeah. He's been over here from Romania two
or three times, trying to stick his nose in where it isn't wanted.'

'Why should that be a bother to you?' asked Detective Inspector Fitzpatrick. 'You're not involved in the drugs business any
more, are you? That's what you swore to Judge O'Shea, did you
not, the last time you were up in the District Court?'

Ştefan Făt-Frumor took a long drag on his cigarette before he
answered, and when he spoke every word was punctuated by
puffs of smoke coming out of his mouth and his nostrils.

'That's right. I'm into the mobile phone business these days,
that's all. But I'm spending more and more of my time in Dublin.
I'll be going up there Monday and in fact I'm thinking of moving
up there permanent, so why should I be worried about the likes
of Lupul?'

'Exactly,' said Detective Inspector Fitzpatrick. 'So you won't
mind giving us some idea where we might find him?'

'What did I just say to you, sham? I'm no fecking sneak.'

Detective Inspector Fitzpatrick was aware that Ştefan Făt-
Frumor was looking over his shoulder with his one good eye
when he said that, and not at him. He turned around and saw
three men standing on the corner, watching them.

'Okay,' he said. 'Honour among thieves and all that.'

'Who are you calling a fecking thief? I told you like I told the
judge, I'm going straight these days. I don't give a tinker's shite
for Lupul or any of his gang.'

He paused for a few seconds, his eye still fixed on the men on
the corner. Then he said, 'You could ask the same question of
Vasile, mind you.'

'Vasile?'

'He works evenings at The Parting Glass, behind the bar. He
washes cars during the day but I don't know where. But slip him
a few yoyos and you might find that he points you in the right
direction.'

'Fair play,' said Detective Inspector Fitzpatrick. 'We won't be troubling you any further, in that case.'

'Good man yourself, Ştefan,' said Detective O'Donovan. 'Enjoy the rest of your afternoon, now, won't you?'

Ştefan Făt-Frumor stared at the two detectives as if he couldn't decide if they were taking the rise out of him or not, but without saying another word he slammed the door in their faces.

'Jesus!' said Detective O'Donovan, in mock surprise. '"See you later, horse!" to you, too!'

They walked back to their car. The three men on the corner were still watching them, and Detective O'Donovan gave them a cheery wave before he climbed in behind the wheel.

'Well, that was illuminating,' said Detective Inspector Fitzpatrick, as they drove away.

'I totally agree,' said Detective O'Donovan. 'If Fatty Flew More isn't in the drugs business any longer, or any other racket, why is he still bothered about this Lupul character?'

'Exactly.'

'He said he couldn't give a shite about him, but if that's true, why did he tip us off about the barman at The Parting Glass?'

Detective Inspector Fitzpatrick said, 'You know something, Patrick? You'd make a good detective, so you would.'

Twenty-One

Down in the conference room, Katie gave the media a short briefing about the fatalities at Deepwater Quay.

'We suspect that the two deceased persons in the Toyota were foreign nationals, and we know that the vehicle was stolen from the multistorey car park at Merchants Quay, but so far we have no clear indication as to motive.

'We extend our heartfelt condolences to the family of the gentleman who lost his life, and our sympathy to all those injured, with best wishes for their speedy recovery.'

Dan Keane from the *Examiner* put up his hand. 'Detective Superintendent Maguire, it appears that you were personally in pursuit of this Toyota. Can you tell us why?'

'Only that I had good reason to believe that they had committed an offence.'

'What offence would that be, exactly?'

'Threatening behaviour.'

'Threatening behaviour against *who* would that be? And threatening to do *what*?'

'That's all I'm prepared to say for now. This inquiry's in its very early stages and I don't want to prejudice our findings in any way.'

'Would it be impertinent of me to ask if you've passed the CBD2 driving test?'

'Yes, it would. But yes, I have. Is that all?'

*

Katie returned to her office to find that Detective O'Crean was waiting for her. He stood up as Katie came in, holding up the search warrant that had been granted to him at the District Court.

'Sorry it took so long,' he told her. 'Judge Brennan was the only judge available and you know how many questions he's always after asking. "Who's the complainant? What evidence do you have that their complaint isn't fictitious or malicious? Who are they complaining about? How extensive a search do you have in mind? What specifically are you looking for?" Et cetera, et cetera, and so forth.'

'He's only bored, if you ask me,' said Katie, shaking the warrant out of its envelope, giving it a quick look to make sure that it was all in order, and then sliding it back in again. 'I think he enjoys exerting his authority, too. I saw him with his wife at the Lord Mayor's charity ball last year and the way she was giving out to him all evening, I think he's your classic henpecked husband.'

She looked at her watch. 'I was considering going up to Foggy Fields later this afternoon, as soon as it got dark, but there isn't the time to organize a search now. DS Ni Nuallán will be coming along with us and I'll want you, too, as well as a couple of uniforms, and of course two technical experts at the very least. I'll have a word with Bill Phinner and see if we can't set it up for tomorrow morning.'

'Anything special we're going to be looking for?' asked Detective O'Crean.

'Well, as you'd expect, any trace of blood that matches Conor's, or any other indication that he was assaulted while he was there. But it'll also give us a chance to take a good look at the McQuaide sisters' puppy-breeding set-up, too. Conor said that they're flouting almost all of the regulations. The bitches are shut up in boxes twenty-four hours a day, and they're filthy. It makes you wonder why the Dáil ever bothered to pass the Dog Breeding Act when nobody ever makes the slightest effort to enforce it.'

The phone on her desk rang. It was Detective Inspector Mulliken.

'We've fetched the coffin-maker in for questioning,' he said. 'He's down in interview room two, shivering like a jelly and looking more than a little sorry for himself.'

'Be nice to him, Tony. Give him a cup of tea in his hand, and a sandwich. I'll be down in a minute so.'

Katie could smell the coffin-maker as soon as she walked into the interview room. That thick, sweet, musky smell of somebody who hasn't washed or changed their clothes for weeks, and the sourness of alcoholic breath. He was sitting with his head bowed, the tip of his prominent nose almost touching the table. His man-bun was tied up with grubby red string, and a sprig of dead heather was pinned to his filthy bronze anorak.

He glanced up briefly as Katie came in and sat down between Detective Markey and Detective Murrish, but then he dropped his head again and continued to stare at the tabletop. He had been given a mug of milky tea and a pink meat sandwich, but it didn't look as if he had touched either of them.

After a few moments Katie heard footsteps along the corridor outside and Detective Inspector Mulliken came in to join them, along with Murtagh, the balding interpreter, who was wearing a three-piece suit of dark green tweed with red flecks in it. If the size of his shoulder pads was anything to go by, he had bought it in the early 1990s.

Katie reached across the table and tapped the coffin-maker's hand to get his attention. He looked up again, and she said, 'I want you to understand that you've not been arrested. You're not in any kind of trouble. We simply need to ask you some questions. Do you understand that?'

The coffin-maker slowly rubbed his unshaven chin, all the while staring at Katie as if he were trying to remember where he had seen her before.

Murtagh cleared his throat and said, '*N-ai făcut nimic rău. Vrem doar să vă punem câteva întrebări. Intelegi?*'

'*Da, inteleg*,' said the coffin-maker. 'I understand good. I was in England for three years. Manchester. Leaver-pool.'

'What were you doing there?' asked Katie.

'All kind. Building. Work in McDonald. Also pub.'

'When was that?'

'Two thousand fourteen to two thousand sixteen.'

'What made you go back to Romania?'

'My father die. I have to take care of my mother. But last year *she* die. I hope maybe she leave me some money but she leave nothing.'

'Don't let your tea get cold,' said Katie.

'Oh,' he said, and sipped it, and while he was sipping it, Katie said, 'What's your name?'

'Gică... Gică Petrescu.'

Murtagh let out a *pfff!* between his lips. 'He's winding you up, ma'am. Gică Petrescu was a famous Romanian singer. He used to sing all kinds of dirty folk songs.'

Katie sat back. 'Listen,' she said. 'You may not be in any trouble right now, but you will be if you start messing. Two people have died and one's missing and that's nothing to be getting humorous about. Do you have me?'

'*Ceea ce spune este că nu este o glumă*,' Murtagh put in, and then turned to Katie and said, 'I told him that this isn't a joke.'

'So what's your real name?' Katie asked him.

The coffin-maker reached into his anorak pocket, took out his ID card in its plastic cover and handed it over.

'All right. Andrei Costescu. Twenty-four years old. Who brought you over here to Cork, Andrei?'

'Nobody. I come here by myself.'

'You came all the way from Romania to sleep in the street?'

'I look for work.'

'Oh, really? You're dirty and you smell and you've been drinking. Who do you think is going to give you a job?'

'I don't know. Maybe coffin-maker.'

'So how many coffin-makers have you asked for a job so far?'

'I am asking soon. Maybe tomorrow.'

'So you haven't approached anybody for a job yet?'

'Maybe tomorrow. If I cannot get job with coffin-maker, maybe building house – or McDonald, like last time.'

'You may get a job on a building site, but they won't even let you in the front door of McDonald's, not smelling the way you do. And you have a dog, don't you?'

'It is not my dog. Only stray.'

'I don't believe you, Andrei. I don't believe a single word. It was Lupul who brought you over here, wasn't it? Dragomir Iliescu.'

Andrei puffed out his cheeks like a small child and violently shook his head. 'I don't know that name! I never hear that name, ever in my life! Never!'

'Well, I'm sorry, Andrei, but I think you do. I think it was Dragomir Iliescu who fetched you over here to Cork and I believe you have no intention of looking for work, either as a coffin-maker or a hod-carrier or a burger flipper or anything else. You're just going to sit on the pavement in St Patrick's Street looking like some poor unfortunate wretch and beg for money.'

'This is not true! I look for work tomorrow! I go to public toilet and wash! I clean up! I get job!'

'Oh, sure like,' said Katie. 'But I don't think that Lupul will be very pleased with you if you do.'

'I don't know that name,' Andrei insisted. 'Who is this Lupul? I come here by myself only to find job.'

'I'm afraid you're out of luck. Under the Immigration Act 1999, as a foreign national I can arrest and detain you without a warrant. You've been caught begging aggressively, in contravention of the Criminal Justice Public Order Act 2011. Not only that, you've been wilfully obstructing a major Garda investigation into two unexplained deaths, as well as a disappearance that's related to one of those deaths. In fact, *two* disappearances. Obstructing a Garda investigation in any way at all, that's *also* an offence under the Criminal Justice Act.'

Andrei looked around the interview room in a panic. 'You say I am not in trouble! What are you saying now?'

'I'm saying you need to co-operate with us, that's all.'

'All we want is a little information about Dragomir Iliescu,' Murtagh explained, in Romanian. '*Unde?* Like, where is he? for instance.'

'I tell you again. I don't know this fucking name.'

Katie shrugged. 'Fair play to you. If you don't know who he is, then you don't know who he is. So thank you for telling us that. We appreciate your co-operation, I can tell you. In fact we'll be making an announcement on the TV this evening that we've been interviewing you, and that you've helped us tremendously. Because of your assistance, we're much nearer now to finding out how our two rough sleepers died – *and* where our two missing women disappeared to. It's all down to you, Andrei, and we'll make sure that everybody knows it.'

Andrei stared at her, gripping the edge of the table. His mouth opened and closed several times before he was able to speak.

'On the TV?'

'That's right. The *Six One News*. They've been calling us all day asking if we've made any progress with this investigation. Now we'll be able to tell them that a homeless fellow from Romania, Andrei Costescu, has given us no end of help.'

'You can't say that. I don't help you.'

'Yes, but you did. You don't even realize how much.'

'You can't say that! He always watches the TV! He will hear my name! He will kill me!'

'Who are you talking about, Andrei? *Who* always watches the TV? You're not talking about Lupul, are you?'

Andrei didn't answer that, but abruptly stood up, so that his chair tipped backwards with a clatter. Detective Markey stood up, too, and then Detective Murrish, followed by Katie and Detective Inspector Mulliken. Murtagh remained seated in the corner, biting his thumbnail.

'Andrei, sit down,' Katie told him, in her calmest tone – the same tone she used when Barney was getting overexcited. 'Just sit down, and we can talk this over a little more.'

Andrei was breathing hard, and he kept glancing towards the door.

'Andrei... we don't have to give your name to the TV people. But you've just admitted that you *do* know Lupul, don't you? All we need to know from you is where we can find him. He never has to know that it was you who told us.'

Andrei stayed where he was, still breathing hard. Then without any warning he lunged towards the door. Detective Murrish was the nearest to him, because she had been sitting right at the end of the table. She stuck out her foot and tripped him up, and he fell sideways on to the floor, hitting his head against the skirting board, but not before he had snatched at her sleeve and pulled her down on top of him.

He was kicking and struggling, but Detective Murrish gripped him by the throat with her left hand and held his left shoulder against the floor with her right. Detective Markey came around the end of the table and snatched at his ankles to pin him down even further and shouted, 'That's it, sham! Stop that fecking kicking, will you?'

Andrei's anorak had flapped open, and with his right hand he reached for his belt buckle. He tugged at it, and out came a knife with a short double-edged blade.

'*Bedelia, watch out!*' Katie shouted, and Detective Markey scrambled forward and made a grab for Andrei's arm. But he was too late to stop Andrei from stabbing Detective Murrish straight in the left eye, so forcefully that Katie heard a sharp crunch, and when Detective Murrish fell backwards against the wall, the knife stayed embedded in her eye socket, with the decorative buckle-shaped handle sticking out of it.

'Ambulance! Now!' snapped Katie. She reached across to the panic button beside the table and hit it hard with the heel of her hand. 'And drag this bastard out of the way!'

Detective Inspector Mulliken called 112, while Detective

Markey gripped Andrei by his shoulders, lifted him up a little, and then banged his head hard against the floor. He did that three times before Detective Inspector Mulliken came around and said, 'That'll do, Nicholas. Jesus Christ. Let's get him over here.'

Detective Murrish was lying on her back, shivering and twitching. Blood was sliding from the side of her eye into her ear. She reached up to pull the knife out of her eye socket, but Katie knelt down beside her and grasped her cuff and said, 'No, Bedelia. No. I know it probably feels like hell itself and I can understand how much it's hurting but wait until a doctor can take it out for you.'

The door to the interview room burst open and two uniformed gardaí came in. They looked down at Detective Murrish and one of them said, 'Holy Mother of God, how did that happen?'

'It doesn't matter how,' said Katie. 'Just get this scummer out of here, lock him up and charge him with assault causing serious harm. Don't forget to caution him.'

The two gardaí took an arm each and heaved Andrei on to his feet. One of them handcuffed him, while the other recited his rights. As he was frogmarched past Katie towards the door, he twisted his head around and panted, 'I tell you! I never knew no Lupul! You don't say that on TV!'

'Get him out of my sight,' said Katie, without looking up. She was holding both of Detective Murrish's hands and shushing her. 'Don't worry, sweetheart. The ambulance will be here in just a minute and I'll be coming with you to the hospital.'

Detective Murrish was in deep shock now. Her right eye was closed and she was trembling from head to foot. Katie prayed that her injury wasn't more serious than being blinded in one eye, but the knife blade was very short and hopefully it hadn't penetrated her brain.

Detective Inspector Mulliken came and hunkered down beside her.

'Oh, Jesus, the poor girl. What a desperate thing to happen to her. How in the name of God did that fellow manage to fetch a knife into the station? Wasn't he *searched*, for Christ's sake?'

'He was of course,' said Detective Markey. His face was ashen and he sounded as if he had suddenly developed a bad cold. 'He was given the once-over with the security wand all right, and he was patted down, too, but his belt buckle showed up as nothing more than a belt buckle.

He coughed, and coughed, and then he said, 'The fellow was only fetched in for questioning, after all. It was not like he'd been arrested for assault or public disorder.'

Katie kept hold of Detective Murrish's hands. She prayed that some of the compassion she was feeling for her would help to keep her warm.

Twenty-Two

Katie held Detective Murrish's hand in the ambulance and stayed with her right up until she was taken into the operating theatre. Detective Murrish whimpered two or three times, and murmured, 'Mammy, is that you, Mammy?' but for most of the time she remained unconscious.

When Katie came back down to the hospital's reception area, she found Chief Superintendent O'Kane waiting for her. He was wearing a long black overcoat, and underneath he was wearing a dark grey suit and a black tie.

'I came here as soon as I heard,' he said. 'How is she?'

'She'll lose the sight of her eye, I'm sad to say. I have my fingers crossed that it's not more serious than that.'

'I've already rung her parents. They live in Mayo but they're on their way. Robert said that your man pulled a knife out of his belt buckle.'

Katie nodded. 'I've seen them a few times before, those belt-buckle knives. But I kind of assumed that he'd been thoroughly searched, do you know?'

They sat down next to a tired-looking potted palm. 'I'm afraid we'll have to be holding an official inquiry,' said Brendan. 'I'll be insisting, too, that anyone brought into the station from now on in connection with a crime will have to be rigorously screened. It won't matter if they're a suspect or if they're only brought in for questioning. That young woman's career has been ended and I

never want anything like that to happen at Anglesea Street again
– not while I'm in charge, anyway.'

He looked around, and then he looked at his watch. 'Are you
going to be staying here or do you want a lift back to the station?'

'I'll be staying here for a while. I'm hoping to see Conor.'

'Oh, yes. Your fiancé. How's he getting on?'

'Not too well, to be truthful with you, sir. He was fierce badly
beaten and he's going to need two or three operations on his
face. He's a bit depressed about it, as you can imagine.'

'He was beaten? I thought I overheard Michael Pearse saying
something about that.'

'He's a pet detective – you know, he finds lost and stolen dogs
and all that. But he's also something of an activist for animals'
rights. Well – a *fanatical* activist for animals' rights. He was
investigating a puppy farm up at Ballynahina and they caught
him poking around on their property.'

'And they beat him that bad?'

Katie nodded. 'Yes, sir. They beat him that bad.'

'Katie – I've said it before – I'm off duty right now and when
we're alone together you don't have to call me "sir". As a matter
of fact, I was over at St Michael's Cemetery laying some flowers
on my late wife's grave when Robert rang me.'

'Oh. I'm pure sorry. I didn't know.'

'There's nothing for you to be sorry about. It's something I
don't choose to talk about all that much.'

'Were you married long?'

'Six-and-a-half years, that's all. Radha, her name was. You read
about other women dying of breast cancer when they're young,
but you never imagine that your own wife is going to be taken
from you before she's thirty-five.'

'Any children?'

Brendan shook his head. 'She wanted to be a barrister. She'd
completed her Kings Inn training and passed her BL degree,
but we decided to wait until she'd finished her year of devilling
before we thought about having a child.'

He looked away. Katie could tell that he wasn't looking at the people coming in and out of the hospital doors, but at something that he could remember. Radha, perhaps, walking between an avenue of summer trees.

'She was diagnosed with the cancer on June the ninth. She had all the chemotherapy but she passed away on December the eighth. We didn't even have the chance to spend a last Christmas together.'

He looked back at her. She didn't know what to say to him. She had lost Paul and she had lost John, as well as baby Seamus, and she knew that however well-meant they were, words of condolence were never enough. Each loss was too personal, and too different.

He was silent for a few moments, and then he said, '*So*—' in a different tone of voice altogether, '—are you taking any action against whoever it was who beat up your fiancé? Are you going to charge them?'

'I am now,' said Katie, and she told him about Conor's probation, and why she had waited until now to search Foggy Fields for evidence.

'I hope you find the bastard,' said Brendan. 'I hope you find him and charge him and I hope that he gets what's coming to him.'

They talked for another ten minutes, before Conor's nurse came down to tell her that she could come up to his room and see him.

'Good luck, then,' said Brendan, as they both stood up. 'Let me know how it goes tomorrow with the McQuaides.'

There was an awkward pause, in which Katie felt that Brendan was tempted to kiss her. This was the first time she had talked to him intimately since his appointment, and she could feel the same attraction that she had first felt for him when they were training at Templemore. She could almost believe that all the years that had passed since then had never happened, except that they were both much more experienced now, and mature, and both bruised by tragedy.

'I'll see you in the morning, sir,' she said, and gave him one of her tight, professional smiles.

He said nothing, but he stayed where he was as she walked across the reception area towards the lifts, and when she stepped inside the lift and turned around, she could see that he was still standing there watching her.

Conor was sitting up in his armchair in his dark blue dressing gown, watching television. He switched it off as soon as Katie knocked and came in through the door. His face was much less swollen now, although his bruises had become rainbow-coloured, so that he looked as if he were wearing a Chinese carnival mask.

'I didn't expect you until later,' he said. 'And even then I wasn't sure that you'd have the time to come.'

She sat down on the bed next to him. 'There's been a fierce nasty incident, that's why I'm here at the hospital. Although I *was* planning to come and see you before I went home.'

She told him how Andrei the coffin-maker had been brought in for questioning and how Detective Murrish had been stabbed in the eye.

'Oh, God,' he said. 'And she's such a sweet girl.'

'Well, we're all praying for her.'

Next she told him that she was all set to go up to Foggy Fields tomorrow morning to question the McQuaide sisters about his beating, as well as searching their puppy farm.

'I decided it was worth the risk, Con. The damage that was done to you, it's changed your life, and I can't see that any judge is going to give you a hard time for breaking the conditions of your parole.'

Conor grimaced. 'To be honest with you, Katie, I truly don't care any more. There's no punishment that could be worse than this. I'd happily serve ten years in prison if I had a choice between that and being a eunuch.'

'Haven't I told you not to use that word?'

'Why not? It's what I am. And anyway, I've come to a decision.'

He paused, and she could see his Adam's apple rising and falling as if he were trying to keep his emotions under control. She reached over and laid her hand on his arm.

'It's over, Katie,' he said. 'It has to be over. I came to you as a man and I proposed to you as a man but now I'm no longer a man. I don't want you coming to see me again because I can never be the same Conor Ó Máille that I was when you fell in love with me.'

'Con... you mustn't talk like this. It's early days yet. You're still getting over a major operation and you have more operations to go through. And you heard what Mr Sandhu said... there are plenty of prescriptions that can help you.'

'Prescriptions! I want to be able to make love to you because you turn me on, not because I've swallowed some little blue pill from Ringaskiddy. No, Katie, it's not going to work. Come on – you know as well as I do that it's not going to work. And I know we never talked about having a child together, but there's no chance of that now, is there? You need a man, not me.'

'You're still a man, Con, no matter what you say. Are you trying to tell me that some soldier who got blown up and suffered the same injuries as you, or worse, that he's not a man? Besides, I can't stop seeing you if I'm going to be charging the fellow who assaulted you, and the McQuaide sisters for inciting him, and for running an illegal puppy farm. I'll have to interview you, for a witness statement.'

Conor was silent for a long time, just looking at Katie with hurt in his eyes. 'Wait till you see those breeding bitches,' he said at last. 'Filthy dirty, all shut up in boxes, their coats thick with fleas. They've never known anything all of their lives but misery.'

'I know, darling, and I'm going to try to do something about it. I want to make sure that you haven't made your sacrifice for nothing.'

There was another long silence between them, and then Conor said, 'Do you know what they've told me? When they operate on my face, they'll have to shave off my beard.'

★

Katie stayed with Conor until it was suppertime. She kissed him gently, and said, 'Listen… concentrate on getting yourself well. You'll be thinking differently when you're better, I promise you. I love you.'

Conor took a breath as if he were about to say something, but then he didn't. As she went out of the door, though, he raised the tips of his fingers to his lips and blew her a kiss. She was tempted to go back and kiss him again, but at that moment his nurse came bustling along the corridor with the supper menu, and said, 'Oh, hallo there, ma'am! How're you coming on?'

Katie took one last look at Conor and then she went to see if Detective Murrish had come out of the operating theatre yet.

She found her surgeon, Mr David McGrath, by the nurses' station. He was deep in serious conversation with one of the nursing managers and two of the staff nurses. For a consultant ophthalmology surgeon he looked surprisingly youthful, but a little old-school, too. He was concave-chested and round-shouldered, with large black-framed spectacles and hair parted in the centre. He reminded Katie of a young Woody Allen.

'Ah, Detective Superintendent Maguire,' he said, as she walked up to him. 'I was on my way to find you.'

'How's Bedelia?' asked Katie.

'Still under anaesthetic, of course. We've extricated the knife blade from her orbit, and we've sutured the upper and lower eyelids. Sadly her eye was eviscerated, but fortunately the point of the blade didn't penetrate any further than the sphenoid bone, and even more fortunately we were able to suture the scleral shell, and most of the extraocular muscles were left intact.'

'That sounds grand altogether. What does that mean?'

'It means that we can fit her with an ocular prosthetic, and that her prosthetic will have motility.'

'You're talking about a glass eye?'

'That's what they're popularly known as. Actually, most of

them are made of acrylic. But her prosthetic eye will move in harmony with her real eye, so that nobody will be able to tell that she's lost it. It'll take her a little time to get used to monocular vision, but we have a brilliant ophthalmology team here, as well as counsellors, and they'll do everything they can to help her to adapt.'

'Thanks a million, doctor,' Katie told him. She was relieved, because she could imagine that when Detective Murrish recovered she might still be able to use her on her team. She would probably be restricted to desk work, at least to begin with, but she was a clever and sophisticated detective, and Katie would be sorry if she didn't come back to Anglesea Street. That was supposing that she had the nerve to come back, after being stabbed and half-blinded.

Katie looked up at the clock. With any luck, Dr Mary Kelley might still be down in the morgue. Katie knew that she often worked very late, especially when she was carrying out post mortems on homicide victims. Dr Kelley was keenly aware that the sooner the cause of death could be established, the sooner the Garda could identify the killers and start to build a case against them.

'The second we breathe our last, it's frightening how quickly we start to decay,' she had once said to Katie. 'It's like God is in a hurry to disassemble us, so that he can use our atoms to make new people. So if we want to find out how somebody has passed away, we need to get our skates on, before God erases all the evidence.'

She had already pressed the button for the lift when she heard somebody calling her name. She turned around and saw Dr Ryan O'Keefe waving to her.

Katie had first met Dr O'Keefe when she was a young garda in Crosshaven, and a teenager had been pulled from the water after his dinghy had capsized. Dr O'Keefe had been yachting there, and had given the teenager CPR, which had saved his life. After that, Katie and Dr O'Keefe had found that their paths had crossed repeatedly, usually after some drowning or stabbing or road accident, and they had become affectionate if infrequent friends. They had seen less of each other since Katie had been promoted to Detective Superintendent, but Katie thought that he hadn't changed. Still big and bluff and blond and striding along as if he were crossing the deck of a ship in a heavy swell.

'Katie! Great to see you! What's the story? Haven't seen you in donkeys'!'

'How's it going, Ry? Oh... I'm after visiting my fiancé. He's been badly injured so he's going to be in here for a while.'

'Sorry to hear that. What happened?'

'To cut a long story short, he got into a fight with another fellow but he came second. His nose and his cheekbone are broken, among other things.'

'That's desperate. But he couldn't be anywhere better than here. You're getting married again? You didn't tell me that.'

'I haven't seen you since he proposed, that's why. We need to have that lunch at Greenes you kept threatening to treat me to.'

'I'm still saving up, Katie. I'm only a poor underpaid medical professional. But I'm glad you're here. I was going to ring you anyway. We've had a young girl fetched in who was rescued from the river at Blackrock.'

'I heard about that, yes. How is she?'

'She's been in and out of consciousness, do you know? But the reason I was going to ring you was that the last time she came to, the nurse who was with her said that she was mumbling about some fellow having knocked her into the water on purpose.'

'Oh, Jesus. Not the Lee Pusher again.'

'Well, of course there's no way of telling for sure. She's still semi-comatose. I'm fairly hopeful that she's suffered no brain damage but we'll be giving her an MRI in the morning just to make certain.'

'Okay, grand. Let me know when she's fully conscious again and I'll send somebody over to have a chat with her. Do we know who she is?'

'Saoirse Duffy her name is. Nineteen years old. One of her neighbours knew where she lived, so they were able to notify her parents. Her ma and her da have been here sitting at her bedside for most of the afternoon, but they've gone off now for a bite to eat. Do you want to see her? She's only just along here.'

'Go on, then. But let's be quick. I was hoping to catch Dr Kelley before she finished for the day.'

They walked along the corridor together, with Dr O'Keefe occasionally breaking his stride with a little skip so that Katie could keep up with him. Although he was so large, Katie felt as if she were walking beside one of her little nephews. They reached a door at the end of the corridor and Dr O'Keefe opened it up.

Saoirse was lying with her eyes closed. She had an oxygen mask over her face and she was attached to an intravenous drip and a vital signs monitor. The monitor was connected to the nursing station in case there was any change in her temperature, pulse, breathing or blood pressure while she was unattended. But Saoirse wasn't alone. Standing close to the left-hand side of her bed holding a pillow in both hands was Brianna, still wearing her fluorescent paramedic jacket. When Dr O'Keefe and Katie came in, she backed away from Saoirse's bedside, stumbling over the plastic chair behind her so that she almost sat down.

'Brianna? What are you doing in here?' Dr O'Keefe demanded. 'This young woman's still in intensive care.'

'Yes – well, yes, sure like, I know that,' Brianna flustered. 'But I was fierce worried about her. I just wanted to see how she was getting along, like.'

'So what are you doing with that pillow?'

'This pillow? Oh, *this* pillow! I thought she looked uncomfortable, and she seemed to be having trouble breathing, so I was going to prop her up a little more. You know, so that she could breathe more easy.'

'Fair play, Brianna, but that's not for you to decide. If you thought she looked uncomfortable, you should have called for a nurse.'

'Yes, well, I suppose you're right. Although I do have the training of course.'

Dr O'Keefe turned to Katie. 'Brianna's one of the paramedics who fetched Saoirse in from Blackrock,' he explained.

'I thought she'd passed over, to tell you the truth,' put in Brianna. 'But as it turned out, I saved her life. If it hadn't been for me, like, she would never have made it. I didn't realize that I'd saved her at the time, and I was mortified – *mortified* – thinking that I'd lost her, but when Dr O'Keefe here told me she was going to recover – well, you can imagine how I felt. I was like, *hallelujah*! I can only give thanks to the Lord in His infinite mercy.'

'I see,' said Katie. As she was gabbling away, Brianna was looking left and right, trying to see where she could put down the pillow, and Katie thought that she had rarely seen anybody look so rattled and so guilty. Whatever her reason for being here, it wasn't to make Saoirse more comfortable, Katie was sure of that. She had interviewed enough thieves and frauds and murderers to recognize the way in which they subtly changed the subject so that they wouldn't directly have to lie about the crime they had committed – or the crime they had in mind.

Brianna finally laid the pillow on the chair and pressed down on it hard, as if to make sure that it stayed there. 'I'd best be making tracks,' she said. 'Keep me up to date with her progress, won't you, doctor?'

'Yes,' said Dr O'Keefe. He may not have been quite as suspicious about Brianna's behaviour as Katie, but he still sounded quite guarded. When Brianna had left the room, he looked at Katie and said, 'What do you think that was all about?'

'I don't know. She may be totally well-meaning. But if I were you, I'd make sure that she doesn't have access to this young woman again – at least, not without supervision.'

'You're not suggesting –?'

Katie looked over at Saoirse. Her face beneath the clear plastic oxygen mask was as white as the pillow that she was lying on, but she was breathing steadily, and possibly dreaming, from the way in which her eyes were darting from side to side, under her eyelids.

'What? No, it's not my job to suggest anything,' said Katie, but she laid her hand against Dr O'Keefe's shoulder as if to show him that they were more than incidental friends, they were guardians, too.

By the time Katie reached the morgue, Dr Kelley had gone home. The doors were locked and the lights were all turned off, so that the dead were left in darkness. *As if they're frightened of the dark*, Katie thought. But when she returned to her car and checked her emails on her laptop, she saw that Dr Kelley had sent her a preliminary report on the cause of Matty Donoghue's death.

The deceased had been suffering from several of the common diseases associated with homelessness and drug addiction: alcoholic polyneuropathy, crack lung and hepatitis C, as well as chronic eczema, rhinitis and athlete's foot.

What killed him though was the 9.5255mm drill bit that penetrated the back of his head and shredded his medulla oblongata, his brainstem. This immediately stopped the functions of breathing, heart rate and blood pressure.

I might comment that if we had not carried out a full post mortem, the entry wound at the back of the deceased's skull could easily have gone unnoticed or been mistaken simply for another of the many sanguineous crusts (scabs) on his arms, body and neck. Death in that case would have appeared to be attributable to sudden cardiac arrest, probably brought on by his inhalation of crack cocaine.

On another matter, I have completed my examination of Ailbe O'Malley. In spite of unusually severe bruising around her neck, there was no evidence that this was caused by manual pressure, or by strangulation with any kind of ligature, but only by torsion of her neck muscles as she fell downstairs. Her death was the direct result of dislocation of her cervical vertibrae.

Well, she thought, *at least we don't have to put poor Peter O'Malley through the third degree. As if he hasn't suffered enough losing his wife and unborn boy.*

Katie drove home steadily, playing 'Báidin Fheilimí' on her car CD to calm herself down. She tried to turn her mind to her search tomorrow morning of the McQuaide sisters' puppy farm, and the killing of Matty Donoghue, and how she was going to have to press Andrei Costescu even harder to tell her where she could find Lupul. She thought briefly, too, about Brianna the paramedic, and what she had been doing in Saoirse Duffy's hospital room – or what she might have been intending to do. She was an experienced paramedic and she had saved Saoirse's life – surely she couldn't have intended her any harm. It was disturbing, though, that she had appeared so shaken when Katie and Dr O'Keefe had walked in. Katie knew guilt when she saw it.

She tried to concentrate on all of these distractions, but again and again she could hear Conor saying, *It's over, Katie. It has to be over. I came to you as a man and I proposed to you as a man but now I'm no longer a man.*

She didn't cry. She was too tired to cry. But when she got home and closed the front door behind her, with Barney and Foltchain snuffling around her and wagging their tails, she simply stood still without taking off her coat and she felt like a statue of the Madonna, in some rainy shrine somewhere, in the darkness, motionless and sad and alone.

Twenty-Three

Bowser was still awake when the two gardaí came past his encampment in the back doorway of the Crane Lane Theatre. He was barricaded behind three of the empty beer kegs that lined the pavement and all that could be seen of him under the mound of blankets and plastic sheeting was his black-bearded face, with a maroon tea-cosy hat on.

It was past midnight, but when one of the guards shone a flashlight into the doorway, they could see that his eyes were open, shining orange with jaundice like two agates.

'How's yourself, Bowser?'

'Still living and breathing,' Bowser growled back. 'No thanks to any fecking fecker excepting myself.'

'Well, we're just warning you to keep sketch for some scummers who are going around the city at the moment attacking the homeless like you. We believe they're Romanians, or Eastern Europeans of some flavour anyway.'

'I heard about it. Jimmy from the Simons told me. Don't you worry about it, boy. I can look after meself. Didn't I win the Elite heavyweight title three years in a row? I would've won the WBO heavyweight title, too, if I hadn't broken me fecking ankle two days before the fight. You're looking at a world champion here, boy. World fecking champion.'

'Okay, Bowser. But be wide anyway. And don't hesitate to call us if there's any trouble. We have special patrols around the city at the moment, so we can be with you in minutes.'

'Oh, call you, shall I? And how do you think I'm going to do that? Mowsie along to the nearest phone box, shall I? Or shall I send you a message by pigeon? There's a rake of pigeons around but I don't have pencil and paper.'

'G'luck, Bowser,' said the guard, and he and his companion carried on walking along Phoenix Street until they turned the corner into Smith Street and disappeared.

Bowser groped underneath his blankets until he found his bottle of Paddy's whiskey. He unscrewed the cap and took a swig of it, which he swilled around his few remaining teeth before he swallowed it. He held it up to the street light and saw that he only had a couple more swigs left. He had intended to keep these until the morning to warm him up, but now that the guards had unsettled him he decided to finish them off now. Maybe John, the manager of O'Donovan's off-licence, would take pity on him and lend him a borrow of another bottle until he had begged sufficient money to pay for it. John was a great boxing fan and never tired of hearing how Bowser had knocked out Declan Higgins at the National Stadium in Dublin in 2003 – or at least he said he was never tired of it.

Bowser finished off the bottle and screwed the cap back on. Now that it was empty he would keep it to piss in, in case the temperature dropped too low for him to heave off all his layers of blankets and shiver his way down to the shore twenty metres along the lane to strain the potatoes.

He began to nod off to sleep. As he did so, he gradually began to hear the roar of applause from the crowd at the National Stadium, swelling louder and louder, and his right arm jerked up as if the referee were holding it up, as he had that night when Bowser had floored Declan Higgins.

He could barely remember now how his life had fallen apart after that. The drinking, and the fights, and the arrogance. He could hardly remember Marie's face, or what her voice had sounded like, but he could remember punching her, and how she had crouched on the kitchen floor with her hands clasped over her head to protect herself, weeping.

In the past three years he had been taken into five different shelters, including St Vincent's House, Clanmornin House and Tir na nÓg, but he had been expelled from every one of them for drinking and violent behaviour. *You're looking at a world champion here, boy. World fecking champion. And don't you forget it.*

By two in the morning he had fallen into a deep, drunken sleep. At a quarter past two, three men came walking up Crane Lane, past the wall paintings on the back of the Crane Lane Theatre – a giant eye and two bewildered-looking cartoon birds. One of the men was tall and broad-shouldered, and wearing a grey leather jacket. The other two were shorter, dressed in black anoraks and black jeans, but they were just as stocky. They reached the doorway in which Bowser was sleeping behind the empty beer kegs and they stood there for a while, watching him. He might have been asleep but he was still sitting upright. Only his bearded face and his woollen hat were visible.

'It looks like he's sleeping,' said the man in the grey leather jacket. 'Let's make sure that he stays sleeping for ever.'

He went to the corner of Crane Lane and Phoenix Street and stood there keeping watch for Garda patrols, while the two shorter men rolled the beer kegs out of the way as quietly as they could. After they had done that, they dragged aside the thick plastic builders' sheeting that covered Bowser's blankets and folded down the layers of stinking blankets as far as his waist.

'*Futu-i!*' said one of the men, flapping his hand in front of his nose. '*Ce miros rău!*'

'Never mind about the smell, Danut!' snapped the man in the grey leather jacket. 'Kill him!'

One of the shorter men bent Bowser's head forward and rolled up the back of his woollen hat, while the other man unbuckled the canvas bag that was slung around his shoulders and took out a cordless drill. He gave it three quick whizzes in the air to make sure that it was working.

'Okay,' said the man in the grey leather jacket. He took another quick look down Phoenix Street, and then gave Danut the thumbs up.

Bowser was snoring. Danut knelt down in the doorway on top of his folded blankets, feeling with his fingertips through his thick wiry hair for the guiding lump at the back of his head. Once he had located it, he said to his companion, 'Marku... tilt head a bit more.'

Even when Bowser's head was pushed forward even further, Danut still found it awkward to position the drill so that the spur would spin cleanly into his neck and leave the smallest entry wound possible. He had to bend his right wrist at a forty-five-degree angle and rest his elbow against the side of the doorway.

'What's taking you so long?' hissed the man in the grey leather jacket.

Danut started drilling, and the drill bit's cutting edges tore into the skin at the back of Bowser's head. But the flutes became instantly entangled with his hair, and with a nasal whine the drill was brought to a stop.

Bowser let out a horrible roar, shaking his head violently from side to side and swinging his arms around as if they were clubs. Marku fell backwards on to the pavement, and Bowser's empty whiskey bottle rolled noisily after him. Danut tried to stand up, but Bowser slammed him against the side of the doorway, so hard that his vertebrae crackled like fireworks. He managed to lift his drill and drilled into the side of Bowser's face, so that the spur skidded across his left cheekbone, tearing a ragged red line, and then ripped into the flesh at the side of his nose. Blood sprayed across the blankets, but Bowser was impervious to pain, and he punched Danut hard on the jaw, and then he punched him again even harder on the side of the head.

The man in the grey leather jacket pulled a pistol out of his pocket and came over to the doorway shouting, 'You! Stop! Hands up! Don't move! You hear me, you *nenorocitule*? Don't move!'

Bowser punched Danut again, so that Danut dropped the drill. Bowser picked it up and slung it at the man in the grey leather jacket, hitting him on the knee. Then he struggled to his feet, kicking his blankets aside, and came lurching out of the doorway, with both of his fists lifted.

'Ye want some, ye langer? Come on, then! C'mere to me! I claim ya!'

He staggered towards the man in the grey leather jacket, his fists milling, ducking his head as if he were coming after his opponent in the boxing ring. *And – in the blue corner – Billy 'Bowser' Barrett, the Ballincollig Bruiser!*

The man in the grey leather jacket took a step back, lifted his pistol higher and shot Bowser in the right eye. The bang was deafening and it echoed all the way down Phoenix Street. Bowser's eye socket exploded and half of the back of his head flapped open, so that his tawny brains were spattered over his blankets.

He came to a dead stop, with his fists still uplifted, as if he couldn't understand what had happened to him. While he was still swaying, the man in the grey leather jacket shot him again, just below his nose this time. His upper lip was split apart, so that he looked like a grisly parody of a giant rabbit. He waved his fists feebly, like paws, and then he pitched over sideways into the road, with his blood running from his head into the gutter.

The three men said nothing. Danut was so badly beaten, it was obvious that they couldn't drag Bowser's body away with them. He probably weighed close to 120 kilos. They heard a Garda siren, too, echoing along St Patrick's Street, and they couldn't be sure that somebody hadn't heard the two shots and dialled 112.

Marku picked up the cordless drill, and the three of them hurried back down Crane Lane to South Mall, with Marku and the man in the grey leather jacket supporting Danut between them. Danut swore under his breath with every agonizing step. '*La naiba, la naiba... Jesus... la naiba!*'

Their green Hyundai was parked on the opposite side of the street. Marku and the man in the grey leather jacket helped Danut into the back seat and then they climbed in themselves. The man in the grey leather jacket sat behind the wheel for a moment before he started the engine, breathing hard. Then he thumped the wheel with his fists and said, '*Futu-i!* Why is God always punishing me?'

Marku shrugged, and sniffed. 'Maybe God is worried that you will take His place.'

Twenty-Four

Katie was dreaming that she was walking along the beach at Garrettstown, on the Old Head of Kinsale, where now and again they used to take Barney and Foltchain for a run. She was trying to catch up with Conor, but he was walking so fast that he seemed to get further and further away, and smaller and smaller, until he was almost out of sight.

Her bedside phone rang. When she sat up to answer it, she saw that it was three minutes past seven already, and she usually woke up at six.

It was Detective Inspector Mulliken. 'Hope I haven't disturbed you, ma'am. I left it as late as I could. There's been a fatal shooting in Crane Lane. A rough sleeper we know as Bowser. It happened about two thirty this morning.'

'Oh, God. He's been shot, you say?'

'Twice, in the head. Most days he used to sit begging outside the General Post Office but at night he dossed down in the back doorway of the Crane Lane Theatre. When he was found, though, his blankets were thrown about all over the shop and he was lying dead in the road. His full name's William Barrett. I'm told that he used to be quite a useful professional boxer before the drink got to him.'

'Any witnesses?'

'Not so far. But the two shots were reported at two twenty-six by a fellow who lives over Counihan's Bar on the corner. He said he used to be in the army, so he recognized a gunshot when he heard it.'

'This doesn't sound like our killer driller, does it? We're hardly likely to mistake two shots in the head for hypothermia, are we, or a heart attack?'

'There's three technicians here now, anyway, ma'am, and the street's cordoned off.'

'Don't move his body until Dr Kelley has a chance to examine him in situ. She's a bit of a stickler when it comes to shootings. She likes to work out where the bullets were most likely fired from, in case it was a suicide or there was more than one shooter.'

'Well, I seriously doubt it was suicide. There was no gun in his hand and I don't think he would have been able to shoot himself twice in the head. Most of his brains are plastered all over his bedding. I'll send you some pictures if they won't put you off your breakfast.'

'All right, Tony. I'll be in by eight thirty because I'm going up to Ballynahina to interview the McQuaide sisters. You should be able to ring Dr Kelley now. She's usually up at the crack.'

Katie rolled out of bed, showered and dressed. Today she chose her black trouser suit and a grey polo neck sweater. She wanted to look as severe as possible. She also put on her black suede concealed-wedge boots, because they made her taller.

She fed Barney and Foltchain with Irish Rover beef burgers. She would have loved to take them for their walk this morning. but she knew that Jenny would give them all the exercise they needed, and with any luck she would be able to take them out when she returned home this evening. Dog-walking was always good for thinking.

She didn't eat any breakfast herself, but she sat at her kitchen table with a mug of lemon tea, checking her emails first and then looking at the photographs that Detective Inspector Mulliken had sent her from Crane Lane.

Bowser was lying on his back with his arms by his sides, staring up to the night sky with one glistening eye. Where his other eye had been, there was nothing but a black hole. In the background Katie could see one of the technical experts in his white Tyvek suit, on his hands and knees, caught in the camera's flash like a strange animal glimpsed in the forest.

Why in the world shoot a rough sleeper like Bowser? she asked herself. Granted, he might have had a profitable day outside the post office, because it was on the corner of Oliver Plunkett Street and opposite the corner of Winthrop Street, which made it a prime location for begging. But even so, it was doubtful that he would have made sufficient money for anybody to risk killing him for it.

It was still possible that Lupul and his gang had shot him, so that they could take over his pitch. Maybe they had realized that the Garda were wise to their drilling technique and now they simply didn't care if they killed Cork's domestic beggars openly. Even if they brazenly replaced them with Romanian beggars, Katie knew from experience what a tedious and long-drawn-out process it would be to deport them. EU law protected the weak and the vulnerable, and so she couldn't simply arrange to have them driven up to the airport and put on the first Ryanair flight back to Bucharest. It was what Assistant Commissioner Frank Magorian called 'that human rights shite' – although he had never said that in front of the media.

So long as the Romanian beggars didn't admit that they were part of Lupul's begging ring, and they didn't lose their nerve and commit violent assault like Andrei Costescu, they would proba-bly be able to delay deportation long enough to make their trip to Cork more than financially worthwhile. For Lupul, anyway.

Katie tugged Barney's ears, which he loved so much that it made him growl in the back of his throat, and then she stroked Foltchain under her feathery chin. She shrugged on her coat, left the house and drove towards the city. It was a steel-sharp morn-ing, cold and cloudy but dazzlingly bright, and she felt that today was the day when she was going to make a dramatic difference in her life.

★

By nine thirty a.m., Dr Kelley had examined Bowser's body where it lay in Crane Lane, and authorized it to be taken to the morgue at CUH. Afterwards she texted Detective Inspector Mulliken to tell him that Bowser had been shot from a distance of less than three metres – both shots from the same direction and fired by the same gun, most likely a semi-automatic loaded with 9x19mm Parabellum bullets. She had not yet discovered any other significant injuries, apart from the usual scabs and bruises associated with rough sleeping, but she would carry out a more extensive examination in the morgue.

Detective Inspector Mulliken was waiting for Katie when she arrived at Anglesea Street. He had loosened his tie, his hair was sticking up at the back like a middle-aged cockatoo, and he needed a shave. Katie noticed how many of the prickles on his chin were silvery-grey.

'Still no witnesses, ma'm,' he told her. 'There's no CCTV covering the back of the Crane Lane Theatre, but I'm having the footage from Oliver Plunkett Street and South Mall checked through. You never know, that may give us a lead – for instance, if we see any of the same vehicles that were parked along Oliver Plunkett Street or Pana after that rough sleeper Matty Donoghue was murdered.'

Katie sat down at her desk and peeled the lid off her cappuccino. 'What about our nasty little coffin-maker?'

'Apparently he was shouting and banging on his cell door for a while, but then Sergeant Molloy told him to shut his bake or he'd give him the mother of all clatters, and you know the size of Sergeant Molloy. After that your man was quiet for the rest of the night and he hasn't uttered a squeak all morning. He'll be up in front of the District Court this afternoon and I expect he'll be granted legal aid.

'Little—' he added, but then he stopped himself. Katie was sure he had been going to add 'bastard' or 'scumbag' or something similar, but he rarely allowed himself to express his feelings out loud.

'Go on,' she said. 'Go away home and get yourself some sleep. I'll catch up with you later when I'm back from Ballynahina.'

She called Kyna and Detective O'Crean to make sure they were ready to accompany her to Foggy Fields. Sergeant O'Farrell told her that two uniformed gardaí were standing by, and Bill Phinner confirmed that his two forensic experts were all set up, too.

She was standing by the window finishing her coffee when Detective Inspector Mulliken came back into her office. He was wearing his bronze-brown anorak with its nylon fur collar, so he was obviously ready to go home, but he was holding up a clear plastic evidence bag.

'Sergeant Delaney just handed me this,' he said. 'One of his officers was clearing up Bowser's mucky old blankets and he found it lying in the back of the doorway. It's a necklace, and I can't see Bowser being the kind of fellow to be wearing it himself, like. And take a lamp at what's on it.'

Katie went over to her overcoat and took out her black forensic gloves. Once she had snapped them on, she tipped up the evidence bag and dropped the necklace into the palm of her hand. The catch of its tarnished silver chain had been broken but attached to the chain was a circular silver pendant, scratched and worn, about the size and thickness of a Krugerrand. The pendant was embossed with a face that Katie immediately recognized. It was identical to the face on Ana-Maria's mother's ring – the sorrowful-looking woman with a deep cleft in one side of her forehead, Saint Philothea of Argeş.

'This can't be a coincidence.'

'Exactly what I thought,' said Detective Inspector Mulliken. 'Same as that ring that was found in the mince. Whoever did for this Bowser fellow could have been wearing this necklace, don't you think? Like I said, Bowser was an ex-boxer, so maybe he put up a fight, and it could have snapped off during the struggle.'

'I'd agree with you, Tony. Because where else did it come from, if it wasn't taken off poor little Ana-Maria's missing mother? What are the chances there's been more than one woman who's been walking around Cork with some unpronounceable Romanian saint on her jewellery. And, besides, what would *any* woman have been doing round the back of the Crane Lane Theatre in the middle of the night, when a fight was going on – even a brasser? You know me. I don't like to theorize, but I'd say this is a fierce strong indication that it was Lupul who killed him, or one of Lupul's gang anyway.'

Katie took out her iPhone, took a picture of the necklace, and then handed it back to Detective Inspector Mulliken. 'Take this down to the lab, Tony, so that Bill can take DNA samples. I'll show Ana-Maria this photo of it, and see if she recognizes it. I don't want to distress her any more than she is already, but we need to know for sure.'

'Well, I hope we have the time to interview our coffin-maker again today. Jesus – he *must* know where we can find Lupul.'

'It depends. I should be back from Ballynahina around four or five, but even if he's granted legal aid this afternoon I'd be amazed if any duty solicitor will show up until tomorrow morning, if then. Still and all – it might soften your man up if we let him stew in his own juice for a few hours. And there's another thing. Did Robert tell you about that Făt-Frumor fellow? He wouldn't say where Lupul was himself. Probably scared of being shot himself if he did. But he did tip off Robert and Patrick O'Donovan to have a word with some Romanian barman up at The Parting Glass.'

'Yes, he mentioned it, like. But I don't know whether they've managed to.'

'Not yet. The barman didn't show up for work yesterday, so Robert said, and nobody up at the Glass knew where he lived, but he's expected to come in for his shift this evening. So – with any luck at all – maybe we won't need our coffin-maker to tell us how to track down Lupul. I hope not, to be honest with you. After what he did to Bedelia, I hate to think that we might have to rely on him for any help at all. In fact, the thought of even looking at him makes me craw sick.'

'How is Bedelia? Have you heard?'

'She's had emergency surgery, and she's in recovery, but that's all I know. It's going to be devastating for her, being blinded in one eye like that, and such a clever girl. There are times when I wish we were back in Old Testament days. You know – if your enemy hurts you, show no pity – hand for hand, foot for foot, and eye for eye.'

Twenty-Five

'It's a fierce pity we're on duty,' said Detective O'Donovan, as they walked down Castle Street to The Parting Glass. 'I could murder a pint of Murphy's.'

'On this occasion, I'd say you're allowed,' Detective Inspector Fitzpatrick told him. 'We don't want to be drawing attention to ourselves by only ordering a Tanora, or a cup of tea. It's not the Roundy. Besides, I've a desperate throat on me myself.'

The Parting Glass was halfway down Castle Street in the city centre, a dingy maroon-painted pub with bars over its windows. Above the lintel hung a faded sign depicting a raven perched on a bearded man's shoulder as he lifted a pint of beer, with the legend '*An Gloine Slán*'. Detective Inspector Fitzpatrick and Detective O'Donovan pushed open the door and stepped inside.

The bar was small and crowded with thirty or forty drinkers, mostly men. There were half a dozen tables on the left-hand side with multicoloured art nouveau lamps on them, which gave the faces of all the men sitting around them a mottled appearance, as if they were afflicted by some medieval skin disease. On the right-hand side there was a curved counter behind which two people were serving, a short, black-haired woman with a deep cleavage and white wobbly arms and a skinny young man with an undercut hairstyle, a scobe tache and a faded red T-shirt with the Cork GAA badge on it.

Conversation in the bar stopped when Detective Inspector Fitzpatrick and Detective O'Donovan walked in, and everybody turned around to stare at them. Detective O'Donovan was relieved that he didn't recognize anybody, and after a few moments the drinkers' backs were turned again and the craic carried on as before. Cork was a small enough city, and there was nothing more mortifying than walking into a pub undercover and finding that he had arrested half the whole clientele at one time or another for assault or robbery or falling dead drunk into the gutter.

Detective Inspector Fitzpatrick went up to the barman and said, 'Two pints of Murphy's, would you, please?'

Then, when the barman was pulling the pints, he said, 'Vasile, is it?'

The barman glanced across at him suspiciously. He didn't say yes, but then he didn't deny it either.

'I've been looking for Dragos. The last time I saw him, we were talking about doing a bit of business together, like. He gave me his number but like an eejit I deleted it.'

The barman set the two pints on the counter. 'Dragos, you say?'

'That's your man. Dragomir Iliescu. Most people call him Lupul.'

'I don't know. Well, maybe I do know. But—' The barman inclined his head towards all the drinkers, and Detective O'Donovan could see that at least two of them appeared to be watching them.

'How much for the drinks?' asked Detective Inspector Fitzpatrick.

'Ten euro.'

Detective Inspector Fitzpatrick took a €10 note out of his wallet and held it up in front of the barman's nose, but before he handed it over, he said, 'How much for letting me know where to find Lupul?'

'I don't know. It's not safe.'

'How about a hundred?'

The barman looked down at the counter and shook his head.

'How about two hundred?'

There was a long pause. One of the drinkers sitting nearby

had been telling a joke, and when he came up with the punchline – 'You stupid bollocks, Tonto! I said "posse", not "pussy"!' – all the men sitting at his table roared with laughter, and the barman took advantage of the noise by saying, very quickly, 'You finish your drink, okay? Then I meet you around the corner, in the Cornmarket Street, by the bicycles.'

Detective Inspector Fitzpatrick and Detective O'Donovan found a small sticky-topped table under the window and sat down.

'You should go for promotion,' said Detective Inspector Fitzpatrick. 'We could use some sergeants with your kind of experience.'

'No, thanks,' said Detective O'Donovan. 'I don't like being the one who's telling everybody else what to do. My da was on the council and always shouting at everybody and I swore to myself that I'd never end up like him. Besides, I like being out on the streets and talking to people. That way, I can find out what their problems are – drugs or drink or the lack of a job or whatever – and then I can advise them how to get themselves some help. I think I can do more good like that. It's like solving crimes before they happen, do you know what I mean?'

Detective Inspector Fitzpatrick stared at him for a long time, almost regretfully, as if he were remembering the time when he was only a detective garda. Then he said, 'Sup up. We've a murderer to find.'

He downed the rest of his drink, wiped his mouth with the back of his hand, and looked across at the counter. The barman must have seen that they were almost finished, because he had already disappeared.

When they turned the corner into Cornmarket Street they found the barman sitting under the trees by the bicycle stands, smoking. He was wearing a black hoodie pulled down so low that they could only see his nose and his chin. He stood up when he saw them, and looked over their shoulders, to make sure they weren't being followed.

'You have the two hundred?' he asked Detective Inspector Fitzpatrick.

'Sure like, when you tell us where we can find Lupul.'

'What you said is true – you met him before and he wants to do business with you?'

'Spot on.'

'I want to see your money first, before I say.'

'Okay,' said Detective Inspector Fitzpatrick. He took out his wallet and counted out four €50 notes. He made sure the barman couldn't see the other six €50 notes that he had brought with him in case he demanded more.

The barman took the money and tucked it into the back pocket of his jeans. He looked around again, and then he said, 'Sidney Park, third house. I don't know number.'

'You're talking about Sidney Park in Montenotte?'

'I don't know. I go there only once. Sidney Park, that's all.'

'But up the hill there, on the northside?'

'That's right. Yes, up there. Past St Luke.'

The barman sucked nervously at his cigarette. As he breathed out a stream of smoke from under his hoodie, Detective Inspector Fitzpatrick laid a hand on his shoulder as if he were congratulating him after winning a cycle race.

'Thanks a million for that information, Vasile. All I can say is, you'd better not be codding us. If you are, boy, we'll be back, and whatever you think Lupul will do to you if he finds out that you've been ratting on him, we can do it a hundred times worse.'

'I tell you the truth. That was the house where I see Lupul. Sidney Park, third house.'

Detective Inspector Fitzpatrick clapped him on the back and said. 'Off you go, then. And not a word to no one.'

'Do I look like I'm crazy?'

As he disappeared around the corner, headed back to The Parting Glass, Detective O'Donovan said, 'No, not crazy. Just feening for a dose of China white.'

Twenty-Six

It took less than half an hour for their convoy of four vehicles to drive north into the countryside to Foggy Fields puppy farm. A Garda squad car led the way, followed by Katie and Kyna and Detective Cairbre O'Crean in a dark blue unmarked Mitsubishi Outlander, and then a Technical Bureau van and another squad car bringing up the rear.

As they passed The Blackman pub at Kilbarry Cottages, three men who were out smoking on the pavement raised their glasses to them.

'Jesus – I wouldn't have thought that we were so popular around here,' said Detective O'Crean. 'The last time I arrested a fellow in Dublin Hill for disorderly conduct I had a whole bowl of tripe and drisheen thrown over me. And it was piping hot, too.'

They drove down the long hedge-lined boreen and then turned into the steeply sloping front forecourt. Around the side of the farmhouse they could see a silver Mercedes coupé, so the second squad car parked diagonally across the gate to block it.

As they were climbing out of their vehicles, the front door opened and Blánaid herself appeared, dressed all in black – black roll-neck sweater and tight black jeans and stiletto-heeled boots. Caoilfhoinn came out close behind her, in a pink cardigan that made her look like Peppa Pig.

'So what's *this* all about, then?' she asked, as Katie approached her, spreading her hands wide and looking bewildered.

'Blánaid McQuaide?' said Katie.

'That's me all right. What's the story?'

'My name's Detective Superintendent Kathleen Maguire from Anglesea Street Garda Station. I've a warrant from the District Court to search these premises in connection with a serious assault that was alleged to have taken place here three days ago.'

'What? You said what? I don't know what you're talking about. What serious assault?'

'A prospective customer came to visit you looking to buy a pug puppy for his daughter. He claims that while he was here he was attacked by a male member of your staff who caused him life-changing injuries.'

Blánaid slowly shook her head. 'You have me totally bamboozled there, Detective Superintendent. We've had no customers calling in here for weeks, and we've no members of staff at the moment apart from my sister Caoilfhoinn here. The thing of it is, Caoilfhoinn hasn't been at all well, have you, Caoilfhoinn? Usually she takes care of everything here but she's been suffering terribly from the asthma ever since before Christmas so we haven't really been properly open for business for a while, except online. But listen, why don't you come on inside? It's cutting cold out here.'

Katie said, 'I'd like to take a look around first. Are your outbuildings open?'

'Well, sure, let me fetch my coat and I'll give you the guided tour. I'm afraid the place isn't really up to standard at the moment so you'll have to forgive us for that. But I'm planning to have it all cleaned up and renovated as soon as the weather starts to improve. Caoilfhoinn, will you get yourself back by the fire, for the love of God? You'll catch your mortal death standing out here.'

Katie and Kyna and Detective O'Crean gave each other meaningful looks as they waited for Blánaid to put on her coat. The uniformed officers and the two forensic technicans circled around, stamping their feet and blowing on their hands to keep warm. A large hooded crow landed on the farmhouse gable and croaked harshly at them, as if it were warning them not to cause any trouble.

'She might be acting surprised, but I definitely have the feeling that she's been expecting us,' said Kyna. 'It's all a little too glib, don't you think, "the place isn't really up to standard at the moment"? And her sister doesn't look shook at all.'

Katie put her fingertip to her lips and said, 'Ssh! She's talking on the phone to somebody. Listen!'

The front door was only half open, so that Katie couldn't make out exactly what Blánaid was saying, but her tone of voice was urgent and firm, as if she were telling somebody what to do, and whatever it was, to do it now. After a few moments she came out, buttoning up a short chocolate-coloured duffel coat.

'How many breeding bitches do you have altogether?' Katie asked her, as they walked around the house towards the five yellow-painted sheds. The ground around the sheds was covered in shingle, so their footsteps crunched.

'We have forty-five, of different breeds. Pugs, rough collies, labradoodles, shih-tzus, Kerry blue terriers.'

'I suppose you're aware that the Irish Kennel Club recommends that no puppy farm should have more than ten.'

'I am, yes, but the Irish Kennel Club doesn't have to make a living out of breeding puppies, and if we had only ten here at Foggy Fields we wouldn't even be able to break even. It's only a recommendation, anyway. I've visited a puppy farm above in Cavan where they have more than a hundred and fifty.'

'But you *are* registered?' asked Kyna. 'I didn't see your certificate of registration up on display outside, like it's supposed to be.'

Blánaid climbed up the wooden steps of the first hut. 'Oh, the certificate! We did have it hanging up by the front door there, but the painters took it down last month and to be honest with you I clean forgot to put it back up again. Thanks for reminding me.'

She opened the door of the shed, switched on the lights and

led them inside. The sweetish stench of dog faeces and urine and rotten meat was overwhelming. Katie took out the scent-soaked handkerchief that she kept in her coat pocket for visits to the morgue and held it against her nose. Kyna flapped her hand in front of her face, and Detective O'Crean said, 'Jesus. The smell in here, like. If a farmer smelled like this, I'm telling you, all his fecking cows would fall over sideways.'

'I know,' said Blánaid. 'I'm truly sorry about it, but Caoilfhoinn hasn't been well enough to clean it out for a week or two. I've tried to hire somebody to do it for her, but you try finding any casual labour, out here in the middle of nowhere at all, in the middle of winter. I'd have more luck finding a snowman.'

'Could you not have done it yourself?' asked Katie.

'Not really. I've all my time taken up with administration, do you know, and I've the chronic asthma, too.'

In this shed the wire cages were almost all empty, unlike the cages in the shed that Conor had looked into, except for two scruffy brown cockapoo puppies who were lying listlessly together, one on top of the other for warmth, and did nothing more than roll their eyes to see who had entered their dingy prison.

Along the right-hand side of the shed there were ten wooden whelping boxes, all of them covered with plywood lids.

Katie said, 'Would you let me see inside those, please?'

Blánaid lifted one of the lids and Katie and Kyna looked inside. A young labradoodle bitch was lying asleep on her bed of torn-up newspaper, her stomach swollen with impending puppies. Her water bowl was empty and her food bowl contained only a few broken dog treats.

'And the others, please,' said Katie, and one by one Blánaid lifted the rest of the lids. Every one of the whelping boxes had a sleeping or miserable-looking breeding bitch inside it, and six out of the ten were also swarming with new puppies, blindly crawling over their mothers and each other.

'I can't believe this,' said Kyna, turning to Blánaid. 'Why would you breed these poor creatures just to be so cruel to them?'

Blánaid turned to her quite calmly.

'I admit we're not looking our best just now,' she told her, replacing the last of the lids so that a rough collie bitch and her three puppies were returned to darkness. 'But as soon as Caoilfhoinn's fully recovered we'll be cleaning and clearing out all of these whelping boxes and you simply won't recognize us. At the minute, though, there's not too much I can do to put things right. Where else can these poor animals go? Who else is going to house them and feed them?'

'Can we go and look at the next shed, please?' said Katie. She was finding it difficult to contain her anger.

'Well, of course.'

They went from shed to shed, and each shed was gloomy and dirty and packed with sad, unwashed bitches and their puppies. Katie didn't speak again until they had come down the steps from the last of the five sheds. Then she said, 'Right. Cairbre – would you go and tell the technicians that they can start examining all of these outbuildings. They know what they're looking for.'

'May I ask what it is that they'll be looking for?' said Blánaid.

'Evidence,' Katie told her, without looking at her.

'Oh. I see.' A pause. Then, 'Evidence of what, exactly?'

'Well, Ms McQuaide, we'll know that if and when we find it.'

Dressed in their white Tyvek suits, the forensic technicians waddled noisily up the steps of the first of the sheds. Blánaid stood and watched them for a few moments, with an expression on her face that Katie found hard to interpret. It was a curious mixture of resignation and contempt, but something else, too. Amusement? But what could she possibly find to amuse her?

'Come on inside and get yourselves warm,' said Blánaid. She led Katie and Kyna and Detective O'Crean back to the farmhouse and into her lime-green living room. Caoilfhoinn was sitting by the smouldering peat fire with a plate in her lap, eating a large hand pie, with a mint-coloured milkshake standing on the table beside her.

They all sat down. Kyna took out her digital voice recorder, switched it on, and laid it on the coffee table in front of her. Katie said, 'Ms McQuaide – I'm going to ask you again if you've any male employees, full-time or casual, or if you know of any male who might have been around the farm here three days ago.'

'The answer to that is no,' said Blánaid. 'How about you, Caoilfhoinn? You're always outside more than I am. Did you see any strange men lurking around at all?'

Caoilfhoinn, with her mouth full, vigorously shook her head.

'The victim of this assault says that he came here to ask if he could buy a pug puppy for his daughter. But you're saying that you had no customers whatsoever, let alone him.'

'That's right. We've had two online enquiries this week – one about a cockapoo and the other about a pit bull terrier, but the person who was asking about the cockapoo never got back to us. I think the price might have put them off. And we don't breed pit bulls, out of principle.'

'So you're absolutely denying that he came here?'

'I'm sorry. You can't ask me to invent a customer we never had.'

'Let's get on to another matter then, shall we?' said Katie. 'And that's the appalling state of this farm.'

'I totally admit that it's not in the tip-top condition that we want it to be, ideally,' said Blánaid. 'I put my hands up to that. But as I've told you, all that is very soon going to be dealt with.'

'You know that if you keep more than six female dogs more than six months old and they're capable of breeding, you have to comply with the Dog Breeding Establishments Act 2010,' put in Kyna.

'I do of course.'

'And you say that you're registered?'

'We are, yes.'

'Can we have sight of your certificate?'

'I have no idea where it is, just at the moment. It was the painters took it down and I have to admit that I haven't a baldy where they might have put it. I can dig it out, though, and fetch it down to the Garda station for you, next time I'm down in the city. Or scan it and send you a picture of it, by email.'

'In any event, we'll be notifying the ISPCA of the poor condition of this farm,' said Katie. 'We'll also be recommending to the council that they give Foggy Fields an urgent inspection. It's not up to us to decide what action they take. They might give you an improvement notice, or even a closure notice. Personally, as a dog owner myself, I'd like to see you shut down here and now.'

Blánaid half-smiled and bit the tip of her tongue, as if she wanted to say something but decided it would be wiser not to.

Katie and Kyna and Detective O'Crean stayed at Foggy Fields for another forty-five minutes, watching the forensic technicians as they shuffled around the sheds on their hands and knees, shining their infrared torches on the linoleum flooring.

As it began to grow dark they still had two more sheds to examine, so Katie decided to leave them to it and return to Anglesea Street. She still had work to do on the murders of the three rough sleepers, as well as the disappearances of Máire O'Connor and Ana-Maria's mother, and the near-drowning of Saoirse Duffy. Chief Superintendent O'Kane had also been pressing her for an update on her budget, and she had a speech to prepare for a meeting next week with the Joint Policing Committee.

She felt disappointed and frustrated that she hadn't been able to find out more this afternoon about Conor's assault, but she had seen for herself how squalid the conditions were at Foggy Fields, and she was confident that she could eventually get it closed down, which was what he had been trying to do when he was attacked.

As they drove back, Kyna said, 'Did you believe one single word that Blánaid McQuaide was coming out with?'

'Not one,' said Katie. 'I'm only hoping that those technicians can find some trace that Conor got beaten up there. Or even some trace that he was there at all.'

'And what if they can't?'

'Well – like Blánaid said herself, Ballynahina is the middle of nowhere. Everybody knows everybody, and everybody knows everybody's business. There must be somebody who can tell us the name of whatever sham-feen the McQuaides had around their farm that day. Don't tell me that Caoilfhoinn really feeds and waters and exercises and cleans all those dogs by herself. Under the Breeding Establishments Act, they're supposed to have adequate staff to keep the place in good order, and their animals healthy.'

'Yes, but I think she was lying about being registered, so she's never been afraid of a council inspection. I'll check with the council when we get back.'

Katie was silent for a while. As they reached Dublin Hill, and the lights of the city began to spread out winking in front of them, she said, 'I can't help thinking about all those poor bitches, lying there now in total darkness. They're hungry, and thirsty, and they must be exhausted with all those puppies to take care of. Do you think dogs ever feel hopeless?'

Her iPhone played '*Mo Ghille Mear*'. It was Detective Inspector Fitzpatrick. He was as terse as usual. 'We've found a possible address for Lupul, ma'am. Sidney Park, Montenotte.'

Twenty-Seven

'I'm *starved*,' said Detective Markey, stretching back in his seat.
'I could eat a nun's arse through the bars of a convent gate.'

It was dark now, and they had been sitting in their car on
Shandon Street since taking over from Detectives Walsh and
Cullen at two o'clock. They had found themselves a space in a
parking bay less than fifty metres uphill from Eamon Buckley's
butcher's shop, on the opposite side of the road, so that they had
a clear view of the shop's front door. Occasionally they had seen
Eamon Buckley himself, when he had appeared in the window to
take down a leg of pork that was hanging on a hook, or a chicken,
or a string of sausages; and twice he had come out to stand on the
pavement and smoke a cigarette.

At half-past five, they saw his acne-spotted young assistant
leave the shop, wheeling his bicycle, and cycle off up the street.
Ten minutes later, all the lights in the shop went out, and Eamon
Buckley appeared, wearing a short brown overcoat with the collar
turned up and a chequered tweed cap.

Detective Markey started the engine. 'All he's going to do is
drive back home,' he said. 'I'm beginning to think that this is a
total waste of time.'

'Just remember what Denis MacCostagáin used to say,' Detective Scanlan reminded him. '"If nothing's going on, that shows
that we're winning."'

'Yes, and look what happened to *him*. He should have told
himself that when he looked in the mirror every morning.'

They waited until Eamon Buckley had walked downhill as far as Dominick Street, a narrow lane that led sharply off to the left, where he had parked his car that morning. Once he had disappeared around the corner, Detective Markey pulled out of the bay and followed him.

Eamon Buckley's red Mondeo was parked next to a high concrete wall. Painted on the wall was a mural that Detective Scanlan had always found disturbing. It depicted an open stable door with an elderly woman smiling out into the street, as well as a living-room window with two children's faces peeping out from behind a pair of red curtains. A black dog was sitting by the door, painted as if it were chained up to the parking sign.

'Gives me the heebie-jeebies, that mural,' said Detective Scanlan, as they drove slowly past it. 'It's like they're living in another dimension, like, do you know what I mean, and looking out at us, and thinking, "One day you'll all be lying dead in the cemetery but we'll still be here on this wall, still smiling our heads off."'

'I reckon you need a holiday,' said Detective Markey.

They followed Eamon Buckley's tail lights all the way up Dominick Street, which was oppressively narrow, with terraces of run-down houses on both sides, and a pub with dusty windows that had long closed its doors. At the end of the street, they expected Eamon Buckley to turn left, and drive himself back home towards Farranree. Instead of that, though, he turned right, down towards the river, and turned right again at Pope's Quay.

'So where the feck's he going now?' asked Detective Markey. 'I'll tell you, if I don't get my mouth round a cheeseburger pretty soon, I'm going to be dying of the malnutration.'

Eamon Buckley drove along Pope's Quay as far as Griffith Bridge. Then he crossed over the river and turned down Grenville Place and Dyke Parade, heading west. It was when he joined the Western Road and kept going that Detectives Markey and Scanlan realized they might be in for a much longer night than they had expected.

As they reached Victoria Cross and Eamon Buckley took the

main N22 towards Carrigrohane, Detective Scanlan put a call in to Katie.

'How's it cutting, Padragain?' said Katie. She had only just returned to her office from Ballynahina. 'How's it coming along with Eamon Buckley?'

'He's closed the shop but he's not going home. He's driving west right now on the Straight Road, so we have no idea at all where he's headed.'

'Give me a second to see where you are,' said Katie. 'Yes, I have you now. Are you okay to stick with him?'

'We can, yes. I'll keep you posted so.'

'The way he's driving, do you think he has any notion that you're following him?'

'It doesn't look like it. He's not speeding or jumping lights or doing any tricksy overtaking.'

'Okay, then. We'll be tracking you constantly. Be careful.'

Eamon Buckley passed Carrigrohane and kept on westward towards Ballincollig. Detective Markey said, 'We should have stuck a tracker on his car, shouldn't we? Then we could have gone for a McDonald's and followed him later, like.'

'I've some jam mallows if that'll help,' said Detective Scanlan.

Detective Buckley looked across at her. '*Jam mallows?*' he said, as if she had uttered the ultimate blasphemy.

They followed Eamon Buckley through Ovens, Crookstown, Bealnablath and Dunmanway, kilometre after kilometre, mostly in complete darkness. Only the lights of farmhouses and pubs and occasional petrol stations reassured them that they and Eamon Buckley were not the only living souls in County Cork.

A few minutes before seven they arrived in the town of Skibbereen, on the River Ilen, eighty-four kilometres to the west of Cork city.

'Please God may this be as far as he's going,' said Detective Markey.

But Eamon Buckley drove through the centre of the town and crossed the stone bridge over the river, turning west again on the road that led to Schull. He didn't drive much further, though. When he reached the small overgrown cemetery at Abbeystrowy, with its crosses and headstones for the victims of the Irish famine, he slowed down. He came almost to a stop, and then he took an acute turn up a steep and narrow boreen, with high hedges and trees on both sides.

Detective Buckley switched off his headlights. This boreen was so remote and rural that if Eamon Buckley saw another car behind him – even as far back as a hundred and fifty metres – he would be sure to realize that it was tailing him.

The detectives followed Eamon Buckley's tail lights for nearly a kilometre. The boreen twisted and turned, and it was so overgrown that sometimes they lost sight of him. Brambles and twigs scratched against the sides of their car like the claws of witches trying to slow them down. Twice Eamon Buckley's lights were obscured by the hedges, and it was so dark that Detective Markey drove into the embankment with a jolt that jarred them both, and he had to reverse before driving forward again.

Only three or four minutes later, Eamon Buckley's lights disappeared altogether and they were left in complete blackness.

Detective Markey stopped the car and pulled up the handbrake. 'This is insane, like. We can't go any further without putting our lights on, and if we put our lights on he's going to see us and reckon that we've been following after him. And maybe he's switched his own lights off anyway because he's seen us.'

Detective Scanlan called in to Anglesea Street again. She was told that Katie was tied up in a meeting with Chief Superintendent O'Kane and Superintendent Pearse, but Detective Inspector Fitzpatrick came out of the meeting and went back to his office to talk to her.

'We've lost him, sir. We're up this pitch-dark boreen and he's totally vanished.'

'I can see where you are on my screen, Padragain,' said

Detective Inspector Fitzpatrick. 'You've no idea where's he gone to at all?'

'None, sir.'

'Tell him what it's like here,' Detective Markey put in. 'Black as the inside of an undertaker's cacks.'

'It's possible that Buckley's caught on that you're tailing him,' said Detective Inspector Fitzpatrick. 'If he hasn't, though, we don't want him to realize that you are. Turn around now and head back to Cork.'

'Really?' said Detective Scanlan.

'Yes, really. Tomorrow morning I'll call Superintendent O'Shea at Clon and ask him to send a couple of his officers up that boreen so that they can check out where Buckley might have gone. It doesn't seem likely that he's coming back to Cork himself tonight, wouldn't you think? Maybe he has a country cottage up there, or maybe he has some friends living there that he's going to be staying with. We can check the satellite image and see how many properties there are. But tonight, no – there's no future in you blundering around in the dark.'

'Okay, sir. I have you.'

They crossed back over the rippling River Ilen. On the south side of the bridge stood the West Cork Hotel, a light grey four-storey building with a decorative first-floor balcony. It was lit up white at the front and green on the side facing the river.

'My cousin Dara came to a wedding here once,' said Detective Markey, slowing down. 'She thought the restaurant was the berries. How about we stop here and have a bite of something to eat before the sides of my stomach stick together? I won't be able to make it all the way back to the city without some sustenance.'

Detective Scanlan tutted. 'Next time I go on a stake-out with you I'm going to fetch along a picnic hamper full of sangers. But all right, let's stop. I've a bit of a mouth on me too, to tell you the truth, and I could use the facilities.'

They parked at the back of the hotel, facing the river, and went inside. Detective Markey found them a table in the corner in the Kennedy Restaurant next to a large potted palm while Detective Scanlan went to the ladies. When she came back she rested her elbows on the table, dropped her head forward and ran both hands through her short-cropped hair.

'I'm beat out,' she said. 'I hope this hasn't been a total wild-goose chase, and Buckley hasn't just come here to visit his aged granny or something like that.'

'Well, we'll find out in the morning with any luck, when the local boys go up that boreen to take a look. How do you fancy the Castletownbere crab and salmon cakes? Or the Gubbeen bangers and mash?'

'I'll stick with a pizza, thanks, Nick. Something that's easy to eat. And a lemonade. If we weren't on duty and we didn't have to drive all the way back I'd go for a treble gin, I can tell you.'

Once the waitress had taken their order, Detective Markey said, 'Do you honestly believe that Buckley minced that little girl's mother up?'

'Are you trying to put me off my pizza?'

'No, of course not. But there doesn't seem to be any other explanation of how her ring was found in the mince. But if he *did* mince her up, who killed her, and where did he get her body from, and what did he do with the rest of it? There wasn't a trace of it in his shop, like.'

'We don't even know for sure if she's dead,' said Detective Scanlan. 'But the main suspect has to be this Lupul, doesn't it? Especially since that matching necklace was found in Crane Lane, where that ex-boxer was shot.'

'Maybe the ex-boxer killed the little girl's mother, and that's where he got the necklace from,' Detective Markey suggested. 'Or maybe he helped Lupul to do it, and Lupul shot him because he was going to rat him out.'

'That still doesn't answer how the ring got into the mince. It also doesn't answer why Lupul wanted to get hold of the little girl so badly – nor those two Eastern European fellows who ended up incinerated down at Cobh. Were they working for Lupul or did they want her for some other reason? And it doesn't answer why the little girl's mother disappeared. And there's that other young woman who's still missing, too, Máire O'Connor. It's more than likely that her partner was murdered by the same person or persons who murdered that rough sleeper by the Savoy Centre. Same MO, like, the power drill. Was that Lupul? And if it *was* Lupul, what's he done with her?'

'You know who you're beginning to sound like?' said Detective Markey. 'You're beginning to sound like DS Maguire. She always says that she doesn't like to speculate, but then she goes off into the longest specumulation that you ever heard in your life.'

'Yes,' said Detective Scanlan. 'But that's how she gets things done. She thinks of all the possibilities, even the maddest possibilities.'

'Now you're beginning to sound like fecking Sherlock Holmes.'

'Anyway… let's talk about something else, shall we? Here's your bangers and mash.'

Twenty-Eight

Once they had finished their dinner, they ordered two double espressos to keep themselves alert on the ninety-minute drive back to Cork. Then they left the hotel and walked back around to the car park, their breath smoking in the cold night air.

'I'm fecking stuffed,' said Detective Markey.

'Well, I'm amazed you ate all that chocolate cake.'

'The place was almost empty so who else was going to eat it? It would have been a crime if they'd had to throw it away. I'd have had to arrest them under the Wilful Disposal of Chocolate Cake Act, 1981.'

Halfway across the car park, Detective Scanlan suddenly stopped and caught Detective Markey's sleeve. 'For the love of God, Nick,' she said. 'Look at our car.'

In the greenish light from the hotel's riverside illuminations they could see that the back window of their grey Ford Mondeo had been shattered, so that it looked as if it had been thickly encrusted with ice; and as they came closer, they saw that the side windows had been shattered too. All four door panels were deeply dented and all four tyres were flat.

'Shite,' said Detective Markey, circling around the car to assess all the damage. 'I'll bet this was Buckley. He must have seen us following him. This is going to be a fecking write-off.'

'I'll call for the local guards,' said Detective Scanlan, taking out her phone. 'Skibbereen's open twenty-four/seven, aren't they?'

She hadn't even started to prod out the number before she

heard footsteps pattering towards them. She looked up and saw a man dressed in black running up behind Detective Markey with a club hammer raised above his head. She was just about to shout out a warning to him when she was hit herself on the side of the head, just behind her right ear, a stunning blow that knocked her over sideways on to the ground. Her forehead banged so hard against the asphalt that she could feel her brain being jolted inside her skull. Her phone skidded away and disappeared under one of the parked cars.

For a few seconds, she couldn't think what had happened to her. She tried to sit up but then she was hit twice more, once on her shoulder and once on the back of her head. She blacked out.

She opened her eyes and she could see somebody's face in front of her, although her vision was so blurred that she couldn't make out who it was. When she reached out with her left hand she touched sheets and a blanket, and she realized that she was lying in bed. She tried to lift up her head, but she felt as if her brain had swollen to twice its normal size, and it was throbbing painfully with every beat of her heart. Her right shoulder was agony, too.

'Where am I?' she croaked.

Whoever it was sitting beside her bed reached out and took hold of her hand.

'You're in CUH, Padragain. They assessed you at SouthDoc in Skibbereen and then they fetched you here. How are you feeling?'

The face came gradually into focus and she realized it was Detective Superintendent Maguire.

'Oh Jesus,' said Detective Scanlan. 'I must have been hit on the head. Same as that fellow was going to do to Nick.'

'That's right. You'll be going for an MRI scan later, just to make sure there's no brain damage.'

'How is Nick? Did that fellow hit him too?'

'I'm afraid so. His skull's been fractured, although the doctor reckons he'll be making a full recovery. Again, they have to check there's no trauma to his brain. He suffered worse in a way, though – all his fingers were broken. That's going to take a long time to heal.'

'Mother of God. Poor Nick. We haven't caught those fellows, have we?'

Katie shook her head. 'Not a trace of them. How many were there, did you see?'

'I saw only the one who was running up behind Nick. Then, *bang!* and that's all I remember. So there must have been at least two of them. Our car was all smashed up – windows broken, doors dented, and all the tyres let down. We were taking a lamp at it when we were attacked. They must have been waiting for us.'

'The sergeant from Skibbereen told us that you'd stopped at the West Cork Hotel for something to eat, and that you left the restaurant about ten past nine. You weren't found till half-past ten, when one of the kitchen staff went out of the back of the hotel to dump some rubbish.'

'Oh Jesus, I hope Nick's going to be all right. We only stopped there because he was hungry.'

'You're only human, Padragain. You'd been sitting in that car since lunchtime.'

'Did DI Fitzpatrick tell you? We followed Eamon Buckley up some fierce narrow boreen but we lost him and it was too dark to go on. When I say dark – honest, there could have been an elephant sitting in the road right in front of us and we wouldn't have seen it.'

'Yes, DI Fitzpatrick brought me up to date,' said Katie. 'And we were thinking that it might well have been Buckley who arranged to have you two beaten. But listen, I'm not going to bother you any further. It's nearly two o'clock and I need to be getting some sleep myself. We can go through it all tomorrow when you're feeling up to it. We've been given an address where Lupul might be staying – a house in Sidney Park – so we'll be paying the place a visit at the crack of dawn.'

'Serious? That'll be some result if you can haul him in. Nick and me were talking about it, and we both reckon that it's him behind the murders of all those rough sleepers, and those two women disappearing – that little Romanian girl's mum and Máire O'Connor, too. Well, that's what I think and Nick says he agrees with me, bless him.'

'I tend to agree with you, too, Padragain. But even if we manage to lift him, we can't charge him on a hypothesis. We're going to need evidence. Sleep well, though. I'll try to visit you again tomorrow afternoon, pressure of work willing. If not, I'll ring you.'

Before she left the hospital, Katie walked along the corridor to Conor's room. When she gently pushed open the door, she found that it was in darkness, except for a faint light shining from underneath the bathroom door. Conor was asleep, with the upper part of his face thickly bandaged. He had undergone surgery on his cheekbone and his eye socket today, and in three or four more days he would be having his nose restructured.

She stood beside his bed watching him breathe. His beard had been shaved off, which made him look younger, but in a way it made him look more vulnerable, too. Behind the beard of a virile hero like Brian Boru there was somebody altogether more sensitive – somebody who had risked his life to save mistreated puppies, and who could be easily hurt by the way the world was.

Katie leaned over his bed and kissed him, and then she left. She loved him, but she was too tired to think any more about their relationship. She would have to stay at Anglesea Street tonight, because there wouldn't be time to drive back home to Cobh, and she would be lucky to get more than three hours' sleep.

As she was waiting for the lift to come up to the second floor, she saw a door open halfway along the corridor – the door to the room in which Saoirse Duffy was being treated. She made a mental note to ask Dr O'Keefe tomorrow how she was, and when she might be ready to be interviewed.

The lift arrived with a *ping!* and its doors opened. But just as Katie was about to step into it, she saw a nurse coming out of

Saoirse Duffy's room. The nurse started to walk quickly towards the lifts, but suddenly she stopped and turned around and walked just as quickly back in the opposite direction.

The lift doors closed, and Katie had to press the button to make them open again. She hesitated, because it had appeared as if the nurse had turned around as soon as she had come close enough to recognize her. But then she thought: *No, you're overtired, and you always get hyper-suspicious about everything when you're overtired.* The poor nurse was working the graveyard shift and she had probably forgotten for a moment which patient she was supposed to be tending to next.

Whenever she had to stay overnight at the station, Katie was restless. She was used to the mournful hooting of ships in the harbour outside her home but not to the constant stopping and starting of traffic on Anglesea Street. Tonight, though, she fell deeply asleep as soon as she climbed into bed. Her sleep was usually dreamless, too, but she began to imagine that she had arrived at the Foggy Fields puppy farm together with Conor, and that they were trying to find the McQuaide sisters. Conor still had his chestnut-coloured beard, although he was wearing a hospital gown and slippers, and a strange white hat like a turban.

Suddenly they heard a piercing chorus of agonized screams from the five yellow-painted sheds. In a slurring voice like a slowed-down record, Conor said, 'It's the puppies! They're hurting them!' and he started to run around the side of the farmhouse, with his hospital gown flapping.

Katie tried to run after him, but her stiletto-heeled boots had become wedged in a crack in the paving stones. She tried to unlace them but the knots were too complicated and she could only succeed in tying them even tighter. She was still struggling with them when she heard the McQuaide sisters shrieking with hysterical laughter, even louder than the puppies' screaming. Conor reappeared. Both of his legs had been severed above his knees so that he was rocking his way slowly towards her on two bloody stumps, like a man wading through treacle. His nose had been hacked off, too, so that there was nothing more than a dark triangular cavity in the middle of his face. He stopped, reaching out his arms to her, but she couldn't move.

'Katie! Don't leave me, Katie!' he begged her. His voice was bubbly with blood. 'Please don't leave me!'

'DS Maguire?' said a voice, out of nowhere.

Startled, Katie opened her eyes. She stared at the wall for a moment and then she turned around. A young garda was standing beside her bed with a cup of tea in her hand.

'It's five-thirty, ma'am. DI Fitzpatrick said to tell you that he's ready when you are.'

Twenty-Nine

When they drove up to Montenotte it was still dark, and a soft rain had started to fall.

Sidney Park was a steep narrow road with a row of semi-detached houses stacked up the hill on the left-hand side, but nothing but railings on the other. The third house had ginger-coloured pebble-dashing and peeling white paint and its front garden was scruffy and untended, with a broken plastic chair in it. A van was parked in the road outside it but no cars were standing in its driveway. All the curtains in the upstairs windows were drawn tight.

Their convoy of two unmarked cars and four squad cars stopped opposite the front gate, blocking the road to all other traffic.

'Looks like they're still in their scratchers,' said Detective Inspector Fitzpatrick, when he and Katie and Detective O'Donovan had climbed out of their car.

The fine drizzle was trailing across the road so Katie put up the pointed hood of her black raincoat. Conor always said it made her look like one of the *Sidhe,* the fairy-folk, because in Ireland the fairies were never tiny, but the same size as humans. Under her raincoat she was wearing a ballistic vest, so this morning she looked even bulkier than a human.

She looked around for Sergeant O'Farrell. 'Ryan,' she called to him. 'Do we have the back covered yet?'

Sergeant O'Farrell came up with his walkie in his hand, followed by seven gardaí, all of them dressed in black. Three of them came from the Regional Support Unit and were armed with Heckler & Koch sub-machine guns.

'The back's covered all right. Just say the word, ma'am, and in we go.'

'Right, then,' said Katie. 'Let's do it.'

Sergeant O'Farrell and the rest of the gardaí hurried to the front door, their jackets rustling as they jogged across the garden. One of them knocked loudly, and pressed the doorbell too. Then they waited, tensely positioned on either side of the porch.

There was no answer from inside the house, so the garda knocked again. After thirty seconds there was still no response, so Katie said, 'That's it. Break it down.'

A garda went up to the front door with an Enforcer battering-ram. He slammed it into the lock stile three times, and with a loud splintering crack the door swung wide open. The gardaí from the RSU bustled into the house first, screaming, 'Armed gardaí! Armed gardaí!'

Katie and Detective Inspector Fitzpatrick and Detective O'Donovan and the rest of the gardaí waited in the rain, which was soft as dandelion puffs. After two or three minutes, one of the armed officers appeared in the doorway and called out, 'There's nobody here, ma'am! The whole place is empty!'

'You're sure of that? You've checked the attic?'

'We have of course. Not a soul.'

'Fair play,' said Katie, resignedly. What surprised her was that she wasn't really surprised. As they had driven up from Anglesea Street she had felt almost certain that they wouldn't find Lupul here. Even if they had, it would have been the beginning of a legalistic nightmare. They could have brought Lupul into Anglesea Street for questioning, but they wouldn't have been able to arrest him without reasonable evidence. She might have accused him of assault for knocking her over in Winthrop Street, but little else. Being Romanian wasn't a crime in itself, and the human rights lawyers would have been swarming around like bluebottles over a dead cat as soon as she charged him.

'*Shite,*' said Detective Inspector Fitzpatrick, under his breath.

'Let's take a sconce inside, shall we?' said Katie, and they stepped in through the broken door and into the hallway.

The house was gloomy and cold and smelled of damp, like so many of the older houses in Montenotte. Outside it was gradually beginning to grow lighter, but Katie borrowed a flashlight from one of the gardaí. They didn't switch on the house lights as a matter of normal procedure, in case the electrical system was booby-trapped or they compromised any incriminating DNA on the light switches. Not only that, flashlights illuminated rooms at different angles, so that they were able to see footprints and objects that might be invisible under overhead lights, such as hairs or crumbs of food or dropped contact lenses.

The living room looked as if it had recently been occupied. Facing a large flat-screen television was a grimy cream leatherette sofa with squashed purple cushions, which had clearly been sat on recently. A coffee table with a large Guinness ashtray on it was heaped with cigarette butts. The room smelled strongly of stale tobacco and another odd smell, which Katie couldn't immediately identify, but which reminded her of toilet freshener blocks.

She tugged on her black forensic gloves and picked up a folded newspaper, which had been dropped on the floor next to the sofa. It was yesterday's *Echo*.

'Well – whoever was here, it looks like they hopped off at very short notice,' she said. 'Who does the house belong to?'

'It's a rental, managed by Cudahy's,' said Detective O'Donovan. 'They told me the owner lives in Málaga these days, a retired fellow by the name of Bell. He used to be something to do with the building trade.'

'Did they tell you who was renting it now?'

'Nobody, according to them. The last tenant left six weeks ago after renting it since April last year. A couple with two young children.'

'So whoever's been staying here, they've been squatting?'

'I'd say so, yes. But at least they won't be able to deny it was them if we find them. They've left a rake of evidence.'

'*If* we find them. They seem to be one step ahead of us, don't they?'

They went through to the kitchen, which was cramped and dark with a chipped red-tiled floor. Katie looked out through the rain-beaded window and could see two gardaí standing outside by a dilapidated garden shed.

The kitchen sink was stacked with dirty plates and all the work surfaces were crowded with empty baked-bean tins and crumpled Brennans bread wrappers and empty Smirnoff bottles. On top of the gas cooker, a casserole dish was encrusted with burned mince and potato.

'Counting the bean tins, I'd say they'd been here about a week,' said Detective Inspector Fitzpatrick. 'And judging by those vodka bottles, I'd say they weren't Irish.'

They climbed the steep stairs to look at the bedrooms. In the main bedroom there was a double bed with no sheets but two duvets heaped on top of it, both of them grubby and covered in brown stains, as if somebody had suffered a nosebleed. The orange-and-green wallpaper was rippled with damp and at a skewed angle above the bed hung a reproduction of Leonardo's *Last Supper*. There was a sour, underlying reek of body odour and again that toilet freshener smell.

They went into the bathroom. A sodden maroon towel lay on the floor, and the bath itself had several rings of grey soap scum around it. The toilet was filthy, too, and the last person to urinate in it hadn't flushed it.

'Holy Saint Peter,' said Detective Inspector Fitzgerald, wrinkling up his nose. 'When I was a lad that was a wooden spoon offence, no excuses accepted.'

On the window sill there were two disposable razors, both used, and a black spray can of men's deodorant with the name Erou on it. Katie picked up the can and sniffed it and now she understood where the toilet-freshener smell had come from.

At the back of the house were two other bedrooms with single beds, although only one of them appeared to have been slept in;

its blue blanket was rumpled and there was a head-shaped dent in the pillow.

Katie said, 'Lupul may well have been staying here, but this isn't the house that Ana-Maria was talking about, where all of his beggars were being put up. She said there were twelve of them at least. I suppose they could have slept on the floor but it doesn't look like it. Where's all their clothes and all their possessions? Even beggars have rucksacks.'

She opened the cheap pine wardrobe but there was nothing inside except for a few wire coat-hangers. When she bent over and looked under the bed, though, she saw a single pale-pink trainer with white stripes on it. What attracted her attention was how small it was. She took out her iPhone and took three flash photographs of it, and then she reached underneath the bed and fished it out.

'Adidas, size thirty-eight,' she said, turning it over. 'This would fit a woman or an older girl. And did you know that most Adidas shoes are made in Romania?'

'Are you thinking what I think you're thinking?' asked Detective Inspector Fitzpatrick.

'Nothing. Except that I'm going to take this back to Bill Phinner and have him test it for DNA. And then I'm going to show it to Ana-Maria.'

'Then you *are* thinking what I think you're thinking.'

They went back downstairs. Sergeant O'Farrell said, 'Well? The birds have flown, haven't they? But why would they fly if they weren't the birds that we were looking for?'

'More to the point, who warned them that we were coming?' said Katie. 'What do you think, Robert? Maybe your man at The Parting Glass lost his nerve and decided that two hundred euros wasn't worth getting himself killed for.'

Detective Inspector Fitzpatrick shook his head. 'This is all still supposition, ma'am. If only we could find one solid piece of evidence that linked Lupul to Ana-Maria's mother disappearing, and her ring turning up in that mince, and her necklace turning up where that Bowser fellow was shot. Not to mention those rough sleepers having the brains drilled out of them.'

'So what are you saying?'

'I'm only saying that maybe none of these things are connected, do you know what I mean? At least, not in the way that we've been thinking they are.'

Katie looked around the hallway, and then back up the stairs. 'You're right, of course, Robert. But there's no future in trying to put the pieces of a jigsaw together if you don't have at least some idea in your mind of what it's going to look like when it's finished. Maybe we haven't found Lupul himself here this morning, but I have the strongest feeling that he's left that link here that you're talking about, even if we're not sure what it is.'

She turned to Sergeant O'Farrell. 'You can cordon off the house now, Ryan, and I'll ask Bill Phinner to send a technical team up and go through it top to bottom. We'll be interviewing all the neighbours, too, when they've woken up – that's if we haven't woken them all up already.'

They left the house and returned to their car. It was still raining, but it was spitting now, rather than soft, and judging by the low grey clouds that were rolling in from the west it would soon be pelting.

'I knew it would be a cat day today,' said Detective O'Donovan, as he slammed the car door. 'The forecast didn't say so, but I could feel it in my bones.'

Katie didn't answer because she was staring at her iPhone. Before she could fasten her seat belt, she had been sent a text by Superintendent Pearse.

'Mother of God,' she said, softly.

'What's the story?'

'That young woman who was pushed into the river at Blackrock. They've found her dead in her bed.'

'That's sad. That *is* sad. Do they know what the cause was?'

'Not yet. They were worried that she was suffering brain damage because she was under the water for so long.'

Detective O'Donovan drove further up Sidney Park so he could turn down the zigzag lanes that would take them back to Wellington Road, and then down Summerhill to the city. They passed the Gabriel House guesthouse, where Conor and she had first made love, and quite unexpectedly she found that she had a *tocht* in her throat, and she pressed her hand over her mouth to keep her emotions under control. She was far too busy to cry.

As soon as she had sat down in her office, Moirin came in with a cappuccino for her, and a sticky raspberry bun from Heaven's Cakes in the English Market.

'Holy Mary, Moirin, I'm trying to keep my weight down.'

'Well, so am I, ma'am, but I bought two of them and if I hadn't have given one of them to you, I would have been forced to eat it myself.'

'Have you thought of buying only the one?'

'Not really. That would make it look as if I had no friends.'

Chief Superintendent Brendan O'Kane tapped at her door. He was looking spruce and freshly showered in his crisp white shirt and Katie could smell that he had sprayed on a little too much Eau Sauvage. *At least it wasn't Erou*, she thought.

'So like, I understand that Lupul wasn't at home.'

'No, sir. That's if it was him who was staying there. But as Sergeant O'Farrell rightly pointed out, why did they leave so quick if they weren't the fellows we were looking for?'

'True. So what's the plan now?'

'The house wasn't nearly big enough to accommodate all of the beggars that Lupul brought over from Romania, so he must be renting or squatting another property somewhere else. What we need to do now is find that.'

'Any clues?'

'None so far. But we're keeping a close watch on all the beggars and rough sleepers around the city, as far as we can anyway, and it will take only one of them to lead us back there.'

'Okay, grand. Have you heard from Dr Kelley about our ex-boxer yet?'

'Not yet. But his head was in a desperate mess so it will probably take her some time to piece it all back together again. You know how scrupulous she is. She'll even be scraping the bits of brain off his blankets and weighing them, just to make sure there isn't too little or too much.'

'And I heard that girl passed away. The one who was rescued from the river.'

'Yes. It could have been that she was starved of oxygen for so long that she didn't have a chance of surviving. All the same, I'll be after asking Dr Kelley to carry out a post mortem on her, too, just to be certain about the cause of death.'

'It could only have been natural causes, though, couldn't it? If you can call being pushed into the river a natural cause.'

'I'm not sure. I have a funny feeling about it, that's all.'

Brendan raised his eyebrows. 'I remember you at Templemore, you and your funny feelings.'

Katie didn't answer that. Instead, she said, 'I went to see Padragain Scanlan yesterday evening. She was knocked about something desperate but it looks like she's going to be okay. I'm still waiting to hear about Nicholas Markey. His skull was fractured and all the bones in his hands were shattered so I don't know how long it's going to take him to recover. If he doesn't regain the full use of his hands – well, we'll just have to wait and see and say a prayer to Saint Stanislaus Kostka.'

Brendan frowned, so Katie added, 'Saint Stanislaus Kostka – the patron saint of broken bones.'

'I see. Okay. You must have been paying attention in catechism. Do you think it was that butcher who did it?'

'Eamon Buckley? It's highly likely, but so far we don't have any proof. No witnesses, as usual.'

'Tell me the old, old story. Thanks for the updates, anyway. Oh – and how's your fiancé? Colin, is it?'

'Conor. He's had an operation on his cheekbone and his eye

socket. He has to have another operation to straighten his nose, but he looks like he's bearing up all right.'

Brendan nodded thoughtfully. Then, after a long pause, he said, 'I've been thinking about that pug dog, Walter.'

Katie had started to look through the messages on her desk, but now she looked up and said, 'Walter? What about him?'

'Can his owners raise enough money to have him fixed?'

'I don't know for sure. I shouldn't think so. They were talking about crowdfunding but I'll be amazed if they can raise as much as three thousand.'

'So they'll probably have to have him put down?'

'It'd be heartbreaking if they have to, wouldn't it? He's such a little dote. But, yes, I expect so. It'd be cruel to let him go on living in that condition. Every single breath is a struggle for him, like.'

'Find out how much his owners have managed to raise so far,' said Brendan. 'However much or how little it is, I'll pay for the rest of it.'

Katie stared at him. She didn't know what to say. Brendan looked back at her, and gave a shrug, as if to say, *Whatever you thought of me, I'm not like that at all. Maybe I cheated on you once, when I was years younger, but that's not the kind of man I am now.*

'Serious?' said Katie, at last.

'Serious. I took a shine to the little fellow. And maybe we can persuade the media to run a story on him. We could use him as a warning to anybody else who's thinking of buying a puppy. You know – tell them to check that it comes from a proper registered puppy breeder, and that it's old enough to be taken away from its mother, and that it's been given all its vaccinations and been wormed and whatever.'

'You're sure about this? You might end up paying the whole three thousand, or near enough.'

'They gave me a very generous bonus when I left the Operational Support Unit. What else am I going to spend it on? Since I lost Radha, I don't have anybody to take on holiday, or buy surprises for. I might as well use the grade to do something worthwhile.'

'That's – well, that's pure generous of you, sir.'

'Brendan.'

'I'll give Walter's owner a ring later and tell them. I'm sure she'll be over the moon.'

Brendan came over and stood beside her, with his hand resting lightly on her desk next to her paperwork. She looked up at him, and then looked down at her desk, and then looked up at him again. They both knew what was going on between them.

Katie's phone warbled. She reached across and picked it up and said, 'DS Maguire.'

'It's Bill Phinner, ma'am. We've tested all the samples we brought back from the puppy farm. There's no matches at all to Conor Ó'Máille's DNA. No fingerprints, no blood, and no fibres either to match his coat.'

'I see, Bill. That's a disappointment, but thanks a million anyway. What time can you send a team up to Sidney Park?'

'They'll be leaving in about twenty minutes. I was just waiting for Deirdre Hagerty to come in. She's especially good with hair. And that trainer you left with us – I should have an analysis for you by late this afternoon.'

'Thanks, Bill.'

Katie put down the phone. Brendan was still standing close beside her.

'Bad news?' he asked her.

'More like no news. There's no trace at all at Foggy Fields that Conor was assaulted there. I knew it was a bit of a long shot, but the McQuaide sisters are totally denying that he was ever there, and without any forensics we have no way of proving that they're lying. I'm thinking of sending Cairbre O'Crean up to Ballynahina to snoop around and see if he can find out who might have beaten him up, but that's another long shot and I don't have a bottomless budget.'

She looked up at him again. 'You don't have any more of that generous bonus to spare, do you, sir?'

Thirty

Vasile beckoned the next car to come forward to be hosed down and washed. He felt tired and hungover. Because it was raining, only three cars had come in to Handwash so far this morning, and only one driver had given him a tip. Apart from that, his throat was sore and he was sure he had caught a cold. There had been one old man in The Parting Glass last night who had sneezed repeatedly in his direction and hadn't once bothered to put his hand over his mouth.

He stood in front of the car and signalled it to stop. It was a black Audi saloon with dark tinted windows. Mihai came forward with the pressure hose but before he could start spraying, the Audi's two rear doors opened up and two short, stocky men in black anoraks climbed out. Vasile recognized them – Danut and Marku. They had come into The Parting Glass two or three times for a drink and once Vasile had caught sight of Danut in McDonald's on St Patrick's Street with Lupul.

Danut came straight towards him, while Marku raised his hand to Mihai, signalling him not to start spraying. Vasile knew immediately that he was in trouble. He dropped the wet chamois leather that he was holding and started to run towards the Texaco petrol station, but he had managed only five paces before Marku came bustling around the front of the car and viciously snatched his right arm. Danut caught up with him from behind and gripped his shoulder.

Vasile tried to twist himself free but the two men were far too strong for him.

'Get the fuck – *off* me, will you?' he panted.

'Shut your trap and get in car!' Danut told him.

'Mihai!' shouted Vasile, but Mihai was already backing away. 'Mihai, call the cops!'

Danut and Marku forced Vasile into the back of the car, with one of them wedged on either side of him. He kicked at the back of the seat in front of him but Danut smacked him hard around the side of the head.

'Stay still, *nenorocitule,* or else I hit you again!'

The two men slammed the Audi's doors and the car drove off at speed, its tyres slithering on the wet concrete forecourt. The driver slewed across the road to the right, towards the city centre, causing an oncoming truck to blast its horn at them.

'What's this all about?' asked Vasile. 'I've done nothing.'

A man was sitting in the front passenger seat with the collar of his jacket turned up. He turned around and stared at Vasile with such grey-eyed frigidity that Vasile shivered and couldn't stop himself from letting out a little squirt of pee into his jeans. It was Lupul, unshaven, his grey eyebrows tangled, his grey hair sticking up as if he had just survived an electric shock.

'Oh, you've done nothing, have you, you skinny piece of shit?' he said, in Romanian. 'How about giving my address to the law? Doesn't that count?'

'I don't know what you're talking about. I don't even *know* your address.'

'So it was a coincidence, was it, that you were seen talking to two cops in street last night, and that my house was raided this morning?'

'I never spoke to any cops. Somebody's just stirring up trouble.'

Lupul took out his mobile phone and held it up so that Vasile could see it. Although the picture on the screen was quite dark, and the car made the phone jiggle, Vasile could see that it was a video of him on Cornmarket Street, talking to Detective Inspector

Fitzpatrick and Detective O'Donovan. It also showed Detective Inspector Fitzpatrick taking out his wallet and it was clear that he was counting out money.

'There – proof,' said Lupul. 'And don't try to pretend that those two men are just friends of yours, paying you back some money that they owe you. We know them. They're *poliţai şpăgar*. Dirty cops.'

'I wasn't talking to them about you. How could I tell them where you live when I don't know where you live? They paid me because I gave them some information about two young guys at the pub selling drugs.'

'Don't bother to make up stories. I know you give tip-offs to that *porc sălbatic* Făt-Frumor. And I know you know where I live – even though I don't know how you found out. Maybe some druggie told you. Maybe some pizza delivery boy. It doesn't matter. What does matter is that I had to leave my house last night with about five minutes' notice and I'm more than upset about it. I'm *înfuriat*.'

'It wasn't me. I didn't tell them anything about you. Why would I?'

'For the money, you miserable motherfucker. Why else?'

Lupul kept on staring at Vasile for several long seconds, unblinking, his mouth turned down with contempt. Then he turned his back and didn't speak again.

They continued to drive through the rain with the windscreen wipers squeaking monotonously, crossing over St Patrick's Bridge and then heading up the long steep hill to St Luke's Cross. Vasile desperately tried to work out some excuse for having taken money from Detective Inspector Fitzpatrick that Lupul might be persuaded to believe, but he was too frightened now to be able to think coherently. He was even too frightened to beg Lupul not to hurt him, in case Lupul didn't intend to, but beat him up just to show him that whatever he begged for, he was going to be given the opposite.

When they reached St Luke's Cross they turned into Alexandra

Road, a terrace of tall damp-looking houses, most of them painted grey or brown or beige, and half-hidden behind high cement-rendered walls and overgrown trees. They stopped about halfway up the road and all climbed out. Vasile was unsettled to see that their driver, despite having black close-cropped hair and broad shoulders, was a woman. She had piggy little Slavic eyes, a blob of a nose, and a large mole on the left side of her chin. When he looked at her, she looked back at him with total dispassion, as if he had no more humanity than a cardboard cutout with a picture of a young man printed on it.

Lupul unlocked the maroon-painted front gate of number thirteen and went inside. The woman driver went after him and, with a polite gesture, Danut indicated that Vasile should follow.

'I have a choice?' asked Vasile, and Marku let out a sharp bark of laughter, like a mongrel.

The house was four storeys high, and probably dated from the 1890s, when there was a British military garrison in Montenotte. As they walked up the black-and-white mosaic path towards the porch, the front door was opened, and a young man appeared, in a pea-green sweater and jeans. Vasile noticed that he didn't look particularly pleased to see Lupul, and when Lupul stepped inside the hallway, he pressed himself back against the wall to let him pass, breathing in and turning his face away, as if he were afraid of him.

Vasile looked at the young man as he entered the house, but the young man still kept his face turned away.

Inside, the house was dark and smelled of damp and burned sausages. Lupul went first to the high-ceilinged drawing room on the right of the hallway, and looked inside. Vasile was going to follow him but Danut held his sleeve so that he had to stay where he was, at the foot of the staircase. From there, only one end of the drawing room was visible, but Vasile could see two scruffy-looking bearded men standing with their arms folded and a young woman in a baggy blue tracksuit top sitting beside them, and he could hear the voices of several more. He guessed there must be at least ten people in the room altogether.

'I am back now. Give me half-hour and we will get you all down to city and out on streets,' Lupul told them.

He came back to Vasile. 'Right,' he said. 'Let's go upstairs, shall we, and you can tell me exactly what you said to those cops.'

'I swear that I'm telling you the truth, Lupul. I didn't say one word about you.'

'*What* did you call me?'

'I'm sorry. I thought that was your name.'

'My name is Dragos. I should smack you across the face for that. But you know what? I'm not going to. And do you know why I'm not going to? It's not because I'm Mr Nice Guy. It's because I don't want to leave my handprint on you, or any of my DNA.'

Vasile stared back at Lupul, and gradually the implication of what he had just said began to dawn on him. He let out a childlike whimper and dropped to the floor, scrambling on his hands and knees towards the front door, which was still open. Before he could reach it, though, the young man in the pea-green sweater slammed it shut. Vasile stood up and tried to snatch the doorknob, but both Danut and Marku took hold of him and threw him violently back against the stairs.

'Now, are you going to climb upstairs by yourself or will we have to drag you up by your balls?' asked Lupul.

Vasile leaned sideways, wincing. He felt a sharp pain in the right side of his back and he was sure that at least two of his ribs had been cracked. Lupul stood waiting for him as he turned himself over and slowly began to crawl upstairs, taking in squeaky snatches of agonized breath with every step.

Eventually he reached the landing, which had a threadbare carpet that smelled of damp and rotting string. He grasped the banisters to pull himself on to his feet, and once he was standing up, Danut and Marku shoved him roughly across to an open bedroom door. The knife-like pain in his side was unbearable, and he was terrified of what they were going to do to him. As he stumbled into the bedroom, he started to cry.

A half-broken blind was drawn down over the bedroom window, and there was a single bed with a filthy striped mattress on it, but no blankets. On the wall above the bed hung a curled-up calendar showing March 2002, and a faded picture of Jesus surrounded by children.

Lupul came in. 'What are you blubbing for?' he demanded. 'Are you a baby? You think that I wouldn't have been blubbing if those cops had hauled me in this morning? And it was all because of you, you little *poponar*! I could have been kicked out of Ireland and everything I've been working on so hard would have gone straight down the toilet!'

Vasile smeared the tears away from his cheeks with his fingers. 'I swear I didn't give those cops your address. I swear it in name of my mother.'

'*Futu-ţi Cristoşii mă-tii!*' Lupul retorted, and waved to Danut and Marku to force Vasile on to the bed, face down. Vasile screamed in pain, but they ignored his screaming and Danut climbed on top of him, sitting astride his back.

In the corner of the bedroom stood a tall chest of drawers with flaking veneer, and on top of it rested a black cordless drill. Lupul picked it up and said, 'Marku.'

Marku took the drill and handed it to Danut. Then he gripped Vasile firmly by the ears, squashing his face into the mattress so that he could barely breathe. Danut felt for the sweet spot at the back of Vasile's skull, and then positioned the drill bit just below his thumb.

'Go ahead,' said Lupul. 'The sooner we're rid of him, the better. Little *poponar*.'

With a nasal whine, the drill bit bored into Vasile's head. He jerked and jumped, but Marku was holding his head so tightly that he couldn't move it, and Danut's weight on his back made it impossible for him to roll off the mattress. He gave one final shudder as Danut wiggled the drill bit around and around, making sure that his brainstem was ripped into shreds, but after that he lay still.

Danut eased out the drill bit and climbed off him, and Marku released his grip on his ears.

'So – what are we going to do with him now?' asked Danut, looking around for something to wipe the drill bit.

'Same as others, of course,' said Lupul.

'You're sure he'll take him?'

'Why shouldn't he? We pay him enough, don't we?'

'Yes. But the cops were searching his shop, weren't they? Maybe he'll want to give it a rest for a while.'

'They didn't find anything because there was nothing to find. That is the whole beauty of it. I'll ring him anyway and he can come around here later and pick him up.'

'Okay.'

Lupul looked down at Vasile's body and crossed himself. 'Rest in peace, little *poponar*,' he said, and then he grinned. 'That'll teach you to rat on Dragos Iliescu.'

Danut and Marku were waiting for him out on the landing. He left the bedroom, closing and locking the door behind him and taking out the key.

'Right,' he said, 'let's take our poor unfortunate devils down to the city to start making us some money.'

Thirty-One

Katie was eating a Marks & Spencer cheese salad at her desk when Dr Kelley emailed her the results of her post mortem on William 'Bowser' Barrett. As she read it, her chewing slowed down, and then stopped, and then she put down her plastic fork.

The cause of death was two gunshot wounds to the head. One of the bullets remained lodged inside the decedent's skull, a 9mm Parabellum round. The entry wounds to the front of the head are identical, which indicates that both rounds were fired from the same weapon. The trauma to the back of the head was catastrophic, as would be expected. Apart from the damage resulting from the gunshot, however, I found a minor twisted contusion in the skin, which appears to have been made by a drill bit, in almost precisely the same spot as the penetrative wounds that I found in the necks of Gearoid Ó Beargha and Matthew Donoghue. It would appear that a start was made on drilling into William Barrett's neck but for some reason this was not completed, leaving him with only a superficial wound.

Dr Kelley's report was accompanied by several close-up photographs, as well as an MRI scan of Bowser's skull, showing the bullet still buried inside his head. Katie hadn't yet heard from Bill Phinner if his technicians had found the other bullet. Maybe it was stuck in the door at the back of the Crane Theatre, or maybe it had ricocheted off the wall and rolled down a nearby shore. But they would need only one bullet to identify the gun that had shot him – so long as they found the gun.

Detective Inspector Mulliken knocked at her door.

'Sorry to interrupt your lunch, ma'am, but our nasty little coffin-maker's lawyer has arrived. J.P. Foley, of all people.'

'Oh God. Not J.P. Foley. Ireland's answer to Atticus Finch. He likes to think he is, anyway.'

'Kyna's down there now. She's dealt with all the paperwork. How do you want us to approach this?'

'What I'd really like to be doing is shooting him in the knee-caps. But it's Lupul we're after, more than a miserable streal like him. So we need to win his confidence, like, do you know what I mean? Make him feel that if he co-operates with us, things may not turn out so bad for him.'

'So long as Foley doesn't advise him to say nothing at all.'

'We'll see. Even the great J.P. Foley knows that you can't stab a garda in the eye in front of witnesses and expect a judge to let you off. But there's one thing more, Tony. Don't mention that we know that Gearoid Beargha and Matty Donoghue were both murdered. Whoever did it, Lupul or not, I still want them to believe they've got away with it.'

They went downstairs to the interview room. J.P. Foley was sitting next to Andrei Costescu, and he stood up when Katie and Detective Inspector Mulliken came in. He was tall, at least six feet three, with a long face but small wide-apart eyes that gave him the appearance of a haddock. His grey hair was combed into waves, and as usual he was wearing a dark blue three-piece suit with a freemason's lapel pin.

'Detective Superintendent Mag-*waah*,' he said, in his rich Dublin baritone, holding out his hand. 'When was the last time you and me crossed swords? The O'Flynn trial, wasn't it? I still like to think of that encounter as a draw.'

'Really?' said Katie. 'Well... Tomás O'Flynn was only sent

down for manslaughter instead of for murder, so I suppose you can give yourself some credit for that.'

She ignored his outstretched hand and sat down at the table next to Kyna. She thought that Kyna was looking exceptionally smart and pretty today, with her blonde hair braided in a circle on top of her head and a hint of blusher on her cheeks. She smelled fresh, too, of some perfume with top notes of bergamot and neroli.

Detective Inspector Mulliken sat beside her and opened up his copy of the charge sheet.

'My client here, Andrei Costescu, is accused of assault causing serious harm,' said J.P. Foley.

'He stabbed Detective Garda Bedelia Murrish in the eye, blinding her,' said Katie. 'I'd say that comes under the heading of assault causing serious harm, wouldn't you?'

'He doesn't deny for a moment that he was holding a belt-buckle knife, which inflicted an injury on Detective Garda Murrish. But he asserts that he wounded her purely by accident when she suddenly and unexpectedly seized him, which made him lose his balance. He had absolutely no intention of hurting her and is extremely remorseful about what happened.'

'Mr Foley, I witnessed the assault myself, and so did DI Mulliken here,' Katie told him. 'Your client jumped up and attempted to escape from the room in the middle of an interview. Detective Murrish tried to restrain him, and it was then that he took out his belt-buckle knife and deliberately stabbed her. There was absolutely no question of it being any kind of an accident.'

'But *why* did he jump up and try to leave the room?' said J.P. Foley, dramatically lifting one finger as if he had just received a message from the Angel Gabriel. 'The reason was, you had threatened him that you would tell a certain Dragomir Iliescu that he had given you information about him, that's why! *Ratted* on him, as they say. And since this Dragomir Iliescu is infamous for his violent retribution against anybody who betrays him, my client was naturally petrified, and in mortal fear for his life.'

Katie shook her head. 'We never threatened to tell Dragomir Iliescu that your client had informed on him, Mr Foley. Quite apart from anything else, we had absolutely no idea where to find him. Not at the time, anyway.'

'All the same, that was the impression that you gave my client. His grasp of English is extremely limited, remember.'

'Even if he was scared witless, he still had no reason to pull out a knife.'

'He did it only to defend himself. He was in a state of panic. And, let's be legalistic about it, he wasn't under arrest and so he was entitled to leave whenever he wanted to. What happened to Detective Murrish was highly regrettable but entirely unintentional and my client will be entering a plea of not guilty.'

Katie looked at J.P. Foley for a few moments, her eyes half-closed as if she were thinking hard. Then she said, 'Don't make any mistake about it, Mr Foley. I will personally be testifying that your client stabbed Detective Murrish with the obvious intention of causing her serious harm. So will the other officers who were present at that interview – Detective Inspector Mulliken here and Detective Markey. I will also categorically deny that your client was threatened.'

'Besides,' put in Kyna, 'how is it that your client even knows this Dragomir Iliescu, and why is he so afraid of him?'

'What?' said J.P. Foley. He shuffled through his papers as if Kyna were simply being tiresome, and then he added, 'No comment.'

Kyna, however, persisted. 'As well as several other offences, Dragomir Iliescu is suspected of running a begging ring here in Cork. Your client was picked up in St Patrick's Street with a sign saying, *No Work Please Generos* and a bowl for passers-by to drop money into. He's Romanian. He entered the country at the same time as Dragomir Iliescu and several other Romanians. Can he tell us with a straight face that he isn't one of Iliescu's gang of beggars?'

'No comment,' said J.P. Foley. 'Besides – simply happening to *know* a criminal isn't a criminal offence in itself, otherwise all of *us* would be behind bars, wouldn't we, ha-ha?'

'That's a spurious point, Mr Foley,' said Katie. 'But I can tell you now in confidence that we were informed by another separate source where we could find Iliescu. He's been squatting in a house in Sidney Park, in Montenotte. We carried out a raid on the premises early this morning and I can guarantee that your client no longer has anything to fear.'

Andrei had been staring down at the table, but as soon as Katie said 'Sidney Park' he jerked his head up to look at her, and when she had finished speaking he leaned over towards J.P. Foley, cupping his hand against his face so that the Garda officers couldn't hear or lip-read what he was saying. J.P. Foley nodded, and nodded again.

'We're still looking for more information, though,' Katie continued. 'We found where Iliescu himself was staying, but we believe there's another address in the city where the members of his begging ring are being accommodated when they're not out on the streets. Not surprisingly, Iliescu isn't going to tell us where this is, so I'm prepared to make your client an offer.'

'DS Maguire – are you telling me that you now have Dragomir Iliescu in custody?' asked J.P. Foley.

'Did you not hear what I said? I said that I can make your client an offer. If he gives us the address of this house, and if we find the rest of the begging ring there, I'll consider reducing the charge against him to one of assault causing harm. As you well know, that can be dealt with as a summary conviction in the District Court, with a fine of only fifteen hundred euros or a maximum of twelve months in prison if the judge should find him guilty.'

'So you've arrested Dragomir Iliescu?'

'Mr Foley – I'm not going to repeat the offer again. Iliescu has not yet been charged, but I can guarantee your client that he has nothing more to fear from him.'

'Very well. But we'll need a few minutes to confer.'

'Of course,' said Katie. She stood up, and Detective Inspector

Mulliken and Kyna stood up, too, and together they left the interview room.

Out in the corridor, Detective Inspector Mulliken said, 'I con-
fess I'm a little confubbled here, ma'am. We haven't lifted Lupul,
have we?'

'No, of course not. All I said was, he hasn't yet been charged,
and of course he hasn't, because we haven't yet found him, let
alone lifted him.'

'But you've just promised your man that he needn't be frightened of him any more,' said Kyna.

'He won't have any cause to be frightened of him, will he?
Not if he's safely locked up in Mountjoy for assault causing serious harm.'

'Hold on. You said that if he gave us the address of Lupul's
other house, you'd reduce the charge to assault causing harm –
but not *serious* harm.'

'No, I didn't. I simply said that I'd consider it. And after I've
considered it, what final decision do you think I'll come to, after
that creature half-blinded poor Bedelia? It was a pure miracle he
didn't kill her.'

'Surely Foley caught on to the way you phrased that, wouldn't
you think?' said Detective Inspector Mulliken. 'He wins most of
his cases by splitting hairs.'

'I expect he did. But he doesn't have a whole lot of room to
manoeuvre, does he? He knows he'll never be able to get the
coffin-maker acquitted, so he might as well go for the possibility
of a lesser charge, even if it isn't a certainty.'

'Well, it's going to be interesting to see what they decide.'

'Tony – we need to nail Lupul like *yesterday*, and if we can
find out where his beggars are dossing down when they're not
out in the city sleeping rough, then we have a much better chance
of finding him. They're all over the shop at the moment, his beggars, but they're fierce cautious about anybody following them.
Not only that, we have to be careful about hauling them in for
questioning. We don't want the Simons or the Good Shepherds

coming down on us like a ton of donkey manure because we've been harassing the homeless. That kind of publicity is the last thing we need. And I'll bet half of them don't speak English and the other half don't even have a notion what country they're in.'

The door to the interview room opened and J.P. Foley appeared. 'My client has come to a decision,' he said.

Katie and Kyna and Detective Inspector Mulliken filed back into the interview room and sat down. Andrei was looking nervous, with one leg furiously jiggling under the table.

'If the charge against my client is reduced to negligence then he is prepared to co-operate and give you the information that you're asking him for.'

'*Negligence?*' Katie retorted. 'Are you serious?'

'He admits that he shouldn't have attempted to leave the interview room so precipitately, but he was seriously alarmed by the threats that you made to him. He withdrew the knife blade from his belt buckle purely by accident as your detective tackled him. During the struggle between them, the blade unfortunately penetrated her eye. He was negligent, yes, admittedly, but no more than that.'

Katie looked at Kyna, and then at Detective Inspector Mulliken, and then she snapped shut the folder in front of her and said, 'Good afternoon to you, Mr Foley. This interview is terminated as of now.'

J.P. Foley leaned back in his chair and drummed his fingertips lightly on top of the table. 'You won't get your information out of my client any other way, DS Maguire.'

'In that case, he can keep his information. We'll be charging him with assault causing serious harm and, as you're well aware, that's an indictable offence, so he'll be looking at a maximum of life imprisonment.'

'Assault, then,' said J.P. Foley.

Without answering or showing him any response at all, Katie stood up again, picking up her folder and tucking it under her arm. Kyna and Detective Inspector Mulliken stood up too.

'Very well,' said J.P. Foley. 'Assault causing harm.'

Katie remained standing. Without looking at Andrei, she said to J.P. Foley, 'What's the address?'

'Give me your assurance first, Detective Superintendent. Assault causing harm only. Not *serious* harm.'

'No address, Mr Foley, no assurance.'

There was a long moment of extreme tension. J.P. Foley sucked in his lips until they almost disappeared, and his eyes bulged so that they looked even more haddocky than usual. Andrei stopped jiggling his leg.

At last Katie said, 'Very well, have it your way,' and turned to go.

'DS Mag-*waah*!' said J.P. Foley loudly. Then, more quietly, 'Please stall it for a second, if you'd be so good.' He passed Andrei a sheet of legal paper and a pencil. Andrei wrote down the address and passed the paper back to him. J.P. Foley folded it and handed it to Katie.

'Thanks a million,' said Katie. 'Before I consider reducing the charge against your client, I'll have to confirm of course that this is the correct address, and I'll have to discuss it with Chief Superintendent O'Kane, and possibly with Assistant Commissioner Magorian as well. After all, we're talking about a serious and life-changing assault on a police officer.'

'Is this what you call a deal?' J.P. Foley protested. 'You may have given my client assurances about his safety, but he could well have put his life in jeopardy by giving you that address. And what have you given him in return? Nothing! Nothing at all! I could file a complaint to the Ombudsman about you for this piece of confidence trickery.'

'That's your privilege, Mr Foley. But don't be surprised if the Ombudsman turns a blind eye to it – just like Detective Murrish will have to do to everything, for the rest of her life.'

Thirty-Two

Katie returned to her office, and Kyna and Detective Inspector Mulliken came too. The address that Andrei Costescu had scrawled across the piece of paper was in Alexandra Road, up by St Luke's Cross. Katie switched on her PC and found the Google map and the satellite image of it.

'Those are big old houses up there, aren't they? Let's find out who that one belongs to and if it's rented. If it is, whose name is on the rental agreement. I'll bet you a cat to a codfish that it isn't Dragomir Iliescu.'

'Well, that little girl, Ana-Maria, reckoned he'd brought over twenty-one beggars, didn't she – so even if half of them are out sleeping rough on the streets, we'll still have to be mounting a fair-sized operation, wouldn't you say?' said Detective Inspector Mulliken. 'We'll need to call in at least a couple of immigration officers, won't we, and maybe Tusla too if there's any more kids involved.'

'I'm after sending Daley and Cailin up to Alexandra Road now to keep a watch on the house, in case Lupul makes an appearance,' Katie told him. 'Mind you, I don't know if they'll be able to recognize him from the sketch I did. I made him look like a cross between Dáithí Ó Sé and Conor McGregor and Bono without his glasses, so let's pray that he's wearing the same grey leather jacket. I don't think the EvoFIT is a whole lot more like him, either.'

'So when were you thinking of going in?' asked Kyna.

'I reckon about four o'clock tomorrow morning would be the best time. Maybe there's only a few beggars staying there overnight, but we should catch them napping, as it were. We could do it earlier, but most of the clubs like Havana Browns and the Voodoo Rooms will have closed by four o'clock, so any beggars who aren't sleeping in the street won't still be hanging around the city centre trying to panhandle money off drunks. Can I leave it to you to start setting things up, Tony, along with Robert Fitzpatrick? I have to go and see how Bedelia and Nicholas and Padragain are getting along. I swear to God, I feel like I've more detectives in the Wilton Hilton than I have here at Anglesea Street.'

'Right then,' said Detective Inspector Mulliken. 'I'll go downstairs with Robert and start sorting things out with Michael Pearse. I'd say we need about a dozen uniforms at least, including at least four RSU – plus the immigration. And we'll need at least one coach on standby. What time do you think you'll be back?'

Katie crossed herself. 'With the Lord's help, they'll all be making a speedy recovery, so not too long. I'm running out of saints to pray to.'

As she was buttoning up her thick navy-blue coat to go to the hospital, her phone rang. It was Superintendent Declan O'Shea from Clonakilty.

'No luck so far,' he told her. 'A couple of the lads from Skibbereen went up that boreen this morning but they found nothing at all up there except for three private houses and a piggery right at the very end of it. None of the residents in the private houses had ever heard of your man, and neither had the fellow who runs the piggery. Cathal Kilmartin his name is. He's well known in Skibbereen, especially in The Corner Bar. Bit of a toper but harmless enough.'

'A piggery? Did they take a look around it?'

'They did, yes, just to see if there was any evidence at all of your man having been there.'

'Did they find anything?'

'Well, pigs of course.'

'Of course pigs. But anything unusual at all? Anything you wouldn't expect to find in a piggery?'

'Nothing that caught their eye. They asked this Cathal Kilmartin about what's-his-name but he denied any knowledge of him.'

'Eamon Buckley.'

'That's your man. Eamon Buckley.'

'And what about what happened at the West Cork Hotel? Have they found no witnesses to Detectives Markey and Scanlan being attacked, or who saw their car being vandalized?'

'No. They interviewed all the hotel staff who were on duty at the time. Plus the assistant manager. But no. Nobody saw nothing. Nobody heard nothing, neither. Their car's been picked up on a low-loader, by the way, and it should be in transit by now to the Technical Bureau workshop – that's if it's not there already.'

'Okay, Declan, thanks. But please ask your lads to keep their eyes peeled for Eamon Buckley, if he ever happens to come driving through Skibbereen again, and to follow him, if he does. You have the details of his car and his index number, don't you?'

'I have, yes. And I will. Don't worry.'

Katie put down her phone and repeated, '"*Pigs of course*",' just as Moirin came in to collect her empty coffee cup.

'"Pigs" did you say, ma'am?'

'Yes, Moirin. But it would take too long to explain.'

She found Detective Scanlan sitting up in her room at CUH, wearing a white roll-neck sweater and jeans and watching television. Both of her eyes were bruised charcoal-black like a raccoon and her right cheek was puffed up, but she gave Katie a smile when she came in and said, 'How are you, ma'am?'

'Not so bad, Padragain, all things considered. But more to the point – how's yourself?'

'Oh, Jesus. I still have the mother and father of all headaches. They've given me the ibuprofen for it but I think I'm going to ask them for something stronger. I've had a CAT scan, though, and there's no brain damage, thank God. They've told me I should be able to go home later today, once the consultant's signed me off.'

'How much time do you think you'll be wanting off duty? Not that I'm pushing you, like. You can take as long as you need to get yourself straight.'

'Maybe three or four days. Not more. I'm itching to get back and track down those thugs who hit us. Have you been to see Nicholas yet? One of the nurses promised to tell me how he was coming along but I haven't seen her since.'

'I've just looked in on him,' said Katie. 'He's asleep, or under sedation anyway. His nurse told me that his skull had been fractured but it's only a simple crack, not depressed, and they expect it to mend by itself in five to ten weeks. I'll be talking to his specialist after, Mr Murphy, when he's free. It seems like a bus went into a cement lorry below by Innishannon and there's several passengers with head injuries, so he's up in the operating theatre, coping with them.'

'And what about Eamon Buckley?' asked Detective Scanlan. 'Have we found out where he was going, when he led us up that boreen?'

'Superintendent O'Shea rang me from Clon before I came here. He said there was nothing up there except for some private houses and a pig farm. The pig farmer had never heard of Eamon Buckley – or claimed he hadn't, anyway. Think about it: it's possible that Buckley led you up there on purpose, just to shake you off. He obviously knew that you were tailing him, and what car you were in.'

'I can't believe we fell into that. *And* we stopped in Skibbereen for something to eat, too, like a right pair of eejits. If I'd thought for one second that Buckley was going to turn around and follow us, I'd have told Nicholas to put his foot down and shoot us back to Cork as fast as humanly possible. If not faster.'

Katie reached out and squeezed her hand. 'Don't go blaming yourself, Padragain. It could have happened to anybody. I'm having Buckley kept under surveillance twenty-four/seven now. He was back to open his shop first thing this morning so it's unlikely that he spent the night down in Skibbereen. As soon as he parked his car we attached a GPS tracker to it so we won't be needing to tail him like that again.'

'Well, maybe not,' said Detective Scanlan. 'But as soon as I'm well enough, I'm going after him, don't think that I won't. And when I haul him in, I'm not only going to throw the book at him, I'm going to hit him over the head with it, as hard as I can.'

Katie shook her head in amusement. She spent another ten minutes talking to Detective Scanlan, mostly about her family and when her boyfriend was going to come and visit her, and then she went along the corridor to see Detective Murrish.

Detective Murrish was awake, propped up on two pillows, with a thick white bandage over her left eye socket, but she was still sedated and her speech was very slow and blurry, with long pauses in between her sentences. All the same, she managed to ask Katie how the hunt for Lupul was progressing, and when Andrei Costescu was likely to be appearing in front of the circuit court.

'The consultant said that they can give me a nocular – an *ocular* prosthesis. A glass eye, in other words. He said that it'll move around, the same as my good eye, and nobody will know the difference. So I'll be able to come back to work, won't I?'

'You're sure? You've had a pure traumatic experience, Bedelia. You can take as long as you like to get over it, and make up your mind if you really want to come back.'

'What? You're codding me, aren't you? Of course I want to come back! Being a detective, that's all I've ever wanted to do, ever since I was a little girl. I used to hide my brother's Lucky Leprechaun lollies and tell him that a thief had taken them, and then I'd take out my magnifying glass and look all around the house and make a big show of finding them.'

Katie couldn't help smiling. 'We'll still have a place for you at Anglesea Street, don't you worry. And you won't only be on lolly-hiding duties.'

'I mean, there's no reason I can't carry on being a detective, is there?' said Detective Murrish. 'Look at that Columbo. He had a glass eye, didn't he, and his glass eye didn't even move.'

Her last call was to Conor. His whole head was wrapped up in white crepe bandages now, except for his eyes and his mouth and two holes for his nostrils.

'I know I look like the Invisible Man,' he told her, in a dry-throated voice. 'My nose is all blocked up and I can hardly see you, but believe it or not I'm feeling a whole better. I think it could be the morphine. It's wonderful. I can understand now why people get addicted.'

'Has Mr Sandhu been in to see you?'

'Yes, and he's very happy. He says I'm healing up down there much quicker than he expected.'

Katie was silent for a few moments, and then she said, 'Like I told you, we went up to Ballynahina yesterday. Me and Kyna and two technicians. I came in to see you last night and tell you but you were dead to the world.'

'Oh, yes? And?'

'Nothing, I'm afraid. No forensic evidence that you'd been there, in any of the huts, nor of the fellow who attacked you. No blood, no hairs, no fibres. Nothing.'

'Did you talk to the dreaded McQuaide sisters?'

'Yes, we did – and Mother of God, they're a right pair of gankies, those two, aren't they? But they totally denied that you'd been up there to see them, and they also denied that they knew of any fellow who could have given you a beating, even if you *had* been there.'

Conor turned his head away, as if he didn't want Katie to see how angry and disappointed he was.

'Con?' she said, laying her hand on his blanket. 'Con – I haven't given up. There's bound to be somebody around Ballynahina who knows him, a fellow like that. And the desperate state of that puppy farm – we're considering prosecution, probably in conjunction with the ISPCA.'

Conor turned back. 'They'll still deny that they had me beaten, won't they? And if you can't find any proof—'

'Not necessarily. Not if we give them a loophole. We can promise them that we won't be after applying for a court order to have them completely closed down – not if they admit to what happened to you, and not if they point the finger at the gowl who did it.'

'But that's the whole point, Katie! They *need* to be closed down! Those two sisters should be thrown in jail for the way they've been mistreating those poor breeding bitches, and those puppies! Christ Almighty, if they'd done anything like that to a human, they'd be looking at five to ten years in the women's wing in Limerick!'

'Con… you know yourself that closing down these puppy farms has almost no political support, and that most of the public simply don't care. What's wrong with breeding little puppies? They're so sweet! And in any case, once they've stopped being so sweet, once they've peed on the carpet a few times or cost a couple of hundred euros in vets' bills, it's easy enough to abandon them in the middle of nowhere, or throw them out of your car window when you're driving up the N8.'

Conor didn't answer that. He reached across to his bedside table and poured himself a glass of water. Once he had drunk it, and wiped his mouth with the back of his hand, he said, 'Tell me what else you've been up to.'

'Con – I promise you I'm not going to let this rest.'

'Forget it, Katie. It doesn't matter any more. What's been done to me, it can't be undone, so what difference does it make if the fellow gets a few months behind bars? He'll have TV to watch, and three square meals a day, and his wife or his girlfriend will be able to come and visit him, and he'll be able to tell her what they can get up to together when he's released. Which is something that I can't say to you – not now, not next week, not next year, and never will be able to, ever, for the rest of my life.'

'I think it would be a good idea if you talked to a counsellor, like Mr Sandhu suggested,' said Katie. 'I'll have a word with him later.'

'Maybe he knows a magician who can conjure me up a new pair of balls.'

'It's not funny, Con.'

'It depends on your sense of humour. I'm sure the McQuaide sisters would think it hilarious, if they knew. I looked in the mirror this morning and I didn't even recognize myself. Face all wrapped up in bandages and no beard. I thought: perhaps I've lucked out, and this isn't me after all. Perhaps the real me is still back in your house in Carrig View, waiting for you to come home so I can make mad passionate love to you. And you don't think *that's* funny?'

Katie stood up. 'I'll come and see you again tomorrow, okay? I have to catch a couple of hours sleep now because we're setting up an operation for four o'clock tomorrow morning and I'm beat out, to tell you the truth.'

She leaned across the bed to kiss him but again he turned his face away.

'Don't kiss me,' he said. 'If you kiss me, I'll know that I'm me, and I don't want to be me.'

Katie waited for a few moments, still leaning towards him, but he kept his face turned away. In the end she said, 'Don't give up, darling. Please. You're still in shock, and you're all drugged up. Things will work out, I promise you.'

'You think so? Well, we'll see, won't we? Whatever it is you're doing at four o'clock tomorrow morning, take care of yourself. With or without me, you're precious.'

As she was crossing the car park, her iPhone pinged. It was Dr Kelley, who texted that she had phoned her a few minutes ago at Anglesea Street, only to be told she was at CUH visiting her three injured officers.

If UR still here I need to talk 2 U urgent.

She went back into the hospital and walked along to the mortuary. Before she went into the pathology laboratory, she hung up her coat and took a surgical gown down from the shelf to cover her trouser suit. She also tied on a surgical mask and pulled on a pair of blue plastic overshoes. The double doors squeaked mournfully when she pushed them open.

Inside the mortuary it was chilly, as usual, and as brightly lit as a film set, with that pervasive smell of chlorine, like a swimming bath. Dr Kelley was standing in front of her PC, her eyes looking tired and thoughtful.

'Ah, there you are, Kathleen. I wanted to talk to you face-to-face because this is a difficult one.'

'Difficult? In what way?'

'Oh, not pathologically. The cause of death is patently obvious. But politically. I mean as far as CUH is concerned.'

She went over to the examination table and lifted the sheet from the body lying underneath. It was Saoirse Duffy, her face bloated and grey. The top of her skull had been sawn off and her brain removed for an MRI and other tests, and her chest and abdomen were still gaping open. Her liver and her stomach and her lungs would be bagged up and returned to her body cavity before she was handed over to the undertakers, but it was likely that her brain would be retained and her skull would be packed instead with wadding.

'She suffered acute hypoxia when she was submerged in the river, there's no question about that,' said Dr Kelley. 'Even if she had survived, there was every likelihood that her brain functions would have been severely impaired. The least she would have suffered would have been episodes of dizziness and chronic confusion.'

'But?' asked Katie, behind her mask.

'But the damage to her brain wasn't the primary cause of death.

The primary cause of death was a massive overdose of fentanyl. From the tests on her brain that I've already carried out, I would say that she was injected with more than five milligrams. Three milligrams as you probably know is enough to kill an adult male.'

'Have you told Dr O'Keefe?'

'Not yet. I wanted to talk to you about it first. We'll have to take a look at Saoirse's medical records to see if there's any indication that she was actually prescribed fentanyl or any other opioid – and if so, who prescribed it, and why. She was semi-comatose, of course, but she wouldn't have been suffering any pain, so why fentanyl?'

Katie couldn't help thinking of the nurse she had seen coming out of Saoirse's room last night – the nurse who had suddenly turned around and hurried off in the opposite direction as soon as she had seen her. Perhaps she had been right to be suspicious about her, after all. She would check with Dr O'Keefe to see what arrangements he had made for Saoirse to be checked on by the nursing staff, and also the hospital's security officers to see if they had any CCTV footage from the first-floor corridor.

She looked again at Saoirse. She had seen so many dead bodies, but she was always struck by how messy and repulsive even the most beautiful of humans are, once they're taken to pieces. They were just bones and red meat and gristle, like bodice hanging in a butcher's window, or the tripe and liver in his stainless-steel trays.

One evening, when they were watching a romantic scene on TV, Katie's late husband, Paul, had said: 'You see them two shifting? Doesn't it ever occur to them that they have their lips around one end of a tube that goes all the way down to their lovebird's large intestines?' But that was what Paul had been like: always imagining the grotesque side of life. Katie had to see it for real.

She decided she would assign Detective Sergeant Sean Begley to this investigation, and as soon as possible. Herself, she badly needed some sleep if she was going to be fit for action at four o'clock in the morning.

Thirty-Three

Katie lay in the darkness in her room upstairs at Anglesea Street and tried to fall asleep, but she couldn't stop thinking about Saoirse's dissected body, and the way she had died. Since the poor girl had been injected with an overdose of fentanyl, which was a hundred times stronger than heroin, whoever had injected her had clearly had every intention of killing her.

But why? Was it the same person who had pushed her into the river? Did somebody hold a grudge against her? She was only a trainee beauty therapist, that was all, and so young. What could she have possibly done in her short and innocuous life to make anybody want to murder her? Maybe she'd jilted a boyfriend, but Katie could hardly imagine that even the bitterest of jilted boyfriends would take the risk of creeping into a hospital at night to give her a lethal injection.

She kept thinking, too, about that paramedic that she and Dr O'Keefe had caught in Saoirse's room holding a pillow. She had appeared to be flustered, but it was hard to imagine that after resuscitating Saoirse from near-drowning she would have been out to do her any harm. And if she had, why? What possible motive could she have had?

Maybe it had been a clinical error, nothing more than that. Maybe the fentanyl injection had been intended for another patient, and their notes had been mixed up. Yet five milligrams of fentanyl would kill anybody, so even if Saoirse hadn't been the intended victim, somebody had been intended to die.

She closed her eyes, but only for a few minutes, because she started thinking about Conor; and then Bedelia; and Nicholas; and Padragain. She felt as if her life was a dark tangled mess, with all the people she cared for tangled up in it, too, and that she would never be able to untangle it again.

It was twenty-five minutes past eleven when her iPhone played 'Mo Ghille Mear'. She rolled over and picked it up almost at once and said, 'Tony?'

'Hope I didn't wake you, ma'am,' said Detective Inspector Mulliken.

'Well, you did and you didn't. I was only half-asleep. What's the story?'

'Caffrey's just called me about Eamon Buckley.'

'God in Heaven, this is late. Are him and O'Sullivan still keeping him under surveillance? Don't tell me your man has shot off down to Skibbereen again.'

'No. Caffrey says that after Buckley shut up his shop at five-thirty he drove straight home to Farranferris Avenue, and that seemed to be that. The curtains in his front room were open and they could see him watching TV. At half-past ten, though, just when him and O'Sullivan had agreed to call it a night, Buckley came out again, and got into his car, and drove off, and you'll never guess where he is now.'

'Tony, I'm not actually in the mood for guessing.'

'Sorry, ma'am, but you'll hardly believe it. He's in Alexandra Road, in Montenotte. He's stopped right outside that house where our coffin-maker said that all of Lupul's beggars were staying.'

Katie sat up and switched on the bedside lamp. 'Can Daley and Cailin see him too?'

'They can, yes. They're only a few metres away, on the opposite side of the road. Buckley got out of his car and went in through the front gate. That was only about five minutes ago.'

'They haven't seen Lupul though?'

'No. They've observed only two people leave the house all afternoon, and they looked like rough sleepers. They were carrying rolled-up sleeping bags and rucksacks and one of them had a small dog with him. They were heading down to the city so.'

'You know what this means, though, don't you, Tony? It *proves* a link between Lupul and Buckley. There's no way that Buckley can deny it now. That's the best news I've had in days.'

'So what do you want to do now?'

'Keep an eye on the place, that's all. We don't yet have any evidence against Buckley, so we can't lift him, but if he comes out again tell Caffrey to keep on following him. If Lupul shows up, then I might consider going in earlier, to catch them together. It's possible of course that Lupul's already inside but right now let's leave it till four o'clock, like we planned to. Is everything set up now?'

'Chalk it down, ma'am. I'm still waiting to hear what time the immigration officers are going to show up, but they've promised to get back to me before twelve.'

Katie climbed out of bed. There was no point in her trying to sleep any longer. She pulled on her black sweater and her tights and her trousers, and then she went downstairs to the canteen for a cup of strong coffee. The canteen was almost empty except for three uniformed gardaí eating a midnight fry and laughing loudly and clattering their knives and forks.

Katie felt for the first time that the investigation into Lupul and his beggars was moving forward. From the moment that Ana-Maria had recognized her mother's ring it had seemed highly likely that Lupul and Eamon Buckley were connected, even if it wasn't in the gruesome way that she had first suspected. Even if the mince had been nothing but pork, and the ring had dropped into it by accident, how had it found its way into Buckley's butcher's shop in the first place? On top of that, the discovery of her mother's necklace at the scene of Bowser's shooting was circumstantial evidence at least that Lupul was responsible for the killing of Gearoid Ó Beargha and Matty Donoghue, and for the disappearance of both Ana-Maria's mother and Máire O'Connor.

What Katie needed now was indisputable proof that Lupul was behind the murders and disappearances. She was hopeful that Bill Phinner's forensic technicians would find some incriminating evidence in the house in Alexandra Road; and once she had enough to arrest him, she would order every Romanian beggar that her officers could find to be rounded up and brought in for questioning. If they knew that Lupul was safely locked up, she was confident that two or three of them would feel brave enough to speak out against him, and admit that they belonged to his illegal begging ring. According to Ana-Maria, her mother had detested Lupul, and maybe some of the other beggars felt the same about him.

She was eating the Lotus biscuit that had come with her coffee when her iPhone rang again. When the three gardaí on the opposite side of the canteen heard 'Mo Ghille Mear' they all turned around, but as soon as they realized who she was, they turned back again and started talking among themselves in much lower voices.

It was Detective Inspector Mulliken again. 'Buckley's come back out of the house, ma'am, along with another and they have a third fellow between them. He has his arms around their shoulders and they're supporting him like he's totally langered.'

'What does he look like, this drunk fellow? Can they see?'

'Hold on a second, I'll ask them. The street lighting's not too clever up there. Yes, Daley, okay. Sure like. Grand. Ma'am? You still there? He looks twentyish, ma'am, with dark hair, and he's wearing some kind of a dark jacket, but that's all they can see. Buckley and the other fellow are helping him into the back of the car now. He's steamboats by the sound of it.'

There was a few seconds' pause, then Detective Inspector Mulliken said, 'Buckley's driving off now. He's turning right – down towards St Luke's Cross. Caffrey's going after him but he's keeping well back because we can follow him anyway on the GPS.

We don't want an action replay of what happened to Markey and Scanlan below at Skibbereen.'

Katie quickly swallowed the last of her coffee and took the lift up to the communications centre on the top floor. It was windowless, and hushed as an undertaker's, and dimly lit. Six gardaí in shirtsleeves were sitting in front of a bank of forty CCTV screens, with Detective Inspector Mulliken standing behind them, along with Detective Inspector Fitzpatrick and Kyna and Detective O'Crean. They were watching the progress of the GPS tracker attached to Eamon Buckley's car, as well as the CCTV monitors, which showed him driving westwards on Wellington Road.

They were also listening to Detective Caffrey's running commentary as he followed well over half a kilometre behind him, driving without lights.

'Where's he going now? He's not heading back home to Farranree. He's taken a left into Watercourse Road… and now a right into Cathedral Walk.'

Detective Inspector Fitzpatrick looked across at Katie with his usual expressionless eyes. 'There, look, he's turned into Shandon Street. I'll bet you a hundred to one he's going back to his shop. Now why would he be going back to his shop at this time of night?'

They watched on the CCTV monitors as Eamon Buckley drove down Shandon Street, past the Cathedral of St Mary and St Anne. He was out of range of the nearest CCTV camera once he had passed the cathedral, but Detective Caffrey had stayed close enough behind him to keep him in sight, and Detective Inspector Fitzpatrick had guessed correctly. Eamon Buckley drew into the parking bay opposite his shop and stopped.

'Buckley's out of his car now, but it looks like the other two are staying put,' said Detective Caffrey. 'He's crossed over to his shop – he's unlocking the door – he's gone in. No, now he's come out again, and crossing back to his car – but he's left the shop door wide open.'

Katie glanced at Kyna. 'Whatever Buckley's up to, do you see how arrogant the man is? He must think that after what happened to Nicholas and Padragain when they followed him down to Skibbereen, we'll be too scared to keep track of him any more.'

Kyna laid a hand on Katie's shoulder, and then she realized that Detective Inspector Fitzpatrick was looking at her, and quickly took it away again.

'Maybe there's a reason he doesn't care,' she suggested. 'Maybe he's doing nothing illegal.'

But at that moment Detective Caffrey's voice broke in again. 'Buckley and his pal are helping the drunk fellow out of the back of the car. They're holding him up like they did before, with his arms over their shoulders. Now they're helping him over the road to the shop. Well, not helping him, I'd say, more like *dragging* him, like. He's not making any effort to walk at all. In fact, I can see that he has only the one brogue on.'

There was silence for almost half a minute. Then Detective Caffrey said, 'Buckley's pal is coming out of the shop. Yes, and so is Buckley. Buckley's locking the door, but there's no sign of the fellow they were carrying in there between them.'

'Buckley's locked the door and left that drunk fellow in there?' asked Katie. 'You're sure?'

'Hundred per cent. It's just the two of them now, so your man must still be inside. Now they're crossing back over the road and getting into the car. Now they're moving away. They're turning left up Dominick Street.'

'Keep after them,' said Katie, briskly. Then she turned to Sergeant Brown, the emergency response officer, who was sitting right in front of her. 'Where's the nearest squad car?'

Sergeant Brown squinted up at his monitors. 'MacCurtain Street, outside the Everyman. And there's another on North Main Street dealing with some kind of minor disturbance. Nothing too serious, by the look of it – just some shower of savages pushing and shoving.'

Katie called back to Detective Caffrey, 'Ronan, can you hear me? We're sending you backup. As soon as they turn up, stop Buckley's car and arrest him.'

'On what charge? He hasn't actually done anything illegal.'

'He's locked some poor fellow in his shop, hasn't he, and by the sound of it the fellow was too langered to give his consent, so you can charge him with false imprisonment. Tell him to take you back to the shop and let you see for yourself what kind of a state your man's in. If he's that wrecked that he wasn't able to walk, he might need taking to the Mercy to sober up. Somehow I get the feeling that he's not just sleeping it off.'

'What if Buckley refuses?'

'Then I'll send a team up there to break down the door. Robert – could you organize that?'

'Of course,' said Detective Inspector Fitzpatrick, and for the first time in a long time he sounded as if he agreed with what she was doing.

Eamon Buckley's red Mondeo was halfway back up to Farran-ferris Avenue when it was overtaken by a Garda squad car with flashing blue lights and pulled over on the corner of Wolfe Tone Street and French's Villas.

Detectives Caffrey and O'Sullivan drew up behind it in their unmarked Toyota, almost touching its rear bumper so that Eamon Buckley wouldn't be able to reverse and speed off – not that he seemed to have any intention of trying to get away. Without waiting to be approached by the gardaí, he swung himself out from the driver's seat and slammed the door so hard behind him that Detective Caffrey thought it might fall off its hinges.

'What in the name of feck is all this about?' Eamon Buckley demanded. He was wearing a yellow nylon Puffa jacket, which made him look even bigger and fatter and more threatening than he actually was. 'Can't you fecking shades ever give me some fecking peace?'

Detective Caffrey produced his ID and held it up in front of Eamon Buckley's face. 'My name is Detective Garda Ronan Caffrey and I am arresting you on suspicion of false imprisonment, which is an offence under section 15 of the Non-Fatal Offences Against the Person Act, 1997. You are not obliged to say anything unless you wish to do so, but whatever you say will be taken down in writing and may be given in evidence.'

'*What?* What the feck are you talking about, "false imprisonment"?'

'You were seen not ten minutes ago locking an individual into your shop on Shandon Street – an individual who appeared to be under the influence of alcohol or drugs.'

'What a load of ballsch! *Who* saw me? I'll fecking give them a fecking clatter for telling lies about me. "False imprisonment"!' He spat on to the pavement and said, 'You're codding me, aren't you?'

'*I* saw you, as a matter of fact. Me and my colleague here, Detective Garda O'Sullivan.'

'In that case, you both need to go down to Egans and get your fecking eyes tested.'

'For the record, can you tell me your name?'

'If you don't know my name, how the feck did you know it was my shop?'

'I do know your name, but you need to tell me for the record, like.'

'For the record my name is Fecking Fuming.'

'You do realize that refusing to give your name is an offence in itself, and I could arrest you for that alone.'

'Feck off up the yard.'

Meanwhile, one of the uniformed gardaí had ordered Eamon Buckley's passenger to get out of the car. He was a white-faced youth, with scarlet spots clustered all over his forehead, a blond fade haircut and bulging eyes like green glassy allies. He didn't look particularly healthy but Detective Caffrey could see from the width of his shoulders and the thickness of his neck that he was quite muscular.

'So what's *your* name?' Detective Caffrey asked him, as the garda brought him around the car.

'Tozza.'

'I mean your real name. First and second.'

The youth looked worriedly at Eamon Buckley but Eamon Buckley shook his head and spat again on the pavement, and the youth stayed silent, chewing his lip.

'Okay, Tozza, have it your own way,' said Detective Caffrey. 'I'm arresting you on a charge of false imprisonment, too, and like your pal here I'm telling you that you are not obliged to say anything unless you wish to do so, but whatever you say will be taken down in writing and may be given in evidence.'

'But he's not my pal,' the youth interrupted, in a voice that sounded only half-broken.

'Who is he, then?'

'He's my boss. I have to do what he tells me, don't I, or else he's going to give me the bullet.'

'Will you shut your fecking bake?' barked Eamon Buckley.

'But I only carried your man in there because you told me to carry him in there. I wouldn't have done it else, would I?'

'I said, shut it!'

'But I don't want to be arrested for something I never wanted to do, do I? My old man's going to murder me!'

'You say one more fecking word and I'll murder you myself, before your old man has the chance!'

'But I never false imprisoned nobody!'

'You helped to carry him into the shop and you locked him in there,' said Detective Caffrey. 'He was plainly too langered to do anything to stop you, so that's false imprisonment.'

He beckoned to the uniformed gardaí and said, 'Cuff them both, would you, and take them in to the station.'

'But he wasn't langered!' the youth protested.

'No? He looked langered to us all right,' put in Detective O'Sullivan.

'He's *dead*! You can't false imprison somebody if they're dead, can you?'

Eamon Buckley let out an extraordinary bull-like roar through his nostrils and lunged at the youth with his right fist bunched.

The youth toppled back against the red Mondeo and slid sideways on to the road. Eamon Buckley seized his jacket and was about to pull him up on to his feet again when one of the gardaí hit him a cracking blow across the back of his head with his baton. He was knocked sideways and spun around on one foot before pitching with a squeaky thump of his Puffa jacket on to the pavement, right where he had been spitting.

He lay there with his arms and his legs outspread, breathing hard and staring up at the sky. After a few moments, he lifted his head and glared at the garda who had struck him, but the garda lifted his baton again as if to say that he could have some more if he wanted it. Eamon Buckley said nothing but '*Shite*', and let his head fall back.

Detective Caffrey lifted his radio and said, 'DS Maguire? We've arrested Buckley and his companion and we'll be fetching them in right now. His companion says he works for Buckley. He also says that the fellow they were dragging into the shop wasn't drunk, but deceased.'

'Mother of God. Did he tell you who he was?'

Detective Caffrey turned to the youth and said, 'What's his name, the dead feen?'

The youth shrugged, but said nothing.

'Ma'am? He's making out like he doesn't know. Either that, or he's too scared of Buckley to tell us. Buckley isn't exactly coming quiet-like, and they had to use the stick on him.'

'Okay, Ronan,' said Katie. 'Take the keys from Buckley and fetch them in with you. DI Fitzpatrick is setting up a team to enter the shop. It sounds like he'll be needing a white van and a couple of forensic technicians, too.'

Eamon Buckley was hauled to his feet, handcuffed, and forced into the back seat of the squad car. He grunted, but he said nothing more. A second squad car arrived, and the youth was bundled into that. Before the car's door was shut, he looked up at Detective Caffrey and said, 'I swear to God I didn't have nothing to do with killing that fellow. I was only doing what I was told.'

As the youth was driven off, Detective Caffrey turned to Detective O'Sullivan, chafing his hands against the cold.

'"I was only doing what I was told,"' he mimicked. 'Sacred Heart of Jesus. If I had ten yoyos for every time I'd heard that, I could have bought myself a Lamborghini by now.'

'What would be the point?' Detective O' Sullivan asked him, as they climbed back into their car. 'You'd have it for a week and then somebody would only half-inch it.'

'You're probably right. And even if I caught them, what do you think they'd say? "I was only doing what I was told" like. Makes me sick, how pathetic most of these criminals are. Bunch of jibbers.'

Detective O'Sullivan laughed.

'Why are you laughing?' Detective Caffrey asked him.

'Why? Well, somebody has to.'

Thirty-Four

It was already half-past two in the morning when three squad cars and a Technical Bureau van arrived outside Eamon Buckley's butcher's shop on Shandon Street, followed after a few more minutes by an ambulance.

The thermometer had dropped sharply, and a fine snow was falling, which was rare for Cork, even though it was nearly invisible. It melted as soon as it touched the ground, but it left the street glistening and wet.

Detective Inspector Fitzpatrick stood by while Detective O'Donovan sorted through the large bunch of keys that he had taken from Eamon Buckley back at the station. He had asked him to show him which key would open the door of the butcher's shop, but Eamon Buckley had told him: 'Find it for yourself, you fecking gom, what do you take me for?'

After nearly five minutes of jingling and poking, Detective O'Donovan at last managed to open the shop door, and immediately the burglar alarm went off, a ringing noise so loud that none of the officers gathered outside the shop could hear each other without shouting.

Two gardaí entered the shop, found the alarm box on the wall behind the counter, opened it up and pulled the red and black wires out of the terminals.

In the sudden silence that followed, Detective Inspector Fitzpatrick and Detective O'Donovan stepped inside and looked around. There was no sign of a dead man in the shop. The window display was bare, except for rows of metal trays bordered by plastic parsley, and the shelves under the glass counter were empty, too.

'The fridge,' said Detective O'Donovan, and went around the counter to the back of the shop. He opened up the heavy stainless-steel door and shone his flashlight inside. Chickens and bodices and legs of pork were hanging from hooks from the ceiling, and the shelves on either side were stacked with black puddings and plastic bags filled with lambs' livers and wet white tripe.

Sitting upright on the floor at the back of the cold room, his eyes open, his face whitish-grey like asbestos, was Vasile, the barman from The Parting Glass. He was missing one shoe and his sock had a large potato in it.

'Holy Saint Joseph,' said Detective Inspector Fitzpatrick. 'Vasile the snitch.'

'What do you think, sir?' Detective O'Donovan asked him. 'Reckon this was our fault? Maybe we should have met him somewhere less public.'

'Who knows, Patrick? But he told us where to find Lupul, didn't he, and Buckley picked him up from Lupul's house. I don't think you need a PhD to work out how he ended up in here, along with the sausages.'

Katie was fastening her white Cordura ballistic vest when Chief Superintendent O'Kane came into her office. He was unshaven and his coat collar was turned up and she could see that underneath his open coat he was wearing a mustard-coloured Aran sweater and jeans.

'You didn't have to come in, sir,' said Katie.

'Sure like, I know. But after you sent me that text I knew I wasn't going to be able to sleep, and I was intending to show up early anyway, what with you mounting that raid up at Alexandra Road. How's it all going?'

'We've charged both Buckley and his lad with aiding and

abetting a murder. The lad's name is Thomas Barry and he works for Buckley in his shop as a trainee butcher – but that's the only information they've given us. I haven't been down to see either of them yet because Robert says that they're refusing to answer any questions.'

'And what about this dead Romanian fellow we found in Buckley's fridge?'

'It looks as if he was killed in the same way that Gearoid Ó Beargha and Matthew Donoghue were killed and that boxer was assaulted, with a power drill in the back of the head. We'll have to wait for Dr Kelley to confirm it, of course. She'll be carrying out a toxicology test too. But the technical expert who examined him said that the drill hole is the only visible injury he could find.'

'So, like you said, this all points to our friend Lupul.'

'I'm not jumping to any conclusions yet, but it seems highly likely that he's behind it. He had a strong enough motive, after all, since this Vasile was the fellow who told us where his house was. I've asked Mathew McElvey in the press office to put out an EvoFIT of him on the TV news, so maybe if we're lucky we'll find out a bit more about him.'

'When are you setting off up there?'

'In about twenty minutes. We're still waiting for one of the immigration officers to show up, because he's coming in all the way from Waterford.'

Brendan nodded, looking around her office as if he thought he might have left something there by mistake. Then he looked back at Katie and said, 'You'll be extra careful, won't you? This Lupul's some homicidal maniac by the sound of it. I don't want to lose you, too.'

The way he said 'too' suggested to Katie that he must be referring to his late wife, Radha. Did that mean that he felt as much affection for her? After all, during their brief affair at Templemore, before he had cheated on her, they had even talked about moving in together.

'I will, sir,' she told him. 'I promise you.'

She was about to put on her coat when her phone rang. As she picked it up, Brendan saluted her and said, 'I'll catch you later so, when you're back,' and headed for the door.

She gave him a wave in return and then, 'Robert,' she said into the phone, 'are we just about ready?'

'You're not going to believe this,' said Detective Inspector Fitzpatrick. 'Lupul's house is on fire.'

'Holy Mary, you're codding, aren't you?'

'No, and it's a serious fire too, from what Cullen says. He's rung for the fire brigade already. He reckons there might be people trapped inside there.'

'Let's get ourselves up there, Robert, like *now*. And Patrick. I'll meet you in the car park.'

Brendan had caught the urgency in Katie's voice, and stopped by the door.

'What's the story?'

Katie was pulling her coat on over her covert ballistic vest. 'Lupul's house is on fire. Daley thinks there could be people in it who can't get out.'

'Jesus. This looks like being a night-and-a-half. I'll stay here for now, Katie, but keep me posted.'

'Yes, sir.'

She could see that he was itching to chide her again for calling him 'sir' instead of 'Brendan', but they both knew that this wasn't the time for it.

The fire had already taken a fierce hold on the ground floor when Katie arrived at Alexandra Road. As she climbed out of her car she could see flames dancing behind the smoke-darkened windows of the first and second floors, too, as if demons were having a party.

When she breathed in she could smell burning nylon carpets, and there was an intermittent crackling in the air that sounded like a shooting gallery.

Three fire engines were already lined up in front of the house with their blue lights flashing, and hoses had been run in through the front garden gate. Katie saw that Assistant Chief Fire Officer Matthew Whelan was in attendance, standing beside his red fire-and-rescue SUV with his arms tightly folded and his lower lip stuck out like a big petulant baby, as if this fire had been started with the deliberate intention of disturbing his night's sleep.

She was surprised and concerned to see some of the media here already – Caroline Dooley from the *Examiner* and Adam O'Hearne from RTÉ television news, accompanied by a cameraman in a woolly bobble hat – as well as Micky Murphy from Red FM.

Further up the hill, two squad cars had been parked across the junction of Alexandra Road and Military Hill to block it off, and Katie could see Sergeant O'Farrell and three uniformed gardaí talking to four or five elderly people and a woman with two small children. She guessed that they must have evacuated them from the houses on either side.

She crossed the road together with Detective Inspector Fitzpatrick and Detective O'Donovan. Detectives Walsh and Cullen were waiting for her beside their car, both looking cold and tired. Detective Walsh was only five feet three and looked far too young to be a fully qualified detective. Her hair was dark and close-cropped and she had thick curved eyebrows so that she always put Katie in mind of Sinéad O'Connor. Detective Cullen was tall and bony and red-haired with a long face and a mournful way of talking, as if he had accepted from his schooldays that life was always going to be unfair to him.

'Any sign of how it started?' asked Katie.

'No, ma'am,' said Detective Cullen sadly. 'None at all. Not from where we sitting out here, anyway. Nobody's come in or out of the house since Eamon Buckley and his pal – and that dead fellow, of course.'

'We saw the smoke to begin with,' said Detective Walsh. 'We thought it was somebody's wood stove burning at first but then it started drifting across the road, like, and it smelled really strong, so we went in through the gate there to check it out. We could see at once through the skylight over the door that there was flames inside the hallway, and that flames were climbing up the stairs, too. We knocked and we rang and we could hear somebody shouting – it sounded like a young woman. So Daley broke the front window with a brick to get in but as soon as he did that the whole front parlour went up like a bomb.'

'I tried round the back, too, but it was no use,' Detective Cullen put in. 'The kitchen door was locked and anyway the fire was already raging in there. I burned my hand on the doorknob. I mean, talk about Dante's *Inferno*.'

'Have you heard that young woman again?'

'No. And no sign of her, either, so maybe I was hearing things. Well, let's hope I was, because if I wasn't she might have been burned up, or choked by the smoke.'

Katie nodded towards the group of reporters. They had been joined now by Duncan Power from the *Irish Times*.

'How did *that* lot find out about this fire so quick? I mean, Jesus, they were here before we were, and we're supposed to be the first responders.'

'I have no idea, ma'am. But that Caroline Dooley – she showed up not five minutes after the first fire engine.'

'Okay, Cailin, thanks,' said Katie. She patted her on the shoulder and then went over to talk to Matthew Whelan.

'DS Maguire!' he greeted her, with his deep, grating voice, which sounded like a dead body being dragged over wet gravel. 'We'll have to stop meeting like this. When was the last time? When that dance studio burned down, wasn't it, on Farren's Quay. Tragic. Beyond tragic. All those young lives lost like that. Your officer there told us that she heard a woman calling out from inside this house but my men haven't seen anybody yet and I'm praying they don't.'

Katie stepped in through the garden gate and Matthew Whelan followed her, although they stayed close to the wall and went no nearer to the house. All the windows in the ground floor had shattered now and Katie thought it was like looking into the furnace at a crematorium. The heat was so intense that she could feel it on her face from twenty metres away. Three firefighters in the front garden were jetting cascades of water into the living room and the first-floor bedroom, while two more were on ladders on top of the fire engines directing water cannon on to the upper floors, so that the cold night air was filled with glittering spray.

'Mother of God, I don't think I've ever in my *life* seen a house fire raging like this one,' said Katie.

'Arson, no doubt about it,' said Matthew Whelan. 'We'll have to wait for the fire investigators to report, but there's no question in my mind that this was set deliberate. The way this is going up, it's my guess that accelerant was poured over every floor and down the stairs, too.'

Thirty-Five

Katie watched the firefighters at work for a few minutes, then she went back through the gate and across the road to where the little knot of reporters was gathered, stamping their feet and chafing their hands to keep warm. Detective Inspector Fitzpatrick came over to join her.

'Would you be having any comment for us, DS Maguire?' Caroline Dooley shouted out, pushing back the hood of her duffel coat.

'Not yet, no,' Katie told her. She had to raise her voice so that she could be heard over the roaring of the fire engines' pumps. 'You can see what's happening for yourself, and I know no more than you do.'

'Would you think there's any chance at all that this house was torched on purpose? I mean, Jesus, look at it. It's burning like a Roman candle.'

'Like I say, I have no comment at the moment. I do have a question for *you*, though. Did somebody tip you off about this fire? It seems to me that you showed up here awful quick, like.'

Caroline Dooley looked at Adam O'Hearne, and Adam O'Hearne shrugged, as if to say, *You'd best tell her, she's going to find out anyway.*

'I had a phone call. I don't know who it was from. There was no number displayed and when I tried to ring back all I got was a continuous tone, like there wasn't any such number. It was a man's voice and all he said was that there was a fire at number

277

thirteen Alexandra Road and I should go up and take a sconce at it, because there was a story behind it.'

'I had the same,' said Adam O'Hearne.

'Did you ask him who he was?'

'Of course, yes, but all he did was hang up.'

'Did he give you any idea what the story was?'

'Not to me, he didn't,' said Adam O'Hearne. 'He said something to you, though, didn't he, Caroline?'

'He did, yes. He said, "Now there'll be no more misunderstandings about who's in charge." I asked him in charge of *what*, like, but he just hung up, the same as he did to Adam.'

'What did he sound like?' asked Detective Inspector Fitzpatrick. 'Young? Old? Did he have any kind of an accent?'

'He wasn't a Corkman, I can tell you that for sure. If he had any kind of an accent he was putting it on, like he was trying to disguise his voice, do you know. I'd say he was copying some inner-city Dublin skanger, if he was copying anybody.'

Katie and Detective Inspector Fitzpatrick were still talking to the reporters when they heard screaming. Katie turned around and saw to her horror that the fourth-floor bedroom window of the house had been pushed up, and that a man and a young woman were leaning out of it, both waving their arms and crying out desperately for help.

The bedroom behind them was filled with billowing orange flames, and Katie could see that they were both on fire – their hair and their clothes. She ran back across the road and in through the garden gate, with Detective Inspector Fitzpatrick close behind her, and the bobble-hatted cameraman so close behind both of them that he stumbled and almost dropped his camera.

The couple continued screaming as they tried to climb out of the bedroom. Two of the firefighters sprayed fine sheets of water up at them, and two more quickly hoisted a ladder and shifted it across to the side of the window. But the fire inside the room was still raging, so fiercely that Katie could hear it howling, like a hungry beast.

Before one of the firefighters was even halfway up the ladder, the man and the woman clung on to each other tightly and pitched themselves sideways over the window sill. They fell together on to the mosaic-tiled path in front of the house with a thick wet thump, and the woman's forehead cracked against the rope-top edging tiles.

The firefighters gently eased the two of them apart. The man's blue check shirt had been charred into rags and the back of the young woman's dress had been completely burned away, exposing her scarlet-blistered back and her underwear. Both of their faces were scorched a dark maroon colour and their hair had been reduced to crispy black stubble.

The young woman was staring up unblinking as the fine drops of water fell from the sky and into her eyes. One of the firefighters felt her pulse, but after a few moments he shook his head. The man, meanwhile, let out a thin, wheezing sigh, as if he were resigned to his fate, and a ghost-like curl of smoke rose out of his mouth. Although he sighed, his neck was twisted at an acute angle and it was obvious that he was dead, too.

Two more firefighters came hurrying into the garden with a Samaritan defibrillator and two oxygen masks, but their colleagues raised both hands to show them that they were wasting their time.

Katie crossed herself. Almost as soon as she did so, the roof high above them collapsed with a rending crash and flames leaped into the darkness up to twenty metres high. Dense brown smoke rolled across the neighbouring rooftops, peppered with sparks.

'Come along, DS Maguire,' said Matthew Whelan, taking her arm. 'You need to be well clear of here. The whole house could be coming down at this rate.'

The reporters were waiting for her as she walked back across the road.

'Holy Saint Joseph,' said Duncan Power. He looked utterly shaken. 'We saw those two falling out the window. What's their condition?'

'I'm sorry to tell you that they didn't survive,' Katie told him.

She had to take a deep breath before she was able to say any more. Of all the tragic events she had witnessed, the deaths of this man and this young woman for some reason had moved her much more deeply than most. Maybe it was the way they had embraced each other, even though they were on fire, and even though they must have known that tumbling out of that fourth-floor window would almost certainly kill them.

'Do you know who they were?' asked Caroline Dooley.

'I've no idea at all. All I can tell you is that we believe this house was rented, but as yet we have no information as to who rented it or who might have been staying in it.'

'That fellow who rang Caroline here and Adam, he rang me, too,' said Duncan Power. 'He said nothing about who was in charge, like he did to Caroline, but it sounded to me like he was out to show somebody else who's boss. Like, "don't be getting above yourself, sham, or I'll burn down your house."'

Katie said, 'Let's wait until the fire investigators have done their work. The pathologist, too. The phone calls you all received could suggest arson, sure like, but it could have been that your caller had seen that the house had caught alight by accident and was hoping to make something out of it. We just don't know the circumstances yet, and for all we know there are even more bodies inside. I pray not.'

Detective O'Donovan came across the road. Behind him, the fire brigade were directing great arcs of water into the skeletal rafters of the roof and at last the leaping flames were beginning to flicker and die down, although the clouds of smoke were piling up much thicker. The night air was not only stunningly cold but hazy and eye-wateringly acrid, so that everybody was coughing. Katie saw an ambulance turning the corner from St Luke's, coming to take the two bodies away to the morgue.

Detective O'Donovan beckoned her aside, out of earshot of the reporters.

'Me and Daley, we've been taking a lamp around the back garden. And what do you think we found there? Three twenty-litre jerrycans. Three, all empty, but all smelling of petrol. There's an empty fish pond back there full of nothing but bracken and they'd been slung in there.'

'If those were what the arsonists used to set the house alight, that was pure careless of them, wouldn't you think? We were bound to find them.'

'Maybe they were careless because they simply don't care.'

'Sure like, you could be right. But three empty jerrycans does make it look almost certain that this was arson, and that narrows down our possible suspects. How many chancers do we know in Cork who would have enough nerve to teach a dangerous character like Lupul a lesson? I think we can count them on the fingers of half a hand.'

'The O'Flynns, for a start,' Detective O'Donovan suggested. 'They've an abiding hatred of anybody who wasn't born and bred in Cork. Well, like most Corkonians. But especially blow-ins who try to muscle in on *their* rackets. And our friend Ştefan Făt-Frumor of course, although he claims he's moving up to Dublin and doesn't give a monkey's about Lupul – that's if you can believe a word he says. And he's mostly into drugs anyway.'

'Or maybe the Garritys,' said Katie. 'That John and Dermot Garrity seem to think they've a monopoly on street crime these days, and they're a right pair of shapers. And then of course there's Foxy Collins, but this is not really his style.'

She coughed, and took out her handkerchief to dab at her eyes. The smoke was so dense now that the firemen were walking around in it like ghosts, and the reporters had all backed further up the road.

Sergeant O'Farrell came up to them.

'Just to let you know, ma'am, the houses on both sides are all evacuated now. The residents have been taken in by the Ambassador Hotel, and given rooms, which was pure Christian of them.'

'Good work, sergeant. Listen, I have to get back down to the station. I'll leave DI Fitzpatrick in charge here. Come on, Patrick, let's make tracks. There's not much more that we can do here now. We'll only choke to death. Where's DI Fitzpatrick got himself to?'

As if she had summoned him from beyond the grave, Detective Inspector Fitzpatrick appeared out of the smoke. 'Here, ma'am. Are you thinking of leaving?'

'Apart from not wanting to suffocate, I need to work out a new strategy. And I mean urgent-like. This whole homeless situation – it's got totally out of control.'

She went across to tell Detectives Cullen and Walsh that she was going back to Anglesea Street so that she could stand down the operation she had been planning to raid Lupul's house. She also promised them she would send two more officers up to relieve them as soon as she could.

'So long as they get here before we see anybody else cremated,' said Detective Walsh. Her eyes were crowded with tears but Katie gave her the benefit of the doubt and put her weeping down to the smoke.

'That immigration officer is going to be spitting tacks,' said Detective O'Donovan, as they climbed back into their car. 'The poor fellow's been driving all the way from Waterford in the dead of night for no purpose whatsoever. He hasn't even got here yet and now he has to drive all the way back again.'

'Well, I hope he doesn't throw too much of a rabie,' Katie told him. 'We'll be needing a whole lot of support from the immigration service if we're going to clear this mess up.'

'So what's the plan, ma'am?'

'I'll have to talk to Chief Superintendent O'Kane first, because this is going to be fierce political. Don't get me wrong about the homeless situation. I don't blame the homeless themselves. There can't be anything worse than having to sleep in a doorway in the middle of winter when you're addicted and flat broke and sick as a squirrel. But scummers like Lupul have been preying on them for far too long and I blame myself for not giving out about it sooner.'

They arrived back at Anglesea Street and Katie went immediately to see Inspector O'Rourke. He had already stood down all the gardaí who had been detailed to raid Lupul's house, and notified the immigration officers and Tusla.

Katie said, 'Thanks, Francis. Good man yourself. But this is only the beginning. I'm going up to discuss this with Chief Superintendent O'Kane, but I'd appreciate it if you could start calculating how many officers you'd need to pick up all of the rough sleepers from the city in one fell swoop.'

Inspector O'Rourke widened his eyes in disbelief. '*All* of them? I wouldn't like to guess. How many are there, exactly?'

'It varies from night to night, of course, depending on how many have managed to find themselves a bed at St Vincent's or the Simon Community. But at the last count it was anything between twenty and thirty.'

'All right, ma'am, I'll work on it. We'd have to do a bit of a reconnoitre first to see where they were all located, because some squads could pick up more than one rough sleeper at a time, couldn't they, if they were dossing down reasonably close together – say the Savoy Centre and the doorways of Dunnes. But what are we going to do with them, once we'd picked them up?'

'Fetch them all here for questioning. I'll tell you, Francis, I'm determined now to stamp out this exploitation of homeless people. I mean, Jesus, as if they don't suffer enough.'

She went upstairs to her office first. She hung up her coat, washed her face and hands, and sprayed her hair with perfume to get rid of the smell of smoke. As she was walking along the corridor to Chief Superintendent O'Kane's office, the lift doors opened and Detective O'Donovan appeared, holding two plastic cups of coffee.

'Thought you might appreciate this, ma'am,' he said.

'Thanks a million, Patrick. You'd make some girl a wonderful husband.'

'Well thanks, but not yet. Me and Aibreann, we broke up last weekend.'

'Oh, I'm sorry to hear that. She's a pretty girl.'

'I know, but she couldn't take the hours I was working, do you know what I mean, and whenever I came home I was always flah'd out in front of the telly, like. My own fault, I'd say. I should have paid her more attention.'

'Do you think you'll get back together?'

'No chance. Not unless I change my job, like.'

Katie stopped in front of Chief Superintendent O'Kane's office door. She wanted to say something to Detective O'Donovan to console him, and to reassure him that he would soon meet some other girl to replace Aibreann. But she couldn't find the words. Her devotion to her job had destroyed most of *her* relationships, too – especially her late husband, Paul, and her lover John. Now Conor was lying in hospital broken and impotent, because he had tried to take the law into his own hands and trap the McQuaide sisters, which she hadn't yet been able to do.

'Thanks for the coffee,' she said, and gave him the briefest of smiles.

She knocked on Chief Superintendent O'Kane's door and went in. Brendan was talking on the phone to Detective Inspector Fitzpatrick and at the same time watching a live streaming of the fire up at Alexandra Road on his flat-screen TV. It looked as if the flames had been extinguished now, but when it was intermittently visible behind the drifting smoke, the house was little more than an empty, blackened shell.

'There you are, Katie,' said Brendan, covering the phone with his hand. 'Come on in – sit down. DI Fitzpatrick is just giving me the latest.'

Katie sat down in the chair in front of Brendan's desk. He lifted the phone again and said, 'Okay, Robert, that's grand altogether. Thanks a million. Let me know when the technical team shows up. Sure. I'll talk to you later.'

Then he turned to Katie, looking serious.

'They've found another body inside the house. It's an adult, he reckons, but it's so badly charred they don't know whether it's a man or a woman. Maybe it's this Lupul.'

'Oh, God. It's possible it's him, I suppose, because I don't think there's much question that this was arson, and if it was arson it must have been Lupul they were after. Did Robert tell you that we found three empty petrol cans in the garden?'

Brendan nodded. 'He did, yes, and with any luck we'll find a rake of forensics. But it makes no odds how many fingerprints and how much DNA we discover if we don't have a match on PULSE.'

'We badly need more intelligence about this begging ring, sir. It's my suggestion that we fetch in every rough sleeper in the city for questioning – especially any Romanians. That's the only way we're going to be able to find out the scale of this operation and where the money's going to and why Lupul's house was set on fire.'

Brendan stood up. 'I'm not at all sure about that, Katie. You realize that we'll be facing some serious resistance if we do that. His Holiness Bishop O'Neill will accuse us of being racist and having hearts of stone. The Simon Community won't like it, and neither will St Vincent's – or even Cork Penny Dinners – "We don't judge, we serve," that's what they say, isn't it, when they're handing out their free shepherd's pie?'

'I know,' said Katie. 'They protect the homeless. They take care of them, as much as they can afford. But at the same time they make it ten times more difficult for us to find and lift the scavengers who exploit them.'

'And what are you going to do about the Human Rights Act? I hate to say it, Katie, but you'll be opening up a can of lawyers, and that's even worse than a can of worms.'

'Let's cross that boreen when we come to it. I've just witnessed two people killed in tonight's fire, right in front of my eyes, and now we've found a third. At least three rough sleepers have been murdered already, as well as our informant from The Parting

Glass, and at least two women are missing. I intend to find out who committed these crimes and make sure that they're punished even if it makes me the most detested police officer in Ireland – ever.'

'Oh, stop. To me personally, Katie, you're the most *likeable* police officer in Ireland. But you have to remember that one of my priorities here is to make the Garda popular again with the public, and this isn't going to help me at all.'

'That's beside the point, sir,' Katie retorted. 'How many times have you heard me saying that we have to clear rough sleepers off the streets? How many times have you heard me saying that we should be finding homes for those who genuinely don't have homes to go to and helping them to overcome their addictions. So many of them are chronically sick or mentally ill, and this is the twenty-first century, for the love of God, not medieval times.'

'Katie—'

'No, listen. We should be taking care of our own, yes, but at the same time we should be deporting all those beggars that scummers like Lupul have smuggled over from Romania. When shoppers give them change, they don't realize that they're not helping out some poor destitute soul in rag condition – they're financing a large-scale money-making criminal operation, run by foreigners. And of course there's not only the beggars. There's all those young people who are bullied into shoplifting or dealing in drugs or prostituting themselves.'

'You always were good at giving lectures,' Brendan told her. 'I have to say that you've nearly persuaded me.'

'Then what do I have to do to get your backing for this? Whenever we question these rough sleepers individually, they're always too afraid to give us any information, because they'll only have to go back out on the streets again where they've no protection at all. But let's bring them all in, and tell them that we'll keep them safe until their bosses have been hauled in and charged. Then maybe we'll have a half-decent chance of putting an end to these begging rings.'

'And where exactly do you propose keeping them safe? If St Vincent's and the Simons don't have the room for them, where are *we* going to put them up? Not to mention feeding them. How much is it all going to cost?'

'I'll talk to Jim Phelan at the council's homeless office, sir. I'm sure we can set up some kind of temporary accommodation for twenty people. As for paying for it, maybe you can talk to Assistant Commissioner Magorian. You can tell him that we've had seven deaths already connected with homelessness, and those are only the ones that we know about. You wait until you see the TV news and the *Echo* later today. I know how much you want the Garda to be popular again, but sometimes you have to forget about your popularity and do the right thing.'

Brendan came over and stood very close to her. Behind him, on the TV screen, Alexandra Road was almost totally obliterated by smoke.

She was sure he wanted to say something personal, but again he must have known that this wasn't the time. Eventually, he said, 'All right, then, Katie. If you can set up a plan for how you might organize an operation like this, let's have a meeting later with Michael Pearse. If he thinks it's workable, I'll have a word with Frank Magorian and the council's homeless forum. It's a fierce dramatic way of dealing with this investigation, I have to say, but—'

He didn't finish his sentence. Instead, he said, 'Why don't you go home and get some sleep and something to eat? You've been up for most of the night.'

'Eamon Buckley's lawyer is coming in at ten.'

'Then let Tony Mulliken hold the interview. You have a grand team, Katie, you don't need to run yourself ragged.'

'Yes, maybe you're right. And I think my poor dogs will be pining for me. I'll see you back here at eleven, say.'

'Twelve. And that's an order.'

She looked up at him. Unshaven, and with his hair uncombed, wearing that mustardy-coloured Aran sweater and jeans, she thought that he was even more attractive than when he came in to the station in his smart blue uniform. She felt guilty and unfaithful for even thinking it, but he was right. She had been running herself into the ground in the past few days and right now she was sorely in need of somebody to put their arms around her and tell her that everything was going to work out, and that in their eyes at least she was beautiful.

Thirty-Six

As she drove up to join the Lower Glanmire Road on her way home, she could see the inky pall of smoke that still hung over Montenotte from Lupul's burned-out house. She was exhausted, but at the same time she couldn't remember when she had felt so determined to rid Cork of corruption by foreign gangs. In her view, they had infested the city's streets like writhing maggots, and she was going to take whatever action was necessary to fumigate them out of their hiding places and exterminate them.

When she arrived home, Barney and Foltchain didn't give her their usual ecstatic welcome. Maybe they were sulking because she had left them to be looked after by Jenny Tierney too long. More likely, the smoke from the fire had permeated her clothes and she smelled unfamiliar. She tugged Barney's ears, though, and stroked Foltchain's feathery back, and when she went into the kitchen to pour out a bowl of fruit muesli and make herself a cup of coffee, they came trotting after her, and looked up at her with expressions that unequivocally said, 'All right, you're back now, even if you do have the weird benjy of something burning off of you. How about some Madra roast beef and vegetables?'

Once she had fed them, she took her muesli and coffee into the living room and sat down on the couch with her feet up. It was still intensely cold outside, but the sun was shining through a thin grey haze and no more rain was forecast until Sunday at least. She was still eating when her iPhone rang.

'Superintendent Maguire? I hope I'm not disturbing you so

289

early but I thought it might be better to catch you before your day got too busy. It's Jimmy O'Neill here, Caoimhe's dad. You left a message yesterday to say that if we couldn't raise enough to pay for Walter's operations by the crowdfunding, that your boss was ready to stump up the difference. Is that right?'

'That's right, he did so.'

'I was only ringing you to make sure that I heard you correctly, do you know? I mean, that's a pure generous offer and we could scarce believe it.'

'Yes, it is generous. But Chief Superintendent O'Kane is trying to show that An Garda Síochána is committed to helping the community – just as much as we are to hauling in criminals.'

She paused, and then she said, 'I hope that doesn't sound too much like a TV commercial.'

'Well, not at all, no,' said Jimmy O'Reilly. 'But the thing of it is, our crowdfunding seems to be pretty much stuck now and we don't think it's going to go up much higher. So we're wondering if your boss really *is* prepared to come up with the rest.'

'He said he would. But how much have you raised so far?'

'Two hundred and seventy-five euros. And the promise of a padded dog basket from the Ideal Pet Shop.'

'So... that's going to leave us with a balance of about two thousand, seven hundred and twenty-five euros. I'll have to ask him if he's ready to pay that much. I'm at home at the moment but I'll try to get back to you later today, like. The sooner little Walter has his operation, the better.'

'I feel morto asking for it, to tell you the truth, and if it's more than he can come up with, we won't feel bad about him saying so.'

'*I expect it's going to be fine,*' said Katie. *After all,* she thought, *I don't think he did it so much to make the Garda popular with the public as he did to make himself popular with me. But I have Conor lying grievously injured in the hospital and I love Conor and no matter what Brendan does to impress me, he can never change that. Conor and I will find a way, I'm sure of it. I'm nearly*

sure of it, anyway. At least, I'm praying to Saint Raphael – and to
Saint Adelaide, too.

Once she had finished talking to Caoimhe's father, Katie
finished her breakfast, stowed her plate in the dishwasher and
went to take a shower. As she washed her hair, she couldn't help
thinking of the strange three-cornered relationship between herself, Brendan and Walter the pug. It was almost like a story out of
Táin Bó Cúailinge, the old book of Irish legends, when preglacial
Ireland had been inhabited by the slimy Slipidyslaps and the
crusty Fumebottoms, and the fairies. Magical agreements had
been struck between men, monsters and mermaids.

Before she put on her nightgown, she stood in front of the bedroom mirror drying her hair. Although she hadn't had time to go
to the gym every morning, she had walked the dogs as often as
she could, and as far as she could, and she had lost weight since
she and Conor had been living together. Maybe it was all the
sex. As a lover, Conor was both inventive and passionate – or at
least he had been. It was more likely, though, that her weight loss
had been caused by stress. Conor was devoted to her, but he was
full on, all the time, as if the inside of his head were a constantly
boiling kettle that never got taken off the hob. What with all the
criminal and legal and political problems that she had to deal
with, she needed time and space at the end of each day to be
totally calm, and to meditate.

She slept on and off for three hours. She heard Jenny's key in
the door when she came to walk Barney and Foltchain, but she
stayed where she was with her eyes closed, and she didn't call
out.

When eleven o'clock chimed, she threw back the covers and
forced herself to get up. This was the day when she was going
to start her operation to clear the streets of Cork. Hopefully she
would soon find out who had drilled into the heads of the homeless, and who had abducted the two missing women, and who
had set fire to the house on Alexandra Road.

But her day was going to start at CUH rather than Anglesey

Street, because she believed it was here in the hospital that she would discover the first clues that would allow her to take apart the begging rings, and also the first clues to what was really going to happen to her, in her personal life.

Before she called in at the security control room at CUH, she went up to see Conor.

He was dressed in his navy-blue sweater and grey corduroy trousers and was sitting in the armchair in his room, reading *The Herald*. The headline read: *Shot Dad – Am I Going To Die?*

His face was still bandaged and stuck with plasters, but only a nosepiece like a Viking helmet and a gauze pad across his left cheek. His bruises were turning yellow and dark purple and most of his facial swelling had subsided. Katie went across and kissed him, and he kissed her back. It was a gentle kiss that he gave her – not hesitant, but careful, exploratory, as if he were trying to find out exactly what she thought of him, now that he was damaged goods.

'I didn't know you read that rag,' smiled Katie, sitting down next to him.

'Oh – well, no, but it's the only paper they could offer me this morning. That's my excuse anyway. And besides, it has the best racing tips in it. I won't be able to go back to work for quite a while until I've fully recovered, will I? So I might as well try to make some grade by betting on the horses.'

'You're looking so much better, though,' said Katie, laying her hand on his arm.

'Mr Sandhu ran some more tests on me this morning. He's happy with the way I've been healing up – down there, like, you know. In fact, he says I should probably be able to come home tomorrow – although I'll have to come back here after a few days so they can make sure that my nose and my cheekbone and my eye socket are all knitting together the way they should be.'

'That's wonderful, Con. Barney and Foltchain will be over the moon to see you back. And so will I. There's only one thing I need to know, though.'

'Oh, yes? And what's that?'

'When can you start growing your beard again? I can't get used to you with your bare chin like that! You look about twenty-one years old!'

'Don't you want a toy boy?'

She leaned across the arm of the chair and kissed him again – once, and then twice, and then again. 'No,' she said, looking him directly in the eyes. 'I want Conor Ó Máille. The dog detective. The man with the beard. And the man I fell in love with.'

He didn't answer that, and after a few moments he turned away and looked towards the window, as if he expected to see a hooded crow perched there, which would be an omen of ill luck, or an unusual cloud formation in the sky.

Katie walked along to the security control room, which was next to the main canteen on the hospital's first floor. She would have done anything for a cup of coffee but she knew she didn't have the time. She had called beforehand so that the acting Chief Security Officer, Donal Magill, was sitting in front of his CCTV screens waiting for her. He was a big, bald, cheery man with a large belly, a voluminous white shirt and a wheezing laugh, although this morning he was unusually sombre.

'How's the form, DS Maguire?' he asked her, half-rising from his revolving chair and holding out his hand. 'I've run through all the footage that you asked me to, like, and I believe I have the sequence you want to see.'

'That's brilliant, Donal, thanks. You've saved us a heap of work.'

'Would you care for a cup of coffee in your hand?'

'No, thanks, no. Let's just take a sconce at the footage, shall we?'

Donal Magill dragged a chair across for her, and they sat side

by side as he ran through the CCTV footage from yesterday evening. Katie saw herself leaving Conor's room and walking along
the corridor towards the lifts, facing the camera. While she was
waiting for the lift, the door of Saoirse Duffy's room opened and
the nurse appeared.

'There – *that's* who I want to see,' said Katie, leaning forward
in her chair. 'Is there any way that you can bring the picture up
any sharper?'

'Sorry, no,' Donal told her. 'This is about the clearest I can get
it. One of your technical experts might be able to enhance it, but
the lighting along that corridor's not too clever.'

As the nurse walked towards the camera, she kept glancing
from side to side, and twice she looked behind her as if she
thought that somebody might be following her. Because of that,
her face was constantly blurred, and from this video footage alone
Katie could see that it would be almost impossible to confirm her
identity beyond reasonable doubt. She was wearing the standard
CUH uniform of a clinical nurse specialist – a pale purple top and
dark navy trousers. She might have been a real CNS, but then she
might have simply lifted the uniform from the clothing store.

The nurse slowed, and stopped, and it looked fairly obvious
that she had just caught sight of Katie standing in front of the
lifts. Immediately she went hurrying off, back along the corridor,
and out of sight.

'Well, that tells me not much at all,' said Katie, sitting back.

'Do you want me to run it again?'

'I don't see the point. There's nothing at all in that footage
that I didn't notice at the time. But come here to me, Donal – the
hospital pharmacy keeps a record of all the drugs they use, don't
they?'

'That's right. They do too. And it's meticulous – it's almost
OCD! If there was so much as a single ibuprofen that went missing, they'd know about it all right, and which member of staff
took it. They have to. The pharmacy's packed floor-to-ceiling
with morphine and oxycodone and sufentanil and you name it.

If a patient was to die of an accidental overdose, there'd be lawyers demanding to know where the drugs came from and who prescribed them for what, and there'd be heads rolling, that's for sure.'

'Dr Kelley's fairly certain that Saoirse Duffy died of an overdose of fentanyl.'

'She told me, yes. And of course they have fentanyl in the pharmacy. In fact, we had a bit of a panic last year when a whole box of fentanyl went missing but as it turned out it was only mislabelled. Still, it could have had serious consequences, do you know what I mean? You don't want to be taking fentanyl instead of Zantac, I can tell you that.'

'Would you go down to the pharmacy and check that all of their fentanyl has been accounted for – and in particular any fentanyl that was signed out within the past forty-eight hours to a CNS – or somebody who looked like a CNS, at least.'

'Sure like, I can have Tadgh do that for me right now so.'

'Thanks, Donal. I'll still be around the hospital for the next forty minutes at least. I have to go down and see Dr Kelley in the morgue.'

'Nothing like a few dead bodies to brighten up your day, DS Maguire, that's what I always say!'

Before she went to the mortuary, though, Katie looked in to see Detective Markey. He was sitting up in bed and even though his head was swathed in a white crêpe turban, he was smiling and bright-eyed.

'It's the constant headache, that's all, ma'am,' he told her. 'I'll tell you – it's nearly as bad as when I was a kid and my mam was always giving me cheesers with the wooden spoon. But I can't wait to get out of here and find the gowl who did this to me and do the same to him. Only I'll do it to him with a sledgehammer, like. And several times over.'

'We'll lift him in the end,' Katie reassured him. 'Then you can go and visit him up at Rathmore Road and smile at him through the bars, and that'll be better revenge than any sledgehammer.'

*

Dr Kelley was busy with the incinerated body that had been brought in from the fire at Alexandra Road. It was charred crusty black from head to foot, and it looked less like a human corpse than a blackened tree trunk found lying on the ground after a forest fire. It even smelled like burned wood.

There were four other bodies in the mortuary, sleeping their last sleep under freshly pressed sheets: the couple who had thrown themselves out of the fourth-floor window of Lupul's house, Vasile, and poor Saoirse Duffy, although Katie expected that Saoirse Duffy had been sutured back together again by now.

Dr Kelley's lab technician, Denis, was sitting in front of the screen of a gas chromatograph, testing hair samples for drugs. He smiled as Katie came in and gave her a scribbly little wave. So cheerful, with all these dead bodies lying around him.

'How's it going, Mary?' said Katie. 'Anything new to tell me?'

'Not a lot. Both the man and the woman sustained multiple injuries. For the man, the main cause of death was a fractured spinal cord. The woman died from a massive brain haemorrhage. They were also both suffering from thirty per cent third-degree burns and from smoke inhalation. It would have been touch-and-go even if they hadn't fallen out of that window. Or jumped, or whatever.'

'Approximate ages?'

'The man about thirty-five, I'd say. The young woman about twenty-seven.'

'Anything further to suggest who they were?'

'The man has tattoos on his forearms. I sent JPEGs of them to Bill Phinner. One of them is a shield with the heads of two red dogs in it, and the words *Cânii roşii* underneath, if I've pronounced that right. One of Bill's technical experts knew what that was straight away: the badge of Dinamo Bucureşti, one of Romania's top football teams.'

'Nothing like that on the girl?'

'A butterfly tattoo. But she was wearing some bracelets and rings and I've also sent those over to Bill to see if he can source them. I must say they looked Eastern European, so maybe she's Romanian as well.'

'It fits, Mary. They were trapped in a house that we suspected was occupied by Romanian beggars.'

Katie paused, and then she nodded at the charred figure lying on the autopsy table in front of them.

'How are you coming along with this one?'

'He's male, I know that much. His internal organs are cooked but only medium-rare and not beyond testing. He was a heavy drinker and he also has a tumour about the size of a tomato on his left lung, although it could be benign. He wasn't the healthiest of men, I can tell you that. But I'm running more tests on him and I should be able to tell you a lot more later today or maybe tomorrow.'

'And the fellow who was found in the butcher's fridge?'

Dr Kelley led Katie across the room and folded back the sheet that was covering Vasile. He looked strangely peaceful, like a young man who had been struggling to find some kind of contentment all his life, and had at last discovered it in death. One side of his mouth was even curled up in a smile.

'The forensic technician who first examined him was spot on. Somebody drilled into the back of his head and reduced his brainstem to a smoothie, if you'll forgive the analogy.'

'But no other injuries?'

'Bruising consistent with being manhandled and forcibly held down, but that's all. On the whole he was in reasonably good shape, although he suffered from mild psoriasis.'

'Well, we know his name and his nationality and where he was working, and they were showing a picture of him on the TV news yesterday evening and this morning, too – so hopefully we'll be able to find out more.'

'I forgot to mention... he has a tattoo, too,' said Dr Kelley. She lifted Vasile's left arm and showed her a heart with a dagger through it and the name *Agrapina*. 'I looked it up, Agrapina. It's a Romanian name meaning a girl who was born feet first.'

'That's funny,' said Katie. 'So was I. Born feet first, I mean. My grandma used to say that I came into the world in the same way that I'll leave it. Mind you, she wasn't exactly a laugh a minute, my grandma. My da used to say that if you were sad she'd make you lonesome.'

'I'll be running more toxicology tests this afternoon,' Dr Kelley told her. 'I'll try to get you some results before the end of the day.'

'Thanks a million,' said Katie. She was beginning to feel stifled behind her surgical mask, so she laid her black latex-gloved hand on Dr Kelley's shoulder to bid her goodbye.

Once she was outside the hospital, she stood on the steps for a moment under the cold, anaemic clouds. She inhaled deeply, to cleanse the smell of the mortuary out of her lungs, and then she closed her eyes and said a quick but heartfelt prayer – this time, directly to God.

Please, Lord, grant me a miracle. Please make Conor a whole man again. For his own sake, if not for mine.

Thirty-Seven

Driving back to Anglesea Street, Katie was called by Bill Phinner. He sounded even more miserable than usual, and she guessed that he was trying to give up smoking again.

'We're still combing through the house on Alexandra Road, ma'am. There's all manner of stuff in there and it's going to take us days. There's at least ten suitcases full of clothes, as well as handbags and shoes – and we've found five mobile phones that are still in working order – four of them subscribers to Telekom Romania and the other one to Orange Romania. They'll be invaluable like when it comes to identifying who was living there and how long they'd been in this country and where they are now.'

'No more human remains?'

'No, ma'am, thank God. But—'

'Well, that ties in with what we suspect. Lupul was using that house as a kind of a base for his beggars, sure, but he was sending them out on the streets all day and at night they had to sleep out rough, so they'd be taken for genuine homeless. That would account for all those mobile phones, don't you think? He probably confiscated them before he sent them out begging. I mean, nobody's going to be dropping money into a beggar's cap, are they, if the beggar can afford a smartphone?'

'Diarmuid and Siobhan are checking the SIM cards right now, ma'am. But what I was going to say was, we found a grey leather jacket. You mentioned that in the bulletin you put out for Lupul, did you not? A grey leather jacket.'

'Yes, I did. Where did you find it?'

'It was in the same room as that body we found – the one that was burned totally black. It was hanging up in an alcove so one sleeve was charred all flaky but that was all. There's no name tag in it or nothing, and nothing in the pockets to tell us who it might have belonged to, except for some loose change and a packet of chewing gum. But it was grey.'

'Where in the house did you find them – I mean both the body and the jacket?'

'First floor, facing the back. It was one of the biggest bedrooms, and it had a desk in it as well as a bed, and a sofa under the window.'

'So if Lupul had a room in that house to himself, that room would have been the most likely – him being the boss?'

'We'll be testing the jacket for DNA of course and see if it compares with samples from the body. We found a notebook in the room, too, one of those spring-bound jobs, which looks as if it could be a diary. It was burned to a cinder, but we should be able to prise the pages apart, like, and if we use the infrared reflected photography, we should be able to read what's written on them.'

'Okay, Bill. I'll be back at the station in ten minutes tops. I'll come down and take a look at that jacket then. If it's Lupul's, and that body is Lupul's body, maybe half of our problem has been solved for us. All we'll need to do now is find out who solved it.'

More news was waiting for her when she returned to her office. She had only just hung up her coat and asked Moirin for a cup of coffee when Detective O'Donovan came in. He looked refreshed and smiley and he was wearing a sleeveless purple tank top that she suspected his former girlfriend had bought for him because it was a size too tight.

'How's it going, ma'am? Guess what? One of our TV appeals has actually worked, for a change.'

'You mean the appeal we put out for that Vasile fellow?'

'That's the one. We know that he worked behind the bar at The Parting Glass but what we *didn't* know was that during the day he washed cars up on the Straight Road, by the Texaco petrol station. There's this fellow walked in downstairs who says that he washed cars along with him, and he not only knows Vasile but he knows what happened to him.'

Katie dropped the file that she had picked up to read and said, 'Right. Let's go and have a word. Moirin – I shouldn't be long. Stall the coffee for a few minutes, could you?'

She went down in the lift with Detective O'Donovan to the interview room, and as they walked along the corridor she quickly told him what she had learned in the mortuary from Dr Kelley, and how she had asked Donal Brogan to carry out an inventory of the opioids in the CUH pharmacy.

Mihai was waiting in the interview room, with his black hair sticking up like a paintbrush that somebody had forgotten to clean. He was hunched forward in his blue fleece-lined jacket and his eyes were puffy. He smelled strongly of cigarette smoke.

Katie sat down opposite him and smiled but he didn't smile back. Detective O'Donovan sat on her left-hand side and switched on the voice recorder.

'Well, thanks a million for coming in,' said Katie. 'Would you like a glass of water or anything? No? So can I start by asking your name?'

'My name?'

'Yes.'

'Mihai.'

'Second name?'

'No. Only Mihai.'

'All right, Mihai. Where are you living now?'

'Cork.'

'Are you going to tell me *where* in Cork? Which street?'

'Only Cork.'

'Fair play to you, if you don't want to tell me. I'm guessing you saw that picture of Vasile on the TV news?'

'Yes. Last night.'

'And you know Vasile?'

'Yes. We work together at Handwash. Wash cars by hand.' Here he lifted his right arm and circled it around as if he were washing a windscreen.

'How long has Vasile been working there?'

'Three month about. Yes, three month. I meet him in club one night and we start to talk and he tell me he want extra job for daytime.'

'Okay. You know from the TV news that Vasile has been found dead.'

Mihai nodded. 'I tell him so many times, be dog wide. He know many bad people, Vasile. He meet bad people in his pub where he work, and he do things for them for money. What you call them? Favours. One week he make more than seven hundred euro, only for tell one bad man where other bad man hide stolen cars.'

'When was the last time you saw him?'

'At Handwash, yesterday in the morning.'

'So what happened?'

Mihai looked behind him, and then he leaned forward across the table and said, in a whisper, 'Two men come to Handwash. They take him.'

'Two men came and took him?' asked Katie. 'In a car, or what?'

Mihai nodded again. 'Black Audi. Number plate start with "L". Then maybe a nine, but that is all I see.'

'Limerick plate,' said Detective O'Donovan. 'But probably a jammer anyway.'

'Do you think Vasile went voluntarily? I mean, do you think he *wanted* to go with them?'

Mihai shook his head. 'He know them. And *I* know them, too. They work for Dragos. And with Dragos you don't – you don't – I can't think of right word—'

'You're talking about Dragomir Iliescu? The one they call Lupul?'

'That's right. Lupul. And with Lupul you don't – well, sorry, sorry to speak like this, but you don't fuck with Lupul.'

'I think we understand that,' said Katie. 'So these two men who took Vasile, they both work for Lupul. Do you know their names?'

Again Mihai glanced over his shoulder, as if he were afraid that Lupul's men would be standing close behind him. 'Danut, is one. Marku, is the other one. Marku – they sometimes call him Dinti Ascutiti.'

'Dinti Ascutiti? What does that mean?'

'It mean something like "Sharp Teeth". They say that one day he is angry with his girlfriend because she go with other man. So, he beat her and bite off her—'

He held both hands in front of his chest and twiddled his fingers.

'So – not exactly the sort of feen that a girl should think about dating on EliteSingles dot com,' said Detective O'Donovan.

'Do you have any idea *why* Vasile was taken away?' asked Katie.

'No. I don't know. He never say much to me about this gangsters he know. But I know that Vasile get most of his money from Fat Man and so he is scare of Lupul. Pure scare.'

'When you say "Fat Man", you're talking about Ştefan Făt-Frumor?'

Mihai shivered, as if the proverbial goose had walked over his grave. 'I don't say that name. Vasile never say that name. I know that the Fat Man pay Vasile plenty-plenty money to tell him what he hear in his pub. But Vasile is scare of Fat Man even more than Lupul – and all Fat Man's men. Vasile say to me one day that you have wrong gatch Fat Man kill you quick as look.'

'One foot wrong and you're dead meat, then?' said Detective O'Donovan.

Detective O'Donovan's phone pinged. He took it out of his pocket and squinted at it, and then he said to Katie, 'Talking of dead meat, Eamon Buckley's lawyer has shown up.'

'All right, Mihai, I think that's all we need from you for now,' said Katie. 'You'll leave us a contact number, won't you?'

'Okay. Okay. But you don't say to nobody that I tell you nothing. Don't say my name to TV or newspaper. Please.'

'Don't worry,' Katie told him. 'You can leave out through the car park and nobody will ever know that you've been here. You'll be like a ghost, so you will.'

The interview with Eamon Buckley and his trainee, Thomas Barry, and their lawyers lasted less than fifteen minutes.

Eamon Buckley was represented by Frank Lyons, a smooth old-school solicitor with a navy-blue three-piece suit, a nose that was spiderwebbed with broken veins and a greasy comb-over. He was a partner in one of the most long-established legal firms on South Mall.

Young Thomas Barry was represented by Michelle O'Hara, a thirty-something legal aid solicitor with an irritating habit of coughing and simultaneously tugging down the hem of her skirt.

Katie was accompanied by Detective Inspector Fitzpatrick and Detective O'Donovan.

'Right,' said Detective Inspector Fitzpatrick, giving both of the accused one of his long, glacial stares, as if he were disgusted with both of them for wasting his time. 'Jointly and between you, you removed the deceased from thirteen Alexandra Road and shut him in the cold room of your butcher's shop in Shandon Street. The deceased has since been identified as a Romanian national by the name of Vasile Deac. Mr Buckley – Mr Barry – did either of you *know* the deceased before you went to Montenotte to collect his body?'

'No comment,' said Frank Lyons, without looking up from the file he was reading.

'No comment,' said Michelle O'Hara. *Cough*, tug.

'You took him away from thirteen Alexandra Road after he was deceased, but had you taken him there beforehand while he was still alive, knowing full well that he was likely to come to harm?'

'No comment,' Frank Lyons intoned, turning a page, and without even looking up.

'No comment,' echoed Michelle O'Hara.

'Mr Buckley, it's been established by the deputy state pathologist that Vasile Deac was unlawfully killed,' said Katie. 'Were you aware of this when you went to pick him up? Were you contacted and asked to remove his body from Alexandra Road? If you were, who contacted you?'

'No comment.'

'No – the same, no comment.'

'Why did you take his body and store it in your cold room? What did you intend to do with it? Were you paid for removing it from Alexandra Road, or were you promised payment, or some other kind of reward?'

'No comment.'

'No comment.'

Katie briefly drummed her fingers on the tabletop, as if she were sending the two accused a coded message. 'I hope your legal representatives have explained to you that your refusal to answer any of our questions will count heavily against you when you appear in front of the circuit court judge. Don't have any doubt about it, we'll have no trouble at all proving that you were both party to murder, and that means twelve years to life. Thomas, how old are you now? Do you really want to spend the rest of your days behind bars?'

She waited for a few moments, her pen lifted in her hand. Then she said, 'Don't tell me. I know. No comment.'

On her way back to her office, Katie called in to see Chief Superintendent O'Kane. He was on the phone looking irritated, with a half-eaten cheese roll and a half-empty bottle of Ballygowan water on the blotter in front of him.

Katie sat in front of his desk and waited for him to finish his call. At last he tossed the phone down and said, 'You know who needs locking up? Forget the criminals. The Ombudsman commissioners, both of them. Jesus. It's like trying to get sense out of a couple of goats.'

'Did you manage to talk to Frank Magorian?'

'Frank? Yes, I did. I was after coming up to tell you, once I'd had a word with Michael Pearse about the logistics.'

'And?'

'You'll be happy to know that hauling in all of the homeless is a go, as far as he's concerned. Provided we can make the arrangements to have them securely accommodated while we question them, he's prepared to underwrite the cost of the whole operation, up to five thousand euros.'

'That's grand altogether. I'll give Jim Phelan a call at the council. I think I remember reading that St Dunstan's church hall up at Mayfield is disused at the moment, so we may be able to accommodate them there. What about Bishop O'Neill and the Simons and the Penny Dinner people? Did Frank suggest any way that we can sell this operation to them? The bishop's going to be giving us the seven shows of Cork when he finds out about it. It wouldn't surprise me if we were excommunicated.'

Brendan shrugged and raised his eyebrows. 'I think you know as well as I do what Frank Magorian feels about human rights. He said to pick up all the rough sleepers first and worry about the self-appointed saints later, except the language he used was a little more colourful than that. He agrees with you, Katie, and I have to admit that you've persuaded me, too. If we can break these begging rings we'll be giving the homeless a hell of a lot more than a boxty now and then and a bed for the night.'

'That's grand then. If you can talk to Michael Pearse and tell him we have the green light, I'll start getting everything else organized. We won't have time to set it up for tonight, which is a pity, because we need to do it as soon as possible. But I want us to be ready by tomorrow so.'

Katie had almost reached his office door when Brendan said, 'You'll let me know, won't you, when you need the money for Walter?'

Katie stopped. 'You're still okay with that? It's likely to be more than two thousand and Mr O'Neill said that he'd understand if you'd changed your mind.'

Brendan came up to her and from the way he looked at her she could tell that he wasn't really thinking about the bill for Walter's surgery.

'Yes,' he said gently, closing his eyes in that sleepy way that had always attracted her so much. 'I haven't changed my mind. To be honest with you, I never have.'

It was almost five o'clock and Katie was thinking about packing up and going home when Donal Brogan rang her from CUH.

'We've been through the pharmacy records for the past seven days, ma'am. There were a few minor discrepancies, like, but most of those were down to patients failing to pick up their medicines after they were discharged.'

'No fentanyl gone missing?'

'None. In fact, no fentanyl prescriptions went through the system at all. There were several other prescriptions for opioids, but all those have been accounted for.'

'Fair play, Donal, thanks. I'll get back to you if I think of anything else.'

Katie stood up and went over to the window, where her phantom reflection was floating outside in the darkness.

Her first suspicion had been that the nurse in the video might have been the paramedic Brianna. She had looked so guilty when she and Dr O'Keefe had surprised her in Saoirse Duffy's room, holding up that pillow. Yet it made no sense that the same medic who had saved Saoirse's life should then try to kill her. Unless perhaps they knew each other, and there was some kind of blood feud between them, what on earth could her motive have been?

It was not that her motive necessarily needed to be logical, or explicable. Katie knew from weary experience that murders could often be totally irrational, and that even the murderers themselves could be at a loss to explain why they had taken it into their heads to kill their victims. Only last month a woman had deliberately run over and killed a completely innocent man in Dunnes' car park in Ballyvolane because he was the image of the father who had sexually abused her when she was seven – even though her real father had died years ago.

All the same – even if Brianna had no obvious or rational motive for murdering Saoirse – Katie still had to check if there was any possibility that she *might* have done it, if only to eliminate her from their inquiries.

She called Detective Inspector Mulliken into her office. He was carrying a fat green jobs book under his arm and Katie knew that he was going to try and bring her up to date on another serious case that he was supervising. A cache of AK-47s and shotguns had been discovered hidden underneath the floor of a barn up near Ballyhooly, and it was suspected that the farmer might have a hidden store of explosives and detonators too.

'Is that the Moloney case you have there?' she asked him.

He laid the jobs book down on her desk. 'It is, yes. We have at least half-a-dozen witness statements now, and some CCTV that could be incriminating, and I'd say we're very close to making an arrest. Well, five arrests, as a matter of fact. The whole Moloney family are New IRA – even the grandad was, believe it or not, Ruari, but he died a couple of weeks ago so we can't be hauling him in.'

'Good work, Tony. But if you can put the Moloneys aside for an hour or two, there's something urgent I need you to do. I want you to go down to the Southside ambulance station and ask Ardan Fallon if he can give us a complete inventory of all the drugs used by all his paramedic crews over the past seven days.'

'*All* his paramedic crews?'

'That's right. Don't tell him, but what we're looking for is any fentanyl that's unaccounted for. There's one paramedic in particular I have my eye on, a woman, but it's possible that she could have lifted it from another ambulance, not her own. We're not talking about a huge amount, like – only about five milligrams, but even five milligrams can stop a carthorse in its tracks. I'm trying to find out where the fentanyl that killed young Saoirse Duffy came from.'

'Okay...' said Detective Inspector Mulliken. He sounded dubious.

'Tony – the reason I want you to go yourself is that Ardan can be pure tetchy at times. He's only just taken over as Chief Ambulance Officer but he still has a rake of old fleet and staffing issues down there at the Southside to sort out. He doesn't like to talk about them so he usually expects us to direct any questions to the HSE and not direct to him. But I think he'll respect you because of your rank. It's critical, though, that he doesn't realize what we're really looking for, so that the ambulance crews don't find out, either.'

'So what *should* I be after telling him that we're looking for?'

'Make up some story so. Tell him we're searching for counterfeit painkillers that were sold to the HSE by some dodgy Eastern European drug gang. I leave it to you.'

'You really think that Saoirse Duffy might have been done in by a paramedic?'

'It's a suspicion, Tony, no more than that. It could be that somebody sneaked into one of the ambulances when it was unattended and hobbled the fentanyl. It could be that the fentanyl overdose that killed her didn't come from an ambulance at all. I mean, you can buy it at almost any nightclub in Cork if you know who to ask for. But like I say, I have a suspicion, and it's a fierce strong suspicion, and we need to follow it up.'

'Right you are, ma'am, I'm on to it. Meanwhile, if you could find the time to look through the Moloney file—'

'I will of course. I like to think that I'm something of an expert when it comes to the New IRA.'

Thirty-Eight

Loredana had never felt so cold in her life, even when she had been sitting on a bench beside a statue of Vlad Tepes in Târgoviște in December, with the thermometer down to minus 15°C. Now she was crouching in the same doorway in Cook Street that Matty and Máire had once called home, bundled up in a smelly bronze sleeping bag, with a yellow scarf wrapped around her head and a pink baby blanket that she had stolen from Penneys folded across her knees.

She was shaking as badly as if she were having an epileptic fit, and every now and then she would let out a little whimper, like a lost puppy. She hadn't had a fix since seven o'clock this morning, and Marku was over two hours late in bringing her the crystal meth that he had promised. He had never been this late before, because Dragos insisted that his beggars should always be balmed out and smiling. If they looked sick or aggressive or mentally disturbed, passers-by tended to give them a wide berth and they collected far less money.

Two uniformed gardaí came walking slowly along the street, a man and a woman. The woman stopped and hunkered down beside her. All Loredana could see was a plump blurry white face and a smile that seemed to float in the air by itself like the Cheshire Cat's smile in *Alice*.

'Are you all right, girl?' she heard her say. 'You're looking fierce shook there, like. Do you want me to see if we can get you a bed at Riverview?'

'I'm okay,' Loredana whispered, scratching her arm. 'I wait for my friend.'

'Who's your friend?'

'It's okay. He take care for me. What is time?'

'The time? It's twenty past nine. What time are you expecting him?'

'He say seven. But maybe he have problem.'

'Have you tried to get yourself into a hostel? Do you know where to find them? Like I say, there's Riverview for young girls like you but Edel House might take you too if they have the room. They're not far away in Grattan Street. We could take you there if you want.'

'No. I wait for my friend.'

'It's up to you, girl. But you're not looking well at all. What drug are you taking?'

'No drug, no,' said Loredana. 'Only cold.'

'Can't force her,' said the male garda, who was growing impatient.

The female garda stood up. 'All right, love. But I'll be coming back this way in about an hour to check up on you. If your friend hasn't shown up by then, I think we ought to try and find you a bed for the night. It's going to be Baltic tonight, I warn you.'

Loredana didn't answer, but nodded. The two gardaí stood over her for a moment longer and then walked off at a measured pace towards St Patrick's Street.

When they had turned the corner, Loredana picked up the plastic McDonald's coffee cup in which she collected change. She tipped it into her shaking hand and tried to count it, wondering if it would be enough to pay for a fix. The trouble was, she couldn't focus on the coins clearly enough to see what denomination they were, and she wasn't familiar with euros, only Romanian leu. Besides, she didn't know where she could find anyone to sell her any ice, and she was trembling so much she wasn't sure that she would be able to walk.

She had never felt so desperate and alone in her life. Where was

Marku? Dragos had promised that he would always look after her, ever since he had first sat down next to her on that bench at the end of Alexandru Ioan Cuza Street. She had been sleeping rough for over a month by then, after her mother's drunken boyfriend had tried to rape her one night and she had fled from her home with nothing, not even a change of clothes. Her father had died of drink when she was only seven years old, and the only relative she knew was an aunt with early-onset dementia who lived in Bucharest.

Dragos had bought her a pizza at the Casa Veche and then taken her back to his flat. He had promised to find her somewhere safe to sleep every night and buy her new clothes and make sure that she always had enough to eat. All she had to do was come and work for him. Before she had gone to bed he had given her a pill to make her feel 'happy again'.

That night she had tossed and turned and sweated and shivered, but she had felt euphoric, as if all her problems were over and a wonderful new life was opening up in front of her. Next morning, as she began to come down, she had begged Lupul for another pill, and that was how she had become addicted to methamphetamine. These days she smoked it mostly, or sniffed it. The septum of her nose had almost completely eroded away and her molars were all black and rotten with 'meth mouth'. Sometimes at night, when she had enough meth powder to spare, she would 'shelve' it, pushing it into her vagina to give herself a slower, longer-lasting high, although her vagina was blistered and sore and never stopped weeping.

More time went by and she started to shake so violently that she had to clench her teeth and hug herself tight, but she still knocked her head several times against the door behind her. She was sure that if Marku didn't come soon she was going to die of a heart attack. The whole street appeared gradually to be tilting itself up at a forty-five-degree angle, and she was sure she could see dark ghosts sliding up and down it, and hear them talking in high, screeching voices, like chalk scraping on a blackboard.

A face floated in front of her like a balloon. A man's face, round and pale. He had a small black moustache and bulbous eyes, and a large mole at the side of his nose.

'What are you doing here?' he asked her.

'What? I wait for my friend.'

'What's your friend's name?'

Loredana bit her bottom lip to try and stop herself from shaking so much. 'Marku. His name is Marku. Do you know him?'

'Yes, I know Marku. But I can tell you this, you're going to have a long wait if it's Marku you're waiting for.'

'Why? Where is he? He comes, yes? Please tell me he comes.'

'You're one of Dragos' gang, are you?'

Loredana stared at him. She suddenly realized that he had actually said, '*Eşti una dintre gaşca lui Dragos, nu-i aşa?*' in Romanian, and she began to feel afraid. She didn't understand what was happening at all. She needed ice, she needed ice more than life itself, and she needed to be warm, and she needed to sleep. She didn't want to be here with this man's balloon face bobbing in front of her. She wanted to be back home in Târgovişte, in her own bed, cuddling the pink bear that she had called Bomboane, and which she had never seen again after she had left. Did Bomboane ever wonder where she had gone? Did Bomboane lie there, looking up at the moon, glassy-eyed, in the same way that she was looking up at this man's round face?

'You shouldn't be here, in this place,' the man told her, still speaking in Romanian. 'This doorway here, Dragos doesn't own it. He has to learn that.'

'I don't have any other place to go,' said Loredana. 'I'm so sick. Do you have any ice? I only need a little and you can have all my money. Please.'

'Dragos needs to understand that he's pushed his luck too far. I'm sorry that you have to pay for Dragos thinking that he could be king of the castle. Well, I'm not *too* sorry. Anybody stupid enough to join Dragos' gang deserves everything they get. Do you know what we call you lot? *Banda de Nebuni* – the Band of Fools.'

His face rose upwards, just like a balloon, and disappeared.

She thought she could hear him talking, but she couldn't make out what he was saying. She was wracked from head to toe by a shudder so intense she felt that her spine was rattling and all the bones in her body had been dislocated.

She heard him say, '*Bine*, there's nobody coming, do it now!'

She looked up to try and see who he was talking to but as she raised her head, freezing cold petrol was splashed into her face, stinging her eyes and temporarily blinding her. She gave a thin, choking squeal and raised her hands to cover her eyes, but then even more petrol was emptied all over her, soaking the scarf that was wrapped around her head, as well as her baby blanket and her duvet and the sleeves of her coat.

She coughed and coughed and spat out petrol and then she groped out sideways for the door frame, so that she could lever herself up on to her feet. She was too weak, though, and her right knee gave way, and she pitched over on to the pavement, jarring her shoulder.

Virgin Mary, help me. Virgin Mary lift me up in your arms and carry me away from here, to somewhere warm and silent and safe.

She started to drag herself across the pavement, blinking furiously to clear her eyes, even though that made them sting even more. But she had crawled less than two metres when a lighted match was dropped on to her back. With a soft whoomph, she exploded into flame.

For a split second, she could see the flames that were burning her face, flickering blue and yellow in front of her. Then she was overwhelmed by the most terrible agony she had ever experienced. She had burned her hand on an iron once, but this was the same searing sensation all over her body, and she could hear her ears crackling and feel the skin on her face shrivelling up, like crumpled cellophane.

Somehow in her blindness and her pain she managed to push both hands against the pavement and force herself up so that she was kneeling. Then she flailed out with her right hand and gripped the drainpipe that ran down the wall beside her – pulling herself, blazing, on to her feet. She tried to scream for somebody to help her but when she took a breath she sucked in flames, which scorched her tongue and seared the back of her throat.

Jerkily, stiff-legged, she started to walk towards St Patrick's Street, although she no longer knew where she was going, and she was both blind and deaf. With each step, though, the pain was gradually easing and she was beginning to feel numb, which not only gave her relief, but hope, as if she might be saved after all. She didn't realize that her nerve endings had been burned away, and that she would never be able to feel anything, ever again.

Passers-by and taxi-drivers stared in horror as she came staggering out of Cook Street and crossed the pavement, a black stick-figure inside a tall rippling column of fire. She reached the kerb and then she toppled face-first into the road, only five metres in front of a bus. The bus stopped and the driver jumped down with a fire extinguisher. He sprayed her from side to side with foam as she lay in the gutter, with only a few flames dancing from her burning hair, like a living crown.

A small crowd gathered around her and the two gardaí who had talked to her earlier came running across the road from Opera Lane. The woman garda knelt down beside her but if Loredana hadn't still been wearing the charred remnants of her yellow scarf around her neck she wouldn't have recognized immediately who she was. Smoke was still rising from her body and blowing in the chilly wind across St Patrick's Street.

A big-bellied priest came hurrying up, his white hair flapping. With a deep grunt he eased himself down on to one knee beside the woman garda and made the sign of the cross over Loredana's blackened forehead.

'Through this holy unction may the Lord pardon thee whatever sins or faults thou hast committed,' he intoned. He was so shocked that was all he could manage to say. He took off his thick-framed spectacles and pressed his hand over his mouth with his hand as if he were going to vomit, and he couldn't even bring himself to choke out a last 'Amen'.

Thirty-Nine

Katie heard her oven ping to tell her that it was heated up enough to put in her individual chicken-and-mushroom pie, but as she walked through to the kitchen her phone rang.

She turned around and went back into the living room, almost tripping over Barney and Foltchain who had been following her into the kitchen in the hope that she might be giving them a few dog treats each.

It was Detective Sergeant Begley on the phone.

'You'll be seeing this on the TV news in half an hour, ma'am. A rough sleeper's been burned to death on Pana. A young woman, and it looks like somebody's doused her in petrol and set her alight.'

'Mother of God. When did this happen?'

'Less than half an hour ago. And here's the thing: she was sleeping in the same doorway where that Matty Donoghue fellow got himself killed, and where his girlfriend disappeared from.'

'Do we know who she is?'

'Not so far. She had no identimication on her at all. But two officers on foot patrol stopped and talked to her only about an hour before she was burned. They guessed that she was Eastern European by her accent. They offered to help her to find a hostel for the night because she wasn't looking too clever, but she told them no, she was waiting on a friend. The officers reckoned that she was actually waiting on her dealer.'

'Where's her body now?'

'Still on Pana. Covered up and cordoned off, of course. There's three technical experts here already, taking pictures and all, and Bill Phinner's called in that burns specialist from the Mercy, what's his name, Michael Cosgrove, isn't it?'

'Have you seen the girl's body yourself?'

'I have, yes. The last time I saw someone as badly cremated as that was when that Circle K tanker crashed on the Magic Roundabout, you remember, the week before Christmas. But it was definitely petrol that she was burned with, you can smell it, like.'

'Any witnesses?'

'Not to her being set alight, no. But at least twenty or thirty people saw her coming out of Cook Street, all on fire. Two witnesses took video of it, on their phones.'

'What about her possessions?'

'She didn't have much. A spare pair of jeans and some underwear and a packet of cheese-and-onion Taytos and a couple of cans of Red Bull. Oh, and a glass crack pipe. They've all been photographed and bagged up and ready to go back to the lab. There was a coffee cup, too, with about seven euros in cash in it, so it's fairly certain she was begging, like.'

Katie sat down on the couch and turned off the sound on her television. Barney and Foltchain came up close to her and stood staring at her as if they wanted to know if they could be of any help.

'Did you see the back of her neck, Sean?' she asked. 'Is there any indication that her killers might have been trying to drill into her brain before they set her on fire?'

'No, I could see no sign of that,' said Detective Sergeant Begley. 'I asked Declan the forensic fellow who was giving her the once-over to take a sconce for me, but he said her head's burned far too bad to tell for sure. Her skin's flaking off and her hair's all burned to a crisp and he didn't want to mess up any evidence by poking around too much, do you know what I mean? We'll have to wait for the autopsy so.'

'Fair play,' said Katie. 'But even if somebody *did* try to kill her with a drill, they obviously didn't succeed – otherwise they wouldn't have needed to pour petrol all over her and set her alight, would they? On top of that, we still haven't identified that man who was burned at Alexandra Road. Bill Phinner says that they found a grey leather jacket hanging up in the room with him, so it's pure possible that it could have been Lupul. And if Lupul's dead, who's going around killing rough sleepers? Or maybe nobody is. Maybe this was just a one-off. A jealous boyfriend or a drug-dealer she owed money to.'

'That's a possibility, ma'am, sure. But your plan to haul in all the rough sleepers – I'd say that's looking more and more like something we need to do asap – if only to save any more of these poor streals from being massacrated.'

'It's almost all set up, Sean. Listen – give me a ring if anything new comes up. Don't worry if it's late. Otherwise I'll catch you tomorrow afternoon when you get back in.'

Katie put down the phone. After hearing about Loredana being burned to death, she suddenly didn't feel at all hungry any more, even though she knew she ought to eat something. She found the events of the past few days deeply unsettling – mostly because there was no way of telling for certain if they were connected in any way or not. Vasile Deac, the informant, had been drilled in the brainstem just like Gearoid Ó Beargha and Matty Donoghue, and he had been carried dead from Lupul's house on Alexandra Road, so the logical conclusion was that Lupul or one of his henchmen had murdered them all. But who had burned down Lupul's house? And was it Lupul whose burned body they had found in the first-floor bedroom? And who had poured petrol over that homeless girl in Cook Street tonight?

Katie knew that she could easily persuade herself that the murders and the fire were all interlocking pieces in the same puzzle, but she was always reluctant to jump to conclusions before she had irrefutable evidence. She had so many other unresolved questions nagging at her, too. For instance – who had given Saoirse Duffy her fatal dose of fentanyl, and why? And how was she going to present her case to the circuit court against Eamon Buckley and his assistant? And what relationship did Eamon Buckley have with Lupul, if any, apart from removing Vasile's body and shutting it up in his fridge? How had Ana-Maria's mother's ring turned up in Eamon Buckley's mince, and her necklace in the street where Bowser had been shot?

She knew she was doing everything she reasonably could to find out the answers to all these conundrums, but they were making her feel tense and frustrated and worst of all, impatient.

She went over to her drinks table and poured herself a large Smirnoff. Then she went into the kitchen, opened the fridge and helped herself to three lumps of ice. She looked at the individual chicken-and-mushroom pie and decided that she had better bake it, although it made her feel even lonelier than she usually did. There was every chance that Conor would be back home tomorrow, and even if he was bringing even more problems with him, at least he would be somebody to talk to in the evening, and somebody to hold her in the middle of the night when the turmoil in her head made it so difficult for her to sleep.

She just hoped he wouldn't start nagging her about the McQuaide sisters and their puppy farm again. It was difficult to know what action she would be able to take against them just yet, especially since they had promised that they would clean up Foggy Fields and abide by ISPCA guidelines. She had been thinking of sending Detective O'Crean up to Ballynahina to see if he could track down the sham-feen who had assaulted Conor, but so far she hadn't been able to spare him for long enough to sit around The Fir Tree pub at Watergrasshill all day eavesdropping on local gossip.

She managed to eat half her pie while watching *After the Headlines – Charlie Bird*. Then she showered and went to bed. She fell asleep almost immediately, but she was woken up after twenty minutes by a nightmare about her lover John. He was outside her bedroom window, banging on it and shouting for her to help him, although she could barely hear him. Then he suddenly dropped out of sight.

She sat up, clutching her duvet tightly. The house was silent, except for Barney snoring in the kitchen.

'John,' she said, as if there were some way that saying his name could bring him back again.

Forty

By the middle of the morning, Katie had finalized her arrangements for gathering up all the rough sleepers in the city centre. Uniformed gardaí had been patrolling around the streets all morning, discreetly noting down the locations of as many beggars and homeless as they could find. With that information, Superintendent Pearse and Detective Inspector Fitzpatrick had drawn up a schematic, which they could use to pick up at least twenty-three of them in rapid succession.

Katie went down to the squad room to give a briefing to the thirty-five uniformed officers who would carry out the operation. She had named it Operation Labre, after Saint Benedict Joseph Labre, the patron saint of homeless people. She was accompanied by Superintendent Pearse, Detective Inspector Fitzpatrick, Kyna and Detective O'Donovan. Chief Superintendent O'Kane joined them, too, but sat at the back to listen and didn't contribute, although he didn't once take his eyes off Katie, and smiled at her and raised an eyebrow whenever she looked in his direction.

'I can't emphasize enough that it's vital that you treat these rough sleepers with care and respect,' she said. 'We're trying to persuade them to co-operate with us, but most of them are drug addicts or alcoholics or mentally disturbed and almost all of them are guilty of petty theft or antisocial behaviour, so it's quite natural that they don't regard the Garda as their bosom pals.'

Sergeant O'Farrell put up his hand. 'I can't really see any of them *wanting* to be hauled in, ma'am. What if they flat-out refuse to come with us?'

'I'm not so sure that they *will* refuse, Ryan. You know how cold it is outside and the forecast says it's going to be lashing later on. You'll be telling them that we're offering them a clean bed for as long as they need it, and hot showers, and that they'll be fed three meals a day and given free medical treatment – and that will include controlled amounts of drugs. We're not expecting any addicts among them to go cold turkey. You'll also be telling them that we're going to protect them from any gowl who's been controlling them or taking money from them. Later, of course – once they're settled and rested and their bellies are full – we'll be asking them to tell us who their ringmasters are, if they have them, and most importantly where we can track them down.'

'But what if they're not persuaded? What if they tell us to go up the yard and that's an end to it?'

'In that case you'll have to use force, so long as you're careful not to hurt them or injure them in any way. As you well know, it isn't against the law to sleep rough, although plenty of politicians have been calling for it to be made illegal. But we can legitimately lift rough sleepers off the streets on suspicion of trespass – for instance, if they're camping on private property such as bank doorways or the waterways under the city's bridges. We have the same authority if we want to question them about drug-dealing or antisocial behaviour, such as aggressive begging or defaecating in public places.

'I'm hoping, though, that on a bitter wet night like tonight, most of them will be tempted by a warm bed at St Dunstan's hall and a decent hot meal – as well as physical protection from their ringmasters.'

'What about their possessions, or any dogs they might have with them?' asked Inspector O'Rourke.

'I've arranged for three follow-up vans that will collect and seal and label their bedding and their belongings. There are only two dogs that we know of, and they'll be picked up by a handler from the dog unit.'

'How long are we going to be able to hold them?'

'Technically, we're not holding them, we're simply giving them some humane relief from sleeping outside in the middle of winter. They'll be free to leave whenever they want to, just like anybody else we fetch in for questioning. But we're not going to tell them that, unless they ask, and I'm confident that they'll come to trust us enough to give us the information we're looking for.'

'Supposing they do, and because of that information we haul in their ringmaster or ringmasters plural, and successfully prosecute them. What do we do with them then?'

'Any non-natives we'll be after deporting back to their countries of origin. As far as Irish natives are concerned, that's up to the council. But even if they have to go back on to the streets, they'll be far safer than they were before, and they won't be having to hand over the money they make from begging to some gangster, on pain of being beaten up.'

Sergeant Rooney put up his hand. 'If you don't mind my saying so, ma'am, there's a whole lot of people going to say that this is one hell of a trick to play on some poor vulnerable down-and-outs. A bed and a hot meal as the price for ratting on their bosses.'

'I fully appreciate that, sergeant,' said Katie. 'I expect His Holiness the Bishop and some of the homeless charity workers are going to be raging. But we've seen at least five murders now in the past few days, as well as two women gone missing, presumed dead. I know that Cork city to our discredit has the highest homicide rate in the country but it's only January and we've only one more murder to go to reach our five-year average of eight. All these murders appear to be related to begging rings, and even if we are playing a trick, it's a trick that could save more rough sleepers from being drilled to death or shot or set on fire.'

Mathew McElvey, the press officer, raised his hand too. 'DS Maguire and I have already been discussing how we're going to present this to the media. We'll be emphasizing that Operation Labre is another initiative in Chief Superintendent O'Kane's PR effort to win back public confidence in the Garda. A random act of kindness to the homeless. We won't be mentioning that we'll be questioning them to discover the location of their ringmasters.'

Superintendent Pearse stood up and said, 'H-hour is twenty-two-thirty. You'll be divided into five teams of seven with two squad cars, an SUV, and a van for each team. Sergeant O'Farrell has all the details on how you'll be organized and which teams will pick up which rough sleepers from where. Any questions?'

The briefing ended, and most of the gardaí drifted out of the squad room to go and get themselves some lunch. Brendan came up to Katie as she was putting away her notes, and said, 'If you can pull this off, you know, you could change the whole way that this country treats its homeless.'

'Oh, you think so? I think most of our TDs are too hard-hearted for that.'

'You're one in a million, Katie, do you know that?'

'I'm taking a serious risk, sir, because I don't see any other way of putting a stop to these begging rings. I'm hoping it's going to work, but on the other hand it could be the biggest public relations disaster that Anglesea Street has ever known.'

Brendan smiled at her. 'We'll see,' he said. 'Meanwhile, I have my bet on Kathleen Maguire to beat all runners.'

Early in the afternoon, along with Detectives Walsh and Cullen, Katie walked up to the newly refurbished criminal court buildings at the top end of Anglesea Street to present the book of evidence against Eamon Buckley and Thomas Barry. Since they were charged with an indictable offence, their hearing was deferred until the first sitting of the circuit court on 5 February, and they were both remanded in custody. Standing in the dock, Eamon Buckley shouted out, 'It's a fecking joke, this! A fecking charade!' while Thomas Barry burst into tears. Both were promptly man-handled out of the courtroom and down to the cells.

On her way back to the station, Katie received a text from Conor. Mr Sandhu was allowing him to go home at two-thirty p.m., once Mr O'Connell, the maxillofacial surgeon, had taken another look at him. *If the scumbags of Cork give you a couple of hours' peace*, he had texted, *do you think you can pick me up?*

I'll be there XX, she texted back.

When she returned to her office, she found Detective Inspector Mulliken waiting for her.

'What's the story, Tony?' she asked him. 'Do you fancy a coffee? I've a terrible throat on me from talking all morning. Moirin!'

'I'll go for a cup of the scaldy if that's all right,' said Detective Inspector Mulliken. 'And you'll be pleased to hear that I have a result from the ambulance station. The Chief Ambulance Officer has just PDF'd me the pharmaceutical records from all his rigs over the past seven days.'

'Was he grudging about it?'

'Not at all. I told him that cock-and-bull story about fake drugs from Eastern Europe and he couldn't have been more helpful. It seems like all the opioids that are carried in HSE ambulances are kept in a sealed box, which only the paramedics themselves can open. At the end of their shift they hand over the box to be kept in a security cage, because addicts sometimes try to prise the doors off ambulances to get at the drugs. If a paramedic team use any opioids while they're out on a shout, they hand the box at the end of their shift to the hospital pharmacy, who supply them with a fresh one.'

'And?'

'Each box contains morphine, atevan, diazepam, dilaudid and fentanyl. In the past three days, only two paramedic teams used fentanyl – one for that traffic accident up at Blarney on Monday evening when that auld wan got knocked off his bike by a tractor and had half his leg torn off. The other team claim that they "accidentally dropped and broke" a fentanyl citrate phial while checking their supplies.'

'I see. Do they have names, these clumsy paramedics?'

'The driver's name is Darragh Ó Dálaigh. His partner's name is Brianna Cusack.'

'Brianna... that was the name of the paramedic that Dr O'Keefe and I found in Saoirse Duffy's room, holding up a pillow. She said she was only going to prop Saoirse up in bed, but if that was all she intended to do, she looked fierce guilty about it. If I'd seen her doing that in a play, on the stage, I'd have said that she definitely had it in mind to smother the poor girl.'

'So what are you going to do? Fetch her in for questioning?'

Moirin brought in a cup of cappuccino for Katie and a mug of tea for Detective Inspector Mulliken, as well as a plate of shortbread biscuits. Katie stirred her coffee for a while, thinking, and then she said, 'Of course, even if this Brianna *was* that nurse, and even if she *did* inject Saoirse Duffy with fentanyl, all she has to do is deny it. We have the CCTV footage, sure, but it's far too unclear to make a positive ID. Before we fetch her in for questioning, we need to try to discover if she had any kind of a motive.'

'So how do you suggest we go about finding that out? Always assuming that it *was* her.'

'I think I'll start by sending Cailin down to make friends with her partner. Those paramedic teams, they go through some desperate moments of stress together, don't they, when they're coping with a car crash or a fire or a stabbing or something like that? In between the stress, though, they have pure long stretches of boredom. Don't tell me that while they're waiting to be called out they don't chat together and share a few personal details about themselves.'

'Well, Cailin's good at the chat, no doubt about that.'

'Exactly. She looks so young and innocent, like. Hardly anybody ever guesses that she's a detective, and she's equally cute at wheedling information out of people as Kyna. She'd hadn't been here long, do you remember, only a couple of months, but she coaxed that AIB bank manager into telling her that he'd been having an affair with his secretary and fiddling the bank's receipts so that he could take her to Santa Ponsa.'

'Right you are, then,' said Detective Inspector Mulliken. 'I'll see if I can track down where he usually goes after the end of his shift, this Darragh. I know that some of the paramedics drink at The Hawthorn in Togher when they're off duty because it's not too far off.'

He finished his tea and stood up, but before he left he said, 'The Moloneys – did you have the chance to look over that jobs book yet? Before we go any further with it, I'd like your opinion on what charges we should be bringing, and whether you think the evidence we have will stand up in court. It's pure sensitive, the whole case, what with Billy Moloney being so close to Councillor McVeigh.'

'Yes, I'm concerned myself about that particular connection,' Katie told him. 'It's going to be kid gloves time, no mistake about that.'

Katie knew that the head of the Moloney family was a lifelong friend of Councillor John McVeigh, who was deputy chair of the Cork City Joint Policing Committee. Councillor McVeigh had never made a secret of his strong Republican views, which was one of the reasons he was so popular in Cork. His grandfather Tom McVeigh had been a member of the Anti-Treaty IRA when they had taken over Collins Barracks in Cork in 1922 and tried to hold out against the National Army. He had been shot dead during the fighting in the hills around Douglas.

Councillor McVeigh still gave fiercely Republican interviews, and frequently lauded his grandfather's bravery. 'Michael Collins betrayed Ireland, but not Tom McVeigh!'

'We'll just have to be careful that it doesn't look like we're persecuting IRA sympathizers simply for their politics,' said Katie.

'Well – you'll see from the jobs book that so far the Moloneys insist that they knew nothing whatsoever about the guns that were found underneath their barn, and they totally deny any knowledge of explosives that might be stored away somewhere else on their farm.'

'I'm going home this afternoon, Tony. I'll take the book with me and read as much as I have time to. Once I've done that, though, I'll have to talk it over with Chief Superintendent O'Kane. He's on the council's Policing Committee too, along with Councillor McVeigh, and the last thing he'll want to be doing is putting the committee's nose out of joint.'

She couldn't help thinking that was an ironic thing to say, considering that she was going to the hospital now to pick up Conor.

Forty-One

Conor was waiting for Katie in the reception area at CUH, and when she came in he stood up at once and held out his arms, almost as if he couldn't believe that she had kept her promise and actually turned up to collect him. Apart from the white plaster covering the bridge of his nose, he was already beginning to look like his normal self. His bruises were fading and his lips were no longer split and swollen and he was already growing chestnut-coloured prickles on his chin.

They held each other tight for a few moments, and Conor kissed her, first on the forehead and then on the lips.

'I knew you'd come,' he told her hoarsely. Ever since he had been beaten up he had been forced to breathe through his mouth.

'Of course I've come. You didn't think that I wouldn't?'

'It's not every day you're asked to give a lift to a eunuch.'

She took his arm and together they walked out of the hospital doors. The rain that had been forecast for this afternoon had just begun, pattering all around them like an audience that couldn't quite decide whether to start clapping or not.

'You're not to use that word again,' Katie told him, as she unlocked her car.

'What, eunuch? Why not? It's true. It's what I am.'

'You're not. You've been badly injured, that's all, and we're going to do everything we can to make you better.'

'There *is* no way to make me better. You heard what Mr Sandhu said.'

'Then we'll have to make the best of what we have. That's what my da always used to say.'

'And look what happened to your da. He ended up doing the riverdance.'

Katie steered out of the hospital car park and turned south towards the Bishopstown Road. 'Don't make fun, Con,' she said. 'My da was pure mortified by what he'd done. He couldn't see any other way out of his guilt than drowning himself.'

'I'm sorry, darling. It's just that if I don't make fun I'll break down and cry.'

Katie reached across and laid her hand on his thigh for a moment. The rain was easing off a little as they reached the South Ring Road, and the windscreen wipers started to squeak.

'Big boys are allowed to cry if they want to,' she told him. 'And who knows – a few tears might water that stubble of yours, and make your beard grow back a bit quicker.'

Conor shook his head. 'Do you know what you are, Katie Maguire? You're a witch! The best kind of witch, don't get me wrong, but a witch all the same.'

They were able to spend three hours together at home before Katie had to go back to Anglesea Street to start off Operation Labre.

Barney and Foltchain were delighted to have Conor back, although Foltchain sniffed suspiciously at the gauze padding and the plaster on his nose. Conor lit the fire in the living room while Katie made cheese and tomato rolls for them, and then they sat on the couch, saying very little, but basking in the warmth of the fire and the contentment of being back together again.

'You'll have to forgive me if I do some reading,' said Katie, when they had finished eating. 'I have this investigation to catch up on. The Moloneys. They have a farm up near Ballyhooly and we found some guns under their barn.'

'The Moloneys? You're codding me, aren't you? I know the Moloneys. Their German Shepherd went missing about a year-

and-a-half ago and I found him for them. He'd been hit by a car and the car driver took him off to the vet because he didn't know who he belonged to, and when he was well enough he'd taken him home. But you say they had *guns*? I mean, serious?'

'Five automatic rifles and three shotguns. We were tipped off by one of their neighbours after he and the Moloneys had some bad-tempered dispute about boundary lines. The neighbour also hinted that they might have Semtex hidden on their farm somewhere.'

'That's unbelievable. They seemed like pleasant enough people to me. They paid me €150 for finding their dog for them, and they gave me a couple of cabbages, too.'

'Well, if they do have explosives hidden anywhere, I should think they've been hidden for at least twenty years – probably since the Good Friday Agreement.'

'Doesn't Semtex have a shelf life?'

'No. It doesn't degrade any more than a car tyre would. Car tyres and Semtex are both made of roughly the same things – rubber, polymers, stuff like that, except Semtex has explosive instead of carbon. About three years ago we found nearly a quarter of a ton of explosives stored in an old cowshed in Rathcormac. That dated back more than sixty years, and it was all still live. Half the village would have been blown to kingdom come if that had gone off.'

Conor pulled a face but said nothing. Katie opened up Detective Inspector Mulliken's jobs book and started reading it, and he sat beside her with his hand on her shoulder watching television. After about ten minutes, though, he turned around and peered out of the window.

'Look – it's only soft rain now, if it's raining at all. Maybe I'll take the dogs for a scove.'

'You won't be long, will you? I have to go back at six at the latest.'

'No, no, I won't be long. I need to get myself some fresh air, that's all, after being cooped up in that hospital. I need to have a think, too.'

'A think? What about?'

'I don't know. Everything. You, and me. My dog detective business. Everything.'

'Con, I still love you. I'm not going to leave you dangling.'

Conor let out a sharp, sardonic laugh. 'That's a grand promise to make to a man with no balls!'

'Con—'

He leaned forward and kissed her. 'Don't worry about me, darling. I'm bound to be kind of bitter from time to time. You know yourself what life can take away from you when you least expect it. Your looks, and then your friends, and then the ones you love. If life was a person, it'd be a thief.'

Darragh Ó Dálaigh wasn't hard to track down. Detective Walsh found a clear picture of him on the NAS website, from the time last summer when he had been awarded an HSE certificate of excellence. Once she knew what he looked like, she went down to the Southside ambulance station, pretending she was delivering a parcel from Amazon that he had ordered. Another paramedic told her that he had finished his shift about an hour earlier, but that he almost always stopped for a scoop or two at Flannery's Bar before he went home to his sister's house by the Lough. If he wasn't there, she might be able to find him in The Harp.

She came across him in Flannery's, a shabby-looking pub on the Glasheen Road painted raspberry pink. He was sitting on a stool at the end of the bar with a half-finished pint of Murphy's in front of him. The pub was gloomy and almost empty, but there was music playing and Darragh was snorting with laughter at something the barman had just told him.

Detective Walsh sat up at the bar about three stools away from him and asked for a Woody's pink grapefruit.

'You're over eighteen are you, love?' the barman asked her. She rolled up her eyes, took out her driving licence and held it up in front of his nose.

'I'll have a couple of chunks of ice in that, too, and two straws,' she told him.

She took two or three sips of her drink before she turned to Darragh and said, 'I reck you, don't I?'

'I dunno, girl. Do you? Where would that be from, then?'

'You're an ambulance driver, isn't that right?'

'I am.'

'You came out when my grandpa had a heart attack last year. You only saved his life, like. I never had the chance to thank you, you and your partner. You were brilliant. He's passed now but he would have passed a lot sooner if it hadn't been for you.'

'Where was that, then?'

'Outside the Spar shop at Ballyphehane. I don't suppose you remember, the number of the times you must get called out. I bet you can't tell one auld wan with a dicky heart from the next.'

'No... I'm fair sure that I remember. Give me a minute so and it'll come back to me.'

'Come here – I have to buy you a drink, like. You more than deserve it. It's a pity your partner isn't here, too, she was amazing doing all that PRC.'

'CPR.'

'Yes, that too. Listen, what's your name? Mine's Cailin. Barman, do you want to pour this good fellow a pint of whatever he's drinking?'

Detective Walsh bought Darragh a pint of Murphy's and then they sat down together at one of the tables at the back of the bar. Darragh told her his name and how long he'd been working for the National Ambulance Service and how he'd been engaged once but his fiancée had broken it off the week before the wedding.

'After that I never found anyone else I wanted to spend the rest of my life with, like.'

'What about your partner?'

'Brianna? Oh, she's good-looking enough, and we get along all right. At least we did at first, but a few months ago she started to have personal problems. These days she spends a lot of time all wrapped up in a world of her own. When she does talk to me, she's kind of sarcastic, which she never used to be.'

'That's a shame. What sort of problems does she have? Do you know?'

'I don't like to be too nosy, like, but I'm fair sure that it's money. She has a boyfriend who's a bit of a gambler and from what she's told me I've put two and two together. It sounds like he's got himself into the height of loberty.'

Cailin nodded understandingly. 'I remember my da lost his job once, and the stress it put on him, it was unbelievable. While he was still in work, he was the sweetest fellow you could ever meet, but as soon as he was unemployed and he started running out of money, you couldn't go near him, he was that moody. I've no proof of it, but I think he was stealing stuff, too, just to make ends meet.'

'How about a refill?' said Darragh, pointing to her empty glass.

'No, let me get this,' said Cailin. 'It's the least I can do to repay you. You gave my grandpa seven more months of life and you can't put a price on that.'

They had another drink and carried on talking. Cailin left the subject of Brianna alone for a while, and concentrated on Darragh himself, and whether he was happy. He confessed that he was lonely at times, especially in the evenings, and that he was worried that he was growing too old to find a wife.

'I'm only forty-seven, like, but every time I meet a girl I like the look of, she's already wed, or living with somebody, and I don't fancy them online dating services – that Kindling or whatever you call it. Christ knows what kind of a munter you're going to end up with.'

He confessed, too, that he was often traumatized by the accidents that he and Brianna had to attend.

'You always have to be totally calm and professional, because that's your job and that's what you're trained to do and people like your grandpa are depending on you to save their lives. But when you see some toddler who's been smashed into a pulp in a car seat, or some farmhand who's got his arm all tangled up in a combine harvester, or a young woman who's been floating around in Tivoli Harbour for a week – all green and blown up twice the size like a fecking dolphin. Well – it's not easy to get pictures like that out of your mind. Here – sorry – I don't mean to give you the gawks.'

'No, not at all, Darragh,' said Cailin. 'How about Brianna? Does she cope with the accidents any better, or does she get upset the same as you?'

'I reckon she's tougher, to tell you the truth. A whole lot tougher. I think women generally are, do you know what I mean? Like they have to deal with the monthlies and having babies and all that kind of malarkey. Some of the things that would make men pass out – well, women just take them in their stride. It's good that they do, because we've been having a fierce bad run of fatalities lately, me and Brianna – you know, quite a few of the people we've been picking up have been giving up the ghost before we could manage to get them to hospital. Many more than normal. I told her the other day that I've been feeling more like I'm driving a fecking funeral car than an ambulance.'

'Really? How many deaths altogether?'

'Seven since the beginning of December. And that's just us. Me and Bree.'

'Seven. Wow.' Cailin didn't tell Darragh that she already knew the statistics for fatal accidents in Cork for the past six months. They had been unusually high, but up until now she hadn't been able to tell how many of those accident victims had died in ambulances on the way to the Mercy or CUH, or how that figure was broken down between individual rigs.

'Sure like, they all died of natural causes,' said Darragh. 'But it's like the lotto, I suppose. Some people's numbers come up, week after week. Other people never get nothing.'

'What does Brianna think about it? I mean, she was trying to save their lives, those seven people. She must feel desperate.'

'She hasn't been saying too much these past couple of months, to be honest with you. I think it's like I said, and women are tougher. They can give *birth* to life, so maybe they're more philumosophical about the *end* of life. One door opens and another door closes, like.'

'Let me get you another,' said Cailin.

'Holy Saint Patrick, I'm going to be wrecked at this rate. But all right, then, sure, why not? It'd be rude to refuse a pretty young woman such as yourself.'

'Now then, Darragh,' smiled Cailin. 'I have a boyfriend already. He's going to be fierce jealous if he knows that I've been spending the afternoon drinking with a handsome paramedic.'

Forty-Two

By ten forty-five that evening, Operation Labre was all set to go. Eight squad cars, three large vans and four unmarked SUVs had been lined up along Anglesea Street and now they all started up and drove off towards their prearranged pick-up points in the city centre. A strong wind had risen and the rain was blowing across the streets in curtains.

Katie sat in the front passenger seat of a silver Toyota Land Cruiser with Detective O'Donovan driving. Detective Inspector Fitzpatrick, Detective Sergeant Kyna Ni Nuallán and Detective Cullen sat in the back. Katie was wearing her black raincoat with the pointy hood, but underneath she had strapped on her ballistic vest. They all knew that this was going to be a highly unpredictable night.

'I'm praying to the Lord that none of the rough sleepers gets hurt tonight,' said Katie. 'Otherwise we're going to be all over the front pages in the morning and for all the wrong reasons. You know how quick the media can turn you from a hero into a villain.'

They drove along South Mall in a convoy with two squad cars in front of them and a large van bringing up the rear. Once they had picked up the rough sleepers, another van would follow to bag up and take away their belongings. Katie had been anxious to avoid any delay or dithering or arguing about their possessions on the street, or to give them the chance to go for any knives or other weapons they might have hidden among their bedding.

Only two weeks ago they had arrested a rough sleeper and found a plastic bottle of battery acid folded into his blanket – 'in case any scummer tries to hobble my hard-earned grade.'

Katie turned around and saw a second convoy turning up Oliver Plunkett Street, where three homeless men had been seen sleeping rough outside the post office. Her own convoy continued along Grand Parade and then turned into Paul Street. For the first hundred metres Paul Street was only wide enough for single-file traffic, but then it opened out into a red-brick plaza in front of the Tesco superstore. During the afternoon, a Garda patrol had noted at least five rough sleepers in the doorways around the plaza, both men and women. Not only could they find shelter here, but Tesco was open until ten p.m., which meant there was always a chance of being given extra change by late-night shoppers.

The two squad cars stopped a few metres short of the plaza, so that the rough sleepers wouldn't be able to see them arrive. Detective O'Donovan steered Katie's SUV into Saints Peter and Paul Place and parked in front of them. The large van drew up and blocked the road behind them. The instant the squad cars came to a standstill, their doors were flung open, and the van doors, too, and eleven uniformed officers scrambled out. They ran around the corner into the plaza and headed for the rough sleepers, who were huddled in the corner under blue plastic sheeting and makeshift tents. Katie jumped down from the SUV, tugged up the hood of her raincoat and followed them.

There were seven rough sleepers altogether – four men, a middle-aged woman and two young girls. The officers dragged the plastic sheeting off them, and hauled them to their feet in the rain. They looked bewildered rather than angry, and Katie could tell that three of the men and the middle-aged woman were drunk, and that the two young girls were almost certainly stoned.

Only one of the men seemed to be sober, although he kept lurching to one side and it took two gardaí to hold his arms to stop him from falling over.

'What in the name of feck are you doing?' he demanded. 'I've done nothing at all wrong, for feck's sake. I'm only trying to get myself a decent night's sleep, for the love of Christ.'

The lurching man had straw-like shoulder-length hair like a scarecrow and he was wearing a filthy beige tracksuit with a wide wet stain between his legs. In spite of his dishevelled appearance and a rather large nose, Katie saw that he was actually quite good-looking and probably ten years younger than he seemed.

She went up to him and said, as gently as she could, 'You're not in any trouble, sir, and you're not under arrest. We've come to offer you shelter out of the rain, and a decent meal.'

The man blinked at her uncomprehendingly, as if he suspected that she could be some ghostly apparition – a sister of the Dulla-han, perhaps, the headless horseman who rode around Ireland to round up the dying and the dead, whipping them into line with a human spine.

'*Shelter?*' he spat. 'What kind of a shelter? Where? What? And what about our things? I have a hang sangridge and a napple there all ready for my breakfast, so I do.'

'Don't worry, we'll collect all your belongings and fetch them along after you. If you want to know, we're taking you to St Dunstan's church hall in Mayfield. There's beds waiting for you and a change of clothes and medicine too if you have need of it.'

The other three men and the middle-aged woman and the two young girls were already allowing themselves to be ushered around the corner by the uniformed gardaí and into the waiting van. Two of the gardaí were picking up their clothes and their bedding and stuffing them into large see-through polythene bags.

But the lurching man twisted himself away from the officers who were holding him upright, and shouted, 'No! I'm not fecking going fecking nowhere! I *can't*! I'll be fecking cremated if I do! Leave me alone, would you? Leave me alone!'

Katie reached out and gripped his hand. He staggered back and collided with the wall behind him, but she took hold of his elbow as well to steady him, and to stop him from sliding down to the pavement.

'Listen – you don't have to be scared,' she told him. 'We won't let anybody hurt you, I promise! That's another reason we've come to take you to St Dunstan's, to take you out of harm's way.'

The lurching man stared at her. His chest was rising and falling and his wild hair was sparkling with raindrops. He licked his lips, and tried to speak, but he couldn't.

'I mean it,' said Katie. 'We know that you have to give up some of your money every day, and we know that you have to do it under threat of being beaten, or worse. But I swear to you on my life that we're not going to let that happen to you. From now on, you're going to be safe.'

She paused for a few moments, and then she said, 'Tell me your name.'

The lurching man closed his eyes, and staggered again. Then, without opening his eyes, he yanked his hand free from Katie's, reached into his sleeve and pulled out a long kitchen knife.

'Watch out!' shouted the garda who was standing close behind Katie's left shoulder.

The lurching man slashed wildly at Katie's face and the tip of the knife slit her left cheek, only about three centimetres below her eye. Katie ducked down to the right and snatched his wrist with both hands, bending it back so hard that his tendons crackled and at least two of his bones were dislocated. He let out a strange honking roar, more like a sea lion than a man, and dropped the knife with a clatter on to the ground.

'You fecking *witch*!' he screamed at her. 'You've busted my fecking wrist, you fecking witch!'

'Take him in, would you?' said Katie to the two gardaí. They roughly seized his arms and hauled him out of his doorway, but Katie added, 'Now, then – go easy on him, lads. Go easy. We came here to make his life better, not worse.' Then, to the lurching man, 'You still didn't tell me your name, sir.'

'Go feck yourself, you witch.'

'Well, whatever. But we'll see that your wrist gets treated. And we'll also make sure that nobody else gets to hurt you.'

'Why the feck should I be scared of some fecking Romanian when you've just busted my fecking wrist, you fecking witch!'

Kyna came back around the corner. She had been helping the middle-aged woman and the two young girls to climb up into the van, since the middle-aged woman was so wrecked she could hardly stand and the two young girls had kept stumbling and collapsing into helpless giggles every time they tried to mount the steps.

'Katie, oh Jesus, you're bleeding.'

Katie dabbed her cheek with her fingertips, and they came away slippery with blood. 'No. It's only a scratch. Don't worry about it.'

Kyna took a folded handkerchief out of her jacket pocket and gently patted Katie's cut. 'It's not too deep, thank God. But we should put some antiseptic on it. You don't know what else that knife could have been used for.'

'I'm more worried about what I've done to him. There I was saying that I didn't want any rough sleepers hurt and the first thing I do is snap the stupid gowl's wrist.'

'He attacked you, Katie. And he called you a witch. I heard him.'

Katie couldn't help giving her a wry smile. 'That's the second time today.'

'Serious? Who else called you that?'

'Never mind. Your man said something else much more important. He said, "Why should I be scared of some expletive-deleted Romanian?"'

'Really? "Romanian"?'

Katie dabbed her face again and nodded. 'So what does that tell us? He's not Romanian himself but he could be one of Lupul's ring of beggars. We've seen it before, haven't we, ringmasters threatening the homeless if they don't hand over a proportion of the money they've made begging. And maybe he's still scared of Lupul because he doesn't yet know that Lupul could have been burned to death. Or maybe he knows for sure that he *isn't* dead.'

Kyna laid a hand on her shoulder and Katie could see in her eyes how much she wanted to hug her, and kiss her cut better. She was shivering slightly from the cold and the shock and she would have done anything to feel Kyna holding her close.

But, 'Come on,' she said. 'Let's hear how the other two squads have been getting along.'

All five squads in Operation Labre arrived within five minutes of each other at St Dunstan's church hall. It was on Knight's Hill on the Old Youghal Road, opposite Keohane's Funeral Home and next to the Top petrol station. The rough sleepers that they had picked up from the city centre were all hurried inside, with umbrellas held over their heads to shield them from the relentlessly hammering rain.

Inside, a team of eleven Garda volunteers and the caretaker from St Dunstan's church had done everything they could to make the hall warm and welcoming. They had turned up the central heating, and divided the main body of the hall into twenty cubicles with blue fence tarpaulins, the sort that were usually used to screen off building sites. In each cubicle they had laid down a single mattress on the floor with a pillow and blankets. On top of each pillow they had left a folded bath towel, as well as a washbag with soap and toothpaste and a toothbrush and a razor. They had set up a wooden box beside each mattress for the homeless sleepers to store their belongings, with a lamp on top of it, and a packet of Kimberley ginger biscuits.

On the raised stage at the far end of the hall they had erected a trestle table with chairs all around it, where the homeless would be served a hot meal. Katie could already smell mutton stew from the kitchen at the back of the hall.

She had stuck a plaster on to her cheek from the first-aid box in the leading squad car. Now she took off her raincoat so that she wouldn't look so witch-like, and was standing by the doorway with Kyna to welcome the homeless as they straggled and shuffled into the hall. Most of them looked around as if they thought they were dreaming. The Garda volunteers guided each one of them individually to one of the cubicles that they had set up, and also showed them where the toilets were, and where they could wash.

A young woman came creeping up to Katie and Kyna, swaddled in a damp maroon blanket tied around with string. Her face was deathly white and she had smudges of dirt on her cheeks. Katie could see by the needle-marks in the veins on the backs of her hands that she was probably a heroin addict. She had tears clinging to her eyelashes and when she spoke she could barely manage more than a whisper.

'Thanks a million million,' she said. 'I didn't think a single soul cared for me any more. I couldn't even work out if I was asleep or awake most of the time. There didn't seem to be no difference between them at all. I thought I might even be dead without knowing it.'

One of the Garda volunteers came up to them, a stolid woman with a russet-red bun and a motherly smile. She put her arm around the girl's shoulders and led her gently to the cubicle where she could sleep.

Detective Inspector Fitzpatrick appeared through the main doorway behind the last of the homeless, an elderly man wearing a green overcoat that was far too large for him, and which dragged along the floor. The elderly man walked with a peculiar hop, which told Katie that he needed a hip replacement.

'This is pure amazing,' said Detective Inspector Fitzpatrick. 'It's almost enough to make me believe that I'm in the wrong job.'

Katie glanced at Kyna and raised her eyebrows, but said nothing. Detective Inspector Fitzpatrick usually seemed to be emotionless. His eyes were like two steel nail-heads and never gave anything away, but once or twice he had let out a comment that made Katie realize that – deep down – he was a man with some very turbulent feelings. He didn't want any of his colleagues to know it, that was all.

'I know what you mean, sir,' said Kyna. 'But I'd say it takes a very special kind of person to help these poor wretches long-term. You'd need to be a saint, wouldn't you, and I know it's not their fault, but you'd have to have a very poor sense of smell.'

Detectives O'Donovan and Cullen emerged from behind the tarpaulin screens.

'That's nineteen rough sleepers we have altogether,' said Detective O'Donovan. 'Three refused to come no matter what, and we've sent your man with the broken wrist to the Mercy.'

'So now we simply let them settle down, feed their faces, and get themselves a good night's sleep?' said Detective Inspector Fitzpatrick.

'That's right,' Katie told him. 'Superintendent Pearse has assigned six officers to be on rotation all night, in case of any trouble, plus four volunteers. As you know, I've arranged for a doctor and a nurse to come around early tomorrow morning and give all the rough sleepers a quick check-up. If any of them have any critical medical problems they can be dealt with, within reason, and the doctor can prescribe methadone or buprenorphine to help any drug addicts. As I said before, we'll be allowing the alcoholics among them a limited amount of drink, provided they don't become abusive or violent. The whole point of Operation Labre is to win their confidence and get information out of them, not to rehabilitate them.'

Katie stayed at St Dunstan's hall for another two hours, introducing herself to the rough sleepers one after another and making sure they were settled. Their belongings all arrived, and the bags were set down by the main doorway so that they could pick out their own. The two dog owners were shown pictures of their dogs in the Garda kennels, and reassured that they would be well taken care of, and given any veterinary treatment if they needed it, like worming or injections.

By one-thirty in the morning, after the hungry had been fed, and everybody had visited the toilet and washed, the lights were lowered, and the hall fell quiet, except for snoring and the mumbling of one man who was endlessly repeating 'The Old Men Admiring Themselves in the Water' by W.B. Yeats, over and over again.

Katie stood with Kyna by the door, ready to leave.

'How's Conor?' asked Kyna. 'He's back home now, is he?'

Katie gave her a non-committal shrug. 'Yes, and he's mending all right. But being beaten up like that, it did a lot to dent his self-confidence. And, well—'

She was tempted to tell Kyna that Conor was now having to face up to being celibate, and so was she, but she was interrupted by one of the sleepers who had heard 'The Old Men Admiring Themselves in the Water' more times than he could tolerate.

'Jesus, Mary and Joseph and all the disciples, will you shut your bake about them old men with their fecking thorny knees! I'm trying to get some fecking shut-eye here!'

When she arrived home at Carrig View, Conor was deeply asleep and she knew that he was on painkillers so she didn't try to disturb him. Only Barney was awake and he sat up in his basket in the kitchen when she came in to pour herself a glass of water. They looked at each other, Katie and Barney, and Katie was sure that she could see sympathy in Barney's eyes, if not understanding, and this was one time when she really wished that dogs could talk.

Forty-Three

The first person Katie called into her office the next morning was Detective Cailin Walsh. She came in wearing a red tartan tweed suit with a very short skirt, thick brown tights and brown leather boots. Katie thought she looked more like a young Sinéad O'Connor than ever.

'So – how did it go with your ambulance driver?' she asked her.

'Fan-*tas*-tic! We got along together like a house on fire. Sorry – that wasn't exactly the most tasteful way of putting it, was it?'

'Not to worry, Cailin. Did you manage to get much out of him about Brianna Cusack?'

'I did, yes. Almost *too* much. About the only thing he didn't tell me about her was her bra size. Brianna's not been herself lately, that's what Darragh told me. It seems like her boyfriend's a gambling addict and they're sore strapped for cash. She used to be chatting all the time but now she barely speaks to him at all.'

'Anything else?'

'You're not joking. He and Brianna have lost seven of the patients that they've been sent to pick up, and that's only since the start of the year.'

'*Seven?* Mother of God.'

'Well, right. That's what I thought. And according to Darragh that's more than they lost in the whole of the past eighteen months. And on top of that it's more than all the rest of the Southside ambulance crews have lost this year put together.'

'When you say they've lost them – you mean they passed away

in between the time Darragh and Brianna picked them up and the time they arrived at the emergency room?'

'That's it, yes, exactly. And of course it's during that time that they were in Brianna's care and nobody else's.'

'Have the ambulance service themselves not looked into it?'

'Darragh says all seven died of natural causes, so there's been no need for the coroner to take it any further.'

Katie sat back in her chair and frowned. 'So what in the name of God is going on here, do you think? Brianna's our most obvious suspect in the murder of Saoirse Duffy, so if she's capable of murdering one patient, perhaps it's conceivable that she did for all those other patients, too – or some of them, anyway. But then – if the coroner's satisfied that they all died a natural death – maybe she didn't. Maybe it's just bad luck.'

'Seven dead in less than six weeks? That's not just bad luck, ma'am, that's *desperate* bad luck. That's the kind of luck I have with scratch cards.'

'Yes, but what would her motive be, always supposing she's not just a homicidal psychopath? Your new friend Darragh's told you she's broke, so lack of money could be a motive – but how do you make money out of accident victims dying in your ambulance? You can't set up some sort of life insurance scam because you've no way of knowing who they're going to be, have you, before you're called out to pick them up. They're probably unconscious or in pain, so it's not likely that you can persuade them to ring up their solicitors to change their wills. I suppose you could threaten them with not reviving them unless they hand over their bank account details, and then *not* revive them. But even at the best of times I can't remember my bank account details off the top of my head – let alone if I had to do it after I was run over by a bus or had a heart attack or I'd been drowning in the Lee.'

'Couldn't we track her ambulance for a week or so, every time she gets called out? Then we could assess the victims she picks up, to see how seriously they'd been injured, and what the odds are on them dying before they make it to the emergency room.'

'That's not such a bad idea in principle, Cailin, but how are we going to carry out examinations like that without her noticing, and without her realizing that she's being followed wherever she goes? And how are we going to know what she's doing inside her ambulance on its way to hospital? Even if her patients haven't been dying of natural causes, maybe Brianna can make it *appear* as if they did. She's an advanced paramedic, after all.'

At that moment, Detective Inspector Mulliken and Detective Sergeant Ni Nuallán knocked at Katie's door, and Katie beckoned them in.

Kyna tapped her own cheek in the same spot as Katie's plaster, and said, 'How's the walking wounded?'

'I'm grand altogether, thanks, Kyna. It's almost healed up already. I might end up with a twinchy scar there, but I reckon that'll only make me look tougher, like, do you know what I mean?'

She turned to Detective Walsh. 'Cailin – tell DI Mulliken and DS Ni Nuallán everything that Darragh the ambulance driver told you. Maybe they can come up with some ideas.'

Detective Inspector Mulliken and Kyna listened while Detective Walsh recounted the conversation that she and Darragh had shared in Flannery's. Then Detective Inspector Mulliken said, 'You're right, of course, ma'am. There's no way that we could examine this Brianna's patients before she took them off to hospital, not without her being aware of it, and then of course she'd only make sure that they were still alive and kicking when they got there.'

'That's right,' said Katie. 'Darragh's busy driving, so apart from Brianna herself, there's only one person who can tell us what goes on inside that ambulance, and that's her patient. But… what if her patient wasn't really sick or injured or unconscious, but was only putting it on?'

'What do you mean?'

'I mean what if the "patient" was really one of us?'

'You took the words right out of my mouth there, ma'am,' said Kyna. '*I* could be a patient, couldn't I? I could easy make it look like I'd had an accident – maybe fainted and fallen down the escalator in Merchants Quay shopping centre or something like that. I was always good at drama when I was at school. I won a prize for when I played Estragon in *Waiting for Godot*. "Nothing happens, nobody comes, nobody goes, it's awful!"'

Katie said, 'It could be fierce risky, Kyna. We don't know the full details of how the other seven patients died, but Saoirse Duffy was injected with a lethal overdose of fentanyl, wasn't she? The same could happen to you before you had the chance to say ouch.'

'Ah, but Saoirse Duffy wasn't awake and alert, was she? She was heavily sedated and I don't suppose for a moment that she was trained in Wing Chun like me.'

'Oh yes, the Wing Chun,' said Katie, and couldn't help smiling. 'I don't think I'll ever forget you knocking out that gobdaw who grabbed that waitress's bottom in O'Brien's sandwich bar. For starters, though, we'll need the Chief Ambulance Officer to know what we're up to, so that we can be sure that it's Darragh and Brianna they dispatch to pick you up, and not some other crew. What do you think, Tony?'

'That shouldn't be too much of a problem, ma'am. He's the Area Operations Manager as well as the Chief Ambulance Officer and I'm sure I can cook up some story so that he'll co-operate. Leave it to me so.'

'Do you know when Darragh and Brianna are next on duty?' Katie asked Detective Walsh.

'Darragh said they have two evening shifts coming up – one tonight and one tomorrow night – six till two in the morning – then they have the weekend off.'

'In that case we could go for it tonight. Merchants Quay closes at six. But Brown Thomas is open till seven and you could make out that you've tripped on their escalator.'

'This Brianna's bound to check your vital signs, though, isn't she?' said Detective Inspector Mulliken. 'Wouldn't she be suspicious if they're normal?'

'That's one thing about Wing Chun,' Kyna told him. 'They teach you to slow your heart rate right down. You may look like you're dancing the fandango, but all the time your heart's beating slow so that you're calm and calculating and you know exactly where you're going to hit your opponent next, so as you can make the maximum impact.'

'Okay, grand, let's go for it, then,' said Katie. 'Tony – if you can fix things up with the ambulance chief and then have a word with the manager at Brown Thomas to explain what we're planning, we'll meet back here at seventeen hundred.'

When Detective Inspector Mulliken and Detective Walsh had left, Katie went up to Kyna and took hold of both of her hands.

'You don't have to do this, you know. It's possible that this Brianna's innocent, and totally harmless, but my gut feeling about her is that she's pure dangerous, and clever with it.'

'Don't worry. I'll be fine. You know that I can take care of myself.'

Katie looked over her shoulder to make sure that Moirin's door was closed, and then kissed Kyna on the lips.

'There's something wrong, isn't there?' said Kyna. 'Is it something between you and Conor?'

'Nothing that the future won't sort out.'

'You know what the Dalai Lama said. "There's only two days in the year when nothing can be done, yesterday and tomorrow."'

'The Dalai Lama doesn't have a dog detective from Limerick for a lover.'

At noon, just as Katie was buttoning up her coat to go out, Bill Phinner rang her.

'Nothing much to report, ma'am, I'm sorry to tell you. We found nothing on those jerrycans that were dumped in the back garden at Alexandra Road. No fingerprints, no DNA. They were bought from Halfords at Mahon Retail Park on Tuesday morning. The barcodes told us that. Nobody else bought jerry cans that morning, but whoever bought them paid cash. There's some footprints but the grass was too overgrown and weedy for them to be of any use for identification purposes, and so far we've come across no other forensics in the house itself.'

'I see, Bill. How's it going with the notebook?'

'Very, very slow, as expected, but coming along. It's incredibly delicate work, separating the pages. But I'm confident that we can make most of them readable.'

'Okay. Thanks a million. We're on our way up to Mayfield in a minute to talk to our twenty rough sleepers so maybe we can cajole some incriminating evidence out of them.'

'Good luck with that, ma'am. Have you heard from immigration yet on who those three fire victims might have been?'

'No. I'm still waiting. It's likely that they were all members of Lupul's begging ring, and one of them could be Lupul himself, but immigration warned me that they could be difficult to trace. They could all have arrived in Ireland on different days from different countries and at different ports of entry. One into Rosslare, for instance, and one into Shannon, and the third into Ringaskiddy. And of course their passports could have been forged, or stolen, which makes it a hundred times harder to find out who they are and where they've come from.'

Once she had finished talking to Bill Phinner, Katie went down to reception to meet up with Detective Inspector Fitzpatrick and Kyna and Detective O'Donovan. Murtagh the balding translator was there, too, in a baggy green waxed jacket, breathing on his glasses to clean them and holding them up to the light. They went out to the car park together, climbed into an unmarked Land Cruiser and drove up to Mayfield. It started to rain again, but only a sprinkle.

The rough sleepers had all been fed a fry-up for their breakfast, with bacon and eggs and black pudding, and given a change of clothes if they wanted it. A flat-screen TV had been set up for them at the far end of the hall and some of them were sitting on the floor watching *Doctors*. Others had returned to their cubicles to sleep, while a GP and a nurse from the Knight's Hill medical centre were going around from one cubicle to the next, examining any who felt ill, and handing out methadone for any with a heroin habit or lorazepam for those addicted to spice.

The lurching man was there, too, sitting cross-legged on his mattress with his right arm in a sling. As Katie passed by his cubicle, he scowled at her and mouthed the word 'witch'.

Katie stopped, and went into his cubicle. Detective O'Donovan stood and waited for her, in case he turned aggressive again.

'Come here, I'm sorry I hurt you,' said Katie. 'You can scarce blame me, though, can you, the way you pulled that knife on me?'

'You could have left me alone, couldn't you? Why didn't you leave me be? I was okay back at Paul Street. I don't even know why you've fetched me here.'

'Why do you think we fetched you here? We want to help you to turn your life around.'

'You're codding, aren't you? How can I turn my life around if I'm going to be clattered to a fecking pulp, or cremated?'

'Nobody's going to hurt you. We'll see to that.'

'I don't give a shite what you say, if I'm not back down by Tesco to give them their share of the fecking money I've begged, which I won't be, they fecking *will* hurt me, and don't you have the slightest doubt about that.'

'No, they won't, because we're going to go after them and haul them in and make sure that they're convicted and locked up.'

'Oh, right! Like, how come you've never done it before now? All you've ever done before is move us on, or do us for obstruction.'

'That's because we had very limited resources and beggars weren't being killed before now, not like they have been recently. Rough sleeping isn't illegal but organized begging is and so is murder.'

Katie waited for this to sink in. She noticed that the man was grinding his teeth and that his left hand was trembling.

'Do you want a drink?' she asked him.

He looked up at her. She could see now that his eyes were

yellow with jaundice. He said nothing but Katie turned around to Detective O'Donovan.

'Patrick, there's some baby Powers in the kitchen. Could you fetch me a couple? In fact, make it three.'

Detective O'Donovan went off and Katie turned back to the lurching man. 'Are you going to tell me your name? I'll have to write a report about breaking your wrist, and I don't want to admit that I didn't even know who you were. You could be entitled to some compo, too, but we can't pay compo to Mr Anonymous.'

'Phelan,' he said, grudgingly. 'Phelan O'Meara. Of no fixed abode, as if you didn't know.'

Katie knelt down on the floor beside his mattress. 'And how long have you been homeless, Phelan?'

Phelan closed his eyes and counted on his fingers. 'Three years now. Three-and-a-half, to be precise.'

'So how did you become homeless?'

Detective O'Donovan returned with three miniature bottles of Powers whiskey. Katie screwed the top off one of them and handed it to Phelan. He lifted it up, said, '*Sláinte*', and downed it in three noisy gulps. When it was empty he licked the neck of it and shivered and wiped his mouth with the back of his hand. Katie could see that his eyes were already fixed on the second bottle, which she was holding up in front of him but keeping tightly clenched in her fist so that only the stopper was showing. They both knew perfectly well that a deal was being negotiated here, whiskey in exchange for information.

'I was working in the Honda garage at Victoria Cross. Mechanic. I lent a borrow of a customer's car one Sunday and drove it down to Kinsale with two pals.'

'Go on,' said Katie, making it clear that she wasn't yet ready to give him the second baby Powers.

'We got langered, didn't we? Wrecked. Totally buckled. On the way back to Cork I knocked an auld wan off his bike and came close to killing him. That was the end of my job and the end of my marriage and the end of everything.'

Forty-Four

Katie screwed the top off the second bottle and gave it to him. This time he drank it more slowly, swilling it around his mouth and breathing in deeply while he did so, so that he could smell it as well as taste it.

'Tell me about this Romanian.'

He shook his head. 'I can't. I told you before. He'll fecking cremate me alive.'

'We're here to protect you, Phelan. But we can't protect you unless you help us to protect you. If you can tell me how to find him, I can make sure that he never threatens you again – ever. He's Romanian, so we can have him deported back to Romania, and never allowed back into Ireland again.'

'He has five gowls that work for him, and they're going to be looking for me now. He'll be fecking raging when he finds out that I'm not outside of Tesco. He wants his grade every morning five o'clock sharp.'

'How much do you have to give him?'

'Half. He takes it from every rough sleeper in the city centre, every fecking day. And it's no good trying to give him less because those gowls that work for him, they'll strip you bollock naked and throw your stuff all over the shop if they think you're hiding any. One young feen tucked a johnny full of rolled-up twenty-yoyo notes up his arse hoping that they wouldn't find it, but they did, and after they pulled it out with a pair of pliers they shoved an empty Tanora bottle up there, for a punishment, like.'

'These fellows who work for him, are they Romanian, too?'

Phelan sipped more whiskey, and nodded.

'Are you going to tell me his name?'

'I can't, I've told you. He'll fecking kill me. And if *he* doesn't kill me, then the other ones will.'

'What "other ones"?'

Phelan dropped his voice so low that Katie could hardly hear him.

'Them other Romanians. They only showed up last week, like, but ever since they did, there's three of us lot have snuffed it. Don't nobody try to spoof me that they froze to death or OD'd or died of old age, because three of *them* lot took over their pitches, almost as soon as they were carted away.'

'Stall it a moment. The Romanian you have to give your money to – isn't that Dragomir Iliescu? Dragos? The fellow they call Lupul?'

'Loophole? I never heard of nobody called Loophole.'

'So what's the name of *your* Romanian?'

'What, do you think I'm thick as a ditch, do you? If I rat him out, that's my one-way ticket to St Catherine's cemetery, and no fecking two ways about it. You shades couldn't protect me twenty-four hours a day, could you, and any road I wouldn't want a razzer in the shitter with me.'

'All right, but what do you know about these other Romanians? How many do you think there are?'

Phelan said, 'Ssh! Be whist, would you? There's at least seven or eight of the feckers in here and they're not all bombed out of their brains even if they act like it. Why do you think I'm not telling you nothing? Not that I *know* nothing – not about *them*, any road.'

'Fair play to you, Phelan, if that's the way you want it,' said Katie, and stood up.

Her mind was racing. Phelan might have refused to give her any names, but he had told her something of critical importance, even if he had done it unwittingly. She couldn't believe that she hadn't found out about it before today, and neither had any of the gardaí on street patrols. It made her feel both unprofessional and uncaring, as if the Garda hadn't considered that it was worth paying attention to the homeless except when they obstructed doorways or left rubbish strewn in the streets.

Even though she had no witnesses or incriminating evidence, Lupul had to be her number one suspect for the drilling murders. He had turned up in Cork with his ring of Romanian beggars and he had set to work almost at once to commandeer all the most profitable locations, like the Savoy Centre and Cook Street and the doorway in front of Moderne. But what Katie hadn't known was that almost all of the existing beggars were already being forced by another Romanian ringmaster to hand over half of the money that they collected every day. This was before Lupul had even arrived, and *this* ringmaster clearly resented Lupul's bid to take over the streets.

Of course she was aware that the homeless were desperately vulnerable. Some of them were beaten up by drunks or randomly robbed by drug addicts and by other beggars while they slept in shop doorways, stupefied by alcohol or spice. Up until now, though, she hadn't picked up even a whisper that they were being systematically fleeced by an organized Romanian ring, and this could have been going on for months, if not years. Katie guessed that if this ringmaster was taking only half of their donations, he had obviously worked out how much they needed to feed them- selves and pay for any drink or drugs, and this must have helped to keep them quiet. What she found grimly impressive was how he had managed to keep them all so silent for so long. Even a hardened beggar like Phelan was terrified of being beaten or killed if he refused to hand over his share, or if he complained to the Garda that he was being threatened, so what chance did a harm- less alcoholic like Gearoid stand, or a sick crack addict like Matty?

'Well – did you catch that?' Katie asked Detective O'Donovan, as they continued to make their way between the screens.

'Most of it, yes. Un-fecking-believable.'

'How in the name of all that's holy did we not *know*, Patrick?'

'Don't ask me. But you have to be realistic, like, don't you? If people are too jibber to tell us then we're *not* going to know, are we?'

'But it's our job to know. It's *my* job to know. Mother of God.'

'Come on, ma'am, this isn't the first time and it won't be the last. What about all those young Somali girls we found last week in that brothel on Grafton Street? They'd been here for nigh on six months, hadn't they, but if Ronan hadn't earwigged that fellow boasting about them in The Ovens Bar, we'd never have known about them.'

'Oh, great. That makes me feel no better at all, I'm sorry to say. But how about this Romanian ringmaster who's been fleecing these poor beggars all this time – the one that Phelan's too frightened to put a name to. Are you thinking who I'm thinking?'

'I'd say so. It's almost sure to be the Fat Fellow, isn't it? I mean, who else?'

'Ştefan Făt-Frumor? Absolutely. That was the first name that came to my mind, too. But you were so sure, weren't you, that he was winding down most of his rackets here in Cork and moving above to Dublin?'

'I was, yes. I have to put my hands up to that. What a cute hoor, he totally convinced me. But I can't think of any other Romanian who's scary enough to make so many people keep their bake shut for so long. There's that Florin Cojoc fellow in Gurra – the one we lifted for selling monkey dust. He's pure violent, but only because he's off his head most of the time. He couldn't organize a ring on a doorbell, leave alone a begging ring.'

'I agree with you, Patrick,' said Katie. 'Unless it's some Romanian we've never heard of, it's almost sure to be Ştefan Făt-Frumor. And if those rough sleepers who were drilled to death were all making money for him, that would have given him more than enough of a motive for burning down Lupul's house in Alexandra Road, wouldn't you think? On top of which, there was your barman from The Parting Glass, what was his name?'

'Vasile.'

'Yes, Vasile. It's almost certain that Lupul had him killed because he tipped us off that he was staying at Sidney Park – and Vasile was Făt-Frumor's friend, or a contact at least.'

As they pushed their way through the lines of tarpaulin screens, Detective O'Donovan peered into one of the cubicles, where a scruffy grey-haired man with bags under his eyes was sitting cross-legged on his mattress solemnly munching his way through his entire packet of Kimberley biscuits. The man had no front teeth so he was spraying crumbs all over his corduroy trousers.

'If only one of these poor streals stopped hounding biscuits and made a complaint against the Fat Fellow by name, we'd be laughing,' said Detective O'Donovan. 'Or not looking so *duairc*, anyway. Jesus.'

Katie continued to make her way along the row of cubicles until she came to a young woman lying on her mattress with earphones in her ears, listening to a cheap DVD player stuck together with brown parcel tape. She was nodding her head and mouthing the words of whatever song she was playing.

She had small feline eyes and wavy black shoulder-length hair and from the thick grey cable-knit sweater she was wearing, Katie was sure that she was Romanian. She gave the young woman a smile and said, 'All right if I come in and have a word with you?'

The young woman took out her earphones and sat up, tossing back her hair. She was quite pretty, even though her hair was dry and badly needed cutting and her eyebrows needed plucking. Katie guessed that she was about twenty-one or twenty-two years old.

'How's it going?' she said. 'My name's Kathleen and I'm a police officer, but I have to tell you straight away that you're not in any kind of trouble.'

'I am worry,' the young woman replied. 'This place is warm and food is good but I should not be here. I have to go back to street.'

A card was propped up against her bedside lamp. Katie picked it up and saw that it read, 'Elenuta Moraru, outside P. Cashell,

Winthrop Street,' with the time and the date when the young woman had been picked up.

'Elenuta? That's a lovely name, Elenuta.'

'If I am not in trouble, is it all right for me to go? I have to go back to street or I make no money.'

'I'm afraid you won't be able to do that, Elenuta. Like I say, you're not in any trouble yourself, but the man who fetched you here from Romania, *he*'s in deep trouble. It's against the law to organize gangs of people like yourself to beg for money in the streets.'

Elenuta bit her lip. 'But if I do not go back, he will – I do not know words – *el mă va răni mult.*' To explain what she meant, she pretended to slap herself across the face.

'He'll hurt you?' said Katie.

'Yes, hurt me. Hurt me bad. One time he breaked two fingers.'

Katie said to Detective O'Donovan, 'Go and find Murtagh for me, could you? I think we may need some translation here.' Then she turned back to Elenuta and said, 'You're talking about Dragomir Iliescu? Dragos? The man they call Lupul?'

'I don't say.'

'Elenuta, I promise you that Lupul isn't going to hurt you again. We're looking for him because he's wanted on suspicion of serious crimes. He won't be able to take money from you again. He won't be able to hit you again. You won't even have to set eyes on him again, ever.'

Elenuta blinked at her and it was clear that she didn't fully understand. At that moment, though, Murtagh appeared around the screen and waved his hand and said, '*Salut! Ce mai faci? Numele meu este Murtagh.*'

Detective O'Donovan brought in a folding chair for Katie and Murtagh crouched down next to her. Katie couldn't help thinking that he looked like a giant frog in his green waxed jacket and his thick-lensed glasses, but she was grateful that he was there. Elenuta was starting to panic, turning her head from side to side as if she were trying to see if there was any way of escaping from this cubicle, and twisting the silver rings on her fingers around and around.

'You're *safe* now, Elenuta,' Katie reassured her, reaching out and laying a hand on her arm. 'It is Lupul that you're afraid of, isn't it? And did he fetch you here from Târgoviște too? First by plane, and then by ship?'

Elenuta nodded, and her eyes filled with tears.

'Why did you come here with Lupul? Did he force you to?'

'My brother Dumitru was always in trouble ever since he was at school and he was in Lupul's gang. He took some drugs that belonged to Lupul and sold them himself to make some extra money, so that he could buy himself a motorbike. Lupul found out and said that if I didn't pay back what Dumitru had taken, he would kill him, but he would kill him in such a way that nobody would know that he had done it.'

'When you came here to Cork, he took you to a big house first, up on a hill? But then he sent you out on the streets to beg for money?'

Elenuta nodded again. 'He will kill me.'

'He won't be able to get anywhere near you, sweetheart, because he'll be in prison for a very long time. He'll be an old man by the time he gets out. And that's if he's still alive. That big house burned down, did you know that, and they found a man dead inside it. That man could well be Lupul.'

'I heard there was a fire. Danut told me. I wanted to go back there, because I have my clothes there, and my suitcase. Also my phone and my ID card. But Danut said I had to stay away because everything was burned and – and – *poliția este peste tot în casă ca muștele.*'

'"Police are swarming all over the house like flies",' Murtagh translated.

'Danut?' said Katie. 'Is that the same Danut they call Sharp Teeth?'

'Yes. Dinti Ascutiti. But I should not have said his name to you. Please.'

'Danut won't be able to hurt you, either, Elenuta. Did Danut come over from Târgovişte with you?'

'Yes. I hate Danut. He always try to touch me. The other girls too. He stinks. Sometimes he take out his *pulă* and say look, don't you want to kiss it? He make me sick.'

'I don't think I need *that* translated, thanks, Murtagh,' said Katie. Then, to Elenuta, 'Did Danut tell you if Lupul was caught in the fire? Do you think the man who was found dead in the house could have been him?'

Elenuta shook her head. 'He say nothing more. Only house is nothing but ashes.'

'But he expected you to stay there on Winthrop Street, still begging?'

'*Da,*' she said, reverting to Romanian. 'He said that in spite of fire nothing has changed. He will fix my ID card. He said not to talk about fire, not to anybody. He said he'd be back at same time as usual in evening, nine o'clock, to take my money. But of course I won't be there. He will be so angry. *Furios ca diavolul.* That's why I'm so afraid.'

'So Danut told you that nothing had changed. Try and remember everything he said. Did he give you the impression that *he* was running things now? Or that Lupul was still alive and still in business? Did he give you any idea of where he was staying, now that the house on Alexandra Road was burned down?'

'No. All he said was, he will be back at nine o'clock like usual. I have to be there and I have to have some money to give him. Please. He will send a message to Lupul's friends in Târgovişte if I'm not there, and my brother will be hurt.'

'Listen, Elenuta, you mustn't worry. We're going to put a stop to all this begging, and the men who run it. Some people from the immigration service will be coming here later this afternoon. They'll be interviewing all the Romanian nationals like yourself, and they'll be helping you to sort out your identity card and give you any help you need to get back to Romania.'

'You will send me back? What about my brother?'

'You can't stay here in Ireland, not as a beggar. But we have good contacts with the police in Romania, and we'll try to make sure that your brother gets protection.'

Elenuta's eyes filled with tears, and she began to rock backwards and forwards in despair. '*Este sfârșitul lumii*,' she wept. '*E sfârșitul tuturor*.'

'She says it's the end of the world,' Murtagh translated. 'It's the end of everything.'

Between them, Katie and her fellow officers spoke to every one of the twenty beggars. Seven of them were Romanian and had been brought over by Lupul. Nine were Irish, three were Polish, and one was Nigerian, a girl called Kisiwa.

Katie promised them all protection and rehabilitation, and that they could stay here at St Dunstan's church hall until accommodation had been found for them, or arrangements had been made to repatriate them. But although none of the Romanians denied that they were members of Lupul's begging ring, she couldn't persuade any of them to accuse him by name – either him or Danut.

The Irish beggars were equally evasive. Katie asked them repeatedly if it was Ștefan Făt-Frumor who was forcing them to hand over half of their donations, but not one of them would say yes. Yet again, she felt ashamed that the Cork Garda hadn't picked up even an inkling that these beggars had been victims of organized extortion for so long. She was even more ashamed that none of them believed that if they identified their ringmasters, the Garda could guarantee their safety.

All the same, she was confident that she had made a small start at least in winning them over. She was making sure they were being kept warm on one of the coldest days of the year so far, and that they were well-fed, and that nobody was treating them like scum because they were addicted, or alcoholic, or suffering from some psychosis. In a few days, perhaps, they might trust her enough to name some names.

Before she left, she returned to Elenuta's cubicle.

'How're you going on?' she asked her.

'Will you let me go to meet Danut? I am so worry.'

'You're not a prisoner, Elenuta. But I'm seriously advising you not to go. It could make it much more difficult for us to find out where he's based now, and if Lupul is still alive. Apart from that, it could be fierce dangerous for you. He's bound to have caught wind by now that we've taken all the rough sleepers off the city's streets, and don't tell me that he won't be after asking you why, and where you all are. He may even try to take you with him by force, and that means we'll have to step in and stop him.'

'So what can I do?'

'Tell me what he looks like, this Danut. Then – if he turns up at Winthrop Street at nine o'clock, like he said he would – we can follow him.'

Elenuta hesitated for a moment. Then, without raising her eyes, she said, 'Short. But big shoulders. Bald head. Always wearing black jacket with jeans. And one earring, silver, this side.'

'Anything else you can think of?'

'Yes. Ugly like dog with squash face.'

'That's pure descriptive, Elenuta, thanks a million,' said Katie, although she couldn't help thinking of Walter.

Forty-Five

It was six thirty-six p.m. when the call came in from the National Ambulance Control Centre that a woman had fallen on the escalator at Brown Thomas department store on St Patrick's Street and appeared to be seriously injured.

The dispatcher came through to the staff room where Darragh and Brianna were sitting with four other paramedics. Brianna was prodding aggressively at her smartphone while Darragh was slowly masticating a corned-beef sandwich and reading the sports pages in the *Examiner* as intently as if he were translating it out of the Ancient Hebrew.

'Darragh – Brianna – this is one for you. From what the caller said, it sounds like the patient's concussed and she could have broken her left humerus.'

Brianna looked up from her phone and said, 'Holy Mary, Denis, it's not five minutes since we got back from taking that auld wan to the Mercy and I've just made myself a fresh cup of tea. Can't Micky and Nola take this one?'

'The boss says that you're to go. Mine not to reason why, mine but to do whatever the feck I'm told.'

'All right, then. Come on, Darragh. Jesus – if we were donkeys they wouldn't work us as hard as this.'

They clattered downstairs, climbed into their ambulance and headed up the South Link Road with their blue lights flashing.

'I don't know what's got into Ardan these past couple of days,' said Brianna. 'Every time he sees me he does a U-turn and walks off the other way like he doesn't even want to share the time of day.'

'Fair play, Bree, the poor fellow has a rake of problems on his plate still, what with all that reorganization. And he was never Mister Gallery at the best of times, was he?'

Darragh didn't say that Brianna herself had been considerably less than easy to get along with lately. He had learned that if he was critical of her in any way at all, she would snap at him like an angry poodle.

They drove along Merchants Quay and then turned down St Patrick's Street to Brown Thomas. A Garda squad car was already parked outside and Brianna could see that uniformed gardaí were standing in front of the doors. As soon as they drew into the kerb, she picked up her resuscitation bag, jumped down from the ambulance and hurried inside.

A young blonde woman in a long tan-coloured coat was lying on her back at the foot of the ground-floor escalator. Her eyes were closed and there was a large crimson bruise on her right cheek. Her left arm was twisted underneath her at an awkward angle and her thick brown nylon tights appeared to have been shredded by the teeth on the edge of the escalator steps. The escalator had been brought to a stop. It was surrounded by cosmetics counters, so there was a strong smell of Chanel in the air.

A small crowd of four or five onlookers shuffled back out of the way as Brianna came through, with Darragh close behind her pulling a trolley. A plump middle-aged man with a comb-over was kneeling beside the young blonde woman, feeling her pulse on her neck.

'Thank the Lord,' he said, as Brianna knelt down beside him. 'I'm the store's first-aider, but this is a sight more than I can handle. I think she might have busted her arm, like.'

Brianna gave him a quick, humourless smile and took out her pulse oximeter. The young woman's heart was beating slowly, but not dangerously so, and although her breathing was quick and shallow, she didn't seem to be at any risk of myocardial infarction.

When Brianna leaned over her, though, she smelled strongly of alcohol. Brianna looked at Darragh and made a waggling gesture with her hand to simulate drinking. He shook his head sadly. So many of the accident victims they attended were drunk.

Between them, they gently lifted the young woman off the floor and on to the trolley, taking care to support her left arm, which was dangling loose.

'Here's her bag,' said one of the shop assistants. 'It has her purse and her phone in it and everything.'

'Did you see her fall?' asked Darragh.

'No, I didn't. We just heard a kind of a scream and a thump and there she was. There wasn't anybody else on the escalator when she fell – not that I could see, anyway.'

'All right, grand. We'll be taking her to the emergency room at CUH if anybody comes asking for her.'

Brianna and Darragh wheeled the young woman out to their ambulance. A woman garda came up to them before they closed the doors and asked how she was.

'Hard to tell,' said Brianna. 'She's clearly been drinking and she had a fierce bad fall down the escalator. She's in shock at the moment and it looks like her arm could be broken. Look, I have her bag. It has her phone in it so we'll be able to put a name to her and ring her next of kin or her friends at least.'

'We'll be following you to the hospital anyway,' said the woman garda. 'As soon as she's conscious we'll be wanting to ask her what happened. You know, just in case somebody gave her a push, like, do you know what I mean?'

Darragh closed the rear door and climbed up into the driving seat and they set off for the hospital, with the Garda squad car close behind.

Brianna checked the young woman's vital signs again and found that her heart rate was slightly quicker and her blood pressure had risen slightly. Although her eyes were closed and she still appeared to be concussed, Brianna could find nothing seriously wrong with her, although delayed shock could still play some malevolent tricks. It was possible that she had suffered a spinal injury as well as a broken arm, in which case she might be suffering from neurogenic shock, which could prove fatal.

'How is she?' called Darragh.

'Not too good,' Brianna called back. 'I'm giving her oxygen and keeping her warm but her vitals are giving me cause for concern, I can tell you. I reckon she must have had a skinful.'

She reached behind her, but instead of unhooking the oxygen mask, she picked up an ambulance dressing No.3 and tore off its plastic wrapper. It was their thickest gauze dressing, and it was designed to be used after serious car crashes and other major accidents, to stem the blood that came pumping out of catastrophic cuts and lacerations and torn-off limbs.

Brianna leaned sideways and ducked her head down so that she could see where they were. They were just passing Mardyke Street, which would give her at least ten minutes, especially since the traffic along Western Road was nose to tail in both directions. Without any hesitation, she pressed the dressing over the young woman's face, completely covering her nose and mouth, and then she stuck the adhesive tapes at the side of the dressing around the back of her head, as tight as she could, so that it formed a mask.

To make sure that the young woman couldn't breathe at all, she held her left hand over the dressing and pressed it down hard.

Nearly two minutes went by. They had only reached Orchard Road, even though Darragh was weaving in and out of the traffic with his siren wailing and his headlights flashing, and blaspheming almost continuously.

'In the name of the Father, the Son, the Holy Ghost and the Pope's eternal jockstrap, will you ever get out of the fecking way, you gobdaw!'

Darragh was still swearing when the young blonde woman suddenly jolted and snatched Brianna's wrist, wrenching her hand away from the dressing that was covering her face. Then she hit Brianna with her knuckles on the bridge of her nose, a punch like a piston that sent Brianna tumbling backwards on to the ambulance floor.

She ripped the adhesive tape from the back of her head and tossed the dressing away, and then she unbuckled the safety belt around her waist and sat up.

Brianna was trying to climb to her feet, but the punch had stunned her, and at that moment the ambulance swayed from side to side as Darragh overtook a bus, and she fell down on to the floor again.

'What the hell is going on back there?' Darragh shouted.

'Slow down and stop!' the young blonde woman ordered him.

'What? Who's that?'

'I'm Detective Sergeant Ni Nuallán from Anglesea Street Garda Station and I'm arresting your partner for attempted murder.'

'*What?*'

'You heard me. I'm not injured at all. Your partner here tried to suffocate me and she's under arrest. You can turn off that siren, pull over to the side of the road and stop.'

'What? I can't understand you. She's *what?*'

Kyna made her way to the front of the ambulance. Darragh looked up at her and almost rear-ended a van right in front of him.

'Pull over, Darragh. I've arrested your partner and there's a squad car right behind us.'

Darragh switched off the siren and slowly steered the ambulance into the front entrance of Áras Sláinte, the health service building by the side of Wilton Road.

Kyna went back, took hold of Brianna's arm, and dragged her up from the floor. Brianna raised both hands to shield her face and said, 'Don't hit me again, please. Once was enough.'

The back door of the ambulance was opened up and two uniformed gardaí were standing outside. A second squad car was arriving behind the first, with its blue lights flashing.

Brianna stepped down, and the woman garda handcuffed her and led her away to sit in the back seat of her squad car. Darragh came around to the back of the ambulance looking shell-shocked.

'You'll have to come in too, Darragh, for questioning,' Kyna told him.

'What about my ambulance? I can't leave it here. Some knacker might make off with it, and it's full of drugs.'

'Don't you worry about your ambulance. One of these officers will drive it back to the station for you.'

'You're not hurt at all,' said Darragh, in bewilderment. 'Did you really not fall down that escalator? Your face is all bruised, like, and your tights are all torn.'

Kyna took a tissue out of her coat pocket and wiped it against the crimson bruise on her cheek. Then she held it up so that Darragh could see that it was make-up.

'And see this?' she said, pointing to the top button of the cardigan she was wearing under her coat. 'It's a video camera. Everything that your partner tried to do to me, it's all here.'

'I'm dreaming, aren't I?' said Darragh. 'I can't believe any of this. I must be dreaming.'

A garda took his arm and led him back to the second squad car, still shaking his head. He was just being helped into it when Katie arrived, in her own Ford Focus. As soon as she climbed out of it she came walking quickly towards Kyna, almost running, but when she saw that she was unharmed and talking to one of the gardaí, she slowed down.

'I'm fine, ma'am,' said Kyna, as Katie approached. 'She tried to spifflicate me with a big thick bandage, would you believe, but the Wing Chun put a stop to that. It's all recorded on the SD card.'

'Mother of God, what a day this has been,' said Katie. 'And it's not over yet.'

They walked back to Katie's car together. Katie was so relieved that Kyna was unhurt that she didn't know what to say. All she could do was lay her hand on her knee before she started up the engine, and turn to her, and smile, sparkly eyed.

Forty-Six

'What if he doesn't show?' asked Detective Caffrey.

'If he doesn't show I'll treat you to a pint of Murphy's,' said Detective Sergeant Begley.

They were sitting at the bar in The Long Valley on Winthrop Street. Through the pub's front window they could see the doorway of P. Cashell's shop directly opposite where Elenuta had been sleeping rough, but it was five past nine and there was still no sign of Danut making an appearance.

The bar was dimly lit and crowded and noisy, and a trio called the Mischief Makers were playing a jig called 'Tenpenny Bit' on the flute and fiddle and bodhrán.

Although the music and the laughter were so loud, the barmaid heard Detective Sergeant Begley say 'Murphy's' and suggestively lifted up an empty glass, but Detective Sergeant Begley shook his head. They had told her that they couldn't order their drinks yet, because they were waiting on a friend. But ten more minutes went past and there was still no sign of Danut.

'I reckon he's caught on that we've hauled in all of his beggars,' said Detective Caffrey. 'In which case he'll be out the gap and back to Romania if he has any brains. Him and that Lupul both, if he's still alive and kicking, and good riddance.'

At a quarter past nine, Detective Sergeant Begley reached into his pocket for his wallet. He took out a twenty-euro note and was about to call the barmaid over when Detective Caffrey tapped his arm and said, 'Come here to me, sarge – look! That's your man, I'll bet you!'

A bald-headed man in a black anorak was walking quickly from the direction of St Patrick's Street, his hands deep in his pockets and his collar tugged up against the rain. He stopped in front of P. Cashell's doorway for a few seconds, looking around. Then he carried on walking towards Oliver Plunkett Street.

'So, what can I get you lads?' asked the barmaid. But both detectives had already slid off their stools and were heading for the door. As they came out on to the pavement, they saw Danut crossing the road towards the General Post Office. He didn't go far, though. He stopped right in front of the wide green post office doors, and turned around so that he was facing them. Immediately they changed direction and carried on walking down the opposite side of the street so he wouldn't realize that they were following him.

Only thirty metres further down the street, though, stood two eircom telephone boxes. The two detectives managed to cram themselves inside one of them, even though they were both wearing padded waterproof jackets and ballistic vests. Detective Sergeant Begley lifted the receiver and pretended to be making a phone call, so that they could wait and watch through the rain-speckled glass to see what Danut did next. They saw him take out his mobile phone and have a brief conversation, and then he stayed where he was, chafing his hands together to keep warm.

'A hundred to one he's rung for a crony to pick him up, just like we reckoned,' said Detective Caffrey. 'Either that or a taxi.'

'Well, I can't see him standing there all night, freezing his arse off, can you? I'll tell the ERU lads to warm up their jets.'

Their own silver Toyota was parked less than twenty metres down the street, in the loading bay of Penneys department store, but they weren't going to be tracking Danut by themselves, without backup. Katie had also called in four armed officers from the Emergency Response Unit, and since eight-thirty that evening they had been stationed at strategic locations close by. They were in two unmarked cars – one on Grand Parade at the far end of Oliver Plunkett Street, and the second outside the Imperial Hotel on South Mall, in case Danut's car took a left off Oliver Plunkett Street down Morgan Street or Marlboro Street.

Detective Sergeant Begley spoke on his radio to the ERU officers in both of those cars. 'It's your man all right. He's outside the General Post Office and it looks like he's rung for a lift. As soon as a vehicle shows up to collect him, we'll let you know. But remember what DS Maguire was saying. It's critical we find out where these suspects have moved themselves to, so give him plenty of space. If it looks like he has any suspicion at all that you're following him, turn off, and another one of us can take over. We can't afford to lose him or let him take us off on some wild goose chase.'

'Roger, detective, we have you,' said one of the ERU officers. His flat tone of voice suggested that he didn't care to be lectured about basic pursuit techniques.

The rain was pelting down now. Detective Sergeant Begley and Detective Caffrey left the phone box, hurried down the street to their car and scrambled in. They sat watching Danut in their rear-view mirrors for over five minutes, but then they saw headlights coming down Oliver Plunkett Street. A black Audi saloon stopped outside the post office and its passenger door was thrown open. Danut scurried across and climbed inside.

'Black Audi saloon, Limerick number plate,' said Detective Sergeant Begley, into his radio. 'Odds on it's the same car they used when they abducted that Vasile fellow.'

As soon as the Audi had driven past them, Detective Caffrey pulled out of the loading bay and followed it. It turned left down Morgan Street to South Mall, and then turned left again. Detective Sergeant Begley alerted the two ERU officers in the car that was stationed outside the Imperial Hotel, and when they turned into South Mall, they saw the headlights of the officers' unmarked Volvo come up close behind them and flash them. The officers in the second ERU car reported that they had left their parking place on Grand Parade and were speeding along South Mall to catch up.

The black Audi saloon drove north, crossing the River Lee on the Michael Collins Bridge. The three unmarked Garda cars took it in turns to follow it. As they drove along St Patrick's Quay, the Volvo even drew up alongside it. When it reached Harley Street, though, it turned left, and then right, and then left again up York Street.

'Where the hell is he heading?' said Detective Caffrey. 'He can't be going back to that house on Sidney Park, surely? That's all been sealed off.'

But the Audi turned up the long steep slope of Richmond Hill, a narrow road with terraced houses on either side, and then up Goldsmith's Avenue, which was even narrower and even steeper, high above the city centre. Eventually it turned into two rows of single-storey red-brick cottages called Sutton's Buildings.

As they reached the corner, Detective Sergeant Begley said, 'Kill the lights, Ronan. Don't follow him yet. See how far he goes. This goes nowhere, this boreen, except back in a circle to where we started.'

They stopped, and waited, with the rain drumming on the roof of their car and their windscreen wipers squeaking. The Audi drove less than fifty metres up Sutton's Buildings and then parked outside one of the cottages. They saw Danut and the Audi's driver climb out and go inside. After only a few seconds, lights were switched on behind the sagging purple curtains that were hanging in the front room.

'Right, we have him now,' said Detective Sergeant Begley, into his radio. 'Michael – if you carry straight on up Rathmore Park you can come back down Sutton's Buildings from the other direction and block it off. But keep your distance for now. And no lights.'

'Roger,' said the ERU officer, flatly. 'Have we time for a quick stabber?'

★

Detective Sergeant Begley called Katie. She had been up in the top-floor communications room in Anglesea Street since nine p.m., following their progress on their dashcam. Detective Inspector Fitzpatrick was sitting next to her, hunched forward in his chair and looking tired, while Kyna was standing behind her with a mug of mint tea.

'So – what's the plan now, ma'am?' asked Detective Sergeant Begley.

'The driver – I couldn't see him clearly at all,' said Katie. 'I'm wondering if it could have been Lupul.'

'If he wasn't charred to a cinder at Alexandra Road then it might have been. But, no, it was too dark to get a clear lamp at him. Male, wearing a shiny black jacket from what I could see. He had on a cap of some kind so I couldn't say for sure if he was a baldy or not.'

Katie turned to Detective Inspector Fitzpatrick. 'There's two things that we can do, Robert. We can go in and lift this Danut now, and take a guess on whoever's in there with him. Either that, or we can keep the place under surveillance until tomorrow morning and see if any more of those gowls show up.'

Detective Inspector Fitzpatrick sniffed and ran his hand through his prickly hair. 'I'm trying to imagine what their next plan of action is going to be. They know for sure now that their begging ring has been busted, and so they'll be wide that we're keeping an eye out for them. My guess is that they'll be after throwing in the towel and heading for Ringaskiddy or even above to the border. They might even head off tonight. Like, they've nothing to stay for, have they, not now?'

'What – you think they'll leave all their rough sleepers behind?' asked Kyna. 'Just abandon them, like?'

'Of course they will. They don't give a two-toned shite for those poor streals. All they'll do is go back to Romania and press-gang some more. They don't see them as human beings, like. They're just ATMs as far as they're concerned. You remember that begging ring in Dublin last year? They were making well over a grand a day, easy, but the beggars themselves were so fecking hungry they were raiding the bins outside of Bunsen's for out-of-date buns.'

'I'm more than inclined to agree with you,' said Katie. 'I believe they'll probably bail, too, so let's haul them in now. Sean – did you hear that?'

'I did, ma'am. McKenzie and Nolan, they're right behind us. O'Mahony and Kerr are ready in position now up the far end of the boreen. We're all set to go.'

Detective Caffrey steered their Toyota into Sutton's Buildings and crept up without lights until their front bumper was less than five metres behind the black Audi saloon, and then he parked at a forty-five-degree angle across the road. The first ERU team followed close behind them in their Volvo, while the second team rolled silently down from the top of the slope and blocked the Audi from escaping in that direction.

Most of the cottage windows along the street were lit, and when Detective Sergeant Begley and Detective Caffrey climbed out of their car and quietly closed the doors, they could hear televisions and muffled music. A curtain was drawn back on the opposite side of the street from Danut's cottage and a white-haired woman in a red cardigan peered out. Detective Sergeant Begley went across to her, pointed to the word Garda on the front of his jacket, and pressed his finger to his lips. The woman stared at him, blinking, and then she crossed herself as if Saint Patrick himself had come to her window, and let her curtain fall back again.

The four ERU officers gathered around. Two of them were holding Heckler & Koch MP7 sub-machine guns while the other two were armed with Sig-Sauer automatics. Both Detective Sergeant Begley and Detective Caffrey were carrying automatics, too.

'I know these cottages and there's no way that anyone can get out the back,' Detective Sergeant Begley told the four ERU officers. 'On the other hand, that might make them a bit more desperate. One of the victims of this begging ring, a fellow called Bowser, he was shot in the head, as well as drilled, so we have to assume that they have at least one pistol.'

Garda McKenzie said, 'If there's a chance at all that they're armed, it's best to go in hard and fast, like. We'll ram the door open and if it looks like they're going for any weapons we'll toss in a flashbang.'

'Any questions?' asked Detective Sergeant Begley. 'No? Then let's do it.'

They gathered around the front door of Danut's cottage and Garda Nolan came forward carrying a red Enforcer battering-ram. The door had peeling yellow paint and it looked half-rotten so Detective Sergeant Begley didn't think it would take more than a couple of hard blows to knock it open. But as Garda Nolan lifted the Enforcer, and was about to slam it into the lock, the door unexpectedly opened, and there was Danut. He had taken off his black anorak and was standing in the hallway in a T-shirt with a grinning skull on it with a daisy in its teeth, with the slogan 'Dirty Shirt'. There was a crumpled cigarette dangling from the side of his mouth and his belly was hanging over his belt.

Detective Sergeant Begley stepped forward. 'Danut? We're armed gardaí. Don't give us any trouble now, sham, we're taking you in. Who else is in the house with you?'

Danut said nothing, but immediately slammed the door. The officers could hear him shouting to somebody inside. '*Politie! Futu-i! Este poliția!*'

'Go ahead,' said Detective Sergeant Begley to Garda Nolan, almost wearily.

Garda Nolan smashed the Enforcer into the door and the lock was splintered out of it with one blow. Garda O'Mahony was the biggest of the team, at least six feet four tall, and he kicked the door wide open with his boot and strode into the hallway like the Terminator, holding up his sub-machine gun.

The living-room door was closed but he kicked that open, too, and stepped inside, crouching down a little with his sub-machine gun held up ready to fire. The other three ERU gardaí jostled in behind him, while Detective Sergeant Begley and Detective Caffrey brought up the rear, but both with their pistols drawn.

The living room was cramped and furnished with a soiled beige sofa and two armchairs that looked as if they had been rescued from a skip. The pale green wallpaper was damp and stained and even the mirror over the fireplace was freckled with brown spots and misted over. A small, smouldering peat fire had filled the room with a haze of pungent smoke.

Danut was standing behind the sofa, holding up an automatic. Sitting on the sofa in front of him with his hands up was Marku. He, too, was bald, but unshaven, with prune-coloured circles under his eyes. His right arm was wound around with grubby white crepe bandages, all the way from his elbow to his wrist, and he was wearing a blue rubber glove on his hand.

'I come quiet,' he said, slurrily. 'Please no shoot.'

'*Taca-ti gura, tâmpit!*' Danut barked at him. Then, to the Garda officers, 'I go now. Okay? You don't stop me. Marku – *dă-mi cheile maşinii*.'

Keeping one hand raised, Marku reached into his trouser pocket and wrestled out a set of car keys. He held them up and Danut snatched them, still keeping his automatic raised.

Detective Sergeant Begley said, 'Danut, you understand English, don't you?'

'And you – you understand English, also,' Danut retorted. 'So I say very clear, I go now. You try to stop me, I will shoot.'

'Danut, sham, you're not going nowhere. Take a sconce out the window if you want to, and you'll see that your car is totally blocked off.'

Danut hesitated, and then took a step back towards the window. He drew back the curtains and quickly glanced out into the street, keeping his automatic held high.

'You move your cars,' he demanded. 'You move your cars and I go.'

'You don't stand a snowball's,' said Detective Sergeant Begley. 'Can't you see that it's over? You're outgunned and outmanoeuvred and even if we did let you walk out of here, how far do you think you'd get?'

'I don't understand you. I go.'

'Not a hope, Danut. Now, why don't you drop that weapon down on the seat there and then come around here with your hands up high, like your friend here?'

Danut looked desperately from side to side. He could see that Garda O'Mahony had his sub-machine gun aimed at his chest, and that his aim didn't waver for a second.

Suddenly, he reached over the back of the sofa and jammed the muzzle of his automatic against Marku's right temple. Marku tried to duck his head away, but Danut kept pressing the gun against his forehead, just above his eye, and snapped, '*Stai nemiscat!*'

'Hold fire, O'Mahony,' said Detective Sergeant Begley, quickly laying a hand on his shoulder. But to Danut he said, 'I'm warning you now, and this is the last time I'll warn you. Drop the weapon. Drop it. It's over.'

'No, it is not over. We will go now, both. You will move your cars and we will go. If not, Marku will die, and you will be the murderer.'

'Danut, can't you get it through your head? There's no way out.'

There was a long moment of extreme tension. It was broken when Danut started to cough – a harsh, wheezing, clogged-up smoker's cough. His automatic wavered as he coughed, and it was then that Marku twisted around on the sofa and tried to seize it.

Marku was too fat, though, and too slow. With an ear-splitting bang, Danut shot him right between the eyes. The back of his bald head burst open like a broken jug and cream-coloured brains looped all over the arm of the sofa.

'Drop it!' screamed Garda O'Mahony. But before he could let off a shot himself, Danut stuck the muzzle of the automatic under his own chin and blew off his jaw and his upper lip and most of his nose. His eyes stared at the gardaí above the bloody cavity of his face, as if he were a child who doesn't understand what's happened to him, and then he collapsed sideways behind the sofa.

Garda O'Mahony edged around the sofa, still pointing his sub-machine gun, just in case Danut had enough life left in him to squeeze off one final shot. He bent over for a moment, and when he stood up he was holding up Danut's automatic, its grip all smothered in blood.

'Straight to the hot place, this one. He'll be dancing with the Devil already, I'd say. Jesus.'

'Two men down, ma'am,' said Detective Sergeant Begley, over his headset. 'Danut and his pal, whoever he is. It's not Lupul. Doesn't fit the description.'

'None of ours hurt?'

'No. Danut did for his pal and then for himself.'

'Damn. That's exactly what I didn't need. I was hoping he might tell us what happened to Lupul. Listen – if you and Caffrey can do a quick search, Sean. See if there's anything that gives you a clue if Lupul's alive or dead. Mobile phones. Notes, letters, bus or train or ferry tickets. Clothing. I'll be sending the Technical Bureau up there right away, plus the coroner of course. *Damn.*'

Forty-Seven

Katie stayed at Anglesea Street that night, although she rang Conor before she went to bed.

'How're you going on, darling?' she asked him. 'Sorry I can't be home tonight. If I told you that today was total madness, that would be the understatement of the year. You'll see some of it on the news tomorrow morning. Two of those Romanians shot dead, up at the top of Richmond Hill.'

'Shot dead? Not by you?'

'No, of course not. I wasn't even there. Not in person, anyway.'

'Well, it's your job, Katie. I know that.'

'You sound kind of quiet. Is everything all right?'

'No. Yes. I'm grand altogether.'

'Did you take the children for a walk?'

'The children? That's the closest I'll ever be to having children.'

'I'm sorry, Con. I didn't mean it like that. I've always called them the children.'

'I did take them for a walk, yes. But it was lashing too hard, even for them. As soon as they'd done their business they wanted to be back by the fire.'

'I wish I was there with them. And you.'

'Well, sometimes terrible things happen to us and there's nothing at all we can do about them. All we can do is hope that we've done right by everybody else.'

'That sounds pure philosophical. What does that mean?'

'Oh, you know. Something and nothing at all.'

'Con – are you okay? I can come back home if you need me.'

'No, you're fine. You don't want to be driving back to Cobh in weather like this. I'll see you tomorrow so, with any luck. Goodnight, sweetheart. Sleep sound.'

'You too, darling.'

When Conor had hung up, Katie sat on the bed frowning at her iPhone, as if she expected him to ring back sounding all cheerful and saying, 'Really! I was only codding you! I'm not miserable at all! Listen to that pop! That's me whipping the top off a bottle of Satz!'

But her iPhone stayed silent. After a while she lifted the blankets of her single bed and slid her bare feet down between the cold sheets. She lay on her pillow with her eyes open, listening to the rain rattling against the window, and then she reached over and switched off her lamp.

Brianna looked rough. Her hair was uncombed and her eyes were puffy and she had a cold sore on her upper lip. Her paramedic's uniform had been taken away and she was wearing a plain grey woollen dress that was at least a size too large for her. When Katie and Kyna came into the interview room next morning, however, she raised her eyes towards them in a way that Katie thought looked almost hopeful. She had seen that look in a criminal's eyes before – *At last, somebody's here to save me from myself.*

'Good morning, all,' she said. 'How's it going on?'

Brianna was represented by Partlan Devine, a solidly built fortyish solicitor from the same chambers as Frank Lyons, but with more experience of representing the suspects of unusual homicides. He had acted two years ago for the Ballincollig mother who had strangled every one of her five children when they reached their third birthday and hidden their bodies in her press.

Partlan Devine had a brick-red face, a prickly ginger moustache, and an equally abrasive way of talking. The shoulders of his dark blue suit were lightly seasoned with dandruff. He was accompanied by his assistant, a pale but attractive girl called Naoimh with an abundance of shiny black hair and large mint-green eyes, and a legal pad balanced on her black-stockinged knee.

Katie laid her job book on Brianna's case on the desk in front of her but didn't open it.

Instead, she said, 'Before we start to question Brianna about her attempt on the life of Detective Sergeant Ni Nuallán in the ambulance yesterday, Mr Devine, there's something else you have to know. Her flat on Noonan Road was searched yesterday evening by experts from the Technical Bureau, and that search has turned up some evidence that incriminates her in another ongoing investigation.'

Brianna glanced nervously at Partlan Devine, but Partlan Devine kept his washed-out hazel eyes on Katie.

'I see, Detective Superintendent Maguire. I assume that you're going to be good enough as to inform me what this evidence might be, and to what allegation it relates?'

Kyna passed Katie a clear plastic evidence bag and Katie held it up. 'This is a phial that once contained fentanyl citrate – a large enough dose to be lethal if it was all to be injected into the average person. It was found in the wheelie bin at the rear of Brianna's block of flats.'

'Sure anybody at all could have tossed it in there. Some drug addict, for instance.'

'No, not just anybody. It has a partial fingerprint on it, and that partial fingerprint matches Brianna's. All opioids carried in NAS ambulances are scrupulously logged, so we know that this particular phial came from the drug store in Brianna's ambulance.'

'So she threw away an empty phial of fentanyl citrate? What does that prove? She's an advanced paramedic.'

'Yes, but it has more than Brianna's fingerprint on it. Our forensic technicians found that its needle also bears traces of DNA – and it's the DNA of a young girl called Saoirse Duffy. Saoirse was recovering from near-drowning at CUH when somebody came into her room and injected her with this fatal dose of fentanyl citrate.

'It doesn't seem like a coincidence to me that after she was rescued from the Lee, the ambulance that took Saoirse to hospital was crewed by Brianna and her partner Darragh Ó Dálaigh.'

'And what does that prove?' asked Partlan Devine.

'We have CCTV footage of a woman dressed as a nurse leaving Saoirse's room shortly before she was found to have passed away. I have to admit that the footage isn't one hundred per cent clear, but it's a reasonable assumption that this "nurse" was Brianna. Her ambulance was parked at CUH at the time. Their shift had just finished and her partner, Darragh, was having a late snack in the hospital canteen. She had told him that she wasn't hungry but she wanted to go and talk to a friend of hers in the emergency room.'

Partlan Devine pursed his lips in annoyance. Then he said, 'I'll need to have some time in private with my client before we respond to this new allegation. You haven't yet formally charged her, I presume?'

'Not yet, but we will be. She's in custody already and I wanted to see her response first. Let us know when you're ready.'

Katie and Kyna both pushed back their chairs, but before they could stand up, Brianna said, 'Don't bother. Charge me. Read me my rights. Go on. I did it. I admit it. And all the others too.'

'*Brianna*—' said Partlan Devine, reaching out for her arm and gripping it tight. 'Please don't say any more. This is not the way to protect your best interests.'

'I don't care,' said Brianna, shaking her head. Tears were sliding down her cheeks and her nose was running too. Kyna took out her handkerchief and passed it across to her. As she wiped her eyes and blew her nose, she looked up at Kyna as if to say, *God Almighty, I tried to kill you, and here you are giving me your handkerchief.*

Katie said, 'What do you mean by "all the others", Brianna? Who exactly are you talking about?'

'She doesn't have to answer that,' said Partlan Devine. 'As you well know, she doesn't have to say anything at all.'

'I don't care,' Brianna told him, pulling her hand away. 'I've been trying to live with it and it's been giving me nightmares. Yes, I injected Saoirse Duffy with the fentanyl. I thought she was going to die in the ambulance on the way back from Blackrock but she didn't. And she *knew* that I was trying to do away with her, so when she woke up she'd only tell everybody that I'd tried to murder her, wouldn't she?'

'Brianna, for *Christ's* sake, don't say any more,' snapped Partlan Devine. His assistant was sitting next to him wide-eyed, her pencil poised above her legal pad. She hadn't written a word.

'There were five of them altogether,' said Brianna. She was so wracked with emotion that every sentence was punctuated by a harsh, painful intake of air.

'Five? And you're telling us that you ended all five of their lives in the ambulance, on the way to hospital, in the same way that you tried to suffocate DS Ni Nuallán?'

Brianna sobbed, and nodded. Partlan Devine shook his head in exasperation and said, 'Mary and Joseph and Jesus. Brianna.'

'But *why*, Brianna?' asked Kyna, and Katie heard that particular tone of voice that Kyna could adopt, a tone of voice that somehow encouraged almost everybody she questioned to admit to everything, no matter what outrage they had committed. She sounded so gentle and so understanding. Instead of being accusing, she seemed to be offering forgiveness and redemption.

'It started when I met Niall Dabney in the Old Oak last October,' said Brianna.

'You mean Niall Dabney from Dabney's the undertakers?' asked Katie.

'That's right. I'd asked for a Bacardi Breezer but when it came to it I couldn't scrape up enough grade to pay for it, and I was morto. Niall was standing next to me in the bar and he chipped in and bought it for me.'

'So you were broke? Didn't you have your wages?'

'Of course. But my boyfriend, Jimmy, was addicted to betting and he cleaned me out completely, all my savings, everything. He was always saying that a big win was coming up and that he was going to pay me back twice over, but he never did. He even stole the diamond earrings that my granny gave me and pawned them off.'

She turned to Partlan Devine, who was pressing his fingertips to his forehead as if he had suddenly contracted a migraine.

'I'm fierce sorry, Mr Devine,' she said. 'But it's all going to come out anyway and there's no point in trying to pretend that it wasn't me, because they know it was, and they have the evidence, don't they?'

'Go on, then,' said Partlan Devine. 'All I can say is, on your own head be it. But I'll stay here as I'm obliged to and make sure that these officers stick to the rules. You haven't been charged with any other offences yet, apart from assaulting DS Ni Nuallán, so if you decide to retract anything else you've said, you're perfectly within your rights.'

'So you met Niall Dabney,' put in Kyna. 'What happened then?'

'Me and Niall got to talking and I told him all about Jimmy and how I was skint. He said that he'd been having some cash-flow troubles too and maybe we could help each other out. If I was to recommend Dabney's to the next of kin of anybody who passed away, he'd give me a cut of the proceeds, like.

'We had two fatal call-outs in November – one when that chipper up in Ballyvolane caught fire and that poor feen was practically fried alive, and the other when that bus overturned on the N20, and that young lad got beheaded by the window.'

'God, yes, I remember that little boy,' said Katie. 'That was tragic.'

'I went around to visit the families of both of them,' Brianna went on. 'I told them that Dabney's would give them the best funeral they could wish for, and a discount, too – ten per cent cheaper than Jennings or Jerh. O'Connor's. They both took me up on it, and Niall paid me my share of both of them. But of course I was able to buy myself some new clothes and pay for the messages then and Jimmy caught on that I must have made myself some grade. He was sniffing around again before you could say blackjack.'

'You didn't have to give him your money, did you?'

Brianna said nothing, but pulled up the sleeve of her dress and showed them the bruises on her arms. Some of them were yellow and fading, but others were purple and crimson and obviously fresh.

'I see,' said Kyna. 'But what happened then? What about these five other patients whose lives you ended?' Katie noticed that she didn't used the words 'murdered' or 'killed'.

Brianna closed her eyes tight and squeezed her fists together and the tears kept sliding freely down her face.

'I couldn't see any other way out. I was terrified of Jimmy. I still am. I don't understand why, but I still loved him. The thought of losing him was more than I could bear. I still love him now. Why do I still love him now? He kept on asking me for money but there weren't enough patients dying. An auld wan died in a road crash on the North Ring on St Stephen's Day but her family wanted her buried in Mayo, where she came from, so I didn't get any money out of her.'

'So you thought – what?' Katie coaxed her. 'You thought that maybe you could give some of your patients a helping hand to get to Heaven? Is that it?'

'I promised myself that it would only be the ones who were close to passing away anyway – the ones who probably wouldn't make it to the emergency room, or if they did, they'd spend the rest of their lives in a coma, or too badly disabled even to feed themselves, do you know?'

'Do you have to go on, Brianna?' asked Partlan Devine. 'I'm sure Detective Superintendent Maguire has got the point by now.'

Katie ignored him. 'How did you do it?' she asked. 'There were no queries raised by the coroner. All of them appeared to have died naturally or accidentally. Did you suffocate them, like you tried to do with DS Ni Nuallán?'

'It's easier than you'd think, after an accident,' said Brianna. 'Your patients are almost always in some state of shock. Haemorrhagic shock. Neurogenic shock. Even if it's only psychological shock. It doesn't take much to stop their hearts when they're in that condition. Usually it's enough to cut off their oxygen. Not many people can survive for longer than two or three minutes without breathing. After that you're looking at brain death in less than six minutes.'

'Your victims,' said Katie. 'Do you know their names and addresses?'

'I can only remember some of them. Niall has the full list. Ask Niall.'

'Well, I expect Niall was delighted with all these new clients you were fetching him. Does Niall know how they died?'

'I don't know. Maybe he guessed. You'll have to ask him.'

'All right, Brianna, that'll do for now,' said Katie. Then she turned to Partlan Devine and said, 'This will take some considerable time, Mr Devine. We'll have to identify all Brianna's victims and have each one of them exhumed to establish if she really did kill them. Meanwhile, I'm arresting you, Brianna Cusack, on suspicion of murder. You are not obliged to say anything unless you wish to do so, but whatever you say will be taken down in writing and may be given in evidence.'

'I think she's just about said it all, don't you?' said Partlan Devine, zipping up his briefcase so fiercely that he caught the tip of his finger in it.

Back in Katie's office, Kyna said, 'What do you think?'

Katie sat down at her desk, looking abstracted. She picked up a report that had been sent to her by Dr Kelley and then put it down again. 'What do I think? I think she's putting it on.'

'Serious? You think she's faking it?'

'Come here, she knows that we're on to her, and that we have enough evidence to convict her, so she's playing the part of the poor abused woman who was forced to do what she did because she was terrified of her boyfriend. She's an advanced paramedic, as Partlan the Not-So-Devine kept reminding us. Don't tell me she doesn't know all about behaviour under stress. It's part of their basic training.'

'But you do believe that she was bullied by her boyfriend, and that she killed those patients of hers because she needed the grade?'

'Sure, like. I can accept that. But from that performance of hers downstairs, I'd say that she enjoyed killing them, too. It gave her a feeling of power, which of course she didn't have with her boyfriend. It might even have given her a sexual thrill, too. Even confessing to those murders turned her on, in a way. Did you notice how flushed she was, and how she kept lifting herself up and down a little in her chair, like she was squeezing her thighs together?'

Kyna gave her a smile and the smallest shake of her head. 'Holy Mary, Katie, you have a sharp eye all right. Next time you and me are together, if we ever are, I think I'll turn the lights off.'

She looked at Katie for a moment without saying anything. Then she said, 'Bacardi Breezer. Do you think a Corkman called it that, for a laugh?'

Forty-Eight

Ştefan Făt-Frumor was sitting in front of the television in his vest and tracksuit bottoms, with a can of Carlsberg Special Brew in his hand, studiously picking his nose.

His doorbell rang, but he ignored it. When it rang a second time, and then a third, he called out, 'Daciana! Didn't you hear that? Someone's at the door! See who it is, you stupid cow!'

'I can't!' his wife called back, from the kitchen. 'I'm right in the middle of stirring the *mămăligă*!'

The bell rang yet again, and Ştefan said, '*Să moară mama!* What am I, my own fucking servant?'

He heaved himself out of his sticky red vinyl armchair and went out into the hallway, still holding his can of Special Brew. Rain-sodden Uggs and worn-down loafers were cluttering the floor and he kicked some of them out of the way. Before he opened the door, he looked up at the small fanlight at the top of it and shouted out, 'Who is it? What do you want?'

'Mytaxi!' came the answer.

'What? You must have the wrong house, boy. I don't order no taxi.'

'This is number twenty-seven, right?'

'That's right. Number twenty-seven. But I don't order no mytaxi. Daciana! You don't order no mytaxi?'

'No,' Daciana called back. 'I don't order no mytaxi.'

'I can show you the order, sir,' said the voice on the other side of the door. 'Someone at this address ordered a mytaxi and that's for definite, like. If you cancel you have to pay six euros.'

Even while he was reaching for the doorknob, Ştefan knew that he was taking a risk. In Bucharest the *Poliţsia* had come banging on his front door more times than he could count, and twice rival gangsters had blasted holes in his door panels, once with a shotgun and once with a sub-machine gun. Here in Cork, though, he had very few enemies.

Dragomir Iliescu had given him some trouble, but he had arranged for his house to be burned down, with him in it, and he reckoned that he had put the fear of God into Dragomir's beggars by setting fire to that young girl. He was confident that he no longer had anything to fear from the one they called Lupul or any of his gang. There were local gangs, of course, the O'Flynns and the Murphys, but from the day he had arrived here in Cork he had cannily kept them on side by supplying them from time to time with young prostitutes that he had trafficked from Romania, and cut-price heroin, which he smuggled in from Kazakhstan.

It could be the Garda ringing at his doorbell, but he doubted it. He knew they had cleared all his beggars off the streets last night, but they had done that before, especially when the Pope or some other dignitary was about to visit the city. He expected them all to be back on their pitches by this evening, or tomorrow morning at the latest. The council had neither the finance nor the will to provide them with permanent housing.

'Okay, okay!' he called out. 'Stall your bean!'

He had only just unlocked the door, though, when it was banged wide open with such force that Ştefan was thrown backwards on to the untidy heaps of shoes and his can of Special Brew went flying down the hallway and clattered into the kitchen.

'*What's that?*' shrilled Daciana. 'Ştefan! What's happening? Who is that?'

She came to the kitchen door in her apron, with her wooden spoon dripping cornmeal on to the floor. She was just in time to see Ştefan being hoisted roughly to his feet by two burly men in black. He was pulled out of the front door and then frogmarched down his concrete garden path.

'Ştefan!' she screamed. 'Ştefan!'

But it was too late and there was nothing that she could do. The two burly men jammed Ştefan into the back seat of a dark grey Mercedes, slammed the doors, and drove off into the rain.

Daciana's neighbours the Popescus came out, both of them, husband and wife. Their children wanted to come out and see what was happening, too, but Andrei Popescu shooed them back in.

Daciana sank to her knees on the wet concrete path, still holding her spoon. Her shoulders shook and her grey braids sparkled with rain and she let out a hooting sound like a mother whale who has lost her calf.

Every single day since she and Ştefan had been married she had been frightened that he would be taken away from her, or shot, but he was so close to retirement now and in Cork she had never felt as threatened as she had in Bucharest. But now – just like that – he was gone. It had happened so quickly and she hadn't even had time to kiss him one last time. And it would have been the last time, too, because she knew that he was never coming back – not alive, anyway. If she ever saw him again, he would be lying in a coffin.

They had been driving for almost five minutes before anybody spoke, but as they turned up Spring Lane, heading north-eastwards towards Ballyvolane, the man sitting in the front passenger seat turned around and said, 'Ştefu! It's been too long!'

It was Dragomir Iliescu, Lupul. He was wearing a new brown leather jacket and the interior of the car smelled of wet new leather, as well as stale cigarettes.

'You're *shocked*, Ştefu?' said Lupul. 'Oh! I get it! You were sure that you had turned me into burned *chiftele*, is that it?'

'I don't understand you, Dragos, what you mean,' Ştefan told him, although the sight of Lupul had given him a sudden sharp cramp in his belly and made him feel as if he urgently needed to open his bowels. 'I don't know nothing from nothing, I swear it. Nothing from nothing.'

'You, Ştefu, are liar. But you are worse than liar. You are murdering shit.'

'I told you. I don't know nothing.'

'You set fire to house where all my people were staying. I know it was you because we found your pet monkey Bogdi and we beat Bogdi until he told us. By the way, if you've been wondering where Bogdi is today, he's gone for dip in River Lee, only he has shopping trolley tied to his ankle, so I don't think he's been able to swim very far.'

Ştefan bent forward because his belly hurt even more. At this moment he felt that trying to stop himself from filling his trousers was even more critical than trying to stay alive. But the two burly men sitting either side of him pushed him back upright, and he had to grit his teeth and squeeze his eyes shut and concentrate with every muscle in his body on keeping his anus clenched tight.

'What's the matter, Ştefu? You look like you're going to cry. Are you sad? Well, let me tell you, *nenorocitule,* if anybody should be crying in this car it is me. Do you know what you did when your pet monkeys set fire to that house? You killed my sister and her husband. They had come here to Ireland to visit, and you killed them. You burned them to death. But there was somebody else you killed, too, and if you think I could ever forgive you for that – *ever* – then you have no imagination at all.'

Lupul opened his eyes wide and stared at Ştefan with an expression contorted with such rage and hatred that Ştefan couldn't hold on to his muscles any longer, and he flooded his trousers with warm diarrhoea.

'You killed my stepfather,' said Lupul, his voice shaking. 'You killed man who brought me up from when I was six years old. You killed man who was my mother's husband and loved her. You burned him alive.'

Ştefan could do nothing but stare back at him and feel the sticky wetness between his legs. They had almost reached the

Spring Lane halting site now, where there was a large gathering of Travellers' mobile homes and caravans. As they turned up the narrow lane towards it, the man sitting on Ștefan's left side suddenly sniffed and waved his hand in front of his nose and said, '*Maica Domnului, care este acel miros teribil!*'

They drew in to the side of the lane before the halting site itself came into view, and stopped next to a mountain of rubbish – sodden mattresses and broken bicycles and rusting gas cookers and cardboard boxes and torn black plastic bags.

'It was an accident, Dragos,' Ștefan pleaded. 'I told them to make sure that the house was empty. Be sure it's empty, I told them. I never set out to hurt nobody.'

'Oh, same like young Loredana? Don't tell me it wasn't your pet monkeys who set fire to her, too? That's your trademark, isn't it, Ștefu? Burning people alive. Well, now you're going to find out what it's like to burn in hell.'

The two burly men in black started to drag Ștefan out of the back of the car, but he held on tight to the headrest in front of him and wouldn't let go.

'We can do a deal, Dragos! We can share the profits! I didn't mean nobody to get hurt, I swear to God! You and me, we could run all the begging business in Cork together!'

Lupul breathed in and out as if he were on the point of exploding. '*What?* You think I would do business with bastard who murdered my stepfather and my own sister? You are more of a cretin than I thought you were. I will piss out candles on your mother's birthday cake. And you *stink*. Get him out of here, Aleks, before I throw up.'

The two men wrenched Ștefan's vest three or four times, ripping it apart, and at last succeeded in pulling him out of the car. Between them they dragged him up the mounds of rubbish, his feet clinking and clanking as they trailed against empty bottles and discarded tin cans. When they had almost reached the summit, next to an abandoned refrigerator that was leaning at an angle like a gravestone, they dropped him face down on to some filthy yellow sofa cushions and one of the men planted his boot in the middle of his back to stop him from getting up. Ştefan clenched his fists and, very quietly, he started to sob. *If my mother could see me now, lying in all this garbage in the rain, with my pants full like a baby – if she knew that I had died like this, she would die herself of shame.*

Lupul got out of the car and climbed up the rubbish heap until he was standing over Ştefan. In his right hand he was holding a cordless drill. He nodded to the two burly men and they knelt down on either side of Ştefan, pressing his shoulders and his upper arms hard against the cushions.

Lupul looked around with his hand shielding his eyes to make sure there was nobody else in sight, and then he knelt down, too, and prodded the cutting edge of the twist drill into the back of Ştefan's neck. Ştefan stopped sobbing and tensed himself. He stayed utterly still, and made no attempt to break free. He had killed men himself and he knew that victims suffered much less if they allowed their killers to get on with it, without a struggle.

'Give the Devil my best wishes,' whispered Lupul, leaning close to his ear.

With that, he drilled into Ştefan's head, pressing straight down at first and then tilting the drill left and right. Ştefan jerked up and down as the drill bit churned his brainstem into a paste, and then lay still. Once he was sure that Ştefan was dead, Lupul carefully eased the drill bit out of his neck and brushed his prickly white hair over the hole to cover it.

They rolled Ştefan over on to his back. His one good eye was still open and his tongue was lolling out of the side of his mouth, so that it looked as if he were pulling a comical face.

'Aleks,' said Lupul, and one of the men handed him a razor blade, the type they usually used for cutting cocaine. Lupul sliced deep into Ştefan's right wrist, and then his left. Then he carefully pinched the razor blade between Ştefan's right finger and thumb, to impress his fingerprints on it, before letting it tinkle down into the rubbish. Blood welled up in each of the cuts, but because Ştefan's heart had stopped beating it did nothing more than slowly ooze out.

'Okay,' said Lupul. 'Now we have only one more rat to deal with. Then we can say *plimba ursu* to everybody. Police too.'

He went clambering back down the rubbish heap, with his two minders following him. He opened the car door, but before he climbed in, he turned around and lifted his fist in the direction of Ştefan's body, with his thumb squeezed between his index finger and his middle finger, a gesture that meant, 'Screw you, Ştefan. Have a good time in hell.'

Forty-Nine

'State of you la,' said Diarmuid Moloney, blowing smoke out of his nostrils.

'Fell off my motorbike,' said Conor. 'Bust my nose and my cheekbone, but it could have been worse.'

'Didn't even know ye owned a motorbike.'

'Old Yamaha. Used to belong to my uncle. I only take it out now and again.'

'Just as fecking well, I'd say.'

They were standing in the porch of Moloney's farm, a run-down collection of buildings and barns on the eastern side of Ballyhooly. Off to the south-west, through the dredging rain, they could see the low green mountains on the opposite side of the Blackwater river. A few black-and-white cows were arranged around the fields like checkmate in a numbingly slow game of chess.

Diarmuid was broad-shouldered but short, with a bulbous nose and wildly sprouting eyebrows. He was wearing a tightly belted raincoat and a broad-brimmed trilby that gave him the appearance of an IRA gunman of 1922.

'How's Ruari?' asked Conor.

'Ruari? Didn't you hear, like? Ruari passed.'

'Oh, I'm sorry to hear that. When?'

Diarmuid sucked at his cigarette. 'Well, if he'd lived till next Thursday he would have been dead for a month.'

'I'm sorry. I would have come to his wake if I'd known.'

As they were talking, the Moloneys' German shepherd came trotting over.

'Hey, how's it going, Aengus?' said Conor, and tugged at his ears and stroked him. In response, Aengus shook himself violently and sprayed both Conor and Diarmuid with rainwater.

'I think Aengus'll always remember how ye found him after those knackers took him and brought him back home,' said Diarmuid. 'I'll never forget it for sure, myself. Ye're a fecking genius and no mistake.'

'In a way, that's the reason I've called in to see you today, Diarmuid. I need a bit of a favour in return.'

'Ye have only to name it, Conor. What's ours is yours. Except for the cows, like.'

'I'm looking for Semtex. And a detonator.'

Diarmuid looked at Conor narrowly. Before he answered, he took a long hard suck on his cigarette and then tossed it aside across the farmyard.

'Semtex, is it?'

'I have some old outbuildings I need to demolish, and that seemed like the quickest and the cheapest way of doing it.'

'Ye couldn't employ a couple of fellers and a digger?'

'It's a little more complicated than that.'

'Complimicated, is it? How much more complimicated?'

'All right, I'll be square with you, Diarmuid. There's a puppy farm not too far from here where they're sorely mistreating their breeding bitches and their litters. Foggy Fields, run by Blánaid and Caoilfhoinn McQuaide.'

'I know them all right. That Blánaid, she's some sour misery, that one. Ye say how's it going on to her and she sticks up her nose like you've blown off a breezer.'

Conor said, 'I've done everything I can to have them closed down, but so far I've got nowhere. I reckon a well-placed explosion would be a quick way to persuade them to shut up shop. Not hurting any dogs, of course, but blowing up a shed maybe or knocking down a wall. Kind of a warning, do you know?'

Diarmuid thought long and hard. Then he said, 'I don't need to tell ye that nobody's ever to know where ye came by it, the Semtex.'

'Diarmuid, I think that goes without saying. On Ruari's grave, nobody will ever find out. But if you'd ever seen for yourself the sheer outright cruelty those dogs have to suffer, you'd be round to Foggy Fields yourself with a whole barrowload of bombs.'

'Okay, then. Come back tomorrow morning and I'll have it ready for you. A pound of it, with an electric detonator. I must be mad as a box of frogs letting you have it, but a favour's a favour.'

Conor shook his hand, and then clapped him on the back. 'You won't forget this, Diarmuid, I promise you.'

Katie drove to CUH after lunch to visit Detectives Murrish and Markey. Detective Scanlan had been allowed home that morning after a final scan, but she would be taking at least four weeks off to recuperate fully. Detective Murrish's eye socket was healing well, and she was impatiently waiting for her prosthetic eye to be fitted, although she admitted to Katie that she was still having nightmares about being blinded.

'Do you know what I hate most of all?' she said. She was sitting in a chair by the window, looking out at the rain sifting across the next-door rooftop. 'I keep hearing that crunch when the knife went into my eye. Crunch! And it makes me shudder something awful.'

Katie took hold of her hand. 'It was a desperate thing to happen to you, Bedelia. But you're strong. You'll get over it.'

Detective Murrish smiled. 'At least I can still see. That's what I'm thankful for, more than anything else. See those raindrops, falling in those puddles? What if I'd never been able to see them again, ever?'

Katie went along the corridor to see Detective Markey. He was still wearing his white turban, but his last scan had shown that the swelling on his brain had almost completely subsided and that he, too, would be allowed to go home, possibly as early as tomorrow.

She updated him on her interview with Eamon Buckley and Thomas Barry. She had to tell him, though, that she had still heard no word from the gardaí in Skibbereen about the identity of the two men who had attacked him and Detective Scanlan.

'Well, if *they* can't find them, I'll go down there and find them myself,' he said. 'With any luck they'll resist arrest so I have an excuse to take the baton to them. Hard, like, on top of the head. And at least twice.'

'Policing isn't about revenge, Nick,' said Katie.

'I know that, ma'am. But I can't say that I wouldn't enjoy it.'

Katie was walking back to her car when her iPhone played 'Mo Ghille Mear'. She climbed behind the wheel and said, 'Yes... sorry about the delay. I was halfway across the car park and it's rotten out.'

It was Detective Inspector Fitzpatrick and he sounded even grimmer than usual. 'It's Ştefan Făt-Frumor. He's been found dead on top of that rubbish tip off Spring Lane.'

'Serious? When?'

'Only about half an hour ago. Some Pavee kids were playing on the tip and they found him.'

'Any indication how he died?'

'The kids called for an ambulance and the paramedics who examined him say that it looks like suicide, because his wrists were cut. Bill Phinner's already sent a team up there anyway so we should know for certain pretty soon. But I can't believe that Făt-Frumor would take his own life. If he'd ever had the choice between being stung by a wazzer and seeing his mother boiled in oil, I know which one he'd have gone for.'

'How was he identified?'

'He had a final demand from Bord Gáis in his back pants pocket.'

'That was a bit of a comedown for a king of crime. No suicide note?'

'Not unless he left one at his house. O'Donovan's gone there now.'

'I totally agree with you that it's highly unlikely that he killed himself. So who do you think might have done it? From what I've heard about him, he rubbed along pretty well with all the other gangs in Cork. Patrick found out that he was planning to expand his drug-running business to Dublin, though, wasn't he? Maybe one of the Dublin gangs decided to come down here and squash him before he even had the chance to get started.'

'I've heard nothing from the CSB that might suggest that.' Detective Inspector Fitzpatrick was referring to the Crime and Security Branch based in Phoenix Park, who constantly monitored the activity of terrorists and serious criminals.

'Listen, Robert – can you tell Bill that as soon as his technicians have completed their examination of the scene at Spring Lane, I want Ștefan Făt-Frumor's body sent down to Dr Kelley at CUH as a matter of priority for an immediate post mortem. I'm going to call her myself to make sure she's free to do it, or that she can arrange for another pathologist to carry it out in her place. I'm having no more gang killings here in Cork. I don't want this turning into all-out warfare like Kinahan-Hutch.'

She made her way back to Anglesea Street. She knew there was no point in trying to guess who might have killed Ștefan Făt-Frumor. As she drove through the city with its silver-grey river and its high surrounding hills and the spires of St Finbarr's and St Anne's rising through the rain, she had the deadening feeling that this investigation was being played out according to a script that had already been written but which she herself had never seen, and that no matter what she did, it would have a tragic and unexpected but unavoidable ending.

Almost as soon as she returned to her office, Chief Superintendent O'Kane came in, briskly rubbing his hands.

'Impromptu media conference downstairs in five minutes, Katie,' he told her.

'Impromptu media conference about what?'

'Ştefan Făt-Frumor, of course. The news has got out already. One of the Pavee lads who found him had the wit to ring RTÉ and the *Echo* so that they would pay him for an interview.'

'Mother of God, sir, we don't even know yet how he died, or what his movements were before he was found.'

'Then we can say so. But we need to be upbeat, and show the media that we're winning the battle against organized crime. We've hauled in all of Lupul's beggars, after all, and Lupul's either deceased or disappeared, and now we've put an end to Făt-Frumor's begging ring, too.'

'Excuse me, sir, but it wasn't us who put an end to Făt-Frumor. Person or persons unknown did it. That's unless he committed suicide, which isn't very likely. And we didn't even *know* that he was running a begging ring until a couple of days ago, much to my personal embarrassment.'

'We don't have to say that, Katie. In any case, it's all water under the bridge now, isn't it? It's pure important that we come over as positive, active, tough on any kind of crime, and always protecting the Cork community from harm.'

Katie hung up her raincoat. She didn't know how to answer that. She knew how badly the Garda needed to repair their relationship with the ordinary people of Cork, but at the same time she didn't believe in obfuscating or telling half-truths. They had failed to realize that Ştefan Făt-Frumor had been extorting money from the city's beggars, and she felt that they should admit it, even now that he was dead. In fact, it was quite possible that his extorting money from beggars had led to him being murdered, and if so, that might lead them to track down his killer, or killers. Maybe a disgruntled beggar had done it. Maybe a whole gang of disgruntled beggars had done it.

'I can only give the media the barest facts, sir,' Katie told him.

'Don't worry. You can leave the inspirational talk to me. That's why I was appointed, after all. To make An Garda Síochána acceptable again. Not just acceptable. Trusted. Liked. Even – dare I say it – *loved*. And, Katie—'

And I know that you're going to say it again. 'When we're alone together, you don't have to call me "sir".' But what we had between us, Brendan, all those years ago, that too is all water under the bridge.

Brendan was about to finish what he was saying when Moirin came in and said, 'Sorry to interrupt, ma'am. A woman called Breda Behan's on the phone. She wants to know if you'd be interested in giving a talk at the next Thursday evening meeting of the Cork Feminist Collective.'

'Katie?' said Brendan, raising an eyebrow. 'That sounds right up your street.'

The media conference was over in less than twenty minutes. Katie announced simply that Ştefan Făt-Frumor had been found dead at Spring Lane and that their investigation into his death was ongoing. She declined to take questions, saying that there was nothing more she could add. She was so abrupt that Brendan found it impossible to launch into his intended speech about how effectively the Garda were cleaning up the streets of the city and rooting out drug-dealers and people traffickers, and how they were gradually winning over the hearts and minds of the people of Cork.

Instead, he could only stand up and say to the assembled reporters and camera operators, 'Thank you. Watch this space.'

Afterwards, he caught up with Katie in the corridor.

'That didn't go down too well, did it, Katie?'

'We told them all we know, sir. There's no point in speculating. If you speculate, you usually end up looking like a total gom when the truth eventually comes out. I'm sure you know that as well as I do.'

'Katie, I need you one hundred per cent on side. It's vital that I have your support when it comes to our public image. Back in there, all you did was give out to those reporters like a – I don't know, like a—'

'Like a detective superintendent, reporting a suspicious death?'

Brendan was about to answer back, but instead he said nothing and lifted both hands as if to say, *Okay, girl, have it your way for now.*

At half past five, the rain eased off, and Katie drove up to St Dunstan's church hall again, with Detective Inspector Fitzgerald and Kyna and Detective O'Donovan. She wanted to tell the rough sleepers that Ştefan Făt-Frumor had been found dead before they saw it on the *Six One News* – especially those that had been part of his begging ring.

They were having an early supper – most of them sitting at the table on the stage, but some of them sitting on the floor watching TV. This evening it was boiled bacon and cabbage and potatoes, with parsley sauce, and as she walked into the hall the smell of it reminded Katie that she hadn't had anything to eat since breakfast.

'Could you mute the telly, please?' she called out, and when the hall was silent she climbed halfway up the steps that led to the stage and said, 'I've some news for you... something that I know some of you will be very glad to hear.'

'The Pope's said he's sorry!' one of the men shouted.

'Well, he has, as a matter of fact,' said Katie. 'But the news is that somebody's passed... somebody who had a whole lot more influence on your lives lately than His Holiness. Ştefan Făt-Frumor. The one you call the Fat Fellow.'

A ragged cheer went up from the beggars sitting at the table, and some of them banged their knives and forks. As Katie stepped down from the stage, a freckle-faced young girl with wildly fraying ginger hair came limping up to her. Her shoulders were shaking and she was crying uncontrollably. Katie had talked to her the last time she was here: she was a cocaine addict and if she had spent all the money that she had made from begging on crack, then Ştefan Făt-Frumor's thugs would beat her. Only a month ago they had knocked out all her front teeth.

She held out her skinny arms and Katie hugged her. Underneath her floppy cotton sweater Katie could feel her shoulder blades sticking out, and her ribs.

'Bless you,' she wept. 'Bless you, bless you, bless you. You're a saint.'

But a black-bearded man at the table shouted out, 'Okay, the Fat Fellow's dead, and he was a bastard all right. But who's going to watch out for us now? At least the Fat Fellow stopped us from getting robbed or beaten or pissed on, like.'

'Fair play to you, but I'm going to talk to the council about housing you all on a permanent basis,' said Katie. 'Also – how we can get you into rehab, and how we can find jobs for you, once you're clean. As far as protection is concerned, I'm going to discuss with the policing council how you can be better looked after if and when you go back on the street. Meanwhile, you can stay here at St Dunstan's for as long as you need to.'

The girl called Elenuta stood up. 'What about us, from Romania? What about Lupul?'

The ginger-haired girl wiped her eyes on her sleeves. Katie gave her one more hug and a smile and then let her go.

'I have some good news for you, too,' she said to Elenuta. 'Danut is dead. We found out where he was hiding and he took his own life before we could arrest him. So you don't have to worry about Danut any more.'

'But Lupul? You give to me promise that I would not have to worry about Lupul, too. Lupul is scary one.'

'I'll be honest with you, we're still not entirely sure if Lupul is alive or dead. But we're doing everything in our power to find out. So long as you stay here, though, he won't be able to come near you, even if he is still alive. Did the immigration people come to talk to you?'

'Yes. They are sort out my papers. When they do that, I will go back to Romania. All here from Romania will go back.'

As they drove down to Anglesea Street, Detective Inspector Fitzpatrick said, 'That fellow who asked about protection had a point, like. I can't see the council having the funds to find accommodation for all of those rough sleepers, can you? And some of them would rather be out on the streets than in some shelter. They have to behave themselves in a shelter. But we don't have the manpower to watch over them every minute of the night, do we? And if that's how they choose to live, why should we?'

'We can only do what we can, Robert,' said Katie. 'But even if somebody's halfway out of their head on spice or monkey dust and doesn't want help, we still have to take care of them. It's our job.'

She was leaving her office for home when Bill Phinner came along the corridor.

'What's the story, Bill?'

'You don't happen to have a cigarette on you, ma'am, do you, by any chance?'

'No. Don't tell me you've taken up smoking again.'

'I haven't, no, but I wish I had. I've tried that vaping but, Jesus. It's like sucking in some two-year-old's breath after they've been eating rhubarb and custards.'

'Were you coming up here to see me?'

'I was, yes. It's that Romanian feen who shot his friend in the head and then blew his own face off. We've examined the bullets and they match the bullets we retrieved from that boxer fellow, the one who was shot in Crane Lane.'

'So it was the same gun?'

'No question about it.'

'Oh well, that leads me to one of several conclusions. Either it was Danut who shot Bowser, or if it wasn't, then whoever had that gun before doesn't have it now. Or – I don't know. I'm too flah'd out to think straight. How are you coming along with that burned notebook, by the way?'

'Slow but sure. We've separated all the pages, like, and now we're drying them off. If there's anything written on them, we should be able to see what it is by tomorrow or the day after.'

'Okay, Bill, that's grand. I'll see you in the morning so. Try not to give up the struggle. Think of your lungs.'

'I am, ma'am, believe me. Both of them are crying out for a deep inhalation of Johnny Blue smoke, followed by a good phlegmy cough.'

Fifty

Conor was quiet again that evening. Katie baked two pepperoni pizzas in the oven because she was too tired to cook anything else, but he ate only one slice of his.

'What's on your mind, Con?' she asked him.

'This and that, you know.'

'No, I don't know. What's "this and that"?'

'I was thinking about the future, that's all. Our future – you and me.'

'And?'

'Like I said before... I think you'd be better off without me.'

Katie put down the slice of pizza that she was about to bite into. 'That's for me to judge, wouldn't you say, not you? And if there's one thing I've learned from my work, it's not to eat your sandwiches before you've made them.'

Conor couldn't help shaking his head in amusement. 'Didn't anyone ever tell you about bridges, and crossing them before you came to them?'

'No. My gran always said sandwiches.'

Despite what he had said, Conor held Katie very close in bed that night, even after he had fallen asleep. After she had heard the clock in the living room chime one, Katie had to lever his arm from around her waist and lay it down beside him. He didn't stir, and although his nose was still bandaged, he was breathing so silently that she had to press her hand against his chest to make sure he wasn't dead.

*

'We have to prioritize who we're going to be looking out for,' said Superintendent Pearse. 'Do we look out for the law-abiding people who pay for police protection through their taxes, or the down-and-outs and druggies living off benefits? We can't always afford to do both. It's not only a financial head-scratcher, and a logistical one, it's political. And of course it's humanitarian, too.'

It was ten o'clock the next morning. Katie was holding an informal conference with Superintendent Pearse, Inspector O'Rourke and Detective Inspector Fitzpatrick. They were discussing what it would take to improve security for Cork's rough sleepers once they had left St Dunstan's church hall. They were having to face up to the fact that even though they had broken up the two Romanian begging rings, this had possibly exposed the city's rough sleepers to a much greater risk of violence and abuse.

'Forget about the beggars, I badly need more manpower on the northside at night,' said Inspector O'Rourke. 'This rash of car-stealing and joyriding and setting fire to cars – well, it's more than a rash now, it's an epidemic.'

'I saw your report this morning about that poor woman up in Knocknaheeny,' said Superintendent Pearse.

'That's right. She went out to confront a gang of kids who were trying to steal her car, and they chased her back into her own house. She wasn't hurt, thank God, but she was fierce shaken. These kids think they can rampage around with complete impunity, and the trouble is, they can.'

'Well, like I say, it all comes down to budget cuts. We can't patrol the streets with officers we haven't got.'

Katie's phone rang. She picked it up and it was Dr Kelley.

'Kathleen? Ah, good. I've completed my examination of Ştefan Făt-Frumor. I can tell you straight off that his death was not the result of accident or suicide. Both his wrists were cut but those incisions were inflicted post mortem, so he didn't kill himself. The direct cause of death was a drill inserted into his brainstem from the back of his neck. An exact copy of the way in which all of those other three victims were drilled to death.'

'Thanks, Mary,' said Katie. 'No other injuries?'

'Some bruising on his arms, which would indicate that he was manhandled shortly before his death. His liver was cirrhosed and he was suffering from chronic gout, but nothing else that would have directly contributed to his death.'

'All right. What about that burned body from Alexandra Road? Any progress with identifying him?'

'It hasn't been at all easy, I'm afraid, because he was almost totally carbonized. Usually we can age victims by their teeth, but all his teeth are false. The only thing I can tell you for certain is that they're not Irish false teeth. Most likely Eastern European, and reasonably new. They do excellent false teeth in the Czech Republic and Romania, if ever you need them.'

'I'll remember that, Mary, thanks. Listen, I'm in the middle of a meeting but I'll ring you back later so.'

She put down the phone and all three officers could immediately see that she had been told something significant.

'It's Ştefan Făt-Frumor,' she said. 'He was killed by a drill, just like those two rough sleepers and the barman from The Parting Glass.'

'Maybe that Lupul *is* still alive,' said Detective Inspector Fitzpatrick. 'Like, who would have a greater incentive to do away with the Fat Fellow than him? And who else uses that MO? We still haven't announced how any of those rough sleepers were killed, so it's a million to one that anybody else would think of using a drill.'

'You're right,' said Katie. 'And Dr Kelley hasn't yet been able to identify the body from Alexandra Road so I think we have to assume for the time being that it *isn't* Lupul. We need to step up our search for him, and in the meantime we should start building up a case against him, so that we can charge him immediately when we haul him in – if he's still alive, that is, and we do.'

'So what's the plan?' asked Detective Inspector Fitzpatrick.

'I want to interview Eamon Buckley again, because that ring didn't get mixed up in his mince by magic. Also, I have that trainer that I found under the bed in Lupul's house in Sidney Park, as well as the necklace that was found in Crane Lane after Bowser was shot. Young Ana-Maria should have recovered enough by now to confirm that they belonged to her ma.'

Detective Inspector Fitzpatrick said, 'We're still going door to door around Orchard Court to see if we can find any witnesses to the Fat Fellow leaving his house. No luck so far. His wife swears he simply walked out of the front door without saying where he was going. He was wearing only a torn vest and trackies when his body was found. It was minus two that night so don't tell me he went off for a hod with no overcoat and only slippers on his feet.'

'Sure somebody must have seen him, especially if he was abducted,' said Superintendent Pearse. 'I can't believe that he would have gone quiet-like.'

'They probably did,' said Katie. 'So why aren't they telling us? What are they afraid of? Or rather, *who* are they afraid of?'

She rang Margaret O'Reilly at Tusla first of all, to ask her if she had any objection to her going to the Flynns' house in Glanmire and asking Ana-Maria to identify her mother's necklace and trainer.

Margaret, in her whispery windblown voice, said that would be no problem at all. Ana-Maria had settled in well with Michael and Sadhbh, which was a relief, because the Romanian authorities still hadn't been able to trace her father, or any other relatives.

Katie took the pink-and-white-striped trainer that she had found under the bed in Sidney Park, and the necklace with the image of Saint Philothea of Argeş. She had arranged to meet Murtagh at the Flynns' house so that he could translate for her. She had thought of asking Kyna to come with her, too, but then she remembered how shy Ana-Maria had been. She needed the child to tell her as much as possible about her missing mother, and she didn't want her to be put off by the presence of a stranger, no matter how pretty and sympathetic that stranger might be.

She drove up by the curving Glashaboy River to Glanmire village. It was a bright and sunny afternoon, but freezing, so that the trees and bushes alongside the river were sparkling white. As she drove, she couldn't stop thinking about Conor. This morning he had been even more distant, although he had held her in his arms for a long time before she had left – not kissing her, just holding her, as if he were afraid of falling.

The Flynns lived at the top of Cúl Na Gréine, a hilly cul-de-sac of large white detached houses with grey slate roofs. A navy-blue Range Rover was parked on the sloping driveway outside. Katie parked behind it and climbed out, and as she did so, Ana-Maria appeared around the corner of the house, on a bicycle with stabilizers. She was wearing a red duffel coat and gloves and fur-lined boots.

'*Mătuşă!*' she cried out, scrambling off her bicycle and running towards Katie with her arms out.

Katie picked her up and kissed her. Her cheeks were as red as her coat, and her nose was cold.

'It's so lovely to see you,' said Katie. 'It looks like the Flynns are taking real good care of you.'

Ana-Maria frowned, concentrating hard, and then she said, very carefully, 'Hal-lo. I am happy to meet you.'

'Oh, and they're teaching you English, too! That's brilliant! Listen, sweetheart, I'll just go and have a word with Michael and Sadhbh and then maybe you can come in and you and we can have a bit of a chat, like. Murtagh will be here soon. You remember Murtagh? He'll be able to translate for us.'

Ana-Maria nodded and Katie put her down. 'I don't know why I'm telling you all this, you don't understand a word I'm saying.'

'*Mătuşă, n-ai găsit-o încă pe mumia mea?*'

Katie could guess what that meant, and she sadly shook her head. 'No, we don't know what happened to your ma, not yet. But we will, I promise you.'

The front door of the house had opened and Sadhbh Flynn was standing waiting for her. Katie said, 'See you in a minute, sweetheart,' and went up the steps to the porch.

Sadhbh was an attractive woman in her early forties, with dark bouncy hair. She was wearing a maroon cardigan and a long tweed skirt and she put Katie in mind of those ideal American housewives on 1950s' magazine covers, like *Saturday Evening Post*.

'Come along in,' said Sadhbh. 'Here, let's go through to the living room. How about a cup of tea in your hand? It's so cold today! What should I call you?'

'Kathleen would be fine,' said Katie. 'Is your husband not here today?'

'He's out for his daily run. He does it every single day, no matter what the weather. All the way up to the Old Christians Rugby Football Club and then back by way of John O'Callaghan Park. He says it helps to clear his mind for all the IT stuff he does. Myself, I couldn't make head nor tail of that IT stuff anyway, even if I ran all the way to Fermoy and back.'

'How's Ana-Maria coming along?' Katie asked her. 'Like I told you on the phone, I've a trainer and a necklace that we believe belong to her mother. I don't want to distress her but I need to know for sure if they're hers.'

'She has her moments. Night-times are the worst. She has desperate bad dreams. I gave her a ginger cookie yesterday in the kitchen and she burst into tears. I can only guess that it reminded her of her ma.'

Katie followed her into the kitchen while she filled the kettle to make tea. They were still talking when they heard Ana-Maria scream outside on the driveway. Almost immediately afterwards, someone hammered on the front door with their fist.

Katie hurried to the front door and flung it open. Lupul was standing in the porch, with his left arm crooked around Ana-Maria's neck. In his right hand he was holding his cordless drill, with the drill bit pointing at the top of her head.

Two bulky men in black windcheaters were standing by the wall at the top of the driveway, their arms folded. A dark grey Volvo saloon was waiting in the road with its doors open and its engine running.

'What in the *name* of God do you think you're playing at?' Katie demanded. 'That young girl has done nothing to you at all. You let her go.'

'This young girl is start of all my trouble. Now my trouble end here.'

'I said let her go. Look at her, she's terrified.'

'You have gun?'

Katie took a deep breath. Then she said, 'No,' and she unbuttoned her jacket to show him that she wasn't carrying her Smith & Wesson revolver. It was unusual for her not to be armed, but she hadn't wanted to unsettle Ana-Maria by wearing a pistol.

'Give me phone,' said Lupul.

Katie took out her iPhone and held it out. Lupul whistled sharply between his teeth and called out, '*Aleks!*' One of the men in black windcheaters came strolling down the driveway and snatched the phone away from her, dropping it into his pocket. Katie gave him a long, intense stare, to show him that she wouldn't forget what he looked like, when it came to him being arrested and standing in front of her in court.

'Now you come with me, police detective woman,' said Lupul. 'And *you*—' to Sadhbh '—we see police follow us, this little girl gets *brrrrrrrrrrrr!*' and he mimicked drilling into Ana-Maria's skull. '*Any* police – car, motorcycle, helicopter – any. *Brrrrrrrrrr!*'

Lupul dragged Ana-Maria up the driveway, still holding the drill to her head. The man called Aleks took hold of Katie's arm and said, 'Come.'

Katie turned around to Sadhbh and whispered urgently, 'Call them. Tell them it's Lupul. But they must keep their distance.'

'What?' said Sadhbh.

'*Lupul!*'

'You *come*!' Aleks barked, and yanked Katie up the driveway by the sleeve of her jacket. She was proficient enough at karate to have knocked him flat, but she was sure that Lupul was cold-blooded enough to kill Ana-Maria on the spot, and so she allowed herself to be jostled up to the Volvo and pushed into the back seat. Ana-Maria was sitting in the middle, with Lupul next to her. Ana-Maria was shivering, so Katie took hold of her hand.

'It's okay, sweetheart,' she said, soothingly. 'Everything's going to be fine. I won't let these men hurt you.'

'You shut up face,' said Lupul. 'You know nothing. All my trouble start with this girl.'

'Let me tell you this, sham,' Katie retorted. 'If you so much as scratch either of us, you're going to be spending so long in prison you'll forget what the world looks like without bars in front of it.'

'And I say this to you, police detective woman. You do like I say, exact, or nobody will ever know what happen to you. Ever. You will be gone. *Pfff!* Like never born.'

As they reached the end of Cúl Na Gréine, Katie saw Murtagh in his Honda turning into the cul-de-sac from Church Hill. She opened her mouth wide, silently shouting, hoping that he would see her in the back of the Volvo. He slowed right down, but he didn't look in her direction and then he carried on driving up the hill towards the Flynn house, oblivious.

Aleks drove the Volvo south to the River Lee and then turned westwards on the Lower Glanmire Road. Katie sat back. She had no idea what Lupul intended to do with her and Ana-Maria, but she knew that she had to keep steely calm and clear-headed. There was one small consolation: Lupul had a cordless drill but it appeared that he didn't have a gun. The pistol that Danut had used to shoot himself must have been his only firearm, and he had left it behind that night at Sutton's Buildings.

She was also confident that if Sadhbh had called 112 by now, Detective Inspector Fitzpatrick would soon be alerted and he would set up a pursuit that wouldn't alert Lupul that he was being tracked.

They had been driving only a few minutes, though, before they turned off the Lower Glanmire Road and into the car park of the Clayton Silver Springs Hotel. They went right to the far end of the hotel car park and stopped, and Aleks and the other man opened the doors.

They had parked next to a metallic green Hyundai Tucson. They opened the doors of that, too, and Aleks said to Katie, 'Come. Change car.'

Mother of God, she thought, *as she climbed up into the back seat of the Hyundai. Lupul has really planned this. He must have been following me everywhere I went. He must know where his beggars are, in St Dunstan's church hall, and that was how he found out where Ana-Maria was being cared for.*

But the begging ring he's tried to set up here in Cork, it's all fallen apart. What's the point of abducting me and Ana-Maria? He's like Hitler in his bunker at the end of the Second World War, with Germany in ruins all around him, refusing to believe that it's all over.

'Dragomir,' she said, as they drove out of the hotel car park and continued to head west, 'why don't you let us both go and give yourself up? You'll be given a much better deal by the court if you do.'

'Why don't you keep your face shut, detective woman? You can prove nothing. What can you prove? Nothing. And when you and this girl are gone, nobody can prove nothing.'

Ana-Maria started to cry again, a thin, hopeless whine. Lupul shook her and jabbed the drill at her and said, 'Shut up! No noise! You hear me? Or, *brrrrrrrrrr!*'

Fifty-One

Conor parked about twenty metres away from the front gate of Foggy Fields. He could see Blánaid's silver Mercedes coupé parked outside, so he knew that she must be home. A mud-spattered Land Rover was parked beside it, with a large bull terrier sitting placidly behind the steering wheel.

He felt strangely detached, as if he been smoking weed, or hadn't slept for twenty-four hours. He could hardly believe that this was really him, Conor Ó Máille, doing this. But he had been feeling like another person ever since he had woken up after his operation and Mr Sandhu had told him that he was going to be impotent for the rest of his life. *Other men are impotent. Eunuchs, or octogenarians, or men who have suffered from prostate cancer. Not me – especially not with a beautiful woman in my life like Katie.*

He sat in his Audi for almost twenty minutes. Then he switched on the radio. RedFM were playing 'It Started with a Kiss' by Hot Chocolate, and so instantly he switched it off again. That song had too many painful connotations. But he couldn't stop himself from miming the words '...*never thought it would end like this*'.

He left his Audi by the side of the boreen and walked up to the front door of the Foggy Fields farmhouse. He pulled the doorbell and waited, shuffling his feet a little so that he looked like any normal man kept waiting in the cold.

He was about to pull the doorbell again when the door opened and there was Caoilfhoinn, holding a half-eaten chicken bap.

'Holy Jesus,' she said. 'It's you. What do you want?'

'I've come to set things straight, that's all.'

'What do you mean, "set things straight"?'

From inside the office, Blánaid called out, 'Kee? Who is that?'

'It's that fellow that said he wanted a pug. The one that Shawn found poking around in the shed. MacSuibhne. The one that the law were after asking about. He says he wants to set things straight, like.'

Blánaid immediately came to the door, in her black sweater and her black jeans and her bright red lipstick. She looked Conor up and down and then she said, 'I don't know what in the world you're talking about, Caoilfhoinn. We never had nobody asking for a pug, and Shawn never found nobody poking around in any of our sheds. I told the guards that, and they believed me.'

She turned to Conor again and said, 'So – who are you?'

'You're not a very good liar, Ms McQuaide,' said Conor. 'You know full well who I am and you know full well what your shamfeen did to me. I didn't break my nose and my cheekbone walking into a door and you know it.'

'What do you want?'

'Now that I'm on the mend, I've been talking with my solicitor about a private prosecution. The Garda may not have found enough circumstantial evidence to charge you, but my doctor can supply plenty of medical evidence. On top of that, I have enough witnesses to my movements that day to be able to prove that I could only have been here when I was assaulted.'

Blánaid said, 'You're trying to pull a fast one. Up the yard with you, whatever your name is, or I'll be after setting Shawn on you again.'

She started to close the door, but Conor said, 'Not so fast, Ms McQuaide. I'm not pulling a fast one at all, as you'll find out if you slam that door on me. My solicitor believes I have a fierce strong case, and that I could sue you for hundreds of thousands.'

Blánaid kept the door half open. 'So what's this about "setting things straight"?'

'We could come to some kind of arrangement, that's what I was thinking. Nothing so punitive as I'd be expecting from you if you forced me to go to court. But maybe a small sum by way of compensation for my injuries, and possibly a modest percentage of your income here from Foggy Fields. Nothing eye-watering, do you know? But enough to make up for what I've suffered.'

'Why don't you come inside and we'll discuss it?' said Blánaid. 'It's pure freezing with the door open.'

Blánaid went into the office and Conor followed her. Caoilfhoinn closed the front door behind them. The fire in the office was crackling, and sitting next to the fire was Shawn, bulky and bald and bearded, with that Y-shaped scar above his eye. He smelled just as strongly of alcohol and body odour as he had when he had beaten and kicked Conor. He said nothing, but glared at Conor with his piggy little eyes as if Blánaid would only have to say the word and he would happily beat him up all over again, and kick his head in this time, just to make sure.

Conor closed his eyes for a moment and gave a smile that was almost beatific. *Thank you, Lord. I was confident that both McQuaide sisters would be home this afternoon, but I hadn't dared to hope that the sham-feen who kicked me into impotence would be here with them. If I have never given you adequate praise in my lifetime, then please O Lord I beg you to forgive me, because today you have rewarded me with justice beyond all my expectations, amen.*

'You know Shawn,' said Blánaid.

Conor didn't answer that. He didn't want to end his prayerful thought to the Lord with the foulest obscenity that he could think of.

'Do you want to take off your coat?' Caoilfhoinn asked him. 'It's like an oven in here.'

'No, no thanks. I won't be staying for long. All I want to know is whether you agree to pay me for my injuries, and how much.'

'You realize you were trespassing,' said Blánaid.

'Oh. I thought you told the guards that I wasn't here at all.'

'I'd be interested to know what you were looking for, poking around in our shed. Were you looking to steal yourself a breeding bitch, was that it?'

'I wouldn't steal one of your breeding bitches if they were the last breeding bitches on the Planet Earth, Ms McQuaide. They're all sick, half-starved, wormy and worn out. You and your sister are a stain on the name of Irish dog-breeding. Worse than a stain. You're a fungus.'

Blánaid sat bolt upright. 'If you're going to speak like that to us, whoever you are, you can forget about any kind of recompense. Foggy Fields is one of the most profitable puppy farms in Munster.'

'Profitable, I agree with you. Oh, yes, profitable. Sanitary, no. Nurturing, certainly not. Loving and kind and happy – I don't think either of you have the first notion what any of those words mean.'

Now Blánaid stood up. 'I thought you came here to talk about a legal settlement, not to insult us. You'd best be out the gap before I ask Shawn to throw you out.'

Conor stood up, too. 'I have a better idea,' he told her. 'Why don't we all go together?'

With that, he detonated the pound of Semtex that he had flattened out and attached to his belt. He had filled his coat pockets with ball bearings, too, so that he was blown apart in a fountain of blood and ribs and shredded flesh. Blánaid was standing right in front of him, so that the blast blew her head off and looped her intestines up to the ceiling for a second like a rearing serpent from some hideous Greek myth. Caoilfhoinn's head was blown off, too, along with both arms and both legs, and her torso blasted out of the window, so that it rolled down the driveway like a bloody beer keg.

Shawn's sweater and half his face were ripped off by a hailstorm of ball bearings and he was thrown sideways into the hearth as if an invisible giant had picked him up and flung him. The fireplace and the chimney breast collapsed on top of him, with a clatter of hot bricks and a shower of sparks. Seconds later, the whole ceiling collapsed, and Conor and Blánaid and Caoilfhoinn and Shawn were all given a temporary burial under lumps of plaster and splintered joists.

Gradually the dust settled and the smoke drifted away. Foggy Fields was too far from the nearest farm for anybody to have heard the explosion. The only sound now was the plaintive yelping of breeding bitches and puppies waiting to be fed. The bull terrier behind the wheel of the Land Rover could smell blood in the air, and he sniffed and licked his lips.

Fifty-Two

It was dark by the time they drove up the narrow boreen and turned into the courtyard of what looked to Katie like a farm. She could see a farmhouse, with its windows lit up, and a large barn off to the right, with a corrugated-iron roof.

They had been driving for over an hour-and-a-half, mostly down side roads. The last town they had been through was Skibbereen, and when they had passed the West Cork Hotel and crossed the bridge over the River Ilen, Katie had guessed that they were being taken to the same place that Eamon Buckley had been heading for when Detectives Markey and Scanlan had been following him.

Aleks opened the Hyundai's door and jerked his thumb to indicate that she should get out, and she needed to take only one breath to know that she had guessed right. The chilly evening air smelled strongly of pigs.

A fat man in a brown padded jacket came waddling across from the house to meet them. His double chins were prickly with white stubble and his face was cratered with acne scars.

'Well, this is some kind of an honour,' he said, in a thick country accent. 'Cathal Kilmartin at your service. Why don't you come along inside?'

'I hope you understand what a heap of trouble you're getting yourself into, Mr Kilmartin,' said Katie, trying to keep her voice steady.

'What d'ye say? Trouble? Oh, sure like. I'm always getting

meself into trouble. Me whole fecking life has been one hape of trouble from beginning to now, so one hape more trouble can't hurt.'

'You're aware that I'm a detective superintendent with An Garda Síochána in Cork city?'

'Oh sure like. I've seen you on the telly, like. That's why I said it's an honour. But in real life I have to say that you're smaller than I thought. Do they make you wear special shoes when you're appearing on the telly, like, so that you look taller?'

'We go inside,' said Lupul, impatiently. He was still gripping Ana-Maria's shoulder, and pointing the drill bit to the side of her head.

'Dragomir – I think we need to call a halt to this pantomime right now,' said Katie. 'Like I said before, if you let us go and give yourself up, any judge will give you a much lighter sentence.'

'And like *I* say before, shut up your face. You *poliţişti* can't prove nothing, so I don't get *no* prison. Now we go inside.'

They all made their way over to the farmhouse and stepped inside. It was an old building, with thick damp walls and brick flooring in the hallway, and it smelled of burned sausages and disinfectant. As they filed through to the back of the house they passed an open living-room door, and Katie saw a blowsy, plump woman sitting on a sofa smoking a cigarette and watching television, with a brindled cat sitting in her lap. The woman turned and looked back at Katie and blew out smoke. There was no expression in her eyes at all. She might as well have been looking at pigs being led to the slaughter.

Cathal Kilmartin unlocked a door at the end of the hallway and went inside, switching on a bare overhead bulb. The room smelled damp, like the rest of the house, but it was carpeted with cheap blue carpet and furnished with two beds, a single and a double, both of them covered with damp beige blankets. A small framed poster hung on the wall, blotched with damp and faded with age. It had an engraving of a pig on it, and the words 'Kilmartin's Famous Drisheen'.

Cathal Kilmartin switched on a small electric fire, only one bar of which was working. 'Hope you'll be comfy,' he said. 'There's tea if you'd like some, missus, and I've lemonade if the kid has a throat on her.'

Katie was tempted to tell him what he could do with his tea and lemonade, but she didn't want Ana-Maria to go thirsty.

'Go on, then,' she said.

'You want sugar, or are you sweet enough already?'

Katie still managed to keep her mouth closed, but if her eyes had been lasers she would have killed him where he stood.

'Sit on bed,' ordered Lupul, once Cathal Kilmartin had left the room. 'Aleks! Gheorghe!'

The two black-jacketed men came in. Aleks was holding two lengths of nylon washing line. He lifted his hands in front of him to indicate to Katie that she should do the same, and then he tied her wrists tightly together with a double handcuff knot. He did the same to Ana-Maria, and once he had done that, Lupul sat down on the single bed opposite and laid down his cordless drill.

'What do you want from us, Dragomir?' asked Katie. 'Like, what is the point of you holding us like this?'

Lupul took a packet of cigarettes out of his jacket pocket and lit one. 'You think I run, yes? You think you take all my beggar from the street, you think I give up, go back to Romania?'

'I was hoping that Ştefan Făt-Frumor might have cremated you, if you must know. Burned you to death in your house. That would have saved me a rake of problems, I can tell you.'

Lupul spat on to the carpet. 'Ştefan Făt-Frumor murder my stepfather in that fire, and my sister, and my sister husband. Făt-Frumor is dead now and in hell where he belong.'

'Of course you know that he's dead. You killed him. You, or one of your gowls. But you'll still be charged with murder yourself. It's all the same in the eyes of the law.'

He waved his hand. 'Not me. I don't kill nobody. You can't prove nothing.'

Katie watched him smoking. He looked so complacent that

she realized then that he genuinely believed he had committed the perfect murders, and that they hadn't discovered how Gearoid and Matty and Vasile and Ștefan Făt-Frumor had been killed with a drill.

It was understandable. She hadn't released the details of the post mortems to the media, and in Romania he might easily have got away with it. He might even have got away with it in Cork, if Katie hadn't insisted on autopsies and Dr Kelley hadn't been so scrupulous. After all, the only outward sign of what had been done to them was a small scab on the back of the neck, and the rough sleepers had already been covered all over with scabs.

'Fair play,' she said. 'I can't prove anything. So what is it you want from us?'

'I want *garanție*. I don't know the word English.'

'I understand. You want a guarantee.'

'That's it, *garanție*. You don't arrest. You don't take me to judge. You let my beggars go back on to streets. I need – I need – Aleks! How do you say *îmi dai imunitate față de urmărire penală?*'

Aleks appeared in the doorway. He was carrying a bottle of Paddy's whiskey and a can of Barr's cloudy lemonade, and he too was smoking a cigarette.

'You immunitate me from the law,' said Aleks.

Katie blew Lupul's cigarette smoke away from her face. 'So what you're telling me is, you want An Garda Síochána to allow you to carry on running your begging ring, without any interference? Is that it?'

Lupul nodded.

'And if I don't agree?'

'You agree! No question! You agree because I keep Ana-Maria. If you arrest – if you give me trouble – then *brrrrrrrrrrr!* You understand? *Brrrrrrrrrr,* before you can save her.'

Katie stared at him in disbelief. 'You're some head-the-ball, do you know that? You might be able to get away with pulling a stunt like this in Romania, but you don't stand an earthly here in Cork.'

'Oh, no?' Lupul tapped his forehead and said, 'I think about it careful. You want something bad to happen to Ana-Maria? Of course no. And anyway what problem is it for you, if I have beggars in Cork? No problem at all.'

'And you really believe that we'll let you do this?'

'I tell you this, too, police woman detective. You listen. When we come to Cork first, I speak to my men about my plan for beggars and for Ştefan Făt-Frumor. I don't know then that Ana-Maria is in next room, and she hear me, all what I say. She tell her mother what is my plan. Then her mother come to me and say to pay for her and Ana-Maria to go back to Târgovişte, or she will tell police my plan.'

Katie glanced quickly at Ana-Maria. Then, with her voice lowered, she leaned towards Lupul and said, 'Are you admitting that you were responsible for her mother disappearing?'

Lupul shrugged, and sucked at his cigarette. It was obvious that he hadn't quite understood what she meant.

She leaned towards him again. '*Did you kill Ana-Maria's mother?*'

Lupul looked at Ana-Maria, and winked at her.

'I said—' Katie began, but Lupul raised his hand and said, 'I *hear* what you say. But you can prove nothing. Everything is gone. A bird fly past your window – how do you prove it?'

With that, he unscrewed the cap on the bottle of Paddy's and took three large gulps. Then he licked his lips and burped and said, 'You stay here tonight and you think, yes? Your police friends will know by morning you are gone. We give them time to worry. Tomorrow you can call and say, "I am safe, Ana-Maria is safe. Dragomir Iliescu is a good man and it is okay for him to have beggars on the streets."'

Jesus, you're some climpy, thought Katie. *And a sadistic climpy, too.* But she had come across plenty of criminals who were twice as stupid and even more violent, and so she said nothing. She knew that by now Detective Inspector Fitzpatrick and the rest of her team would be making every effort to find out where she and Ana-Maria had been taken, and that they had the expertise to rescue them once they had. If necessary, they could call in the Garda Negotiation Section, who had a remarkable record of ending hostage situations and barricades without bloodshed.

She realized that she would be wasting her breath if she argued with Lupul any longer. He sat on his bed playing with his mobile phone and sniffing and repeatedly swigging Paddy's. Shortly after eleven o'clock, the blowsy woman came in and took Ana-Maria to the toilet. Afterwards Katie went to the toilet, too, but when she had struggled to take down her trousers and her thong with her hands tied, she had to sit with the door open while Gheorghe leaned against the wall opposite, watching her and grinning.

When she returned to the bedroom, Lupul said, 'You lie down now. Sleep.'

Katie and Ana-Maria lay down back to back on the double bed, and Lupul directed Aleks to fasten the cords around their wrists to the bed frame.

'Please – this is hurting my hand something fierce,' Katie protested.

'Who cares? Shut up your face. Sleep.'

By midnight, Lupul had finished the bottle of whiskey. He dropped his phone on the carpet and lay on his back, snoring.

Cathal Kilmartin looked in on them. He reeked of alcohol, too. He saw the phone on the floor and bent over with a grunt to pick it up. 'Pleasant dreams, girls,' he said. 'Don't let the fleas bite.' Then he switched off the overhead light and closed the door, so that the only illumination came from the single orange bar of the electric fire.

'*Mătuşă?*' whispered Ana-Maria.

'What is it, sweetheart?'

'*O să ne omoare?*'

'I don't know what that means, Ana-Maria, but don't you worry. There are people coming to save us, I promise you.'

'*Lupul mi-a omorât mumia, nu-i aşa?*'

Katie guessed what that meant. Ana-Maria was asking if Lupul had murdered her mother.

'Try to get some sleep,' she said. 'We can worry about that in the morning.'

She felt bruised and exhausted and disorientated, and as if she had wandered into a strange surreal world where nothing made any sense. She closed her eyes, even though she didn't think she would be able to sleep. Aleks had tied her up at an awkward angle so that the heel of her hand was pressing hard against the metal bed frame.

She said a prayer for their rescue – silently, but shaping the words with her lips so that God would be able to see what she was saying.

Fifty-Three

Detective Inspector Fitzpatrick was still in the communications room at half-past eleven. Every Garda station in the southern and eastern regions had been alerted that Katie and Ana-Maria had been taken, and roadblocks had been set up on most of the major roads, but there was still no sign of them.

The Volvo in which they had first been abducted had been found at the Clayton Silver Springs Hotel, but the CCTV coverage didn't extend to that end of the hotel's car park, so the Garda had no idea what make of vehicle they might be travelling in now. It was likely that instead of leaving Silver Springs by the main road they had turned right up Lover's Walk, which was steep and very narrow, and which had no CCTV coverage either, not until St Luke's Cross. From Lover's Walk, they could have turned off in almost any direction, up or down any number of winding side roads – east to Mayfield, north to Fermoy or west to Blackpool.

Detective O'Donovan came in, stretching and smearing his face with his hands after a two-hour nap. He had started his shift at seven o'clock that morning, and after he had nodded off over his desk Detective Inspector Fitzpatrick had told him to take a break.

'Story?' he asked, but Detective Inspector Fitzpatrick shook his head.

'At least we know that it's Lupul who's taken them. So much for him being cremated in that fire. But that doesn't help us much. We've no intelligence at all about where he might have taken himself off to, after Sutton's Buildings. There was nothing on his dead pals' phones except texts about picking up money and drugs, and Romanian porn. And there's been no sightings of him anywhere around the city.'

'What about the beggars? Have they been any use?'

'You're joking, aren't you? I sent Cullen and Walsh up to St Dunstan's church hall with that translator fellow so that they could ask all the Romanians yet again if they had any notion where Lupul might be hiding himself. If they do know, they're not telling. Too scared, if you ask me, now that they're sure he's alive.'

'I'm off to find myself a coffee,' said Detective O'Donovan. 'Can I fetch you one?'

At that moment, though, Bill Phinner walked in through the door. He was wearing a baggy green cardigan with what looked like a striped pyjama jacket underneath it, and he was holding up a blue plastic folder.

'Bill,' said Detective Inspector Fitzpatrick. 'Thought you went home hours ago.'

'I did. But I'd left this file on DS Maguire's desk so that she could see it as soon as she got back in. I rang her half an hour ago to find out if she'd managed to take a sconce at it yet, and that's when Sergeant O'Farrell told me that Lupul had abducted her, like.'

He set the file down on the desk in front of the CCTV monitors and opened it up. It contained at least fifteen 5 x 10cm photographs, all solid black, but with faint white handwriting on them.

'These are pages from the notebook we found in Lupul's burned-out house on Alexandra Road. They were pretty much charred to a cinder, but we were able to salvage a fair number of them, as you can see. We were lucky that all the writing's been done in ballpoint pen, which always shows up a whole lot clearer than fountain pen or gel ink.'

'So how did you get to read what was written on them?'

'We photographed each page under infrared LED light. How much reflectivity your surface gives you, that depends on your incident angles. We tried various angles between fifteen and seventy-five degrees to see which gave us the best contrast between the writing and the paper background.'

'I'm not sure I understood a word of that,' said Detective Inspector Fitzpatrick. 'So what does the writing actually say?'

Bill Phinner passed him the first sheet out of the file. 'Some of it's in Romanian, but that's not a bother because it's mostly figures. It's Lupul's accounts book. It has a complete list of all of his beggars by name, where they're located in the city and how much each one of them has earned each day. You can see that the fellow who took over the pitch outside of the Savoy Centre almost doubled his takings from his previous location, which was on Marlboro Street.'

'Okay... this could be useful background evidence if we ever catch him.'

'Ah, yes, no, but that's not the half of it. On *this* page he's listed his expenses. And look at the very first one, right at the top. *"Pentru E. Buckley, pentru Sorina Bălescu, 250 €."'*

'Sorina Bălescu – that's Ana-Maria's mother,' said Detective O'Donovan. 'Like, it doesn't say so in so many words, but surely that's proof that Lupul knew Buckley, and why would he pay him two hundred and fifty yoyos, except to get rid of her? What's the odds he *did* fecking mince her, the lying scumbag?'

'Look at the next entry,' said Bill Phinner. '"*Pentru E. Buckley, pentru femeia Cook St, 275 €."* That young woman who went missing from Cook Street, Máire O'Connor, he's clearly paid Buckley to make sure that *she* disappeared without any trace, too.'

'And we know for a fact that he was intending to dispose of Vasile Deac's body,' put in Detective Inspector Fitzpatrick. 'There's no other earthly reason he would have put it into his fridge.'

'Sure like, but I think this is the critical entry,' said Bill Phinner. '"*Pentru C. Kilmartin, Skibbereen, 2,000 €."'*

'Kilmartin – that's the name of that feen who runs a piggery down in Skibb, isn't it?' said Detective O'Donovan. 'You know – the one at the end of the road where Nick and Padragain were following Buckley to, that night they got assaulted outside the West Cork Hotel.'

'Well, I didn't know that myself,' said Bill Phinner. 'But I thought, if you're running a begging ring in Cork, why would you be paying that much grade to somebody in Skibbereen, unless maybe they were laundering it for you? Anyway, I looked up all the Kilmartins in the area and the only C. Kilmartin is Cathal Kilmartin who runs Kilmartin's Pig Farm, at the end of Blackthorn Boreen.'

'They sent officers from Skibbereen to interview this Kilmartin fellow, didn't they?' said Detective Inspector Fitzpatrick. 'And they checked out his piggery, too. He was adamant that he didn't know Buckley, wasn't he, and they gave the piggery the once-over, but they couldn't find anything suspicious.'

'Think about it,' said Bill Phinner. 'Where can you dispose of a body so that no trace of it can ever be found, not even by forensics? Not in a bog, or the river. It'll either be dug up one day, or it'll float to the surface. You can burn it, but it still leaves ashes. But if you feed it to your animals, then it's gone and lost forever. Come on, you've read stories about it, haven't you, dead bodies being fed to the pigs, and then recycled, and recycled. If you ask me, that Lupul's been reading the same stories.'

'But if Sorina Bălescu was fed to Kilmartin's pigs, how did her ring end up in Buckley's mince?'

They all looked at each other, and they knew there was only one answer.

'The sick feck,' said Detective O'Donovan.

'Sweeney Todd Syndrome, they call it,' said Bill Phinner. 'The perverse pleasure of making other people eat human flesh without them knowing it. A hundred to one he fetched some back from the piggery and sold it in his shop, along with the crubeens. Cannibalism by proxy. I'll bet it turned him on.'

Detective Inspector Fitzpatrick lifted up his jacket from the back of his chair. 'Whatever his motive was, Lupul did away with Ana-Maria's mother, we can be sure of that. Now he's taken Ana-Maria herself, *and* DS Maguire, so I think we have to face up to the strong possibility that he intends to do away with them, too, if he hasn't already. Let's start by getting ourselves down to Skibb, pronto. I'll wake up Superintendent O'Shea down at Clon so that he can organize a squad asap and get them up to that boreen.'

'What if they're not there, at the piggery?'

'Then at least we'll know that they haven't been fed to the pigs.'

'But, Jesus. What if they have?'

'Then I won't be accountable for my actions, I can promise you that.'

Katie kept falling asleep, and then immediately waking up, and then falling back to sleep again. Her hand had become numb and despite the one-bar electric fire she was so cold that she kept dreaming she was dead, and that she was lying in one of the drawers of Dr Kelley's morgue. Dr Kelley pulled out the drawer, stared at her, and then slid her back in again.

She dreamed about Conor, too. They were standing on the beach at Garrettstown again. It was a grey afternoon, and growing dark. Conor had his back to her and his coat collar turned up, and for some reason he refused to turn round.

She kept shouting '*Con!*' over and over again, but the sea swallowed up her words, and when she tried to run after him, Barney kept jumping up and knocking against her and getting in her way.

She suddenly opened her eyes. For a split second, she couldn't think where she was. She twisted her head around and saw that Ana-Maria was no longer lying next to her. That must have been the jumping up and knocking that she had felt. By the dim orange light of the electric fire, she saw that Ana-Maria had managed to wriggle her hands out of the washing-line knots that had been holding her, and that she was standing by the side of Lupul's single bed.

She had picked up his cordless drill and she was holding it in both hands above his head. Lupul himself was oblivious, deep in a drunken sleep. His mouth was hanging open and he was snoring, rough and uneven. He sounded like a carpenter slowly sawing his way through a sheet of asbestos.

Katie had never seen an expression like Ana-Maria's before, not on a child of nine. It was partly saintly, the pale face of a Madonna in a roadside shrine, but her eyes were wide and glassy, as if the Madonna had become possessed by a demon.

'Ana-Maria,' she said, softly. She didn't want to wake Lupul. He was so drunk that God alone knew what he would do if he found that Ana-Maria had freed herself, and had picked up his drill.

Ana-Maria ignored her. All her attention was focused on Lupul. She lowered the drill until the triangular cutting edge of the bit was pointing right between his untidy eyebrows.

'*Ana-Maria – no!*' Katie cried out, but Ana-Maria squeezed the trigger and drilled straight into Lupul's forehead. She pushed the drill down as hard as she could, right up to the chuck, so it screeched against his skull, and a bloody ribbon of skin flew up.

Lupul let out a roaring scream and tried to sit up, but Ana-Maria tugged the drill out from between his eyebrows and stuck it into the centre of his forehead, just below his tangled grey hairline. His brains were oozing out of the first hole that she had drilled, as shiny and beige as French mustard, streaked with blood. He was thrashing his arms and kicking his legs, but Ana-Maria pressed her knee against his shoulder to hold him down. She managed to drill right into his head a second time, until the drill bit jammed, and she had to let go, and he was left with the heavy drill and its battery swinging from his forehead.

Croaking with pain and shock, Lupul rolled off his bed and fell heavily on to the floor. He kept trying to pull the drill out of his head but his hands jerked and trembled and twitched and he couldn't seem to get them to do what he wanted.

Ana-Maria stood back and watched him, her arms by her sides. She didn't take her eyes off Lupul, but she remained totally expressionless, as if she had sprayed a wasp with insecticide, and was dispassionately watching it die.

The bedroom door slammed open. It was Cathal Kilmartin, in a stained white nightshirt. He was still drunk, and he had to grab the door handle to stop himself from falling over.

'What the feck?' he blurted. Then he tilted forward and saw Lupul lying on his side on the floor, feebly trying to tug the drill out of his head. 'Jesus, what the feck?'

Aleks appeared behind him, and he looked equally drunk.

Katie said, 'For the love of God, you two, don't just stand there! Ring for an ambulance! This man's going to die if you don't!'

'What's he doing?' blinked Cathal Kilmartin. 'What's that fecking drill doing, stuck in his fecking head? Dragos? *Dragos!* Are ye trying to kill yourself or something, ye fecking eejit?'

'Ring 112!' Katie snapped at him. 'Call for an ambulance! Tell them it's desperate!'

Aleks was swaying from side to side. 'No fecking way. Ambulance come, police come too. I go. I'm out of here. Gheorghe! Gheorghe! *Trezeşte-te!* We go!'

He went stumbling off into the darkness. Cathal Kilmartin stayed where he was in the doorway, trying to understand what was happening. A few seconds later the blowsy woman looked over his shoulder, wrapping a pink satin dressing gown around herself.

'Holy Mary Mother of God!' she said, in a voice harsh from decades of cigarette smoking. 'Cathal, out the road, you fat lump! Jesus, the shite you're in now, boy!'

Katie said, 'Untie me, would you? This man needs urgent first aid, and an ambulance.'

The woman knelt on the bed, so that the springs creaked. Leaning over, she tugged at the washing line tied around Katie's wrists. She smelled of cigarette smoke and musky perfume, and her breasts swung heavily against Katie's hip as she gradually unravelled all the knots.

'What's that fecking eejit doing with that drill stuck in his nut? The times I've told Cathal not to bother with these fecking Ramoonians.'

'They've been good to us, girl, you can't deny it,' slurred Cathal Kilmartin. 'Who else would have given us all that grade not to say nothing?'

'Oh, shut your bake, Cah, you're fecking moylo. As if you're not always.'

At last Katie was able to climb off the bed. She said to the woman, 'Ring 112, will you?' and the woman puffed out her cheeks in exasperation.

'I'm only doing this because these langers are so fecking langered,' she said. 'They're worse than fecking kids, I tell you.' She slapped off in her slippers to make the call, coughing as she went.

Katie knelt down next to Lupul. His eyes were half open and he was still breathing but he was utterly still now. She pressed two fingertips against his neck and felt his pulse. It was slow, but she decided that he didn't need CPR. Carefully, she lifted up the heavy cordless drill and twisted the chuck, so that the drill bit was released. Its shaft was protruding about four centimetres out of his forehead but she didn't try to pull it out in case she damaged his brain tissue even more.

She looked up at Ana-Maria, who was holding herself tightly now, as if she were cold, or badly needed a hug.

The woman came back from the living room, holding her mobile phone. 'Ten minutes, they said. They'll be sending a car first, with a paradermic. They said to keep him warm and not to move him.'

'Christ, this has given me the fecking gawks,' said Cathal Kilmartin. 'I can feel them bangers coming back up like fecking Mount Etna.' He lumbered off to the toilet, his shoulders thumping drunkenly against the walls on either side.

Katie stood up and held out her hand for the woman's phone. The woman coughed and said, 'Here you are, girl. But make sure the shades know this is nothing to do with me, any of this shite,' and gave it to her. She took a packet of Marlboro out of her dressing-gown pocket and held a cigarette against the bar of the electric fire to light it.

Katie put one arm around Ana-Maria and held her close. At the same time, she rang the station at Anglesea Street. Ana-Maria's eyes were filled with tears, but she didn't sob. *God in Heaven,* thought Katie, as she gently rocked her, *nine years old, but tonight you've learned to fight back like a woman.*

The duty officer at Anglesea Street asked Katie to hold on for a moment, and then put her through to Detective Inspector Fitzpatrick.

'Robert? I'm just calling to let you know that we're safe, me and Ana-Maria.'

'Thank God for that, ma'am.'

'Lupul took us all the way down to Skibbereen, to Kilmartin's Pig Farm, a couple of kilometres west of the River Ilen bridge. We're here now, and like I say we're safe, although Lupul himself is in a bad way. We've called for an ambulance for him.'

'That's a fierce relief altogether, I can tell you. Most of all because *we're* almost at Kilmartin's Pig Farm, too. We're heading up the boreen and we'll be with you before you know it.'

'*What?* You're codding me.'

'Step outside and see. We're coming through the gate right now.'

Katie took hold of Ana-Maria's hand and the woman stood aside and held her cigarette out of the way as they went along to the front door and opened it. Three Garda squad cars and two unmarked cars were arriving in the farmyard with a crunching of shingle, their headlights criss-crossing the farmhouse and lighting up the pig sheds.

Katie and Ana-Maria stood in the porch as Detective Inspector

Fitzpatrick and Detective O'Donovan walked across the farmyard towards them, their breath smoking in the cold. Detective Inspector Fitzpatrick came up to Katie and looked at her with those steel-grey eyes that never gave anything away.

'Delighted to see you're not hurt, ma'am. Neither of you.'

Katie nodded and bit her lip. It hadn't been part of her training at Templemore, but she knew that detective superintendents weren't supposed to cry – not in front of their fellow officers, anyway.

Fifty-Four

On the way back to Cork, sitting with Ana-Maria in the rear of Detective Inspector Fitzpatrick's car, Katie tried ringing Conor, both on his mobile and at home. She rang and rang but he didn't pick up. She guessed that he had forgotten to recharge his battery, or that he had spent the night somewhere else. Either that, or he had drunk himself into a stupor, like Lupul.

As they passed through Bandon, Detective Inspector Fitzpatrick received a message from the gardaí who had stayed at the piggery that an ambulance had arrived to pick up Lupul. Because of the severity of his brain injuries, he was being taken directly to CUH.

Cathal Kilmartin and his woman partner had both been arrested and would be taken first to Clonakilty Garda Station, although they would probably be sent up to Anglesea Street sometime later in the day.

Less than fifteen minutes later, as they reached Halfway, another message came through that Aleks and Gheorghe had been arrested, too. They had been trying to drive north to Bantry but had only managed to get as far as Ballydehob before they had driven drunkenly into a ditch.

Katie tried ringing Conor twice more before they arrived at Anglesea Street, but he still didn't pick up.

'Do you want to be taken back to Cobh first, ma'am?' asked Detective Inspector Fitzpatrick, turning around in his seat.

'No, not yet. We should have at least a preliminary debriefing before I go home. What's the time now – five to eight – let's all get together at nine. Can you tell Chief Superintendent O'Kane, please, Robert, and Superintendent Pearse? And Mathew McElvey, too. We need to discuss how we're going to present this to the press.'

They all climbed the station steps into the reception area and Detective O'Donovan went to find a garda to drive Ana-Maria back to Glanmire. Katie gave Ana-Maria a hug and gently brushed her hair back. She was white-faced and shivering and still in shock from what she had done and Katie knew that she would need some serious counselling in the days to come. First of all, though, she needed affection and reassurance and warmth and a good long sleep.

'*Mătuşă?*' she said, miserably.

'It's all right, sweetheart. It's been a desperate night but you're not in any trouble. Look – this nice lady garda is going to take you back to Sadhbh and Michael's house. I'll come and see you myself tomorrow, when we've all had a rest.'

Katie had a long, hot shower and changed into a cream cotton blouse and a navy-blue sweater and black trousers. Even then, she imagined that she could still smell cigarette smoke on her, so she squirted herself with primrose and rye cologne.

She tried ringing Conor again. He still didn't pick up his mobile, but when she rang her home number, Jenny Tierney, her neighbour, answered.

'Jenny, it's Kathleen. Conor isn't there, by any chance?'

'No – no, he's not, Kathleen. And it looks like he hasn't been here since yesterday. I've just come in to take Barney and Foltchain for their walk, and they're both starving and thirsty and I'm afraid they've done a bit of a mess on the kitchen floor.'

'Oh. Has he left a note anywhere?'

'Not that I can see, Kathleen.'

'I have a meeting to go to, Jenny, but I should be home in about an hour or so. Don't bother about the mess. I'll clean it up when I get back.'

'It's no bother, Kathleen. I've had to clear up worse. I worked at that old folks' home in Youghal, remember.'

Katie put down the phone. She couldn't understand why Conor wasn't answering his phone and why he hadn't been in touch. Usually he rang her two or three times a day to ask how she was, and what she wanted for supper, or if she wanted to go out for a meal. Lately he had been ringing her even more frequently, because he was bored.

She went down to the conference room. Detective Inspector Fitzpatrick was there already, as well as Superintendent Pearse, Inspector O'Rourke and seven of her team, including Detective Sergeants Ni Nuallán and Begley and Detectives O'Donovan, Walsh, Cullen, O'Crean and Caffrey.

'First, I have to thank you all for tearing down to Skibbereen so fast to rescue us,' said Katie. 'Bless you for trusting your instincts and there's me always telling you not to rely on hunches. DI Fitzpatrick has told me how you managed to find us, and when I see Bill Phinner and his technical experts I'll be thanking them, too.'

Detective Inspector Fitzpatrick put up his hand. 'I'm happy to say that I have more positive news, ma'am. While you were changing, we questioned Eamon Buckley and Thomas Barry again, in the light of the information that we'd retrieved from Lupul's notebook.'

'And? What did they have to say?'

'Buckley refused to answer any questions without his lawyer present. But young Barry spilled the whole jar of beans. Crying his eyes out, he was, saying that he didn't want to spend the rest of his life in prison. He admitted that on two separate occasions he'd helped Buckley to take human bodies down to Kilmartin's Pig Farm in his van. He couldn't describe them because they were all wrapped up in black bin bags, but he'd seen their hair and their feet and he was sure they were both women.'

'One of them was Ana-Maria's mother, most likely,' said Katie. 'Maybe the other one was Máire O'Connor – that young druggie girl who went missing from Cook Street. We still haven't found any trace of her yet.'

'Barry said that they carried the bodies into a shed at the back of the pig farm. There was a butcher's block in there, he said, as well as a gammon boiler and an industrial mincing machine and bone miller. The first time he saw the mincer he thought it was a washing machine, because he'd never seen one as big as that before.'

'Mother of God,' said Katie. 'Why didn't the officers from Skibb see it, when they searched the place? They told me they couldn't find anything suspicious.'

'Well, yes, but a mincer like that, it's not unusual on a pig farm. They use it for grinding up the pig feed.'

'Did Barry see for himself how the bodies were disposed of?'

'No. Buckley told him to go into the house and watch TV until he was finished. It took him nearly two hours altogether, that's what Barry said. When Buckley came out his apron was all stained with blood and he was carrying a big white polystyrene box with a lid on, the same type they got their meat deliveries in.'

'Didn't Barry realize what was inside of it? He must have done.'

'He did, yes. But he said he was so scared of Buckley that he didn't dare to say anything. He was sure that if he told anyone, Buckley would kill him and *he*'d end up as mincemeat, too.'

'That's perfect, Robert,' said Katie. 'You'd best contact Barry's solicitor and have him repeat all that word for word in front of her, because we'll be charging him with murder on the basis of that. And then you'd best contact Buckley's man, Frank Lyons, and tell *him* the good news. That pompous hoor. I can't wait to see the look on his face.'

Katie went over their abduction in detail, describing at the end how Ana-Maria had drilled into Lupul's skull. She could see Kyna wincing, and Detective O'Donovan shaking his head, because he had seen the injuries for himself.

Afterwards, Detective Inspector Fitzpatrick laid out all the pages of Lupul's notebook.

'So – we have a fierce strong case already,' said Katie. 'I'd be prepared to present a book of evidence to the court with what we have now – but if we can find DNA from Sorina Bălescu and Máire O'Connor in Cathal Kilmartin's mincing machine, or his butcher's block, or anywhere else on his farm, that's going to make it watertight.'

'I've been in touch with Superintendent O'Shea, and the farm is cordoned off now,' said Detective O'Donovan. 'He's arranged for another local farmer to feed the pigs. There's more than forty of them and we don't want them dying, too. Not before their time, anyway.'

'I'll have Bill Phinner send a team down as soon as we've finished here,' said Katie. 'The filthy state of that farm, there's a good chance that Kilmartin didn't manage to clean away every last trace of evidence.'

While she was talking, Katie had noticed that the door of the conference room had opened, and that Chief Superintendent O'Kane was standing outside. She beckoned for him to join them, but he stayed where he was until the briefing was over. He could probably hear what was being said, but she wondered why he didn't come in.

As she left the room, she said, 'Sir?' She had never seen him look so grim.

'Could you come to my office, Katie,' he said, and it wasn't a question.

'What's wrong, sir?'

He didn't answer, but led the way to his office and opened the door, allowing her to go in first.

'You'd best sit down,' he told her.

She was suddenly filled with dread. His tone of voice reminded her of all the times when she was a uniformed garda and she had knocked on doors to tell wives that their husbands had been killed in road accidents, or parents that their children had drowned.

She remained standing. She had to remain standing to stay strong.

'It's Conor, isn't it?' she said.

Brendan said, 'Yes.'

She listened numbly while he explained what had happened. A postman had called at Foggy Fields less than an hour ago to deliver a parcel and he had seen that the front window had been blown out and that there was shattered glass all over the driveway. Two gardaí from Midleton had been sent to investigate and they had found Caoilfhoinn's torso underneath the Land Rover. When they had looked in through the farmhouse window they had seen the remains of several other people inside, although they were so badly mutilated that it was difficult to work out how many there were.

'They found an Audi SUV parked by the side of the road not far away,' said Brendan. 'It was unlocked, and there was a letter on the driver's seat. The letter is addressed to you.'

Katie was beginning to feel swimmy now, but still she didn't want to sit down. 'Did they open it?'

'Under the circumstances, yes.'

'What does it say, this letter?'

'They'll be fetching it down here so that you can read it for yourself. But it's signed "Conor" and the gist of it is that it's a suicide note.'

'I see.'

'They checked the Audi's number plate and it's registered to Conor Ó Máille, with an address in Limerick.'

'That's Conor, yes,' said Katie. She took three or four deep breaths, and then she said, 'What do they think happened? It sounds like somebody set off a bomb.'

'Yes. They've called in the bomb squad from Collins Barracks and the fire brigade from Ballyvolane and of course we'll be sending a forensic team up there. I've already informed DI Mulliken so that he can start to get an investigation under way on your behalf.'

He paused, and then he said, 'After what you've been through last night, Katie – I'm sure this is the last thing you want to be dealing with yourself.'

Katie looked up at him and swallowed. *Detective superintendents don't cry. Detective superintendents don't cry. Not in front of fellow officers, and not in front of former lovers.*

'The letter,' she said.

'Of course. As soon as it arrives I'll make sure you get it. What do you want to do now? Do you want to go home?'

'I need a drink,' she said.

Without a word, Brendan went over to the sideboard next to the window, opened it up and took out a bottle of Smirnoff. He half-filled a glass and brought it over to her.

'I've no ice, I'm afraid, but I could fetch you some.'

Katie shook her head. She lifted up the glass and said, '*Sláinte mhaith*, Con.' She took a mouthful of neat vodka, closed her eyes for a moment and then swallowed it.

After about ten minutes, there was a knock at Brendan's office door. Sergeant O'Farrell came in, holding a white envelope in a clear plastic evidence bag.

'I'm supposed to give you this, ma'am.'

Katie was sitting by the window now. Brendan was sitting beside her with his arm along the back of the couch. They had said almost nothing at all, but Brendan had been looking at her sympathetically and that was all she needed.

'Thanks a million, Ryan,' she said. She took the envelope out of the evidence bag and opened it. The letter inside was written on her own headed notepaper from Carrig View.

'*My darling Katie,*

I am not asking for forgiveness because I know you will think that what I have done is unforgivable.'

She lowered the letter, took a deep breath, and held out her empty glass. Brendan brought over the Smirnoff bottle and filled it for her.

'*We never know what the Almighty has in store for us but I have always believed that He gives us what we deserve. I have always tried to do good in my life by helping animals, but in helping animals I ignored too often the human beings who needed my help and my love even more.*

'*God reminded me of my indifference by taking away my ability to become your husband and possibly the father of your new child.*

'*I have accepted God's judgement but in ending my life I have at least struck a last blow for what I passionately fought for, the protection of helpless animals from the cruelty of human greed.*

'*I love you, Katie Maguire, and wherever I am now I will always hold you in my heart. You are the most special woman that I have ever known, so kind but always so brave. I know that you have the strength to bear the pain of what I have done to you, and forget that I ever was.*

'*Your loving Conor.*'

Katie read the letter again, then folded it and tucked it back in its envelope. *There goes my future life*, she thought, *and the baby who will never be.*

'Are you okay?' Brendan asked her. 'Is there anything I can get you? Anybody you want me to ring? One of your sisters maybe?'

'No. No, thanks. I'll tell them in my own good time. I'm just finding it hard to believe that the man I was supposed to be marrying has blown himself up, like one of those terrorist suicide bombers. Jesus, it would almost be funny if it wasn't so sad.'

'What do you want to do?'

'Sit here for a while and try to think about nothing at all.'

'All right, then, whatever. I have some paperwork to be doing but that can wait. You're more important than paperwork.'

Katie finished her drink and held out her glass again.

'You're sure?' asked Brendan.

'I'm in need of a little anaesthesia, sir. And I don't think I'm sufficiently anaesthetized yet because I can say "anaesthesia". And "sufficiently".'

Brendan filled her glass again. 'You can call me Brendan,' he told her. 'If only for today.'

'Yes, sir. That's pure understanding of you, sir.'

She was still sitting by the window when Kyna came in. Kyna came over and stood in front of Katie with her hands clasped tightly together because her natural instinct was to throw her arms around her and hug her and kiss her and tell her how much she loved her, and how sorry she was about Conor. With Brendan present, of course, she had to restrain herself.

'You've heard about Con?' Katie asked her.

'Cailin just told me. It's desperate. I don't know what to say to you.'

'So long as you don't say that he went out with a bang.'

Katie lifted her glass as if she were drinking another toast. Kyna looked over at Brendan. 'I think DS Maguire should be going home, sir, don't you? I can take her if you like.'

'No, you're all right,' said Brendan. 'I'll take her myself.'

'She shouldn't be drinking any more, though.'

Katie finished her glass and held it up again.

'You're not my doctor, Kyna. Although I wouldn't mind if you were. How about a parting glass, Brendan? If it's not bad luck to mention parting glasses. You know, after that what's-his-name. That Vaseline fellow.'

'I don't think so, Katie. I'll be after taking you back to Cobh now. You'll feel better when you've had a good long sleep.'

'Come on, only a twinchy scoop.'

Brendan poured her a last small tot of vodka, which she downed in one.

'Now, let's be going,' he told her. He took hold of her arm and helped her to stand up.

'I'll go to her office and pick up her bag for her,' said Kyna. 'She has a neighbour who walks her dogs for her, a Mrs Tierney.

You should tell her that you've fetched her back – you know, so that she can keep an eye on her.'

'I will, sure,' said Brendan, although he didn't ask how Kyna knew so much about Katie's personal life.

Kyna stood and watched as Katie walked unsteadily out of the office, with Brendan beside her. Katie had managed not to cry, but Kyna was close.

'Oh, dear Lord,' she said, under her breath. 'Please bring her some happiness.' Then she went off to collect Katie's bag.

Fifty-Five

Katie leaned against the front door with her eyes closed while Brendan sorted through her bag to find her keys. Behind the door, Barney and Foltchain were snuffling and scratching, and obviously wondering why Katie was taking so long to come in.

At last Brendan found the right key, and let them into the hallway. The dogs milled around them, their tails slapping against their legs, and they sniffed suspiciously at Brendan as he helped Katie to stumble along towards her bedroom.

'It's all right, children,' said Katie. 'Everything's grand altogether. Your ma's a little rubbery, like, that's all.'

Brendan opened her bedroom door for her and she took three staggering steps before throwing herself face-down on the bed.

'Oh Jesus,' she slurred.

'Listen, Katie,' said Brendan, bending sideways next to the bed so that she could see him. 'I'll stay here for a while, okay, in case you're sick or something. Can I fetch you anything now? A glass of water, maybe?'

Katie looked up at him with unfocused eyes. 'No, you're all right. I *am* home, amn't I?'

'Yes, you're home. Try and get some sleep now and you'll feel a whole lot better.'

'Is this my bed? It feels more like a boat. Why does it keep rocking up and down?'

'That's the vodka, not the bed. It'll settle down soon.'

Katie closed her eyes. She plunged immediately into a deep

drunken sleep, so that she wasn't aware that Brendan didn't leave the bedroom, not at first, but stood next to the bed looking down at her, thoughtfully biting at his knuckle.

Barney stuck his nose in through the bedroom door, and made a wuffling noise.

'Come on, boy,' said Brendan. 'Let's get you two shut up in the kitchen where you can't interrupt us.'

Katie started to dream. She was back on the beach at Garrettstown, on a warm overcast day, but this time she was lying on the soft sand among the dunes, and the long grass all around her was making a soft sizzling sound in the breeze.

Conor came walking up the dunes until he was standing over her. He said something but his voice was muffled and she couldn't understand what it was.

'Con?' she said. 'What is it, Con? What's wrong?'

He didn't say anything, but knelt down in the sand in front of her. He unbuttoned her trousers and started to tug them down, a little at a time, until he had managed to wrestle them right off over her feet. Once he had done that, he pulled down her thong and tossed that to one side, and then he opened her thighs wide so that she could feel the sea air caressing her between her legs.

Conor climbed on top of her, and she felt him part her lips with his fingers and slowly push his hardened penis into her.

'Con,' she whispered. 'That's beautiful. See, my darling, you're not a eunuch after all.'

He slid himself into her so deeply that she could feel his curly hair against her vulva and his balls against the cheeks of her bottom, and the sensation was so arousing that she shuddered, and she squeezed her muscles against his smooth hard shaft again and again.

'Oh my God, Con. It's just like it was. It's *better* than it was. It's wonderful.'

She reached up and wrapped her arms around him and hugged

him, and it was then that she felt that his chest was bare, even though she hadn't seen him take off his clothes. She suddenly felt that something was badly wrong. She lifted up her head from the sand and opened her eyes.

By the light of her bedside lamp she saw that she wasn't lying in the dunes at all, and that it wasn't Con who was making love to her, but Brendan. While she was drunkenly sleeping, he had removed her trousers and her thong and pulled up her sweater and her blouse as far as her bra, so that her stomach was bare. He was completely naked, as fit and muscular as she remembered him, and with the same pattern of moles on his left shoulder. His eyes were dreamily closed as he was pushing himself in and out of her.

She smacked him across the face, hard, and kicked her heels so that she forced herself backwards up the bed and his penis flopped out of her.

They stared at each other. At first, neither of them spoke. Katie dragged the bedspread across to cover herself while Brendan shuffled down to the end of the bed on his knees and then stood up.

He cleared his throat, and then he said, 'Come on, Katie, we *used* to be lovers.'

'Used to be, sir, until you cheated on me. And what you've just done, that's rape.'

'Oh, what?' he protested. 'That was a friendly flah for old time's sake, that's all. You can't call it rape if we were lovers before.'

'Get dressed and get out.'

Brendan went over to the chair and picked up his underpants.

'Fair play, Katie. Maybe I misread your signals. So let's forget it, shall we?'

'Signals? *What* signals? I was totally langered. I still am – except that now I'm angry and totally langered. Now fecking get out of here before I throw you out.'

Brendan pulled up his trousers and buttoned up his shirt. 'This won't go any further,' he said.

'What do you mean, "this won't go any further"?'

'You won't be making any kind of official complaint?'

Katie sat up. She was rigid with rage. 'Last night I was abducted and threatened with my life. Last night I saw an innocent young girl drilling holes in a fellow's head. This morning I found out that my fiancé has blown himself up and other people with him. Because of all that I'm in shock and I'm shattered and I'm excusably drunk. And you thought that was the right time to take advantage of me, and rape me.'

'I'm sorry,' said Brendan. 'Like I said, I misunderstood the situation altogether. I thought you might be needing some emotional consolation, do you know what I mean?'

'If you really believe that "emotional consolation" means fucking a woman while she's so wrecked that she doesn't know what's happening to her, then all I can say is that you're the stupidest, saddest gombeen I ever met in my life. Now go.'

Brendan left, carrying his shoes in his hand. As soon as Katie heard the front door close behind him, she went to the kitchen and let out Barney and Foltchain. Then she went into the living room, where a framed photograph of herself and Conor was hanging next to the fireplace. It had been taken in November, in the grounds of Blarney Castle, and they were both laughing.

She stared at it for a long time and she felt she ought to cry but for some reason she couldn't. She could only think of the way that he had ended his letter. *I know that you have the strength to bear the pain of what I have done to you, and forget that I ever was.*

The following morning, the sky was black and thundery and hailstones were bouncing all over the road as Katie took a taxi into the city.

Moirin had obviously been told about Conor because she brought Katie a cup of coffee as soon as she sat down at her desk and said, 'I'm so sorry to hear your news, ma'am. You have my condolences.'

Her first visitor of the morning was Kyna.

'How's the head this morning?' Kyna asked her.

'What do you think? I feel like my brain's an anvil and all the hammers of hell are beating horseshoes into shape on it.'

She was half-inclined to tell Kyna about Brendan, but before she said anything about it to anybody, she wanted to work out for herself what she was going to do next. She could report Brendan to the Garda's confidential recipient; or she could threaten to make a complaint if he tried to obstruct or overrule any investigations that she was carrying out, or restrict her funding. On the other hand, she could say nothing at all.

Kyna said, 'I've heard from CUH. They operated on Lupul yesterday afternoon but he died during the night.'

'Well, I can't say I'm grieved about it. And it'll save us a rake of work.'

Kyna hesitated for a moment, and then she said, 'Would you like to meet up this evening? Somewhere quiet, where nobody knows us.'

'Yes, I'd like that,' said Katie. 'That's if you don't mind listening to me moaning and whingeing for an hour or three.'

Kyna left, and almost immediately afterwards Brendan came into her office, smiling and looking smart and smelling of aftershave as usual.

'Hi, Katie. How are you going on?'

Katie looked down at the files and messages that had been left on her desk, and started to leaf through them. 'Did you want something, sir?'

'I only wanted to tell you that I've had a thank-you call from Caoimhe O'Neill. Walter's had his operation and all his breathing problems are sorted. As it turned out, the vet's bill was only fifteen hundred euros.'

Katie raised her eyes from her paperwork. 'Good. But that money wasn't really for Walter, was it? That money was for me, to win me over. Well, let me tell you this, sir. I'm going to cost you much, much more than that.'